THE OTHER LIFE OF BRIAN

GRAHAM PARKER

THUNDER'S MOUTH PRESS/NEW YORK

The Other Life of Brian
Copyright © 2003 by Graham Parker

Published by Thunders Mouth Press
An Imprint of Avalon Publishing Group Incorporated
161 William Street, 16th Floor
New York, NY 10038

All rights reserved. No part of this book may be reproduced in whole or in part without written permission from the publisher, except by reviewers who may quote brief excerpts in connection with a review in a newspaper, magazine, or electronic publication; nor may any part of this book be reproduced, stored in a retrieval system, or transmitted in any form or by any means electronic, mechanical, photocopying, recording, or other, without written permission from the publisher.

Library of Congress Publication Data

Parker, Graham, 1950-
 The other life of Brian / by Graham Parker.
  p. cm.
 ISBN 1-56025-549-8
  1. Rock musicians--Fiction. 2. Arctic regions--Fiction. 3.Scandinavia--Fiction. 4. Tasmania--Fiction. 5. Cults--Fiction. I. Title.

PR6066.A578O84 2003
823'.914--dc21

9 8 7 6 5 4 3 2 1

Designed by Paul Paddock
Printed in Canada
Distributed by Publishers Group West

Many thanks to Laurie Fox and the Linda Chester Literary Agency. Thanks to Neil Ortenberg for taking this on with such decisiveness. Cheers to Greg Kihn for including me in the short story collection *Carved In Rock,* and giving me the idea of where to send this book.

Immeasurable thanks to my wife, Jolie, for coming up with the best plot twists, the title, and so much more.

Chapter 1

One summer afternoon as I lay back beside the pool, a lazy eye inspecting two eastern black swallowtails fluttering around the wildflower proliferation I'd planted in the spring, my glazed reverie was pierced by that vicious instrument of technology, the cellular phone.

My wife called out from somewhere in the house (the shower? the bathtub? the giant fitted mirrors designer lit so exquisitely for perfect applications of ultra expensive Christian Dior products?) and ordered me to answer it, which I did, albeit with twisting lip and resigned sigh, hoping it was a mistake, a heavy breather I could swear at, or a telemarketer I could simply hang up on. Alas, such easily overcome prickles of annoyance it was not, and my crazed, errant manager, Tarquin Steed, boomed across the Atlantic in my right ear without a word of the common social courtesy generally reserved for normal people.

"Now, BP!" he bellowed, intoning a seriousness that made my heart sink.

"Hang on!" I ordered, shuffling about, pretending I had important business to take care of.

What *now*?

What grim and foolish promo stunt is about to be thrust my way? To which ridiculous backward nation shall I be hurtled toward like a dying comet? What project has his other rock star client, the Neanderthal guitarist, aborted at the last minute, leaving Steed restless and itchy and hawking over his giant wall atlas, sticking red pins in everywhere—with my name on them?

If only I could have the remains of Summer and the golden Autumn to continue my languid perusal of the changing seasons. To have that fleeting, melancholy period to burrow, mole-like, into the very fabric of nature. To observe the tiny, emerald young of the green snake breaking through their chalky eggs under the snake boards, the

1

fledging of bluebird and tree swallow (born in the very nesting boxes I myself had erected in the meadow behind our house), the pupation and metamorphosis of the monarch butterfly and their clever impersonators, the viceroy, and to track the black bear as they crisscrossed my Vermont mountain acreage, the heat wave driving them in search of succulent leaves and berries. Or to do simply nothing, but hang by the pool and let the guitar calluses of the left-hand fingertips go soft as a baby's bum from lack of use.

I had collected my Sneer Grammy earlier in the year, appeared in front of millions not three weeks ago in some preposterous Donovan tribute broadcast the world over. Why couldn't I, as the vernacular would have it, "veg out" for the rest of the year?

A fat, iridescent green dragonfly dashed down from the meadow, circled the pool twice, zipped by my head, hung motionless for a second not three feet away, and finally, with a barely audible chomp, tore into a black gnat with its powerful jaws. As it shot off across the meadow dancing in the sun, its buzz receding, I fancied my lazy summer receding faster than my hairline.

My wife, fresh from her exquisite toilet, leaned out of the dimpled glass bathroom doors dressed only in a pale fawn silk camisole, a questioning look directed at the phone. A chemical yearn traveled at the speed of light from my brain to my crotch and I had to battle the urge to drop the phone into the pool and slide into the house with her.

Our hyperactive young son was in kindergarten, most probably terrorizing some hapless child of milder demeanor, and before Steed's interruption, I'd been cultivating a lazy lob in my maroon swimming trunks and looking forward to its full expansion within the hour with the help of my lovely wife. But now I could feel the organ lose vigor at the mere thought of what would surely be a lengthy and difficult exchange with Tarquin Steed, for our exchanges were rarely brief, and nearly always difficult.

"Steed?" hissed my better half, and I nodded, still hanging on the pregnant pause renting the ocean of static.

"How's Findhorn, Tarquin?" I asked, hoping to divert my bullish manager from his original intentions. Findhorn, his home in the north of Scotland, was rumored to be an almost magical place, infused by some rare current of warm air carried on the sea from the gulf; a place that attracted oily, permed new agers, crystal enthusiasts, and for some inexplicable reason, rock 'n' roll managers. One could grow giant vegetables in Findhorn, supposedly. But I, despite Steed's many invitations, had never made the ass-numbing drive from London and never would. As far as I was concerned, it was *always* raining, freezing, or both, anywhere north of Watford.

"My eggplants are getting on for twelve inches," I continued, deciding I just might be able to turn this conversation my way if I kept at it. "Tomatoes are huge. I'll send you a Polaroid . . . Oh, and I've got a pumpkin like a mall breeder's butt! So, come on Steed. What are you growing up there?"

But alas, Steed's bulldog fixation on something other than freak fruits of the earth would not be diverted and his only condescension to normal etiquette was a brusque, half-chuckle that made me feel like flinging the telephone into the deep end. What would Tarquin's reaction be? Would he launch into the inevitable speech about touring, compromise, and collaboration, blathering on as the gurgling in his ear grew louder until finally he twigged that something was wrong and he began speaking my initials in a distracted, questioning manner? Perhaps I should actually *dive* into the pool, holding the telephone. That way I'd be able to hear his speech break down into confusion as the device faltered. I recalled reading somewhere that underwater cellular phones were now available, devices snapped up by phoneaholic yuppies for their Caribbean snorkeling vacations, and perhaps I had unwittingly purchased one.

I looked at the heavy, black object in my hand as my manager began his monologue. It was 1983, and in those days cell phones were cumbersome and expensive and came in two separate parts—a heavy mouthpiece and a monstrous receiver. As I studied the device I imagined with a wanton thrill that under water what Steed had to say would sound more appealing, more vital and alive. The idea had taken on the proportions of an experiment, and before I had time to renege on my impulses I hopped off of the deck chair as my wife looked on in amazement, walked casually to the edge of the pool, and stepped in!

Scrunching the phone between my shoulder and my right ear (still gripping its leviathan, separate base in my other hand), I used my free arm to push the water up and thrust myself into the depths, releasing discrete amounts of air from my lungs. In a few seconds, my feet hit the bottom, eight feet down. Unfortunately, the experiment did not affect reality the way I had hoped and I could still hear Steed's voice unscathed, droning on about A&R men, my lack of complicity with the publicity departments of various record labels, obscure singer/songwriters whom he thought I should collaborate with, and a concerted effort on my part to stimulate fresh ideas by "working with" a tally of nerds who might just as well, in my opinion, have been selling rubber plants instead of records. The usual, in other words.

Bereft of some new angle of argument, I merely responded with typically lifeless replies, only instead of sounding like, "Yes Steed," "Right," "OK," all that came out was, "Burble burble. Burble, burble."

By now, my head was beginning to feel like it would split open and an intense buzzing sound went off between my ears. The telephone, though, kept on functioning perfectly (this *must* be the underwater model, I decided), and as I looked up at the shimmering oblique of my wife's camisole as she leaned over the pool prodding down at me with a leaf net, Steed bellowed in a perfectly audible voice: "You're running out of fucking money!"

This remark made me bob to the surface like a cork, gulp down some air, and shout, "What? What?" into the telephone with great alarm. My exasperated wife pulled me from the water but I held up my left hand to indicate silence, even though her eyes begged an answer to my ridiculous behavior.

"What do you mean?" I gasped, heaving like a beached whale. "What do you mean, I'm running out of money? How? Why?"

"Are you all right?" asked Steed in a delayed reaction to my underwater burbling. "You sounded like you were choking there for a bit."

"No I . . . I was drinking a margarita . . . the salt got stuck in my windpipe."

"Well that's the long and the short of it," continued Steed. "Porker Intangibles Ltd. is down to ten thousand in the UK and BP Muzak in the US has got, what . . . fifteen grand in it? Dollars, that is. And we don't expect any significant royalties in the foreseeable future—not till you make another record at any rate, and even if you do record this year it'll be a while before the publishing rolls in—such as it is. I know you've only recently released *Porker, Himself,*" said Steed, referring to my last album, put out nine months previous, "but I'm talking about a *commercial* record, something you seem unwilling to entertain."

I leaned against the deck chair, puffing and gasping, my wife eyeing me with a look that might normally be reserved for a lunatic. Even my dog, the Doberman, Mustapha, one ear cocked and girt red tongue lolling in bafflement, appeared unsettled by my demeanor. Steed pounded on in my eardrum.

"Oh, it's all right playing a Donovan tribute in Madison Square Garden and collecting a Sneery for whatever it was—"

"Best old fucker who isn't dead yet," I prompted, which is what the award might as well have been, seeing as it was actually for "Best Timed Gaps Between Songs on a Pop Record" and handed out as a token to my career's irritating longevity.

"Right, right," Steed continued. "But it hasn't done a thing. For some reason, you remain invisible! Better get out on the road, is my advice. Now, there's this Swedish offer from Yoast Willem. Looks like it's dripping with Kronor—can't see how you can turn it down . . ." And off he went, describing the farcical ins and outs of Swedish contract law as I stood numbly by the pool, watching the summer disappear.

"Are you nuts?" asked my wife. A fair question I thought.

"What? No . . . I'm fine, dear, fine," I answered vaguely. But as she turned back toward the house, the camisole softly hugging her tan skin, I dropped the phone's base heavily onto the concrete siding and flipped the mouthpiece neatly over my shoulder, back into the deep-end, leaving Steed waffling on about the labyrinthine Scandinavian taxation system.

Chapter 2

Let me explain myself. My professional career in music began in the 1970s. January 1974, to be precise. Like most musicians, I had made the long journey from garage and front-room teenage bands, hastily conceived, comprised of old school friends or brief acquaintances, to regular gigging outfits manned mostly by people who were desperate enough to answer ads in local papers *("Bass player wanted. Must have own gear and transport. Into Floyd, Cochise, Stones. No bread heads.")* and throw their lot in with an intense but reasonably easy-going singer/songwriter/guitarist of no fixed ability. The various combos sported a phalanx of different names, usually headed by my own unlikely moniker, and duly slogged around the south of England, hitting the pubs, living rooms, church halls, and workingmen's clubs, parlaying a variety of material, sometimes well received, sometime booed, and oftentimes met with vicious sneers and solid, flying objects. Typical beginnings, in other words.

Names like "Brian Porker and the Wankers" (hard rock with a prophetic, but unnoticed by the press—none of which saw the outfit—punky attitude), "The Pink Porkers" (flamboyant glam with acid-influenced lyrics), "The Brian 3" (stripped-down hard rock minimalism), "Brian Porker and the Surrey Puma" (named after the cryptozooalogical beast frequently spotted crossing the A30 throughout the sixties and early seventies by many a drunk after they'd chucked the pubs out on a Friday night), "The Porker 5" (Little Feat on speed), "The Furniture Men" (no one, not even the band, could ascertain what kind of music this incarnation played), "Brian Porker's Soulbilly Shakers" (Soulbilly, my own invention—Tamla meets Eddie Cochran), and endless variations thereof had, in the form of cheap posters, graced telephone poles from Wapping to High Wycombe, none of them sticking to the poles' creosote or indeed the public's imagination for longer then it takes your average rock band to go belly-up in a dull funk of profound lassitude or a virulent broil of animosity. They all seemed doomed to failure. Then suddenly, out of nowhere and for no good reason it seemed, I had a hit.

In desperation, I had thrown my lot in with a straw-headed music publisher with bad skin who had built his own studio in his garden shed in a bland suburb in Middlesex. Here, I proceeded to record demos backed by a revolving door of musicians whom the publisher—who was acquiring my catalog of songs that I had foolishly signed off on for 50 percent—furnished on a weekly basis for a period of about three months in the summer of '73.

During one of those sessions that had taken place on a long, humid July afternoon, the combination of players unaccountably clicked, and of the five new songs we recorded, one of them, "Knee Trembler,"—a three-and-a-half-minute celebration of vertical sex—stood out like Bolicia beacon. I had virtually invented Soulbilly, a rather skillful mix of Duane Eddy and the Four Tops and had been performing this exciting new genre for six months in my latest incarnation as Brian Porker's Soulbilly Shakers, thrashing out the hammering-on Eddy technique (a signature device employed on almost every tune), combined with Eastern-sounding chord progressions à la the intro to "Reach Out I'll Be There" to stunning indifference from pretty much every audience we stood in front of.

But the original Soulbilly Shakers had never really gelled, and I felt my canny invention was being seriously shortchanged, until that afternoon when Sal Amblewood—the aforementioned straw-headed publisher—brought in an alcoholic Irish bassist whose Motown chops were bang-on, a hashish fanatic keyboard man who finally backed my songs with a marvelous rhythmic subtlety that no other ivory tinkler had so far managed, and an aging (he had to be fifty if he was a day) curly-haired South London drummer named "Spots" Morgan who played a three-piece kit standing up with such alarming yet rock steady ferocity, I wondered how this man had remained obscure for so many years. Turned out that in hard core rockabilly circles at least, Spots was not so obscure and had made a reasonable living at his profession for many years, playing in a small but thriving underground scene for uncountable greasy, quiffed-up outfits who would never let the rockabilly flame die no matter what. Spots, I discovered, was always much in demand and booked up solid for months in advance.

We struck a serious chord with "Knee Trembler," and our mouths dropped as we listened to the playback, having nailed that sucker in just one hell-bent-for-leather take.

"That's a fuckin' hit!" exclaimed Sal triumphantly. "That-is-a-fucking-hit!"

And so it was, peaking in the UK singles chart at number 3 in late January, 1974.

Even Spots Morgan quit his reliance on steady work with the many American acts who came to the UK to ply their ancient craft, using pickup bands that almost always included Spots as the drummer of choice, to join up with me and jog up and down the country in support of "Knee Trembler"'s incredible success.

I owned the name and saw no point in thinking up something else, and so, in keeping with the songs' unique style, the four of us faced the world as Brian Porker's Soulbilly Shakers.

We made an unlikely quartet: "Spots" Morgan with his oversize denims flapping around a soundly overweight frame and his jet-black greasy curls bobbing about his florid, fat face; Mickey "Monkey" O'Hoolan, donning a permanently wrinkled green Irish showband suit, his lanky, drunken frame weaving dangerously close to the edge of every stage we graced; Johny "Ice Man" Gill, stoned, emaciated, his brutally short snow-white hair and orange sunglasses framing aquiline features that never cracked a smile, even though he was ripped every waking moment. And finally myself, Brian Porker (aka BP or Beep to my friends), rather less adventurous in standard rock 'n' roll black jeans and leather jacket but still exuding an oddball intensity as I gripped my white Gretch and ripped into each vocal as if it were my final performance.

You should have seen us on Top of the Pops! Perhaps you did, but ten years on and it's hard to find any but diehard Porker freaks (and to be fair, there have been enough over those ten years to keep me in a tidy living) who remember when "Knee Trembler" rocked the charts and even made page two in the *Daily Mirror*:

'KNEE TREMBLER, VICAR?' screamed the headline.

Brian Porker's racy hit "Knee Trembler" is causing quite a wobble all over the country!' 'The naughty ditty about sex standing up has caused teenagers all over the land to copy its blatant advice. "Stand up and get it up!" goes the chorus, and by golly Missus they are! But when the vicar of St. Mary's By The Gate in the normally conservative village of Bunstead was caught with his pants down, it was too much for the locals. "I comes out 'o' the pub on Friday night, like, and there was the vicar giving it one to some young lady up against the wall behind the social club," claimed Ted Jasper, a local plumber. 'Standin'-up, too, the pair of 'em. Fair makin' the thatch fall off the roof, they was! Mind you, they was doin' it in the standin'- up missionary position, so I suppose it's all right then, innit?" '

But I couldn't follow it up, and my next single (taken from the first album, *Tremble,* and one of ten songs that recycled the same tricks employed on "Trembler," but to much lesser effect) barely reached the top twenty and fizzled in the second week of its release. And besides, I didn't want to follow it up. Even as "Trembler" was shooting up the charts, I was trying to escape the chaos a hit brings and ducked off every time there was a break from TV appearances and tours to concentrate on less one-dimensional compositions, stuff with staying power that really meant something. The genre I had created began to stifle me before it had hit its short-lived peak. In reality, "Knee Trembler" was not much more than a novelty record and I felt at odds relying on the obvious transience of its rather facile lyrics as a base for a lasting career.

I had always been angry. My hostility toward the world was a legend in my own mind, even though my everyday discourse with most people was courteous and polite (unless someone dicked with me, that is, then I'd go off like a firework in their face). But inside I was seething, and I was dying to make music that reflected this boiling angst. Once I went solo, there was no stopping the outpouring of diatribe, although luckily I did have enough dimension of talent to temper the churning lava with songs of love, sex, and betrayal—standard rock stuff, in other words—and I began to create an interesting display of material, much to the chagrin of Sal Amblewood. Sal, of course, became my manager from that day when "Knee Trembler" lashed out of his nasty Sound City monitors with such animal ferocity. He did not last long at the job. The straw-headed sebhoreic producer/manager expected me to repeat the formula, ad nauseam, and I, in my contrariness—after that first album—refused to even attempt to repeat it once. A singer/songwriter is what I wanted to be, not a one-hit-wonder novelty act, and within this earnest format I did achieve a measure of success, albeit of the lower-top-30-for-two-weeks-in-the-album-charts kind, and never made more than a minor dent in the singles charts again. And somehow I have kept this up for over ten years, a goodly run in the fickle world of pop.

But when pressed into service for the sake of a bob or two at the prodding of my latest (and perhaps most eccentric) manager, Tarquin Steed, I sometimes wished I had not shunned the commercial side of the genre with such decisiveness and attempted to adjust and refine Soulbilly into something more lasting, something that would have yielded a few more hits, thus a few more rungs in the ladder of rock currency.

And so, on a sticky, late August morning, I trudged into JFK, leaving America, my second home, bound for the godforsaken Scandinavias to sing for my accountants, and backed by a pickup Swedish outfit at that. That alone was enough to put me in a rather tetchy mood, and the full flight was not going to wash well with me at all.

Steed had faxed over the accounts the moment the phone had finally died in the swimming pool, and their story was irrefutable: I had to go out there and drum up some shekels, even if it meant an abrupt and melancholy end to the lazy summer I'd had planned.

The Gretch Countryman and the freebie Ibanez acoustic/electric were stowed in the hold of the monolithic British Airways jumbo jet, along with my invincible Tumi suitcase.

As I wedged myself into the minute seat I felt a buzz of communication between the immediate passengers. Almost from the moment I sat down, the complete stranger I was to share the next seven hours with projected a moony smile in my direction. It was one of those two-feet-above-the-ground "aren't I just the happiest idiot you've ever seen" smiles, promising a flight of almost unremitting grimness, and within seconds, my neighbor, the Mata Horror, as I had immediately dubbed her, intruded upon me.

"Hello, I'm a Bahá'i," she said without prompting, her drippy, middle-class English accent suggesting a predilection toward religious airy fairyisms.

The Mata Horror, perhaps noticing my distraction as I braced myself for the probable fall of a large brown wheelie suitcase being stuffed into the nearest overhead by a sweating, overweight red-headed gentleman (an item so bulky I couldn't believe the flight attendants had allowed it as hand luggage), finally averted her excessively happy gaze and began reading a small tan leaflet. I surveyed the people around me. Some of them spoke to each other in self-consciously gentle tones, often over their seatbacks, reinforcing my belief that I had landed smack in the middle of a convention of whatever obscure religion the Mata Horror had claimed to be a member of. She noticed my interest, and without a hint of reticence hoisted up the beatific smile once again. "We're Bahá'i. Many of us here." She gestured airily at the wide swath of bodies around me.

I stared at her with a false half-smile, chewing the inside of my cheek in nervous reflex as she launched unbidden into an outline of the genesis of her beliefs with a well-trodden mechanical simple-mindedness. Their guru, she informed me, was some Iranian fellow named Bahá'u'lláh (1817-1892).

She told me this as if it were the easiest thing in the world to pronounce, like Steven Martin saying "Anne Amelmahey," or the brain saying "Dr. Herferferfer," in *The Man with Two Brains*. She thrust a greasy pamphlet into my hands. I noticed the numerous dog turds floating above this Iranian's outrageous moniker and wondered if there was some ancient connection between Sweden, the land I was destined for, and Iran. I glanced at the other members of the religion, wondering how so many people could be so foolish as to follow the advice of someone whose name it must take years to learn how to pronounce; they actually seemed happy to be crammed together in a claustrophobic tube for seven hours, sharing the sour effluvium of each other's bodily odors. What was wrong with people? What desperation brings them to this? Whatever, I might as well hear her out, since she was going to tell me anyway and nothing short of an insistent "fuck off" would clam her up.

With the jackhammer wit of a troupe of boiled eggs, the cult members bandied jollities between themselves as my neighbor made her speech. Much slushy reference was made to their recent satellite love-in at the Jacob Javits Center in New York. Herself, the Mata Horror—after I professed complete ignorance of this sect—gleefully began to fill me in on its prerogatives and history. She outlined a particularly loathesome "love the world" type of philosophy which they stupidly hoped to spread to the rest of humanity. I gritted my teeth, blinked rapidly, and upheld a locked smile as I indulged the great lump and pretended to be interested. I looked her over, taking in the mustache, the red curtain she wore as a dress and the disgusting agricultural experiment she cultivated beneath her fingernails. As she droned on, I continued to observe in fleeting glances the other cult members who seemed interested in the progress of her apparent recruiting technique.

Unceremoniously, the plane began its unsettling rumble down the runway toward seven hours of thin air.

The Bahá'í were as serious a bunch of troglodytes as I have ever laid eyes on, and judging by their excited chattering, most of them were sitting on an aircraft for only the second time in their lives—the first being the flight over here. I also noticed with alarm that every one of them appeared to have thick, sausage-like fingers—a prerequisite of the cult perhaps?

Within moments of being airborne, one of the womenfolk two seats away from me ripped off her shoes and socks, and the fetid pall of toejam tickled my keen olfactory organ. Obviously, I was stuck in the midst of some species of nature cult involving sweating bodily hair. Perhaps it was the strip lights that glimmered dully over the aisle as the giant tube plunged upward, but it looked to me as if these people had hair on their teeth!

But even the visual and olfactory outrages I experienced did nothing to prepare me for the aural abomination I had to endure the moment the jet leveled off. Suddenly, the Mata Horror herself broke into the most banal non-melody imaginable (the words seemed to consist of complex loops of the founder's silly name, e.g., "Bahá'a'u'lláh, u'lláh a hab, ballah'u' a'hall a Bahá'í"), which was quickly taken up by other members of the cult, most notably a wide-arsed tart from Yorkshire whose bulk was practically destroying the seat in front of me.

To add insult to injury, when the stewardess arrived, each acolyte ordered tomato juice with Worcestershire sauce and actually seemed to be enjoying the dry roasted peanuts.

At some point during the group's mesmeric drone, the half Valium I had knocked back with a Bloody Mary in the bar at the terminal gate kicked in and I thankfully drifted off, miraculously remaining at least partially unconscious until the meal arrived.

I awoke a few hours later to a steady mumble of anticipation as the flight attendants crept agonizingly slowly down the aisles, pushing their unwieldy carts before them, handing out the foil-covered meals with smiles every bit as vapid as the Bahá'í's. Perhaps it was the Valium, but I got the distinct (distinct being a relative term when one is on Valium) feeling that the Bahá'í had been staring at me as I slept. Imagination, I told myself. Had to be, surely.

Each member of the cult was of course strictly vegetarian and the slow plod of the stewardesses was halted further as they abruptly did an about-turn when reaching my section of the plane, disappearing just as I was ready to order two or three mini bottles of red plonk with my meal. The flustered flight crew eventually returned, balancing special meals over my head like jugglers, which they distributed to the ever-grateful clan. At last, a young member of the cabin crew wearing enough makeup to put Jezebel in her place, took my order. I went for the steak, more to make a statement to the Bahá'í' than anything else; but the dark-lipped Mata Horror appeared not to notice as she swished her stained red curtain garment, dipped down under the seat tray, and passed me yet more subversive literature fished from somewhere down between her hairy legs.

"I think you're interested," she said between a mouthful of some colorless grains I took to be instant couscous. I had to give her points for enthusiasm, seeing as I'd responded to her robotical statements with nothing more than a few cursory Umhums and Oh, I sees.

I studied the propaganda while guzzling my mealy-tasting wine. "A *world embracing community of . . .*" announced the blurb in the Bahá'í pamphlet, and then went on to bomb me with such brilliant ideas as: *"the Oneness of God"* (original, original) *"equality of men and women," "universal compulsory education"* (I knew it was coming; amid the lily-livered platitudes they sneak in the old mind-control bit. Ha! Spotted it), and *"world peace upheld by a world government"* (presumably all the members of this government will agree on everything owing to the *"universal compulsory education"* they have received from Bahá'í's who are superior, yet strangely equal to themselves). And on it went in this mind-numbing fashion.

It took considerably less gray matter than that of your average gerbil to absorb the gist of this heinous discipline. But something in their monotonous chanting and the drip drip of the Mata Horror's ramblings had created a bizarre lassitude within me, stronger than the Valium, which was in any case wearing off by now, and I found my senses blurring into a half-conscious state in which time elasticized into some strange fluid abstraction.

The Mata Horror, the big tart from Yorkshire, and the slim, almond-eyed dark-complexioned young men who formed the male element of the group droned the tuneless tunes of Bahá'u'lláh, and I began floating in the formless pool of non-melody, strangely unable to break free.

Perhaps, I considered dazedly, the putrid steak I had consumed earlier had been contaminated with hostile bacteria that were infecting my peptic juices. Was it my imagination, or were my digits, sleek and nimble not five hours ago, beginning to fatten out like wieners? And where did that dirt beneath my fingernails come from? And where indeed did those five hours go?

"Mm . . . mm, what?" I mumbled as if awakened from a deep sleep, although my eyes had seemed wide open the entire time.

As my vision came into focus, I saw that the Mata Horror was staring at me with alarming intensity. I returned her gaze as best I could but found myself distracted, further alarmed by the site of her brethren, who, to a man, were leaning over seatbacks and twisting their necks from their various positions around me and applying the same fascinated scrutiny to my face. This was no longer imagination, yet I seemed oddly ambivalent about it.

"I asked if you felt relaxed—about your tour of Sweden I mean," the Mata finally commented. "Are you looking forward to it, Brian?" she asked, her eyes still pellucid and penetrating.

"Mm . . . relaxed. Yes, yes." When had I explained my business to this curtain-wearing cultist? I couldn't remember for the life of me.

I shook myself like a wet dog trying to remove the ridiculous "smile of the beyond" that now seemed plastered across my face. I reached out to my tray-table for more alcohol but found only a bag of dry roasted peanuts, which I stared at dumbly, imagining that they had just dropped through a crack in dimensions, a physical manifestation from the ethera beyond. The droning went on around me, and within that timeless, half-sleep region of consciousness I had a distant sense that I was joining in, committing my very vocal cords to the insipid Bahá'í chants.

Suddenly there was a bump, and the plane hit the tarmac in London's Heathrow Airport. The Bahá'í busied themselves with their obscure items of baggage, rummaging on the floor for loose pamphlets and earth shoes, once again taking up that annoying sense of joviality that had greeted me upon boarding the vessel.

I had entirely forgotten that in order to save money, Yoast Willem, my soon-to-be cohort on the road, had booked me on a flight with a London stopover.

As the Bahá'í collected their carry-ons and waited to deplane, I noticed the sly looks they threw my way. They seemed less stupid and more informed with intent than before, their demeanor even a trifle menacing. The Mata Horror locked eyes with me as I sat there waiting for the flight to clear of London-bound passengers and the inevitable hour or so of monotony before it continued on to my destination, Stockholm.

"Perhaps you'll meet us in Stockholm," she said before swishing off down the aisle. "We like to visit Sweden sometimes."

Chapter 3

*The hooded crows,
mincing carrion undertakers,
drop in on magpies
and steal their pickings
from the dogshit soil.
Women mind strings of
toddlers in bobble hats;
they trundle by plunging
me into melancholy keen
as pain.
Micro-twisters of wind
pick up plastic bags
and straggles of leaves
and spin them in perfect,
eerie circles. The
housing estates of Stockholm,
loneliest places on
Earth.*

Sweden, far from lifting my spirits after my strange experience with the Bahá'í on the flight over, plunged me into an instant blue funk. Not for the last time I found myself silently cursing my manager for dragging me away from that halcyon summer, my well-maintained and soothing pool, and my well-maintained and soothing (and scantily clad) woman. I had a free day before rehearsal to brood through my hotel room window at the blocky, soulless estate behind the building, so vividly portrayed in the above piece of tosh composed in perverse inspiration. People, I have heard, make a niggardly living writing claptrap like this—it's called "poetry," I believe.

Such was my state of mind as I flopped around the hotel and paced the wet streets of Stockholm, now, like the rest of Scandinavia, in the throes of what appeared to be darkest winter—two months before the rest of the world! If I had realized that for four solid weeks I would see no sunlight whatsoever, the debacle that ensued might have been avoided completely, for only a fool would submit himself to such extreme conditions, whatever the money.

Regardless, the following day I found myself in a dog-hair-ridden Saab streaking through the incessant rain toward some godforsaken suburb of Stockholm, himself, Yoast Willem, simultaneously manning the steering wheel and cellular phone. In this setup that is Yoast's specialty, I am but a gun for hire, an international name to hoist in front of his revolving-door Swedish backing band, the Yöbs, and the collector of a fairly hefty bag of kronor at the end of it. I must confess, there is a certain element of ancient wish fulfillment involved, for in my more naive days the idea of being a pop star, to me, was to go to another country, perform for people, and stick money in my pocket the night of each show, instead of seeing it disappear into the ethera of tour managers, checks, bank accounts, wire transfers, and finally a company logo.

Of course, the dosh *would* finally end up in such a construct, but at least I could entertain the attractive illusion that it was indeed all mine as I stuffed fat rolls of Monopoly-like kronor into my pocket after each show. Yoast, a talentless, lying rogue and would-be singer/songwriter/promoter/accountant with the insidious charm of a rock manager, put the band together, stomached the cost of monitors, P.A., and lights, and got the best deals for the headliner, somehow wheedling decent sums from the local promoters and all expenses covered.

But there is always a pound of flesh involved, a transaction involving brain cells, pride and subservience, weather and mood—a price, in fact, to be paid.

The rehearsal room, Yoast assured me, would be bigger than the last time I was here (this being my second outing with the Swede and his ingenious setup). But after a grim forty-five minutes of conversation concerning the paltry sum of bookings Yoast had actually secured for this tour, we arrived at a cavernous building, went through a heavy industrial-sized door, and zigzagged through menacing towers of equipment before finally reaching the actual room, which was, if anything, smaller than last time.

By now, memories of that last time with Yoast and the Yöbs came flooding back like reopened scars: the endless drives on slow, two-lane highways in a cramped van listening to the band members nattering in Swedish against a soundtrack of Swedish Mersey Beat impersonations on the radio; Swedish—that strange convoluted tongue that after five hours of night driving and bottles of Pripps #3 ale began to sound positively Pakistani. At times I indeed wondered if I had been abducted in a doze and whisked off to some bizarre mobile Indian restaurant.

And one freezing night, deep in the mountains of Norway as we hacked through a blizzard in a vain attempt to reach Bergen in time for a show, Gork, the keyboard player, had told me the chilling legend of the Mountain Women. Gork warned me in deadly seriousness that piss stops were verboten here in the Norwegian forests, for it was in these wild and rugged cliffs that the Mountain Women lived. Many's the time, he assured me, that unsuspecting men had stepped from their vehicles after dusk and found themselves, penis in hand, surrounded by large, fur-clad women with horned Viking helmets atop their blond, pigtailed heads. Before the unfortunate victim could barely shake himself dry, he was enmeshed in nets and hauled up the cliffs into the Mountain Woman's "disco love nest." There, he would be forced to perform sexual duties until exhausted, worn to a frazzle, and returned, weeks later, thin and pale and half the man he used to be.

"What the fuck are you talking on about, Gork?" I'd asked, confused.

"Mountain fucking women," he asserted.

Gork had been driving and I had been in the front passenger seat as he had recounted his yarn. The Yöbs snored fitfully in the back. Despite the absurdity of Gork's tale, I felt the chills flow through my spine as the image of that awful creature, decked out in mail and shield, a two-pronged lance gripped in her big hand, passed before my mind's eye in a flash.

I should quit this game, I remember thinking. It's getting to me. Then I started giggling, realizing the potent weed Gork had been feeding me had assisted his deadpan storytelling to a T.

With the frightful memory of Gork's Mountain Women echoing in my head, Yoast and I stood in the doorway of the tiny rehearsal space. I eased my way past a stack of ratty speakers and looked around the cramped pit, stacked floor to ceiling with amps, cables, keyboards, and a drum kit. A man was holding a bass guitar. He introduced himself with a bright grin: "Ja, Brihan, pleased to meet you. I'm Stigma, the bass player." I winced as I shook his hand, studying his ball of brown curly hair and his faded blue, crimped jeans. He looked like a 1969 Lancia salesman, and before the evening's rehearsal was through, the blaggard had given me a detailed description of how he had recently shaved his girlfriend's "poosy." Shaved poosy didn't really turn him on, he was quick to mention, but he enjoyed the actual task of shaving it. He seemed dangerous to me. But what really got my goat was that I was expecting to see Gorm, the Yöbs' usual bass player.

"So, thanks for telling me about Stigma, Yoast," I whined on the drive back after rehearsal. "What happened to Gorm?" I added lamely.

"Gorm?" said Yoast, already bored and reaching for his drug, the cellular phone. He absently punched in a number and tapped on the steering wheel, waiting for someone to pick up. Yoast's dark and beady eyes scanned the rain in the headlight beams as he broke into a sudden and aggressive conversation with his old lady. Rapid-fire sentences popped out of his mouth with the much used word "oor" repeated again and again. I had spent three weeks on a tour bus with him a year ago and no mountain range, no torrential downpour, no distance was extreme enough to deter him from having a damn good ooring session at least every half hour.

"So?" I said, after he had hung up. "Gorm? Gorm?"

"Oh ja. Gorm iss playing in the Theater. We should go in the week on a night off. It's supposed to be worth seeing. What about the other guys? Pretty good, eh? Best in Sweden."

"Yeah, yeah," I agreed, although merely for the sake of politeness. The drummer, whose name I could not yet master, had the time-keeping of a man with Tourette's syndrome, the keyboard player favored heavily synthesized programs, which I had had to take him aside about, and the lead guitarist knew all the tricks of someone who had learned rock guitar from a college course. At least they'd done their homework and the songs on the tape I had sent over had been learned with consummate professionalism, which made the rehearsals skip by with ease.

"And so . . . as yet," I ventured, getting back to the important subject of monetary remuneration, "we've still only got gigs on the weekends, right?"

"No, there's one on Thursday now, next week."

"Yeah, yeah, I got that. But that's it?"

"Well . . . ah, y'know . . . economy iss bad, suddenly like everywhere. But I'm rilly trying to get some more gigs like I'm rilly working my balls off, you know? And like, Stigma's rilly good, ja?"

"Yeah, Yoast, he's great. I just would have liked to *know*, that's all. Just so that I don't feel like a giant dickhead *all* the time, know what I mean?"

"Ja Brihan, also," he went on blandly, "the guys have to fulfill an engagement with the National Skiffle Band on the second weekend, but the guys who are filling in are rilly good, it's no problem."

"What!?" I barked.

"Hang on!" yelped Yoast, as his phone went off like a siren. By the time he'd finished with the convoluted set of Oors and Jas that serve as Swedish conversation, we were pulled up outside The Sticka Bargrill opposite my hotel, and after rehearsal and the onset of deep jet lag, all I wanted was a large cold beer.

"The Kronor got devalued overnight," explained Yoast as we drank Pripps #3 in the Sticka Bar.

"So?" I said, watching a vaguely familiar woman in red slide into the ladies' room.

"So, you know. Your money's not going to be quite as good. But I'm working like fucking crazy on more gigs. Iss so . . . hard, right now, you know?"

At Yoast's pessimistic words, those familiar prickles of annoyance immediately turned into great hammerheads of gloom. I stared at Yoast, wondering what the hell I was doing there, in Stockholm, winter locking in like a vice and the rain falling in sheets outside the bar. My eyes continued to study Yoast, as if noticing him really for the first time. His face appeared more chubby than I remembered and his black hair, hanging in flat strands around his face, looked greasier, more unkempt than on my previous visit here. Yoast, it must be added, also opened the show backed by the Yöbs, performing eight or nine of his own unfortunate and entirely non-ironic bubble gum tunes. That evening, he sat next to me at the bar wearing a type of oilskin fisherman's sou' wester. This man wants to be a pop star? I thought, at that point not even seeing a joke in it. Still, I can't blame the Swedes for their ridiculous fashion sense. Who cares what you look like in a country that's freezing pitch-black nine months of the year?

From across the room a nauseating song buzzed out of the stereo and Yoast perked up.

"Have you heard this? It's Donny Breed. You know him?"

"No."

"I just had him over here. He sold out every show. He's had three hits this year. He's American. You never heard him? He's half Cherokee. 'Iss hard to find a true love, yeh, iss har, har, har, hard.' " Yoast sang along with Donny. I ordered more beer, cursing the success of this Breed fellow, who, it transpired, sang only songs about mating with teenagers. Yoast asked my opinion of these atrocities and I told him in no uncertain terms that the harebrained funkster ought to be committed.

"Ah, ha ha ha!" boomed Yoast. "You are rilly cool, Brihan. Rilly cool!"

As the last pedophilic Breed song faded out and the Rollmöps crashed on with their ersatz sixties bosh, the woman in red whom I had glimpsed earlier suddenly appeared at my side. A vicious shock ran threw me when I realized her identity: it was herself, the Mata Horror! I stared in amazement as she hoisted herself onto the stool next to mine and placed her sausage-like fingers on the Formica-covered bar. A sudden impulse to bolt was quashed by the sight of the rain pelting down beyond the smoke-filled window.

"Bahá'a'u'lláh u'llah a hab i bah bah," she sang gently, right into my face. "Thought I'd come to Sweden after all," she said, and then turned with a googly-eyed smile and headed straight out of the door.

"What the fuck was that?" asked Yoast.

"Just some idiot I met on the plane," I mumbled, actually shaking in my shoes. It was time I got to bed: the beer, the smoke in the bar—it was getting to me.

"Nice tune," said Yoast, in deadly earnest. "I like that."

We sat in silence for a while. Yoast ordered two more beers. A midget sitting at a table behind us appeared to be cracking jokes. His three companions, two of whom were seriously well-built women in furs, were laughing fit to burst.

"So, Brihan, I haf a few irons in the fire right now," said Yoast, apropos of nothing.

"What?"

"*Good* irons," he continued, sounding as if the beer had hit him in a maudlin way.

"Ja, also, apart from this rock business," Yoast continued as I scanned the rain-pelted windows nervously, "I haf a ski hat importing business that's doing rilly well, number three in Sweden."

This boastful statement reminded me of the bogus chart positions my plethora of managers have quoted me over the years in order to convince me to tour countries like this.

"Oh really," I answered, amazed at the number of scams Yoast was mixed up in and suddenly glad for the diversion. On my last visit here under his auspices, he had slowly unfurled his list of dubious businesses, ranging from Afghan breeding to part ownership of a Rastafarian record store specializing in rare sixties ska music.

"Ja," he went on, "they are wool, lined with fleas."

"Fleas?" I repeated, confused.

"Ja, the ski hats—all fleas inside."

I stared at him uncomprehendingly.

"I don't know how you say it in English . . . fleas!"

"Things that suck blood and hop?" I ventured, perhaps thinking of my many managers.

"I don't know," said Yoast, frustrated. "Fleas!"

"Oh," I nodded, finally twigging it. "Fleece!"

"Ja, fleas!" yelled Yoast, bashing his beer glass into mine in a celebratory fashion.

After a few more brews, I walked across the road in the swirling rain and entered my hotel. A labyrinthine establishment with a lobby the size of a cupboard, the Stöokabröton drew a strange clientele consisting mostly of transients, who stayed in the tiny rooms lining the corridor to the right of the lobby, and conservative-looking businessmen, who rented the upstairs suites to the left. Yoast had come through for me on this count at least, and the suite I was booked into was agreeably large if brutally unattractive, done out as it was in a color

I immediately dubbed "suicide pulch," a common Swedish interior decorating nightmare.

I paced through the lounge, glancing despondently at the dense, uninviting brick-red sofa, the forlorn glass coffee table, and the lonely TV set, and made for the bedroom. The one light in the room, which the Swedes responsible for this travesty of comfort had thoughtfully placed smack in the center of the ceiling (having made sure the wiring only allowed for the most powerful lightbulb available this side of an aircraft landing light), glowered down at me as I flopped onto the bed. Right away I began tossing the remnants of old Scandinavian tours around my mind, trying to put them in order, attempting to nail dates on the jagged tumble of random recollections. My jet-lagged mental ramblings continued for a while as I lay there and I did nothing to abate them, finding these interior visions far more diverting than the fare offered on Swedish television, where a balding man playing guitar and singing to a stuffed cat is considered highly entertaining. I glanced over at the clock radio on the bedside cabinet that read 11:30 P.M., just as the phone began ringing.

"Hello," I said throatily, affecting extreme weariness, even though the jet lag had spun its usual cruel trick leaving me wide awake at bedtime.

"Hello, Brian," said a mesmerizingly soft male voice in a lilting Arabic accent. "You don't know me, but you met my friend on the plane. My name is Mukraik. I was on the flight also. We were going to London but then decided to come immediately to Stockholm. Are you well?"

My usual response to strangers who call me up in the middle of the night just because I am something of a celebrity is a perfunctory curse followed by the most violent clank down of the receiver I can muster. I have destroyed telephones in this way, and hopefully eardrums too. But this Mukraik fellow had the most mellifluous and calming voice, snapping me right out of the mind surfing that threatened to keep me awake all night. So I just sat there listening, relaxed and attentive.

"Bahá'í bah u'lláh, ahab i halla bah . . . do you like this tune, Brian?" asked the silken-voiced Mukraik. Not waiting for an answer, he launched into the insipid pap once again and without questioning, I too, joined in.

A curious, numbed feeling flooded through me, and the next thing I knew, I awoke in bed at 9:00 A.M. refreshed and calm but confused as to how the communication with Mukraik had ended, and what, if anything, had transpired after the singsong.

I dressed quickly and drifted down to the breakfast room, where I ran into the guitarist from the English pop group Slade, the one with the head shaped exactly like an egg. Himself and the boys were now choosing to call themselves Slade Two, or so I had read recently. Yoast had informed me that they were over here, battling their way through the Scandinavian disco circuit, minus the main focus of the group, the lead singer. The egg-headed guitarist asked me what I was up to, and when I explained Yoast's little setup he exclaimed in a ripe northern accent: "Ee, it's better than being out of work, in't it?"

I agreed with him vaguely but my mind was on that insidious Bahá'i song, which without question, I had suddenly decided to integrate into my stage act. I determined that I could slide in those puerile rhymes right over the chord changes of one of my old favorites without anyone noticing. This thought came to me as naturally as if I was considering changing the arrangement of a particular song's introduction or conclusion. The idea did not seem odd at all.

Returning to my room I sat down in front of the silent TV screen and remained there for a good ten minutes without questioning the strangeness of my behavior. I felt as though I was waiting for something. Sure enough, the phone rang and the sinuous voice of the Bahá'i Mukraik thrummed in my ear; once again I became glazed and obedient, hanging on to his every word.

"Brian, we've been waiting for you, you know. We've been preparing for a long while now. Are you going to incorporate our song into your act as I have suggested?"

I couldn't remember any concrete suggestion on his part, but something at some time had been inferred, or ordered—I wasn't sure which.

"Yes, Mukraik," I replied, unable to control my words. "I think that's a good idea. I'm going into rehearsal today, I'll work it out with the boys then. It's a nice tune, I think."

"Yes it is," said Mukraik, chuckling softly, his voice like a chocolate brook running over round pebbles.

"Lolla sends love, Brian. She'll see you soon." I knew automatically that he referred to the Mata Horror. "We'll all see you soon, Brian. Good things are in store. Time is a cycle, it throws up repeated expressions of the divine, recurring manifestations of the Oneness of God. You are part of that cycle, Brian, as we all are, but you are, we know, a very important aspect of the cycle. You will find out soon. Carry on with your tour, it will pass the time until the day arrives, the great day of enthronement."

"Um . . ." I mumbled, absolutely mesmerized by this load of old kibosh.

"Until then," said Mukraik, "good Bahá'í Brian, good Bahá'í!"

I sat grinning at his little joke. What a pleasant chap, I thought! And off I went to rehearsals.

Chapter 4

As the Yöbs and myself once again bludgeoned our way through my material later that afternoon, I could not, with many a secret grimace, avoid asking the internal question: do Swedes have soul? This idea popped into my mind that very afternoon as the Yöbs and I worked our way through my songs. For although they have reasonable mastery over their instruments, the root of their expression is obviously more technical than emotional.

Running over my tunes that day I was painfully aware of the wrinkles of aggravation I felt at various points in their performance. Are the drums slightly ahead of the beat as opposed to microscopically behind? Is that a keyboard Pörfen (I *would* get the hang of his name) is playing or a digital reverberation unit from hell? Why doesn't Stigma's bass crackle or fart occasionally? Why is every note so perfect, so rounded? Why does Torke, the guitarist, have to keep stomping on that mega digital effects box every time we launch into a song? Could it be that he prefers that hideous over-affected barrage of blandness (played on his very new, bright red guitar called a Quantum, or a Sceptre, or something) over the earthy tones I have insisted on for my material?

Indeed, playing with these Nordic devils placed one's credibility in no small amount of jeopardy, but at least I didn't have to pay them and my money came off the top, courtesy of Yoast and his admittedly clever business acumen. As we worked that afternoon, incorporating the Bahá'í tune into one of my old raves without a word of dissent from the malleable Swedes, I again thought back to the first tour I had done with Yoast and the Yöbs. Because of the money involved and the fact that I considered Scandinavia too far from critical civilization to matter, I had simply soldiered through, ignoring the string of "why's" as listed above. But in every obscure freezing townships it seemed there was a tiny population of Brits who remembered my days as an icon and purveyor of that sweet, short-lived shining moment in rock history, Soulbilly.

On some nights, a solitary voice would pipe up from somewhere in the back, near the bar: "On yer bike, Porker!" one would yell, or: "They swing like a eunuch's balls!" I ignored these remarks, preferring to indulge the various drunken Swedes named Yorge, or Jarre, who would come backstage after the show and harangue me with spittle-spraying pigeon English, all of it complimentary toward myself and the band.

Still, as these thoughts spiked out at me every time Torke tweaked up his solid-state gloss machine halfway through a song, or when I said to him, "You know, play it more like Steve Cropper," concerning the execution of a solo, and he looked at me like I might be referring to some form of hairstyle, then, I would feel a few pangs of embarrassment—guilt even. But to hell with it. One can't be a hepcat forever, and what's so wrong about being an aging rocker trying to earn a crust? Besides, it was only Scandinavia, I reasoned, and I liked the way that Bahá'í tune was fitting in. That at least appeared to be a nice little touch.

At last the tour began and we skittered around the usual circuit of clubs and discos, the roulette wheels and blackjack tables tucked away in the corners of each establishment in typical Swedish fashion, I experienced an almost narcotic disinterest as we slogged from Gothenburg to Norrköning, Jönköning to Eskilstuna, as if I were watching a particularly dull movie. The only times I felt grounded in the situation was that brief period in the set when I inserted the Bahá'í chant. Then, an interesting electricity shimmered within me which the crowd picked up on, and even their numbers seemed to swell as if the people hanging back in the darkness near the toilets, the bar, or the gaming tables were now drawn onto the dance floor by the limpid simplicity of the tune.

Incredibly, it didn't occur to me that this weird exhibition of triteness was everything I had fought against my whole career. The band was noncommittal and worked up some reasonable harmonies around the piece, and those audience members who appeared from the shadows had a vaguely stunned look about them; they stared up at me as if I was well worth staring at. Then, when the Bahá'í insert was over, they drifted back to the shadows and I resumed the show as detached as before.

THE OTHER LIFE OF BRIAN

At the last minute, Yoast had managed to procure a number of engagements for the week, and so our schedule heated up, assuming the gruesome grind of a more typical tour. On the second Thursday of August we played in an acoustically demented wooden box in Gävle, and then piled into the van for a nine-hour overnight drive to Jokkmokk where we were due to perform on Friday evening. The trek was as tiresome as expected, and nothing of interest transpired, not even tales of the legendary Mountain Women.

Stepping out of the van, finally escaping the stale air, the odor of banana skins, beer, and human breath at 9:30 on Friday morning, was a sweet relief. Outside the hotel in Jokkmökk—a town so far north it could almost be considered part of Lapland—I breathed in the fresh, freezing air and attempted a couple of exploratory slides on the icy pavement while Yoast checked us in to the Hotel Börped. Jokkmökk had that gnomish quality so typical of small Swedish towns where the rampant commercialism of American fast food franchises had been integrated into the cobbled streets and effectively Tom Thumbed.

We went directly to the hotel restaurant and wolfed down boiled eggs, toast, and homemade preserves of fruits I had never heard of along with licoricey tea from Gotland and three different kinds of pickled herring before heading off to our rooms for a day's sleep. As I made my way out of the busy breakfast room—obviously *the* place to start the day in Jokkmökk—I stopped by at a table occupied by the egg-headed guitarist from Slade Two, together with the rest of the band. After a few pleasantries about food, endless drives, and impossible tour schedules, I found the elevator and ascended to the third floor. The moment my head hit the pillow, the phone rang and I picked it up expecting Yoast with some problem, but the familiar svelte voice of the Arabic phantom, Mukraik, greeted me with a sinuous welcome.

"Brian, how are you? The drive wasn't too hard I hope, and you have the day to sleep, don't you?"

"Mm, yes," I mumbled, staring at my free hand which seemed swollen, the fingernails encrusted even though I had just washed after breakfast.

"Don't worry about your hands, Brian," he said, as if reading my mind. "It's a Bahá'í trait even we don't fully understand yet—it is a divine sign from beyond. Perhaps—our wise men sometimes joke—

the great Bahá'u'lláh had pudgy fingers and liked a spot of gardening. Today is very important in our Bahá'i calendar and you are very important to the future of our religion. It has been determined, Brian. It has been written: 'And the messenger of God will appear to you from on high, bearing the likeness of his previous incarnation, Bahá'u'lláh. And he shall point the way. And you shall recognize him and give guidance according to the skills of the masters and in the frozen wastes his eminence shall shine forth and his glory be made manifest.' "

"Ah ha," I said, and the next thing I knew the clock radio alarm was blaring and it was late afternoon, time for soundcheck.

Once that task was completed, the Yöbs and I ate an early dinner, which was steamed up in the gigantic kitchen at the back of the disco. The club's doors weren't opening until 8:30 P.M. that evening, so I decided to explore the cavernous building further. I spent my time climbing vertical steps into storerooms stacked high with chairs and desks, wandering in and out of a series of lecture halls complete with baskets of cheap ballpoint pens and big projection screens and other rooms lateral to, below, and above the chintzy ballroom with the disco globe lights and the tiny stage where we would perform later on. The place was vast, and no clue as to its immensity could be gleaned from entering its small foyer, which was situated diagonally across the street from our hotel lobby. From there, it appeared to be just another Swedish disco/rock club, which are always spacious compared with the club gigs in the US and Britain. But once inside, beyond the kitchen which could well have served a major hospital, I discovered that it was a multilevel utility/arts/entertainment center serving the town of Jokkmokk, and in typical dwarfish fashion, the Swedes had disguised its immensity by building most of it underground.

The conference halls and storerooms of the complex were eerily empty and I felt an odd foreboding as I explored them, an unwarranted nerviness I could only calm by humming the Bahá'i tune in strange loops and configurations that sprang to me with consummate ease.

Eventually, I rounded a bend between storerooms, ducking under huge padded poles and air-conditioning systems, and came across Yoast, fishing through a giant pocket in his oilskin for the cellular phone, a black fedora, pimp-like on his glum head. By serendipity, I had returned to the dressing rooms, next to the bright clanging kitchen, its staff readying the chicken-in-a-basket and burgers for the evening's customers.

"Brihan," said Yoast distractedly, already beginning to punch a number. "You going back to the hotel? We're not on till 11:30."

"This place is massive, Yoast! How do they afford to run it?"

"Not from our ticket sales," he answered with a wry chuckle. "We've sold only fifty—and Slade Two have sold only thirty-eight. Ha ha! At least we're doing slightly better, eh?"

"You mean Slade Two are playing here? In *this* building?" I could well believe there was another dance hall that I had not stumbled across in my ramblings, but I thought it a mite cheeky of the local promoter to put two international acts on under the same roof, on the same night, in a town practically within walking distance of the Arctic Circle.

"I know," said Yoast, the phone pressed to his ear. "Stupid, isn't it? But that's how they are up here: they drink so much fucking alcohol because they are *so* depressed; it's fucking dark all winter, then in the summer, the sun shines at midnight! It drives them crazy . . . Ja! Hello, hello Monica!" And off he went "ooring" and "jaing" into the phone to some little piece of chicken he had stashed away, another rubber-faced blonde, thick as two short planks and with a skinny brunette friend in tow to give to the band.

We strolled back to the gig at 11 P.M.—Yoast with his docile groupies tagging along—and threaded our way to the backstage area, which was conveniently located by the kitchen, on the other side of the hall. The disco lights splashed on the dull-looking couples seated around the room, and I thought it a good thing that we never had packed houses in these insufferable places with their unfriendly layouts. If we did, getting to the stage would be a difficult proposition.

Half an hour later the disco lights went down and the band and I—together with a gormless young waiter balancing plates full of food who chose that moment to emerge from the kitchen where we'd been hanging out—crossed the lonely dance floor to the stage to a few whoops and hollers from the audience, who by now had swollen to 132, still leaving the place cavernous.

We began our show without much enthusiasm (it's not easy to get pumped up at the site of a table full of overweight male Swedes, sitting smack in front of the stage, bellowing instructions to a waiter about who should get what plate of badly cooked chicken parts). As before, I felt unconnected to the music, and only when we reached the point in the set that included the Bahá'í chant did I feel any engagement. True to recent form, shadowy figures seemed to emerge from the recesses of the hall and dot the edge of the dance floor, creating some small semblance of atmosphere, which dissolved as soon as we resumed normal service. Once our final tune clanged to its conclusion, I darted back to the dressing rooms, rudely avoiding the two fans who held out ticket stubs for me to sign. After guzzling a few beers with the band, I sloped off into the bowels of the building to see if I could find the room where Slade Two were performing. This time I got completely lost and found myself in a dank basement, my ear pressed to the wall behind a stack of tattered P.A. equipment, listening to a jumbled version of one of Slade's old hits. I groped in the darkness searching for a door, which I found half hidden behind a rotting projection screen. I opened the door, and there, right in front of me was a slim young man of Arabic descent whom I immediately divined was Mukraik, my previously invisible guide.

"Welcome, Brian," he said, gesturing for me to enter, which I did, instantly becoming passive and languorous at the sound of his voice.

"Lolla is here," he said, pointing behind him to a densely packed group of people. "And all your subjects. Brian, you are the one we've been searching for. You are Bahá'u'lláh incarnate! We've been *expecting* you!"

At this, herself, the Mata Horror, still resplendent in the red curtain garment and with a large group of Bahá'í in tow, beckoned me to follow her through a narrow door. I felt their warm and expectant presence around me as we entered an incense-filled room where I was led to a chair elevated upon some stage-like arrangement hastily knocked together from pieces of old board. They sat me down on this erstwhile throne, draped me with a garland of flowers and Lolla, her eyes wet and googly, pointed to a painting on the wall as the whole lot of them broke into the tuneless tunes of Bahá'u'lláh.

I stared up at the painting, unable at first to grasp its full implications. It was a poster, actually—a reproduction of what was once a reasonably competent watercolor, sticky-looking, as if it had just come from a color copying machine that had dulled the original hues down to a somber ochre. It portrayed a young Middle Eastern gentleman with a blissed-out expression on his face and a gold robe swaddling his shoulders.

It bore an unmistakable likeness to myself.

At that moment I felt frustratingly close to shaking off the torpor that the Bahá'i seemed to be able to induce in me with such alarming ease. I experienced a queasy schizophrenia, which pulled me one way then another as my mind fought some deeper, more primal energy for control. Within nanoseconds I shifted back and forth between outrage at what had actually been going on since I met the Baha'i' on the plane, and bland acceptance that I was, in fact, the reincarnation of himself, Bahá'u'lláh!

My eyes widened as I remained immobilized on the throne, as if nailed there, listening to Mukraik reel off a litany that bespoke the autocracy of my new position. It seemed I would come into bucket loads of loot that the Bahá'i had amassed over the years. I would be able to pass judgment on individuals of the sect, jet around the world preaching the simplistic mumbo I had read in their literature, and, typical of these messianic cults, I could help myself to the womenfolk.

This rosy future was described in poetic form by Mukraik and the Bahá'i who bobbed and fawned around me in full subservience. But something else was nagging at me, spiking through my anesthetized state, something that I felt—if I could only get to it—would free me completely of paralysis. Then I realized, gradually, that I was hearing another song, undercutting the Bahá'i banality like a bracing astringent. It came booming through the wall right behind Bahá'u'lláh's likeness. It was Slade Two, pounding out one of their old hits, "Gudbuy T'Jane."

Suddenly, there was an explosion and a man-sized piece of the plasterboard wall, just left of Bahá'u'lláh's portrait, crashed inward, propelled by an actual man. The Bahá'i stopped in mid-chant, backing away from the wall, and stared at the figure who lay there groaning, a big acoustic guitar in his hand and a number of wires running from the bottom of his trouser leg. He looked up at the Bahá'i with equal surprise. Then he noticed me and blinked rapidly. A small wisp of smoke rose from the guitar's sound hole.

"Ee, booger me. It's Brian Porker!" he exclaimed. " 'Ow was yer gig, mate? We only pulled 38, wanna join us for the encore? It's just a Chuck Berry medley, nuthin' too clever like."

He struggled to his feet, brushing off the drywall dust from his purple velvet jacket. And then he took a good look at the strange gathering, with me at its center, seated on the makeshift wooden throne.

"Funny backstage scene you've got goin' 'ere," he said finally, flashing me a cheeky wink as if he had discovered a fellow entertainer with a particularly interesting sexual peccadillo.

It was the guitarist from Slade Two, resplendant beneath his trademark basin-cut hairdo and sporting a feckless grin on that perfectly oval chicken's-egg face. He appeared to be having problems with some dangerous-looking acoustic amplification system, but the incongruity of his presence among the flaky religious herd had the restorative effect I needed, and with a jolting feeling of physical reentry, my normal senses returned with a bang.

"Jesus!" I yelled.

"No, no," pleaded Lolla, pulling at my jacket as if trying to drag me back into my former tranquilized state.

"No, Brian, not Jesus—Bahá'u'lláh!

"You hypnotized me!" I accused the cult firmly, completely shedding the hypnogenesis like a species of mental dandruff. Mukraik and Lolla fell at my feet.

"We had to! We had to!" Lolla implored. "You would never have believed us otherwise. And it is written: 'The incarnation shall be instated, willingly or coercively.' We knew your cynicism would prevent you from entering the glorious realm of Bahá'i willingly—we had to practice our leader's hypnotic methods to get you to see. But look Brian! The icon! It *is* you! You are he, Bahá'u'lláh returned to earth once more to lead us . . ."

"Hold it!" I demanded. "Enough of this crap."

I looked once again at the picture. Certainly, there was a striking resemblance; it could have been me with a suntan and a bigger nose. I looked over at Slade Two, who had by now all climbed through the hole from the adjoining stage.

"Well," I said, leveling my eyes at the egg-faced guitarist, "that remarkable pickup system you're foolishly employing has had a bracing effect on me; and 'Gudbuy T' Jane' didn't hurt any, either. Thanks, pal. What is it anyway?" I asked, nodding toward his guitar.

"S'called the Stouffer Sonic Set-Up," he answered, holding up the instrument with some difficulty; there seemed to be a massive black pickup inserted into its sound hole, which spat out wisps of smoke at regular intervals. "A genius named Stouffer rigged it up—comes from up north 'e does, not far from me. It's bloody mega when it works right like. Incredible natural acoustic sound, but you 'ave t'wear all this tackle an' all. Fookin' wires and thermostats and suchlike. Something to do with the local power and body temperature. Freaks out occasionally though, know what I mean?"

"Christ, it's . . . *different*," I said, amazed that he'd actually been conned into using this abomination.

"It's explosive when it goes right, and explosive when it goes wrong!" joked the guitarist, opening his eyes wide under his basin-cut. " 'Oo are these twats then?" he added, eyeballing the swarm of Bahá'i.

My attention returned to the cult and with it my expression assumed a set-jaw look of abject outrage. They had used mind control techniques in order to fulfill their obscure prophesies. But the spell was broken; I would have no more of their airy-fairy kibosh.

"Perhaps it does look a little like me," I said finally, studying the guru's image. "But hearing that cracking old Slade hit and seeing this silly bugger blasting through the wall has shaken me out of the foul torpor your evil coercion had me in. Hypnotism? I'm sorry, but that's not fuckin' cricket—you can take the job and stuff it! And besides," I added, enjoying the feeling of having my own comfortable bristling senses back, "I do not eat dry-roasted peanuts!" Glancing down at my fingers I was relieved to see that they had lost the wiener-like quality favored by the cult. I looked over at Slade Two. By now, a few audience members had crept up on the stage and were poking their heads through the hole, wondering if they were going to get an encore. One of them noticed me, a small chap who looked like a rock critic.

"Ja, BP!" he wailed, sounding as drunk as any typical male Swede on a night out. "Getting up on stage, ja, and joining Slade Two for encore, ja?"

"That's it!" I yelled, striding toward the hole in the wall. "Get me a guitar! Let's boogie!"

Chapter 5

That night in Jokkmokk's entertainment complex ended in a fine jam with Slade Two, followed by some serious after-show imbibement in which both the Northern English legends and my Swedish cohorts ended up carousing on the frigid streets of the town before the polite and earnest local police force managed to corral us back to the safety of our hotel rooms before someone suffered an accident. The Bahá'í' had not joined us in our celebrations, even though I was quite prepared to let bygones be bygones and would have gladly hung out with them within the security of my rock 'n' roll buddies. They had simply disappeared. They were not staying in our hotel, that much was obvious, and no one knew where they were spending the night.

Next morning, we departed Jokkmokk in the thralls of a blizzard to yet another lifeless location further south. The back of the tour had been broken and the winning post was in sight. My mood improved markedly, and like all tours, the events of previous days seemed light-years away and this strange Swedish trek eventually ground to an uneventful conclusion with a ragtag of poorly attended shows (for which Yoast duly paid me the agreed amount in full without a word of dissension).

At last, I finally left for London to join my wife and son, who had flown over from America. Somehow, during my rudely interrupted summer and the long hours in Swedish hotel rooms, I had written enough songs for an album and was anxious to arrange recording sessions. After a week of agonizing phone conversations with my brilliant but wayward manager, Tarquin Steed, and his assistant Smyke, I finally managed to convince them that, yes, indeed, my latest material was outstanding, full grown, and of exquisite artistic perception and irrepressible commerciality, and each gem had been evicted from its home in my subconscious with both inspiration and perspiration. Having clobbered the pair of them with much whining, they finally agreed to spend my money on a month of studio time, and before Christmas I had completed my latest record, "Porker in Aspic," ready for rush-release early next year. That task out of the way, I could spend some time toning down my intellect with hours of excruciating television, thus numbing myself enough to get through an English Christmas without climbing the walls.

As fortune would have it, a rerun of The Sneer Grammy's was on at 1:30 in the morning on ITV one Friday, so, armed with large quantities of McEwen's Ale, I stayed up to watch myself for the second time, collecting my Sneer Grammy for "Best Timed Gaps Between Songs on a Pop Record."

It was the usual farce, and before long I was halfway through a bowl of crudités my son had prepared for me as an endless stream of African Americans took the podium and made their speeches of acceptance, thanking God, their record companies, their managers, and various unknown high school teachers.

At last I took the stage to collect my Sneery, awarded to me most incongruously by Tina Turner, whom I kissed and hugged for too long, tilting the applause into a frittering embarrassed ending. At this point, sitting there on the Italian sofa in my beautifully appointed London flat, I had become so wound up that I didn't notice the whole raw jalapeno pepper my rascally boy had slipped onto the plate of cut vegetables. As my image on the screen received the ridiculous looking statuette and intoned my pretentious one word speech ("Justice!"), I bit fully into the pepper and began masticating the seeds, eyes agog in the blue glare of the television set, where by now, I was careening off of the stage followed by a confused looking Turner. The meltdown heat of the pepper had begun to sear the roof of my mouth like a flamethrower, and I stifled a scream and grabbed at the can of warm McEwen's, guzzling the unsavory brew in desperation. But it was none too effective in quelching the vegetable that continued to flay the inside of my mouth in a multitude of nuance I had not dreamed possible.

Eventually, after more beer and some chemical English concoction from the freezer that some shysters had the nerve to call "ice cream," the burning subsided, and I sat at the dinner-stained black wood living room table sweating profusely and resolving to soundly wallop my vicious young son in the morning.

Recovering slowly, I studied the clutter on the table: a new phone book, some junk mail, and a pile of letters Smyke had delivered from our London office. Opening one, I saw that it was from a firm of American lawyers representing a couple who had boarded my dear old half-uncle John "Sir" Bacon, for two years before he died at the age of 91. Being a trifle touched in the head, he had bequeathed to these people—Gaylord and Loretta Baedburger—his entire estate.

I read the letter with disgust and decided right then and there at 2:15 A.M. as the last drunks yelled and reeled in the street below our window, to dash off a terse reply. It appeared that these rapacious vipers were hoping I would just shut up and let some wide-bottomed, God fearing hicks walk off with my old half-uncle's money. No chance. I would make that clear, and the letter I composed backed my resolve with pristine vivacity:

To Messrs. Goldtraub, Cardbaum and Silvermein
Dear Sirs:

John Bacon was, and always had been, as nutty as a fruitcake. My dealings with the man throughout my life, whether in person or in the form of the numerous letters he wrote me during the latter part of his life, were always besieged with lunacy. As he grew older and even more demented (a word used to describe John by his last doctor at Lombardi Memorial Hospital), he moved in with numerous families whereupon he executed almost identical wills to the one the Baedburger's received.

Ever since I can remember, he has recounted to anyone who would listen the story of how he was injured in France in the war and underwent an operation whereby a metal plate was inserted into his head. He awoke to find King George V at his bedside congratulating him on surviving this unique operation. During the many retellings of this story, which my family foolishly regarded as the truth, he would point to his penis and allude to the unfortunate effect that the procedure had had on him. What this effect may have been was never made clear. But seeing as the plate was allegedly inserted when he was but a young man of twenty, and considering the five children he went on to sire, one can safely rule out impotence, at least until well after the prime of his life. Before

THE OTHER LIFE OF BRIAN

he died, a CAT scan was performed on him that revealed no such metal plate: this is the kind of man we are talking about here.

Mr. Bacon would drift in and out of many alleged religions and embrace them and their practitioners with equal alacrity, only to eventually denounce them with great vehemence for reasons entirely nonsensical to all who heard them. He would send me letters which I still have in my possession, the contents of which are bizarre in the extreme. One minute he loved me and wanted to see me again (and of course give me all his money), the next he wished me burned at the stake as some form of heretic, for reasons he alone imagined. You are not (and I'm sure do not wish to be) aware that the man was committed to more than one mental asylum during his lifetime.

Even in his 80's, he would suddenly fly into a rage at whichever family happened to be presently stuck with the noisome task of caring for him, and dash to the nearest bus station and travel across the entire continent in search of the next religion he could embrace, then denounce with complete finality. Once, he appeared in Utah, became a Mormon and married three hapless women lured by his charm (yes, he was mad, but charming too), only to dump them unceremoniously when he discovered that a once famous pop group had been prime exponents of that particular religion. This may seem, given the excruciating nature of said pop group's repertoire, a sensible thing to do. But Mr. Bacon did not denounce the religion because of their banal squealings, but rather because he wished them to reform with him acting as their manager, and when they refused, he threw a fit and punched the most famous member squarely on the nose. Mr. Bacon narrowly avoided a lawsuit by jumping the state line and disappearing for two years into the protective enclave of a monastery populated with monks who practiced the obscure faith of "Silencio," and thus, according to their vows, would not breath a word of his presence.

Make no mistake sirs, I will contest this ridiculously misplaced Last Will And Testament on the grounds of incompetence and am in no doubt that I shall blow your case right out of the water.

Yours sincerely,
Brian Porker, Esq.

GRAHAM PARKER

That completed, I popped another beer and bellied up to the table, pen in hand, my ire flowing in rich veins, the seemingly inordinate supply of hatred for what I perceive to be a world full of very stupid people burning in my head like the mental equivalent of the jalapeno pepper. I suddenly remembered a gig in Halmstad on the Swedish tour that had been canceled by some unscrupulous agents without a word of apology. In my Bahá'í induced stupor, I had not given thought of retribution, but after the cult's spell had been broken, I had picked up the agent's fax number from Yoast, determined to send them a piece of my mind when the mood struck. The mood had indeed struck and the boil of venom I had worked up needed to be lanced, and thus, more hate mail screamed from my pen:

The EMA Agency
Dear Scumbags:

I gather from my associate, Yoast "The Terrible," that my scheduled appearance in Halmstad was canceled due to pressure brought to bear from your agency; something to do with, I believe, one of the ridiculous cabaret acts you represent getting the elbow by the local promoters due to lack of interest, and my innocent self being used as a mere pawn in the game, an intangible object, a faceless name useful only as leverage for cretins like yourselves to get back at those naughty Halmstad boys.

Let me tell you, you puke-headed agents of deceit, that I have a long memory and plans are being hatched, even as you read this, plans diabolical enough to make you unscrupulous creeps think twice before you cross me again.

I am, at this very moment, training an enormous Irish Setter named Mooja. Once fully broken, he will be shipped to my contacts in Sweden and instructed to break into your offices (of which I have received a detailed floor plan, freely available to those who, like myself, have studied Swedish contract law) and spray the contents of his rear end all over your hideously perfect Scandinavian pine wood desks.

The dog in question is being fed a diet of rotting vegetation (perfumed with offal essence to induce appetite) and those obscene salty licorice things you Scandic prannies seem to enjoy so much. True, there have been a few incidents involving involuntary bowel movements in embarrassingly public places during the course of Mooja's training. But these kinks are gradually being ironed out and the animal's back-up sphincter control program is proceeding apace. Before Christmas is upon us, I believe he will be ready for his righteous task.

I myself first got wind—if you'll pardon the expression—of Mooja's talents the first day of this tour. Yoast, bastard that he is, brought the cur on the tour van without a word of forewarning (no real explanation: something about girlfriends, babies, complicated dog-sitting arrangements, Europeans in tight trousers) and the giant beast doused the entire van not 15 minutes outside of Stockholm. Oh yes, make no mistake, Mooja is the dog for the job. That's why I purchased the hound from Yoast and had him shipped back to the UK for complete training.

All this, however, can be avoided by merely sending a cheque for two thousand (my expected fee for the gig) US dollars to my UK management offices at the address below. I feel sure you will swiftly comply with this request if you wish to avoid the consequences of my idle threats.

I did not travel all the way from America to rehearse for four days in a broom cupboard with people whose names I cannot pronounce, and who think that Rod Stewart and Jeff Beck's presumptuous version of "People Get Ready" is the original, to be unceremoniously robbed of 2,000 bucks.

So, to put it simply, in a language that agents the world over can understand—pay up, you fucking bastards!

Yes, incredible as it may seem, there is a human being at the end of your ill-considered actions and I sirs, am it. Please send a bankers cheque to:

Tarquin Steed
75B Harley Street (cul-de-sac)
London
England UK

Yours,
Brian "Sir" Porker

At last, the heat from the jalapeno had all but dissipated, leaving, I imagined, only minor lacerations on my tongue, and I was about to call it a night when I heard a car door slamming in the street below and some boisterous conversation. I gritted my teeth, finding that last ounce of ire that needed to be vented, and shot over to the bay windows, visions of hot oil and buckets of urine flashing in my head.

As I swung the windows open, the cretins below had turned on the car stereo and the moronic bombast of rap music filled the chilly air. Two jokers stood there, hanging on the driver's-side door, double parked and patently inebriated. They were young black men—presumably not the politically correct term any more if American trends were anything to go by, and I supposed they now called themselves "African Englishmen." One of them I had seen recently moving into the building next door, and with that last bung of hostility still clogging my system, I decided to let the blighter know that this kind of ragarousting was not on in the street where I lived. No sir, not at two-something in the morning.

Lacing my sneakers, I bolted down the two flights of stairs to the street. I strode in swift step right up to the car, muscled between the two startled men, and yelled in the direction of the stereo at the top of my lungs, "Come back when you can write a fucking tune, pal! " And with that, I bashed around at the stereo's controls until I found the eject button. I then removed the heinous cassette and threw it across the street.

Setting my jaw in a tight parodic grin, I gave both men a quick eye to eye before I returned, at the same swift step, to my door. They said nothing, but appeared to have sobered up instantly, and presumably, not wishing to annoy this potential psychopath one iota more, slammed the car door; the driver gunned off down the street and the neighbor hurriedly dashed to his flat. The boil of ire now fully lanced and the pus of angst ejected, I crept into the bedroom and went out like a light.

Chapter 6

I had endured the Christmas season with reasonable aplomb, effectively reducing my fecund sensitivities and intelligence with lashings of puerile British TV personalities, earfuls of moronic Radio 1 DJs, stilted phone conversations with old friends ("Little Sodding on Sea, 95325," they would announce in a singsong manner, answering their telephones as if impaled on stick), and bucket loads of stick-to-the-ribs meals boiled up by relatives intent on removing all nutrients and vitamins from the food; and now, on this typically wet and chilly English day, just after 1984 had crawled reluctantly in, already Orwelian with Thatcher's seemingly permanent hold over the country, I found myself in a taxi cab, struggling through the Monday morning traffic on Marylebone Road, heading toward my manager's office in a nameless cul-de-sac off Harley Street.

"Cuh! Wouldn't mind 'earnin' wot these blokes earn, would you?" the cabbie said, flicking his head toward a tall distinguished doctor striding up the stone steps to his practice, dressed in a Saville Row pinstripe and carrying a black leather medical bag. I had long since given up responding to cabbies' banalities. There was no to and fro of normal intelligent conversation with these people. They had absolutely no desire to hear what anyone else had to say and might just as well have been hurling their inane observations and gutter-press philosophies at a stuffed wildebeest.

"Next right," I ordered, my teeth gritting and sweat beading my forehead. I was anxious to get out.

"There ya go, guvnor. What, bein' seen to by one of these posh docs, are ya?"

"Yeah, kidneys are on the blink," I lied.

"S'all right for them that can afford it, eh? Heh heh heh."

He drooled at me anticipating a largish tip, which I foolishly gave him. I cursed myself after handing over what felt like two or three pounds in weight of the latest nasty-looking currency. Every time I returned to England after a tour the money had changed yet again, and I often found myself on the supermarket line, ahead of a string of impatient customers, pulling streams of coins out of my pockets only to be told that most of them in fact were obsolete and no longer legal tender.

The day had begun. It was not yet 11 A.M. and I was already very angry.

I leapt up the steps to my manager's office, turning my extreme hostility into energy. I was wearing a gray running suit, still damp in the armpits from a two-mile jog I'd done earlier.

Anger aside, I was feeling fairly reasonable considering the usual hangover I had battled in order to get out of bed by 8 A.M. To accomplish this early rise I was assisted by a touch of jet lag I had picked up after a one-off solo gig in France, just after Christmas. Normally, a show so near the holidays would be turned down in no uncertain terms by me, not wishing to shed the Valiumish sloth the season affords with adrenaline-producing rehearsals. But in this case (those coffers still clawing toward the red ink) I had accepted the gig on Steed's assurance that they wanted a mere half hour on a TV special for a goodly bundle of francs.

This little jaunt had left my body clock slightly out of kilter and I am an expert at using jet lag as an excuse for sleeping through late afternoon. Even a one-off show in Paris will serve me well as a major disorienting experience that can be used to get out of all sorts of normal endeavors. It's not unusual, for instance, for my long-suffering wife to find me fast asleep on the floor of our London apartment at two in the afternoon and have to push me aside, like a dead animal, as she attempts to Hoover our royal blue carpet, and this after a mere one-hour flight from the continent that took place at least two weeks before.

I pressed Steed's buzzer and announced my presence on the intercom. The door of the ancient stone building opened and I bounded up a flight of stairs, passing an elderly gentleman on the ground floor corridor who, judging by the tubing snaking up his legs under the white hospital gown and the glowing transparent bag in his hand, was undergoing a barium enema. This was not an unusual site—

my manager's workplace was in a building with six other offices, all of them concerned with the profitable trade of healing.

On entering his suite—which was to all appearances as clinical as a doctor's quarters and only the rock music publications on the coffee table gave away its true designation—I found my manager, Tarquin Steed, in a heated telephone conversation. Steed was speaking a stuttering mixture of the Queen's English and what sounded like pigeon Japanese, apparently attempting to clarify some obscure contractual point with whoever was on the other end. I sat down on the green leather sofa and picked through the magazines. One was entitled *Metal Thrash*, another *Teenage Death Rockers!* I flicked through them, sneering at the primped hirsute fashion display that today's youth presumably believed to be prime exponents of rock 'n' roll. I silently cursed Kiss, Motorhead, and Hawkwind for starting this tosh in the first place.

Tarquin, finally satisfied with his communications, put the phone down. "Ah, there you are. You look well—been for a sprint then, laddie?" he asked in a voice (in keeping with his surname) straight out of the Avengers. Tarquin's previous profession was Magistrate's Court Judge and he had the public school voice to go with it. On this morning he wore checked trousers with red leather fox-hunting boots, a Tweed jacket sporting leather patches on the elbows, and a white linen shirt punctuated by a red and white polka dot bow tie. His shock of white hair needed cutting and hovered about his large rectangular head like a snowstorm.

"Oh, just . . ." I began, but as usual was immediately interrupted by my hyperactive manager. First the cabdriver, now Tarquin. Why, I thought, is England full of people who have no intention of listening to what anyone has to say?

"Well my lad, it's looking good, it's looking good!" he trumpeted, bounding from his swivel chair and heading toward what appeared to be an antique map pinned to the wall. I felt a tingle of impotence pass through me as Steed with his august and blithering presence immediately dominated the atmosphere of the room. *What* was looking good? My latest product had been rush-released to yawns the size of the Grand Canyon. The task of promoting *Porker in Aspic* among the numbing dross of the marketplace was so thankless it filled me with a palpable lethargy. And quite frankly, I wasn't that keen on the thing anyway and was now having severe doubts about its veracity. Who wants to have someone constantly poking them in the eye? Who wants to feel besieged, constantly badgered by streams of self-important lyrics set against a backdrop of shopworn rock 'n' roll archetypes that seem to be losing value with each passing year? Not too many, obviously. But I kept these thoughts to myself, and only entertained them in my darkest moments, mostly clinging to the idea that what I was doing was still of some relevance; and much of the time, luckily, I even liked what I'd created.

With the dire reality of another albatross strapped across my shoulders, I had recently bombarded Steed with pointed faxes, haranguing phone calls, and the general whining that accompanies the victims of unfeeling fashion. Much of this lambasting he countered with the usual bland managerese, insisting that some artistic compromise on the next release would surely do the trick, forgetting that my age, hairstyle, intelligence, and sheer bloody-mindedness were so thoroughly against me. So, I thought again, staring up at Steed, who wielded a plastic baton that he tapped around the wall atlas—what could possibly be looking good?

"The tour's looking good," he said alarmingly, ignoring my testy expression. "Yes, look at that! Amazing isn't it? That's where Abel went . . . all the bloody way in a rotting old clipper ship. You can fly though, OK?" he chuckled.

My confusion was evident, but Steed was not about to leave any pregnant pauses hanging in the air.

"So, um . . . you had a little run in with the Bahá'í, I hear," he continued, completely changing the subject before I could respond to his opening gambit. He raised his eyebrows and drew his eyes into slits in a suggestive manner.

"Ah . . ." I sighed, not wishing to get into it.

"Nothing . . . um . . . nothing the missus should . . . ah . . . be worrying about, was it?"

"What the fuck d'you mean, Steed?" I countered, alarmed at the thought of lascivious rumors spreading like wildfire through the biz.

"Oh, nothing," said Tarquin, but not meaning it.

"What the bugger have those Northern twats been saying?"

"Well, Brian, you know how people talk . . . I mean, if anything did occur of a—you know—shall we say *naughty* nature, we could use the press. Scandal's always good for business. That egg-headed guitarist from Slade Two seemed pretty sure—"

"Bollocks!" I interrupted firmly, then added: "They haven't said anything in print, have they?"

"No, no, no," Steed assured me hurriedly. "The boys were just in here the other day—we might be taking over their management." He stated this matter-of-factly, as if it were no big thing, but I didn't like the sound of it.

"Oh, Christ," I moaned.

"Anyway," Tarquin went on, "I'll take your word for it—on the Bahá'í I mean—they were just fans then, that it? I heard they turned up at an awful lot of gigs out there—saved the tour, by the sound of it. I'd watch out for those people, though, if I were you."

"Yeah right, right." I had no intention of going into the details of my cult abduction experience with Steed; I'd still been going through a few weird lurches that I felt sure were related to the Bahá'í's powerful hypnotic skills and did not want to be thrust into a relapse just then, in Steed's office, where I already felt besieged.

"All right then," he said finally, returning to the job in hand. Steed then minced around the great wall atlas, pulling out pins and replacing them in no apparently logical pattern, clicking the heels of his riding boots together like Hitler deciding to invade Poland.

"What tour?" I asked in delayed reaction. "You said something about a tour. You're not teaming me up with Slade Two, are you?"

By now, I felt the morning's anger/energy quota, which had burned so brightly before entering Steed's office, depleting rapidly in the face of Steed's confusing tactics. Tarquin was like some exotic sea creature when faced with adversity. He would put on a misleading display of bristling, puffing, and fin-flashing, effectively leaving any other life-form with predatory intentions swimming off with its tail between its tentacles.

"Smyke didn't tell you?" he said, his eyebrows raising in a glorious display of mock surprise.

"Wha . . ." I groaned, feeling the life go out of my eyeballs and my tail already disappearing.

"Tasmania!" boomed my manager. "Oh for Christ's sake, BP, didn't Smyke call? Well never mind, it's going great. They're really enthusiastic down there, and we'll be the first international act to do a major tour of Tas for years. Now! . . ."

And on he went, outlining in cunning management logic (this logic insists that the only way to improve one's commercial clout is to accept every vile engagement thrown one's way) his ideas for salvaging my career, phase one of which was a two-month tour of the "Ireland of Australasia," Tasmania.

He had purchased the yellowed wall atlas in an antique shop on the Portobello Road, an atlas crisscrossed with the routes taken by a number of early explorers. One of these intrepid travelers was Abel Zanszoon Tasman, the discoverer of Tasmania, originally named Van Diemans Land, after the explorer's boss.

Tarquin's overactive imagination had gone into high gear and I had been cast, without a scrap of consultation, into the role of latter day Zanszoon, and without a shred of research into the feasibility of such a reckless idea Tarquin had begun feverishly faxing and phoning agents and promoters; already, gigs in this unknown antipodes were being penciled in for the months of March and April.

By virtue of extensive self-promotion, rich benefits would be reaped by those daring enough to concentrate on such untapped markets as Tasmania, Steed reasoned, and after my recent complaints he was only doing his job as creative manager.

Steed continued to explain this supposedly brilliant idea with all the badgering force he could muster as I sat there dumbfounded, the drying sweat in my jogging suit re-moisturizing in an uncomfortably pricklish fashion, echoing the impotent tingling going on beneath my skin.

"BP, BP, BP! . . . 'Ello Beep, all right?"

In walked Smyke, Tarquin's verbose assistant, as usual repeating everything like an ack-ack gun.

"Mr. Porker, Mr. Porker, Mr. Porker. Just the man! Fortesque wants to know about guitars for the tour—one acoustic and one electric? One of each, is it babe? And the ondioline?"

Smyke clutched a pile of mail and some photocopies. He was wearing the sort of sweater that folk singers wear—those chaps who constantly stick fingers in their ears as they reach for difficult Celtic notes of obscure nuance. He slapped the stuff down on the table, clapped his hands together, and yelled, "Passport photos!" in my general direction, screwing his face up in an inane grin before joining Steed at the atlas.

"Looking good, looking good, looking good!" he enthused with another clap of his hands.

"It is, isn't it?" said Steed, once more raising his white eyebrows as he poked at the atlas with his baton.

I sat and watched my management team, affecting a wan smile when a look of abject misery would have been closer to the truth, and thought, not for the last time, about bald-faced lying managers, hyperbolic chart positions, and impossible tour schedules. The telephone rang and Steed rushed over to get it, bursting into a loutish Australian accent and guffawing loudly with someone named Shirley, before dropping back into his chair and agreeing that, yes, Brian Porker would be available for extensive phone interviews with Tasmanian rock publications by next week. I winced and looked at Smyke, who was pouring through the mail he had brought in with him.

"There you go, there you go," he enthused, handing some stuff to me. "Reviews of *Porker in Aspic* from America—better than over here, I must say—and some fan letters . . . aaaand, the usual begging junk. Shall I throw that away, Beep my babe?"

Beep my babe? Where was he getting these phrases? A man of his age? I glanced over at the glossy music papers on the table, proudly boasting their parodies of rock, and for a minute thought that the world had gone mad, and that somehow I'd been left out of it, stranded in a lonely sea of sanity.

Nodding robotically, I took the envelope of review copies sent over by Shinto Tool, my latest in a long line of American record companies.

"Dump the fan mail too, Smyke," I whined, determined to at least show someone in this office that I was not happy. Smyke pursed his lips, barely visible under his enormous bushy, brown mustache, and put the fan mail on the desk. He clapped his hands together again and returned to his previous war cry: "Passport photos! Off you go, BP, up to Baker Street, my lad. Need some new passport photos for the visas! Soon be on us, this tour. Soon be on us."

Chapter 7

In my game, time no longer exists as a daily phenomenon, but is perceived as a series of yearly blocks truncated into months by enforced schedules. The year is only remembered by those chunks in the diary devoted to touring and recording, processes that within themselves seem to possess an infinite nature, as if they exist outside of regular, normal time, but later are simply remembered as markers of a life flashing forward like a lightbulb with legs, running for a distant finishing line.

If my game is entertainment—singing, songwriting, playing musical instruments, and, oddly enough, the occasional playwriting—it should also be added that traveling is as much a part of that game as is any creative endeavor. Tuning up, hiring mental cripples who exist under the guise of musicians, winking at the lady with the breasts in the front row to the chagrin of her boyfriend, and working hours and hours on some brilliantly profound third verse that will go completely unnoticed to all but the most fawning, bookish fans—all this is locked within those blocks of time that make up the year, but no more so than traveling.

After Steed had filled me in on the surprisingly generous guarantees the Tasmanian promoters were offering and outlined the profit I would pull in, even after expenses and the inclusion of a two-man crew, I had no arguments to put forward (plus, the bounder had placed the alluring figures in front of my wife first, who was duly impressed and insisted I not miss this opportunity to bolster our accounts with Australian dollars), and I reluctantly agreed to the tour.

And so, before I had time to think, before that strangely vacant period between January and the second week in March had had time to register, I found myself on a nice little thirty-hour flight from London's Heathrow Airport to Hobart International, Tasmania.

I was accompanied by Fortesque, my trusty tour manager, and a young, pie-faced wastrel named Carruthers, whom I was told, was "one of the best soundmen around." Whether he knew his way around a console was yet to be seen, but judging by the ill-fitting emerald green boxing shorts, the oversized T-shirt with the word "Tit" emblazoned on it in bright red letters, and the matted ginger hair that resembled nothing less than steel wool on fire, he seemed to me anything but a sound man. He spoke, if speech it could be called, in some indecipherable Northern brogue and came from an obscure village he referred to as "Kimber." This word also popped up in most of the bizarrely phrased sentences he uttered and seemed commonly to be used in the context of problems, or trouble. When I first met him in the airport terminal he immediately informed me that he'd left some essential equipment in the taxi and that we were "in t'serious kimber, boogger me if we ain't."

"Well," I ventured, staring up at him with an aching neck—for he was at least seven feet tall—"I'm sure we'll be able to pick something up on the other side." His only reply to this was the single syllable, "nibs." What "nibs" meant I could not fathom, and he disappeared into the throng to find the bar. A sinking dread overcame me. I hissed my manager's name under my breath and hoped to God I would not find myself for thirty hours, in a seat next to the improbably named Carruthers. All I knew was that my laziness and reliance on Steed's dangerous choices had landed me with this dubious personage; I had simply gone along with his recommendation and not bothered to even meet the man in whom I would have to trust my presentation to the Tasmanian public. What the hell, I thought. Tasmania? Luckily, Fortesque was a known and well-liked quantity and seemed unfazed by the bizarre spectacle that was Carruthers, and that would have to do for now.

I boarded the plane, sweating like a pig, great swollen shoulder bag bumping ears and backsides, stumbling down the crowded aisle scanning for seat 32D, all the while casting surreptitious glances at Carruthers, who thankfully plonked himself down a few rows ahead of me.

Even without the gangly Carruthers occupying the space of two men in close proximity to myself, I still had nothing to cheer about; the flight was jam-packed and I noticed with a wince that the smoking section, ten rows back, looked absolutely full. Sliding back for a puff was going to be a problem and I would have to seriously consider tampering with the smoke detector in one of the chemical toilets.

I had one aisle seat free to my right, but was forced to leave it vacant under orders from that most dreaded denizen of the air corridors, the Stewardess From Hell. She barked at me, insisting I stay put, at least until after take off, and I sat there praying that no one would occupy it, grimacing and clutching an imaginary talisman every time some massive sweating human came squeezing down the aisle, checking the row numbers. To my left, however, an Arab sat, already rubbing one of his putrid stockinged feet against my leg at every opportunity, cracking pistachio nuts, and smelling like a goat. The stinker leaned over that thin divider, the armrest, as if it didn't exist, as if no encroachment of space were occurring, and smiled at me! He seemed happy at the proximity, undaunted that the plane might become completely full and that the aisle seat next to me taken. He appeared to be, unlike myself, accepting of the cruel fate that nails absolute strangers together for long, long hours, sharing those accumulative odors that hang in stale clouds and permeate one's very clothes. His perky demeanor suggested that he considered our situation to be fair enough—that things could be worse!

I sat there, almost cracking my teeth with irritation until finally the seat belt signs lit up and the tube of metal began barreling down the gray slab, the aisle seat next to me miraculously remaining free. Gasping with relief, I furtively glanced around the cabin looking for the Stewardess From Hell, whom I would most likely encounter many times again on this marathon voyage, and when I could see no sign of her, slipped over to the aisle seat in midtakeoff, leaving the Arab still giving me little grins, happy either way. I jammed on my Walkman headphones, wishing to send him definite signals indicating privacy, and stuffed my bag into my previously occupied seat, thus avoiding a dreaded earful of his unformed philosophies.

Suffering the obligatory two-hour wait for the drinks trolley, I pulled out the reviews of my latest rush released product, *Porker in Aspic*, that Smyke had given me light-years ago in the London office. Why I had left them unread for so long I couldn't say, but there they were, tucked away in my shoulder bag waiting to cheer me during those long odorous hours while my life rested in the hands of some hayseed who called himself a pilot.

Studying the reviews immediately fomented my anger, that bottomless well of creative goo that serves as the essence of my inspiration.

They were practically indistinguishable from one another, as if torn off in some corporate rock charnel house by the carcasses of scribes whose asinine assessments had been preordained by presumptive logic formulated long ago. Neither resoundingly bad nor good, they waffled in the hinterland reserved for artists whose impact had long been diluted by the fierce scramble for new blood.

The bastards were treating *Porker in Aspic* as if its assured and mature brilliance was merely a journeyman's nonchalant, workaday achievement; as if this kind of focused writing and recording popped out of the imagination of every second-rank talent over the age of thirty-five who was lucky enough to have a recording contract!

"Surprisingly strong," said the uppity hack from *Tuning Fork Magazine*. From Moi? Surprisingly strong? I seethed to myself as I delved into the next robotic article, which came from the self-satisfied pages of *Rising Stereo*: "Porker's lyrics show his usual flair and craftsmanship on the uplifting ballad, 'Horse Tangent,' " wrote a woman named Anthea. "Usual flair?" "Craftsmanship?" The words needled into my skin, causing me to reach for my folder of fax paper in order to jot down a series of severe drubbings. The mechanical simpletons of the American music press were going to feel the sharp end of my "craftsmanship" for these preconditioned heresies, without doubt.

"It may not have the stinging one-two punch of Porker's former work," wrote that loathsome guy-rope enthusiast Jay Weinerbaum of *Campers Monthly*, "but for Porker fanatics it will certainly work like a warm compost on these chill evenings."

"Warm compost"? The former gardening columnist Weinerbaum was comparing me to horseshit and humus and fully intending such comparisons to be favorable?

And to make matters worse, Steed's absurd idea of rush-releasing *Aspic* before the vinyl had had time to dry, as if it carried enormous weight and importance, was backfiring with all the force of a clapped-out Honda 50.

I spat bile as I composed the faxes and floated in a sea of immeasurable megrims: was this Steed's way of avoiding the lackadaisical reaction I would no doubt receive if I were to appear in civilized areas of the globe? Was this then, to be my future in the superficial world of entertainment, where the aging hacks in their corporate abattoirs chopped up yesterday's prime cuts and dressed strings of fresh offal in modern packaging, pumping the bloody entrails into the bloodstream of today's dullard, tossle-headed youth?

Was this my manager's answer? Hump me off to Tasmania for two months like a sack of old spuds?

My ire now at peak performance level, I burrowed into the examples from the school of clichéd rock journalism, clobbering the wretched publications and their scruffy little hirelings with a force and venom that eventually pulled me out of my doldrums, giving way to a pure, vibrant state, as if a hefty dose of endorphins had kicked into action.

Yes, this was fine stuff. "Don't let the bastards grind you down!" I yelled inside my head as I signed off on the last smug little snit and capped my fountain pen as if returning a killing sword to its fine leather sheath.

At last, the drinks trolley arrived and the Stewardess From Hell prodded me out of my reverie. She was a middle-aged biddy (which means a lot older than me) with badly dyed black hair, tight facial skin with overlarge pores as if pulled back by an antediluvian face-lift, and an expression long ago hewn from a block of pure hostility. Her blatently accusing demeanor dared me to order something out of the ordinary and not wishing to disappoint, I asked for a Vodka gimlet. Her eyebrows twitched and her black pupils dilated.

"We don't have it," she said, and began to move on, as if dealing with a piece of wood or a concrete post.

"Excuse me, excuse me!" I almost yelled, making heads turn. "I'll have a beer then, *please*. A cold one."

She stepped back and fished out a can, eyeing me with deep suspicion before dumping the warm drink and a plastic cup onto the tray table.

"Excuse me," I repeated, a hiss creeping into my voice as the old viper began to move off. She threw back a glance spiked with venom.

"What!" she exclaimed. "What is it?"

"Nuts," I said defiantly.

Again, she burrowed into the clanking trolley and withdrew a pack of dry roasted peanuts and almost threw them at me.

I lifted the things in front of my eyes between thumb and forefinger, the memory of the Bahá'í debacle still stinging my psyche. With a grimace, as if holding up a dead mouse fished from the skimmer basket of my swimming pool, I tossed them at Carruthers' big red head, where they landed accurately and hung for a split second, the impact absorbed by the wiry thickness of his hair, before the crinkly packet dropped down behind his white neck.

The oaf did not stir, and I realized with irritation that he must surely be one of those people who can sleep on an airplane for fifteen hours straight with nothing short of a crash disturbing him.

The next dull hour of flight settled upon the passengers like a gray cloud and I caved to the nicotine craving tugging at my bloodstream and quickly got up to join the other drug addicts in the back.

A near impenetrable fallout of foul Benson and Hedges smoke greeted me as I picked my way down the aisle, affecting a nonchalance as I searched for an empty seat. Finally, there, second to last row on the port side, I spotted one.

The craving mounted a desperate assault and I almost broke into a run, hustling people in line for the toilets out of my way as I scrambled around the back partition. Arriving at the seat I noticed its unsullied appearance and eased myself down, casually pulling my rolling tobacco out of my pocket as if either way, a smoke might be a pleasant diversion, but if the seat were taken by a particularly light-bodied and tidy soul, then no matter, I would get up and leave, not bothered in the slightest that I might have to wait another *twenty-eight hours for a smoke*!

I settled into the seat casually, as if I wasn't really doing so, teased out a Rizla, and began to build a cigarette, casting a smile at the man in the window seat next to me who sat, drink in one hand, Benson in the other.

"Where are you going?" was his opening gambit, throwing me into an instant withdrawal panic.

"Ah . . . just having a smoke. Is it free?" I asked, gesturing at the seat.

"No, I mean where's your destination. Where are you traveling to?"

Whew, thank God for that, I thought, and continued rolling, any hint of distress now receding as I lit up, inhaled, and felt the weed coarse through my bloodstream. But behind the toxic effect of the smoke, a tiny alarm bell went off. That question, the alcoholic crack in his voice, his cannonball teeth full of gaps like gunsights and crosshairs leveling in for the kill—something here was amiss. I sucked hard at the tube of pleasure, which in my haste to roll resembled more a giant reefer than a cigarette.

Where am I going? Of course, the flight is hardly a direct one, making stops in both Bombay and Singapore. That's what he wants to know.

"Tasmania actually," I replied, confident that I was in fact on the right plane.

"Nice Zippo!" he bellowed incongruously, his placeless English accent definitely leaning toward the twit-like. "What do you want for it?" queried the cad forwardly. "I've been looking for one of those everywhere. You can't get them anymore."

By now, that tiny alarm bell was building to a less distant clang as the tintinnabulator of stress began his good work, continuing to warn me of impending danger. That same inherent process that reminded early man to run like hell from the hungry saber-toothed tiger, or the stampeding woolly mammoth, had evolved to exquisite refinement in modern humans, and was now giving me cause to ponder this potentially threatening predicament.

I took in his garb: brown suit, green socks, dun-colored shirt, steaming bifocals, crumpled gray tie streaked with gravy. Yes, this was trouble. Without doubt, I had plunked myself down next to that scourge of the skies, the Flight Bore!

"A brass Zippo!" continued the moon-faced rotter, swilling his drink back the better to spray me and torching up another king-sized coffin nail. "Come on, what d'yer want for it? Here, just listen to this then," he enthused, suddenly thrusting a pair of headphones and a Walkman at me.

"Do you like Dusty Springfield? What line are you in?"

The man was obviously a complete nutter, and unbelievably, as if I had already lost control of my senses, I blurted out that I was a songwriter going to Tasmania on a tour. This monstrous mistake arrived under what was by now the full church bell alarm system. I knew I was in deep trouble. I felt like a gazelle with a cheetah on its ass and, barely noticing, rolled another cigarette, which again looked like something Peter Tosh might stick in his mouth.

"A musician? Good. Then you'll appreciate this!" He pressed play as I donned the cans and the deafening strains of "You Don't Have to Say You Love Me" pummeled my eardrums. Never had Dusty sounded so awful, so doom-ridden. I dutifully plowed through the song, chain-inhaling the cigarette, watching the line for the toilets, the line that effectively blocked me in, getting longer and longer.

I ripped off the headphones when the song was over and quickly handed the digitally re-mastered monstrosity back to its owner, who seemed locked in a side-on position, the great, grinning crosshairs of his donkey teeth fastened to my face.

"They don't write songs like that anymore, do they? No one like Dusty!"

"No, you're right," I mumbled, resolving not to inform the prat that Dusty didn't write the song, knowing full well that the Flight Bore is not the listening type, that my information would be met with a fixed grin and ignored as if spoken to a statue.

He continued to grill me through his bifocals as I smoked, the sweat beginning to bead into boils on my forehead, my eyes locked haplessly at the line to the toilets, still blocking my exit. To my knowledge, no travel brochure, book, article, TV exposé, or radio show has ever tackled this character. It's as if he doesn't exist. But this cretin of the air corridors is as ubiquitous as dry-roasted peanuts, warm beer, two-hundred-fifty-pound human beings, imitation butter, and that other repugnant demon, the Stewardess From Hell. Fuming at the clown's audacity as he began his obligatory monologue, filling me in on his comprehensive knowledge of popular music up the to year 1966, I resolved to deliver a mighty trouncing at the earliest opportunity. I was still smarting from my encounter with the fiendish Bahá'i, but they were small potatoes compared with the Flight Bore—at least their offer of guruship under hypnosis was original. This devil had nothing to offer other than the vapid emulsion of his own pinheaded existence.

"Whoa! Here we go!" he exclaimed, dipping into his crumpled jacket and pulling out a cheap, tinny looking Instamatic. "Nice cloud formations! Hang on, I'll be back in a jiffy!"

With that, he climbed over me, almost crunching my groin with his ancient brogues and barged rudely into the line waiting for toilets. Once past them, he proceeded to lean over seated passengers as if they weren't there, once knocking the yarmulke off a sleeping Jew's head, merely to snap dull, blurry photographs of empty skies. These, I knew from experience, would be developed as soon as he touched down and fondly exhibited on subsequent flights, thrust into the faces of further innocents, effectively boring the pants off of them.

I looked up at the line, breathing a sigh of relief at my momentary respite, and there standing next to me was my trusty tour manager, Fortesque.

"Forty," I said, "you'll never guess who the one free smoking seat in the entire plane is next to."

"Pegged it," said Fortesque, a savvy veteran of cretin attacks.

"Listen," I said, noticing the metal briefcase Fortesque held. "Pull out a sheet of paper and a black marker, quick!"

Fortesque obliged. I grabbed the sheet and wrote "THE FLIGHT BORE" on it in big black letters.

"You got some cellotape?" I asked.

"No problem, blue," said Forty, fishing out a roll.

I glanced at the bore, still flashing away with the Vivitar, capturing intriguing studies of bulkheads, ashtrays, carpeting—anything that could be used in the future as a weapon of tedium.

"Good. Now, Fortesque, there's a good chap. Stick this on the bastard's back!"

"No problem, sport," said the stalwart road turf, shuffling out of the line and heading in the direction of the Flight Bore, six rows up and conveniently bent over a beer stain in the carpet of the aisle, his worn, shiny trousers sticking up like an old plum.

The plane rocked suddenly and the fasten seat belts sign pinged on. The hayseed in the pilot's seat gave a casual warning of turbulence and the air hostesses began hustling people back to their seats. I seized the opportunity to escape but not before I had reached over to the bore's tray table and tipped the remainder of his scotch and Coke onto his seat. Typical of his ilk, the bore ignored the captain's warning and continued leaning over, snapping away at nothing.

The queue for the toilets now disbanding, I made it easily to the opposite aisle and got to my seat. As I drew parallel to the bore, I noticed Fortesque bump into him and palm the sign onto his back! The symmetry, the precision of Forty's touch, hanging before my eyes like a slow-motion ballet, sent a warm gush to my heart, and I sat in my seat, arching back to eye the forthcoming events with eager anticipation.

Fortesque headed on up the aisle (he had given up relieving his bladder to perform this task—the sign of a great tour manager) as the letters glared from the bore's back like a beacon. A stewardess appeared and almost wrestled the blighter back to his seat, an inane grin on his toothy face all the while.

He sat down and after a few moments registered discomfort on his florid face, but his reaction to the wet seat was disappointing and the vapid grin barely changed; it was going to take some deeper insult to pierce his rhino skin. As luck would have it, this event was immediately forthcoming, for when he half stood to pull at the damp seat of his pants, the passenger in the window seat directly behind him, pointed at his back. Although I couldn't hear it from the distance at which I was sitting, I could lip-read the passenger's comment clearly enough: "There's a sign on your back," he said.

The Flight Bore looked at him, the message slowly penetrating his gray matter.

"A what?" I could see him ask.

When the passenger repeated himself, the bore reached around and grabbed at the dangling paper.

Skin like a Sherman Tank notwithstanding, the bore's face eventually changed expression, and the barest hint of a flush crept up around his neck as he stared at my handiwork held inches in front of his myopic eyeballs. He looked at the man behind who had issued the tip-off. He looked at the fellow in the aisle seat next to the man who had tipped him off, a surly-looking youth with a nose ring and prominent five o'clock shadow. He leaned over the seat back and made some remarks to this rather menacing looking punk.

Incredibly, the Flight Bore made no move to scan the aisles for me, but with boorish tunnel vision waved the paper accusingly at the leather-clad teenager.

"Did you put this on my back?" it looked like he was saying.

The kid, obviously a hard case and not dressed like a ruffian for purely fashionable reasons, glared back at him and offered a perfunctory "Fuck off," to which the Flight Bore, increasingly put out and oblivious to impending danger, shifted into the seat I had so recently occupied, planted his knees on it, leaned over with the thin arse of his trousers glaring, and made a clumsy grab at the youth's throat.

I glanced over at Fortesque, who was also twisted around in his seat, peeking out between lank strands of black hair, his craggy face creased with mirth.

It was all over very quickly. A stewardess rushed to the scene and the paper sign popped into the air momentarily, where it hung like a kite as the nose-ringed ruffian delivered a well-timed punch, right on the Flight Bore's nose! More damage would surely have ensued had not the powerful arm of herself, the Stewardess From Hell, intervened, rushing to the assistance of her weaker associate and grappling the ruffian into an effective half nelson.

The Flight Bore sat down, dejected, a thin trickle of blood issuing from his swollen conk, a handkerchief in his hand with the Instamatic hanging from the wrist.

"I'm not a bore," I saw him mumble. But the skies were safe again; a contusion had been delivered, a comeuppance doled out, and I sat back with lighter heart, more tolerant of the rigors of a long, long journey.

After a two-hour stop in Bombay, where we were allowed to de-plane, we were off again and the grinding hum of the engines once more became my numbing backdrop. Carruthers had indeed slept the whole way from London to Bombay, where, shortly after disembarking, he had gotten into an affray with an Indian gentleman who seemed convinced that the rubber-limbed soundman was a woman.

Shortly after we were back in the air, a bizarre concoction of curried eggs, basmati rice, and ham and cheese sandwiches arrived, and I moved over to a newly vacated window seat to wash it down with a mini bottle of champagne and a brandy. The plane, somewhat emptier after the Bombay stop, where we had thankfully lost the foul-footed Arab, was still jammed in the smoking section, and whenever those nicotine insects began their buzzing in my bloodstream, I would have to creep into the one empty seat in the section, the one next to the Flight Bore, and have a quick puff while our tedium monger sat unconscious, presumably having bored himself to sleep.

Where I sat when not indulging the addiction, however, there was plenty of space and I had just popped the miniature brandy when Carruthers unfolded himself like a human runner bean, stood up, and, spotting the vacant seats, loped over to join me. His ungainly countenance was truly something to behold, and I watched with fascination as he maneuvered those impossible stick insect legs that fired out from the bottom of his lime-green boxing shorts like flesh derricks.

He launched into a one-sided discussion on the intricacies of digital reverb, throwing in a healthy smattering of "kimbers" and "nibs' " and other unique terms, and I, being totally uninterested in the subject, decided to quiz him on the bands he had worked for. My mouth dropped open as he reeled off a list of obscure hard-core groups, most of whom sounded more like methods of deadly assault than musical outfits. This bodes well, I thought. What an outrage it is! There I was, about to play solo, mostly acoustic, to an audience of convict descendants on a Pacific island well off the rock 'n' roll map, and my "soundman," who seemed all of nineteen, had spent his entire "career" working with people who treat their instruments as if they were chain saws! Tarquin, you bastard! I hissed to myself, not for the last time.

Eventually Carruthers returned to his seat, goosing a stewardess on the way over as if it were something included in the ticket price, and I was then joined by Fortesque, who had been up in the front, listening to news on the pilot's radio. He plunked himself down, the tangy odor of his old leather jacket reaching my nostrils and his etched face betraying a familiar sense of gloom.

"Doesn't look good, mate," he said with a sigh.

"What!" I nearly yelled, still irritated after my conversation with Carruthers. "What doesn't look good? If it's about the toggle-headed soundman, I know it doesn't look good!"

"No, he'll be all right, mate," he said blandly. "He's a good un, he is. It's Tas I'm talking about—been raining nonstop there for the last week. They're expecting another month of it, too, and the hotel in Hobart is s'posed to be flooded and the power's out. Might be a while before they get it all workin' again."

"Great!" I responded, almost cracking a tooth. "Well let's stay in another hotel then."

"Mm . . . not a good idea," he replied. "You won't like any of the others." Fortesque, himself an Aussie who had spent a good portion of his early life on a sheep farm in Tasmania, presumably knew something about this hellish island we were about to invade. One of the two major towns in the country and there was not another suitable hotel? What, I thought, with something akin to suicidal depression settling in, is it going to be like in Burnie, or Dunalley, or Margate (Margate?!), or Flinders Island, or Triabunna? These names hurled themselves from my itinerary like aboriginal spears, each one impaling my heart with further dread.

"Don't worry, blue," said the black-haired gnome-like Fortesque, "you'll be great!"

We lifted off from Singapore, where, as with the layover in Bombay, a two-hour stop had found me slouching around the stifling airport, glumly appraising a tropical rainstorm through the dirty windows and hoping to Christ that Carruthers would get abducted by a pack of homosexual Asians. Once in the air again, I was on the verge of nodding off when the Flight Bore appeared, his thick skin apparently healed and the Vivitar at the ready.

"Give us a light with that Zippo then!" he enthused, leaning over the empty seats, a pole-like cigarette in his mouth and breath like an alcoholic canine. I quickly obliged and thankfully the platter-faced bozo headed off toward the front of the plane, belching smoke and leaving a parting shot in his wake: "I'll make you an offer you can't refuse!"

Finally, after a good twenty-four hours in the air, the drinks, the fatigue, and the general stresses delivered at the hands of my preposterous company had now begun to take their toll, and I began to drop off. But before I went out, I heard the dry cackle of the Stewardess From Hell and the strangled English of Carruthers, those two unpleasant auditory phenomena intertwined in a devilish match. My left eyelid sprung up and I saw them sitting together, it being that portion of the flight where the stewardesses begin loosening up and popping what's left of the mini champagnes, often joining passengers for a spot of camaraderie. Could I believe my ears? It sounded like Carruthers was chatting the old bird up!

This noisome idea rattled through my mind as I pulled a blanket over me, slugged back my fourth brandy, and fell into a thick, sweaty sleep.

Chapter 8

The weather in Tasmania, a brooding mix of gray skies, rain, and wind, put a damper on our arrival matched only by the sight of The Abel, our monolithic and flooded hotel. Carruthers, Fortesque, and myself waded into the lobby, where we were greeted by a man with a wetsuit on, wielding a great rusty old pump that he continually banged with a hammer. The ancient instrument, which looked as though it might have been designed in the same year as the hotel, spluttered and farted and smoked into action, sucking dirty water up and propelling it through a stretch of clear plastic tubing that snaked out of a nearby window.

I looked on in amazement as a small, live fish slivered through the tube and shot off toward its doom. This dangerous device was plugged into the wall only inches above the water, which almost came up to my knees, and I feared certain death by electrocution at any moment.

"Hang on, boys, hang on!" the man shouted above the roar of the water pump. "Be right with you!" With this, he thumped the contraption once more and waded off to the registration desk.

We followed dumbly, our socks stuffed in our pockets and our shoes tied around our necks. Touring, fraught with bores, religious cults, evil stewardesses, and dry-roasted peanuts, also elicited the charm of the lost luggage scenario, a treat we had recently undergone on our arrival at Hobart International Airport. It was in Singapore, the loutish lost luggage official had sneered. It would arrive on the next flight in approximately eight hours' time—if we were lucky.

"Ee, fookin' 'ell!" exclaimed Carruthers, looking around the hotel lobby at the cloth-covered couch, the table in front of it with its magazines and ashtrays, the four or five threadbare chairs, the yucca trees that stood with water lapping about the sides of their large ceramic pots, and the tall lamps that reached up toward the echoing ceiling, twenty feet up. The whole scene resembled a Turkish bath without the steam.

" 'Ad a high tide, did thee?" he asked the man in the wetsuit behind the counter.

"High? . . . " he began, looking flustered as he tapped some check-in cards on the counter in front of us. His skin had a sallow complexion and a knobbly wart grew in the crevice at the side of his nose. "Oh this?" he said, as if noticing the flooding for the first time. "No no no. It's the Gooligolli stream runs out back. So much rain, y'see . . . lobby's built like a fuckin' great hole, stream breaks its banks . . . boom boom. Rooms are a bit dampish, but the power's on most of the time, and they reckon the weather's on the mend. Any luggage, boys?"

"It's in Singapore," said Fortesque, one Aussie accent to another.

"Christ!" said the man. "You'll be lucky to see that again! 'Ere's your keys. Bar opens at six, it's round the corner. 'Ave a gutfull of tinnies later an' you won't notice the water sloshin' in your shoes, right?"

The prickles of annoyance, the hammerheads of gloom still danced around me like taunting wraiths, but I was determined to keep at bay that huge planet of depression—nay, *galaxy* of misery—that lurked in my primal cortex ready to swoop down and overcome with its tides of cosmic anguish. It was only my beautiful Gretsch Countryman, my rare and priceless Hohner acoustic and my irreplaceable ondioline that were lost somewhere in Singapore, that's all. Nothing to get all hot under the collar about—like hell. Plus my clothing for two months and various other items totally necessary for survival in a hostile environment. I desperately stifled a pang of misery at the thought of some cookie-boy baggage cretin in Singapore Airport, sliding my ten-thousand-dollar Gretsch into the back of his rusting third-hand Honda, taking it back to his hovel in downtown Singapore, where his fifteen brothers would squeal at each other as they fought for a go, and the wizened old father would come in, a Marlboro hanging from his lips, and stare at the rare beauty, wondering if it was made in Taiwan or Japan, and how much would it be worth—"Ten, fifteen, twenty dollar, maybe?"

I attempted to quash the remorse this image produced and directed a glare at the wart-man in the wetsuit. Hopefully, the rat would electrocute himself before the lobby dried out. Then I despondently took the winding stairs to my accommodations.

THE OTHER LIFE OF BRIAN

My room was a gothic affair with a massive chest of drawers and a high ceiling of white painted metal featuring parallel indentations that resembled cows udders. But the power was on, and I flopped onto the bed to watch TV, ignoring a state bordering on hallucination that exhaustion and jet lag had begun to produce within me. Even in this back-of-beyond they had satellite TV, and I flicked through the channels until something suitably arresting caught my eye. It appeared to be a station from France, and I stared with bug-eyed wonder as the credits rolled.

"Ladies and gentlemen," a lady's voice announced in a French accent. "Welcome, once again to—Les Deux Jerry Lewis!"

Cheering and applause broke out, and the camera showed a close-up of two gnarly, beringed hands thumping out barroom rock 'n' roll on an upright piano. The camera moved up and a stiff and obvious cut was made, for when we reached the face, it was none other then the comedian, Jerry Lewis, his face contorted into it's usual buck-tooth demeanor, á la The Nutty Professor. Down went the camera lens to his legs, which were locked in a spastic, knock-kneed stance, and then up again to his face, but here, our high-speed editing crew flashed to the man playing the upright piano, that notorious legend of the entertainment world, Jerry *Lee* Lewis.

The applause cascaded into deafening roars of laughter as another camera angle, dollying in from between the rows of red-faced audience members, treated us to the two Jerry Lewises standing on the studio floor with a gaudy blue curtain shimmering behind them. One of the Jerry Lewises pulled out a gun and pretended to shoot the other Jerry Lewis. This scene, couched in absolute howls of merriment, made me drop the channel changer on the bed as the Jerry Lewis who had been shot executed a professional pratfall and the Jerry Lewis with the gun spun around and resumed his hammering of the piano keys. He then shook his unruly forelocks and a close-up of his face revealed a maniacal grin. Shots of the studio audience were interspersed, some of them in tears, overwhelmed with jollity. The piano-playing Jerry Lewis then pulled two bottles of colored capsules from his pocket that he opened and began swallowing, following this action with fierce gulps from a bottle of Southern Comfort. The audience maintained the hysterical frenzy as the *other* Jerry Lewis writhed around on the floor, indicating that the pills were taking effect.

Then the lights went dim and the camera snapped to the piano-thumping Jerry Lewis, his face lit eerily as he intoned in a menacing southern drawl—"Bring me a wife!" A blond woman in a cowboy outfit entered the scene and she stood, hand on blue-jeaned hip, between the two Jerry Lewises, who began punching and kicking her until she fell to the floor, blood (presumably from a capsule) trickling down from her mouth.

The two Jerry Lewises then shook hands and slapped each other around a bit as two men wearing berets rushed on stage and carted the blonde away. The cameras wobbled into the audience, a large percentage of whom consisted of bulky, overdressed Frenchwomen. Some appeared so overcome with hilarity that they could barely breath, and a quick backstage insert flashed on, showing a medical crew studying monitor screens, presumably ready to rush to their assistance in case of heart attacks or hyperventilation. Then there was a commercial break featuring Citroën, Pernod, and Gauloise advertisements.

I lay there dumbfounded, any thoughts of lost luggage, checking the local scenery, or swimming to the hotel bar completely forgotten, and I reached for the telephone like an automaton. I dialed Fortesque to see if he was witnessing this remarkable spectacle.

"Clocked it," he answered stoically when I asked if he were tuned in to the show. "Yeah, blue, haven't you heard about this then?"

"No, no," I answered.

"Couple of mates of mine in Aussie told me about it. We don't get it in the UK cos the English hate the French—you know how it is—but it's bloody popular over here. It's the rage in France, of course."

"Oh . . . great. Thanks, Forty," I said, at a loss for words.

"Later," he said, and hung up.

The adverts finished and the action resumed. One of the Jerry Lewises was hammering out "Whole Lotta Shakin' " on the piano while the other, dressed as a schoolboy, convulsed to the music in a lunatic manner exhibiting a startling array of facial gymnastics.

After a minute or so of this, the two changed places and the piano-thumping Jerry Lewis did an excellent impersonation of the erratic-twitching Jerry Lewis and the erratic-twitching Jerry Lewis did an excellent impersonation of the piano-thumping Jerry Lewis. As these antics gathered momentum, it became harder and harder to distinguish one Jerry Lewis from the other, and some audience members were by now receiving medical treatment; one middle-aged lady was panting wildly as a medic thrust smelling salts under her nose and a thin gentleman was being rolled onto a stretcher, having passed out completely.

I suddenly remembered reading fairly recently that Jerry Lewis, the comedian, had left the USA to live in France, where he is considered a genius, having finally had it with his own country, where he is considered an idiot. Who could blame him for going where the respect is? It's a wonder there are any homegrown artists of any description performing in the UK, considering the denizens of that sceptered isle's ingrained habit of giving them a little slack for the first fifteen minutes of their careers, then trouncing them with great buckets of shit for the rest of their lives. I could certainly sympathize with Jerry. Good for him, I thought. He was probably being paid a fortune for this and seemed to be thoroughly enjoying himself to boot.

As for Jerry Lee Lewis (he of the wild antics on stage and off, the consumption of massive amounts of medication, the half a stomach due to a recent medical procedure, and the many wives who have "died" under strange and suspicious circumstances), I remembered also reading recently that he had left the USA for very different reasons—he owed the IRS about seven million dollars. Still, he certainly seemed revered on the continent, judging by the show's success.

The two Jerrys *would* fit neatly into the French canons of greatness, I realized as one of them (I *think* it was the comedian) made a number of particularly unfunny silly walks. The fashion sense of the French, contrary to public imagination, is, of course, awful; Mickey Rourke is perceived as an actor of Olivierian magnitude largely due to his perfect stubble; and not two years ago I witnessed a whole nightclub full of French teenagers in Paris attempting to dance like the ska revival band, Madness. The degree to which they misjudged the style was astonishing—they looked more like pierots on shock treatment than neo moddy boys.

Still, I could not take my eyes from the screen, so mesmerized was I by this stunning format that I had not a thought of even looking out of the window or stepping out onto the street to find the nearest sandwich bar or pinball arcade; I attempted none of the usual rituals that remove me momentarily from the remorseless grind of man's dullest endeavor—travel, and the discomfort it creates. Identifying glandular odors, drubbing Flight Bores, hanging in grimy tropical airports and losing expensive guitars and priceless personal effects—you can keep it all, I thought then. Just give me a satellite dish and access to programs like this recherché spectacle and I would be happy to sit, idle as a post, living on the thin trickle of royalties that occasionally fell through the mailbox.

This jolly, madcap game went on for about ten minutes before the voice-over announced something about Le Grande Finale, coming up right after the commercials.

I reached for the rooming list, spotted Carruthers' number, and grabbed at the phone, barely taking my eyes from the screen.

"Nibs" was his single-syllable greeting.

"You watching this, Carruthers?"

"Aye, clocked it. Forty just phoned up. Fookin' mega, eh, Beep?"

I could hear the blur of his TV set along with the clinking of a glass or a bottle. Someone was with him. I decided not to inquire, having a sinking feeling that the bounder was probably (unlikely as his physical presence might indicate) the sort that pulls women left, right, and center.

"Later," I said.

"Nibs," Carruthers agreed.

I returned my attention to the show where the two Jerry Lewises were announcing—one in a bleating, childish voice, the other in a deranged southern psychopathic slur—that they both have grown sons, both of whom, as fortune would have it, are named Jerry Lewis Jr. The crowd went wild at this suggestion and I got the distinct impression that the format of this show was repeated every week, with nary a fluctuation.

Then the French national anthem played as a backdrop and the junior Jerry Lewises were brought on. Two of the Jerry Lewises thumped the upright piano and performed a hectic version of "Drinkin' Wine Spo-Dee-O-Dee," while the other two Jerry Lewises gyrated across the stage, running the complete repertoire of pratfalls, silly walks, and facial tics that the French find so excruciatingly funny. Finally, to deafening applause, the gleeful female voice-over yelled, "Monsieur, Madame . . . Les Quatre Jerry Lewis!" The original Jerry Lewises then appeared close up on camera and said (each Jerry Lewis taking every other word and delivering them in his own inimitable style, which produced a macabre ping pong effect), "We'll-be-back-next-week-with"—and they hollered this bit together, "Les Deux Jerry Lewis!!!"

So far, Tasmania had been more interesting than I had anticipated, and I decided to toast the local satellite company responsible for delivering the two Jerry Lewises with a celebratory drink, it being early evening in Tasmania and God knows what time for my confused body clock.

I called the front desk, not wishing to ford the deluge downstairs, and got the wart-faced man.

"Could you possibly bring me a couple of beers, please?" I asked. The man sighed impatiently, grudgingly agreed, and after fifteen minutes knocked on the door and entered with two bottles of Boags, the local brew, and a letter.

"Watch the two Jerry Lewises, sport?" he inquired.

"Yes I did."

"Lucky bastard," he whined. "Some of us have to bloody work . . . oh, letter for you here, mate. I forgot to give it to you earlier."

He handed me the beer and the envelope and left, leaving a puddle of water at the door. I tore into both, thirsty, and hungry to discover who could possibly have this address before I had even arrived. I was startled to find it was from those viperous American lawyers representing the Baedburgers, the unrightful recipients of my late uncle, John "Sir" Bacon's estate. Steed or Smyke had probably given them the whole of my wretched itinerary without a word of consent from me. I guzzled the cold brew and read the thing with mounting disgust.

Dear Mr. Borker:

Thank you for your letter regarding Mr. John "Sir" Bacon. It was most interesting and informative but we fail to see the relevance of such information. The Baedburgers were Mr. Bacon's legal guardians for two years and he in his immense gratitude saw fit to bequeath them his entire estate.

We understand your disappointment in this matter, being his sole surviving relative, but under the circumstances feel our clients deserve the full benefit of the legal and binding aforementioned will, and unless you are indeed going to contest said will in the immediate future, we feel we must continue to process the document as it stands and represent the Baedburgers in their rightful claim.

We feel we have waited long enough and now the Baedburgers are desperately short of money, so we are compelled to complete our duties, assuming there is no legal intervention on your behalf. We furthermore believe John Bacon to have been of sound mind when he executed the will, and if you do decide to contest, we shall crush you like an ant.

Very truly yours,
Messrs. Goldtraub, Cardbaum & Silvermein

I steeled myself, stifling an urge to throw the empty bottle of Boags through the window. The telephone rang and on came Fortesque with good news of the baggage and guitars—they were apparently in one piece and would be on the next flight from Singapore. Relieved, I ripped pen and paper from my shoulder bag and composed a reply to those hucksters, a reply I believed that would convince them in short order of my intent to go the distance contesting this farce.

Messrs. Goldfinger, Cardcredit and Silverhoard
Dear Sirs:

"Of sound mind when he executed the will"? Are you joking? To suggest that Johnny had all his deckchairs on the pier at any time during his erratic, errant life would be a misjudgment of the grossest proportion. The examples of his deeply ingrained and hereditary lunacy are legion and well documented by various potentates, medical examiners and lay people. I myself have cause to undergo frequent and various examinations in the event that I too am touched by the rabid and virulent strain of madness it has been my family's misfortune to endure for eons. In fact, I am actually writing this while sitting in a chair he once set fire to.

Are you unaware of the notorious "wall tapping" phenomena of Lurchdale, N.Y.? Let me, good sirs, give you a brief account of that famous and scandalous affair that rocked the spiritualist community to its roots in the 1960s. My late lamented half uncle, John "Sir" Bacon, was at that time employed as curator of the Lurchdale Museum of Jaffa Antiquities. His job was to preside over the small establishment and give detailed information concerning its sacred contents to visitors, many of whom were interested religious parties of often disparate beliefs. "Sir" Bacon, it must be noted, took many forms of employment during his life, but usually his tenure in such employment lasted a year or two at most, owing to the inevitable upsurge of eccentric behavior that consistently ensured his dismissal. The "wall tapping" fiasco was no exception.

After approximately six months on the job, my half uncle was convinced that he heard a series of willful and calculated tappings, as if in code, issuing from a particularly grand Jaffa throne, which was quite a centerpiece of the museum. The tappings, he concluded, were of such a similar nature to those recorded in the famous Fox Cottage in nearby Hydesville, N.Y. (the Hydesville Rappings, 1848), that he managed to convince a slew of eminent religious leaders and Spiritualists that a full-scale investigation was in order.

Before long, paranormal investigators had flooded the tiny museum with cameras and tape machines, and television news teams the length and breadth of the country were questioning "Sir" Bacon and pointing their microphones at the throne, which would generally give up a tap or two on cue. Three noted Spiritualists, Sir Oliver Lodge, W. E. Harriman, and the Reverend "John" Thomas flew to America from the United Kingdom, so convincing was Bacon's assurances of communications from beyond. It was not long, however, before someone thought of moving the throne (an irksome job requiring a hole to be punched through the roof of the museum so that a small crane could be employed in this task) and examining its underside. When this expensive feat was accomplished, it was discovered that a series of small tunnels had been bored into the throne that connected to a hole in the floor. This hole led directly through the floor (it was discovered after much careful and costly excavation) and down to the cellar, where Mr. Bacon kept a large supply of dried dog food for his three mangy strays. Apparently, mice had been tunneling up through the floor and into the throne, attracted, no doubt, by its lush layers of velvet and dry-rotted wood, and with them had dragged hefty quantities of dog food. As they had enlarged their excavations while holding the portions of hard niblets in their mouths, they would (it was estimated by an expensive mammalogist) drop the niblets from time to time in order to chew deeper into the throne, thus causing fairly rhythmic "tappings."

Mr. Bacon was, of course, dismissed in disgrace and the Jaffa organization has never quite recovered its original power and esteem. This was in no small part due to the ridicule henceforth leveled at the religion, and the enormous sums incurred by the investigation.

Please expect a citation to be served upon you via the Pratsville County Surrogate Judge invoking my contestation of Mr. Bacon's will. Be assured sirs, that I am now coming in on this with big guns blazing, and shall mow you down like human nine-pins.

Yours sincerely,
Brian Porker Esq., M.B.E.

After no small expenditure of bile, a weariness gripped me and I lay back on the mildewy, sagging bed and slept like a top.

Chapter 9

It was four days later when Fortesque, Carruthers, and myself arrived in the northern town of Penguin for my third appearance in Tasmania, the tour by now gathering the momentum of a Model T Ford reversing up Mount Everest. We had already survived two shows in two other obscure towns, both loathsome cabaret joints with back alleys serving as dressing rooms and audiences of pasty, confused-looking characters who had no inkling as to who I was, or why I was standing on the stage with just two guitars and a bizarre keyboard instrument for accompaniment. "Where's the band?" some would inquire at the ticket office. "Is he a folk singer, or what?" they would ask lamely. Most of these people had the intelligence of your average marmoset, and remembering my experiences as a young man in the British Channel Islands, where I had spent some time after first leaving home, I suspected mass inbreeding.

I stood on the tilting, sticky stage of Penguin's only rock nightspot, the ingeniously named Marquee Club, and attempted a soundcheck hampered by a loud hum, constant electrical crackling and the odd jolt in the lip from the dented microphone.

Faded posters of sixties English variety acts adorned the walls, making me wonder if any act of international repute had performed in the room since that era.

By far the most annoying aspect of Tasmania, in fact, proved to be the enforced Englishness the natives had glommed onto everything. The English surnames, the abundance of Ye Olde English tea rooms and antique shops, and the plain fact the these people were indeed under the illusion that they were English, when not a short hop away was Australia, about as foreign a place as you can imagine despite the use (or abuse) of the English language. All of this conspired to wind me up like a buzzsaw and I was ready to tear Carruthers' hair out by the roots, deciding that it was all his fault, for want of a more tangible target. (Typically, Steed—a more realistic mark if it were not for the fact that he was on the other side of the globe—had not phoned to check on our progress or sent so much as a fax, despite the fact that he or Smyke had given the Baedburgers' lawyers the address of the first hotel we had stayed in and also forwarded one extraordinarily bad review of *Porker In Aspic* and a note from a radio station in Woodstock, New York, asking if I would do a benefit for the local sewers in two weeks' time.)

Carruthers, the new object of my ire until something better presented itself, lolloped backstage after each performance with comments like: "Ee, toof crowd, but mega by the end!" or: "Thought we were in a spot of kimber tonight, seven power cuts! Crackin'! Pulled it off, by 'eck!"

More than once I almost crowned him with a bottle of Boags but managed to restrain myself realizing I'd need a stepladder to reach his head. Irksome road turf that he was, he'd usually give himself a whopping headache by morning anyway, seeing as he'd be up until dawn carousing and would not generally return to his room until he'd found some blob-like fool female to accompany him.

That very morning in the hotel breakfast room he had sat down next to me, reeking of cheap perfume and pulling putrid articles of female underwear out of his kit bag.

"Ee, got a right ole pastin' last night!" he'd boasted, hanging the smalls out over the table like trophies and upsetting the hotel's resident spinsters across the room.

"Do me a favor, Forty," I said sarcastically as I received another minor electrical charge from the mic in the dingy Marquee Club. "If I get electrocuted up here tonight, just make sure Carruthers touches my still-jolting torso before they turn the power off, okay?"

That evening, the "crowd" filed in, and as I peeked around the tattered gray curtain at the back of the stage I writhed involuntarily, feeling the evening's gloom quotient expand like a dividing amoebae. There were a half dozen locals who lived up to the town's name perfectly, moving as they did in a flock like flightless seabirds. They made straight for the bar near the entrance without even glancing at the stage. But the bulk of the audience—all seventeen of them—were led in by a Hitleresque nurse who chewed gum and carried a billy club, stewarding her charges into the middle of the grimy dance floor as if leading them to a gas chamber.

THE OTHER LIFE OF BRIAN

Fortesque was dispatched to make inquiries, as I at first found this odd group's demeanor unfathomable, even for Tasmania. But before my tour manager had a chance to return with any answers, the strange group's vacant expressions and errant physical contortions tipped me off: they were obviously nutters—"mentally challenged," I believe was the upcoming buzz phrase of the time—most probably on day release from a nearby lunatic asylum. Unless, I thought with a shiver, these half-formed entropic gibberers were normal folk for Penguin.

Fortesque busied himself re-stringing my guitars, not mentioning whether or not he had discovered why my audience that night was composed almost entirely of very insane people. I leaned morosely against the wall of the dressing room—a charming lavatory housing a toilet with no seat—nibbling on some rather toothsome local concoction named lamington (a kind of sponge cake, dipped in chocolate icing and rolled in coconut) that appeared to be all the town's promoter was willing to provide by way of hospitality. Forty mumbled about holding off showtime for another half hour, vainly hoping for a mass invasion of Brian Porker fans, tanking it up in the local pubs until closing time, five minutes hence. But it seemed that the inhabitants of Penguin would stay at home, blubbery in their armchairs in front of their infinite satellite TV programs, oblivious to international renown, an ancient one-of-a-kind English Soulbilly hit single, and my stunning reinvention of myself as a three-and-a-half-minute multiinfluenced pop songster.

"Any more out there yet?" I asked Fortesque eventually.

He poked his head gingerly around the dusty curtain. "Oh, yeah . . . few more 'ave just arrived. They're tankin' it up at the bar," he said chirpily, ever the optimistic road dog.

"Fuck it, let's go."

With that I strode onto the stage, accompanied by a ferocious squeal of feedback, as if the mere presence of a live human anywhere near the Marquee's crappy equipment was bound to cause insurmountable technical problems. After finding an angle at which to approach the microphone without making it produce a deafening howl, I edged up to the greasy thing as if stalking a wild beast and launched into "Knee Trembler," hoping to Christ one person in the place apart from my crew had heard it before. Despite the dangerous stage gear, I was ripping into it pretty good, unfortunately though, to the utter disinterest of the dullard flock at the bar who drank and talked as if a record were playing. And judging by *their* reaction, the loonies, who were gathered together in the middle of the floor like mollusks stuck to a rock, likewise appeared to be under the impression that the stage was empty, that there was in fact nobody up there working his balls off; they flailed their arms, emitted communal facial tics and grunts, intense grimaces, and floods of spittle together with unprovoked screams and roars.

I soldiered on as if nothing were happening, but Carruthers eventually could take it no more. An hour into my performance, he leapt off his console (conveniently located on stage-right not three feet away from me) and dived headfirst into the nearest knot of mentally challenged folk with a cry of "kimber!" Two of the poor devils got their heads soundly cracked together and one poor catatonic whom Carruthers had mysteriously singled out to receive the brunt or his ire had his wheelchair flipped over on top of him, which set off a profuse nosebleed on the dance floor.

The club manager—suitably attired in a threadbare penguin-like tuxedo—a couple of his henchmen, and some ruffian from the bar leapt into the affray and pulled Carruthers off to the side, leaving the unfortunate in the wheelchair spinning on his head like a crippled break dancer and the nurse whacking hysterical members of her party about their heads with the billy club. Carruthers was kicked around for a good deal longer than was necessary and serious damage seemed likely. But at some time during the fracas the barmaid had called the police, who stormed in looking dangerously mental themselves.

The pig-like rozzers almost dragged Carruthers off to a cell for the night, but, after a few moments of appraisal (that evening he wore a huge yellow T-shirt with the word "Bollocks" printed on it), thought better of it, and we continued the show, minus seventeen lunatics, the best part of the audience.

Throughout this entertaining diversion, I had continued to play on, somehow gaining an exhilarating inspiration that was not dampened by the near total evacuation of the club, and my performance became so forceful that the few stragglers left at the bar and the cops who hung around till the end, edged up to the lip of the stage and cheered me on, encouraging a triple encore.

THE OTHER LIFE OF BRIAN

"Fookin mega, BP!" exclaimed an exuberant Carruthers after the show as we gathered around the bar guzzling beer with the minuscule audience.

One of the police officers even rushed outside to his squad car to retrieve a compilation cassette of mine and thrust it into my hand with much enthusiasm for me to sign.

"Glad someone here's heard of me," I said to the burly copper.

"Well, never actually played it, mate—picked it up at some bloke's place in a drug bust—but I will now after seeing your show. Bloody great!"

As Fortesque, Carruthers, and I tramped through the dark sleeping town back to our quarters (an uninviting guest house on the top of a lonely hill) a yell rent the air behind us: "Hang on, Carruthers, I'm comin'!" It was the big, dykey looking nurse who had stewarded the loonies in the nightclub. "Ee, Lindy! Cheers, luv," Carruthers exclaimed as she rounded a bend below us, the severe bun haloing her square head spotlighted by a lone streetlamp. "You got 'em all to bed quickish then. Come on oop to the 'otel for a drink, my beauty!"

How the giant soundman had found the time to pull her was an infuriating mystery to me, and I didn't have the bottle to ask him.

But few shows inspired the intensity of that night, and we plodded on for another three weeks, traveling from one dull mining town or fish-canning community to another, attracting listless denizens smelling of cod liver oil, alcohol, and Brut aftershave. The most applause I had received on the whole tour came one night in the annoyingly named town of Margate, when Fortesque, rushing the stage to adjust an unruly mic stand, tipped over the edge, and executed an awkward swan dive into the thin audience.

And then we had a week off.

What to do with all that free time was bound to be a problem. We'd had enough visits to breweries, mines, and crab factories to last a lifetime, and scouring each town's excuse for record stores had proved extremely depressing: so far we'd only managed to locate a single copy of my product, and that a battered vinyl disc of my first recording. About ten years too late, the Tasmanians were just discovering disco and John Travolta was getting a big push. Donna Summer couldn't be far behind.

It was Fortesque who suggested a boat trip. Rent some sleeping bags and a boat and bop upstream to see a bit of the countryside, was how he put it. Fair enough, I thought. Better then hanging around in these witless towns drinking ourselves stupid every night.

We had been crisscrossing the north of the island following an itinerary that must have made my manager chuckle a great deal, retracing our steps monotonously in Steed's ramshackle attempt to cover every town in Tasmania with the supposedly powerful promotional tool of my living presence. (Tarquin Steed, of course, remained sequestered in Findhorn, although now at least he would occasionally dash off a terse fax to our hotels regarding the enthusiastic "feedback" he was receiving from the Tasmanian promoters, none of whom had actually stayed to watch the shows.)

This ass-backward routing caused us to once again be near Penguin, the site of the best show, and as luck would have it a short drive from Devonport on the mouth of the fiendishly named Mersey River.

One bright morning, nursing Boags hangovers, toting sleeping bags, and carrying a minimum of camping gear, we set off to the brackish harbor and rented a dilapidated ice-blue motor boat from a barrel-shaped man named Tubb, and set off upstream, Carruthers at the helm.

Seagulls squawked in our wake, eyeing schools of tiny silver fish that darted in the roiling foam of the propeller, and a massive blue sky hung over us. The rains of the previous weeks had freshened the air and I felt uplifted staring into the moving water, now suddenly crystalline after a two-week spate.

At first, tedious farmlands flanked our progress, but after two hours chugging along with Captain Carruthers at the helm, the scenery became more interesting and vaguely hostile. The depth and width of the river grew less and gradually a textbook prehistoric appearance began to surround us with upper Cambrian tuffs, lavas, graywacks, and breccias forming the crust on which rich plant life flourished. The more awesome and unusual the flora, the more Carruthers snorted and spat.

"What is it?" I asked him, as we rounded a bend and found ourselves in thick, primeval-looking forest. "This is pretty wild, Carruthers. What's your problem?"

"Kimber," he said flatly, as if to himself. "Headin' for t'kimber here. Farff!"

"Less dangerous than rock 'n' roll," said Fortesque, fishing in his leather jacket for a Boags.

"That's right, Carruthers," I added, edging forward and taking control of the wheel. "Haven't seen any mental defectives or violent cops yet. Enjoy yourself. Relax and float upstream," I quipped.

The river, ever narrowing, took us into a dense patch of what could only be described as rainforest. This created a glum look on Carruthers, who seemed to prefer kicking the shit out of mental defectives than nature studies.

"Could be back in Penguin, boffing barmaids, scoring bint. Kimber, this is," he moaned.

"Oh knock it off, Carruthers," said Fortesque as we gradually entered what looked to me like a lower Silurian landscape sprouting from a base of Gordon limestone.

I had visited a local library before our trip and made a study of the ecology of the island; I'd jotted down some notes, too, which I referred to constantly as the landscape changed around us, hoping at least to gain something more from this worthless tour than hangovers and a litany of complaints. Staring at the abundant foliage, the antediluvian geographical formations, and the panoramic blue sky, I began to think that travel might not always be the miserable experience I had ascribed to it after all; if only one could reach places like this without having first to endure the cattle market that airports and planes had become in recent years.

"I must say, Forty," I said, as we rounded a bend and the sky suddenly darkened under the weight of the forest trees, "it's definitely looking interesting."

"Ah, Tas," said Fortesque wistfully. "Still some wild shit left over here. As much as they wanna chop it all down and mine it—put farms across it and all that—there's still plenty of wilderness left. I think a lot of this *must* be protected land. They'd have knocked all this down by now if it wasn't."

Presumably Fortesque knew a bit about the country, being an Australian himself and having spent a few years of his younger life on a farm on this very island. He was a strange bird: dumped just after birth by his parents—a pair of roaming circus clowns—and shunted around various relatives' homes before settling with an uncle who had briefly tried sheep farming in Tasmania before going back to the mainland to become a bush pilot.

"Certainly could be worse, this tour," I said, feeling an unaccustomed warmness of the heart. He was a good bloke, old Forty, and I was lucky to have him in my employ. In my time, I'd had road managers who'd done some sly and underhanded things, and plenty who had simply fucked up, usually due to excessively hungry noses or veins that constantly needed class-A narcotics pumped into them. Fortesque had been through the rock 'n' roll gristmill all right, but he'd come out the end of it with his sanity intact and his loyalty toward his current steward always unwavering.

"Forty, you're a damn good egg," I said, breathing in the highly oxygenated air, which seemed to be shoehorning a strangely magnanimus demeanor from my typically begrudging, road-worn, cynical personality. And then I looked over at Carruthers, who appeared to have his finger up his nostril almost to the wrist, and felt instantly normal again.

I slowed the boat down to a chug as we craned our necks to take in the towering trees. Long, snaky roots reached out onto the water from the banks, which I scanned for trilobite or dendroid fossils but saw nothing save whorls of mud, bundles of cattails, and a cabbage-like plant that grew from the bank deep into the river, threatening our rudder.

The thick vegetation and onset of evening produced a gloaming that was beginning to make navigation treacherous, and after a brief chat we decided to pull off the main current into one of the pristine tributaries that now sprang from the shores, disgorging their darkly sparkling waters into the river.

Negotiating the entrance to one such stream, we pushed on under a massive blanket of myrtle, she-oak, wattle, sassafras, and eucalyptus, until a peat-bed cove came into view set in a thick carpet of button grass. We disembarked, dragged the boat onto land, and pulled out our provisions: a few cases of Boags, some saltfish, a bag of scones and a tub of clotted cream, a stand-up flashlight, tea bags, tin cups, and a can of condensed milk, a primus stove, three sleeping bags, and finally a shared knapsack picked up in an army surplus store in which we had stuffed bits and pieces of personal property. In the belly of the old craft I fished out a handmade beehive lobster pot, suitable for catching the native freshwater crayfish, which I knew from my studies in Penguin's library could reach an enormous twelve pounds in weight.

The cove stretched back twenty feet into the forest before becoming a narrow, spindly stream that disappeared into the dense vegetation, and we scattered our provisions around, clearing rocks and driftwood for our sleeping bags. I stared up at the darkening sky through the towering trees. This was more like it. Far more stimulating than playing my tired old stuff to minuscule audiences primed by the local media to expect anyone wielding a musical instrument to break into "You're the One That I Want" at a moment's notice. This, I told myself, was really living.

Night came on swiftly and stars twinkled overhead, becoming a backdrop for scores of fruit bats the size of mallards. We drank Boags and ate the scones and salt fish, a little of which I stuffed into the lobster pot before lowering it into a rocky hole among the tree roots that tangled in the stream.

"What a bloody lark," muttered Carruthers, putting a hand to his matted red hair, as if expecting a fruit bat attack. "Wish I'd brought me DAT recorder—listen to the fookin' boogs!"

There certainly was an abundance of insect life, most of it hungry for fresh blood, and I cursed the things as they impaled themselves in my delicate skin.

Above the din of the insects, amphibians, and fruit bats, Fortesque and I began to talk; the need to increase the quotient of male bonding was ripe in unusual touring situations such as the one we now found ourselves in. Forty was a good bloke, yes, but a bit of a sad sack, too. Rootless, single, and oftentimes entertaining the idea of getting enough money together to go back to Oz and start off his own bush pilot service like his uncle Bruce, he was seemingly stuck on an endless rock 'n' roll tour like a mouse on a wheel. We squatted in the glare of the flashlights, swatting bugs and talking quietly while Carruthers huddled in his sleeping bag, a wary eye cocked for flying rodent attacks. Having only been able to acquire a bag for a normal sized human, which barely came up to the middle of his chest, in the dappling shadows cast by the flashlight Carruthers took on the appearance of a giant red-headed caterpillar attempting to cocoon itself.

"So, Fortesque," I said, as we cracked a couple of Boags, "how is old

Bruce, your uncle? Is he still zipping around the outback in that old crate you showed me a picture of?"

"Naw, he had a spot of bother with the law. He's inside for a year."

"Jeez, Forty, you're kidding! What happened?" I was always eager for a story about Uncle Bruce, a man who by all accounts blustered through life like a rogue elephant.

"What's the old sod been up to now?" I asked, a hint of glee creeping into my voice. Fortesque sniffed, guzzled his beer, and shifted in his old brown leather pilot's jacket.

"Got involved with smuggling drugs to New Zealand, silly bastard. The cops ambushed him walking out of a little airport in Wellington. He had a full bag of toad's glands under his arm."

"Toad's glands?" I questioned, for some reason not immediately getting his drift.

"Toad's glands... I dunno. That shit they're all smoking in Oz. They get it from those big ugly cane toads. They made it illegal and there was quite a demand in New Zealand, so Bruce—well, you know what he's like from what I've told you—silly bugger got into it. Good money, you know?"

"Ah, gotcha. Had some meself once as a matter of fact," I said, shivering at the memory. "Fuckin' horrible stuff."

Of course: the parotoid glands of Bufo Marinus, colloquially known as the "cane toad." Those monsters were the size of dinner plates and had been imported from the tropics into Australia to eat the cane beetles, but they made no dent in that pest's population and bred like flies themselves, becoming in recent years something of a plague. The toad's parotoid glands contain an interesting hallucinogen that Australian drug enthusiasts had picked up on. Licking, snorting, and smoking the stuff was fairly popular and the authorities eventually made it illegal. Once, in my more adventurous days, I had given the stuff a go myself and found its effects similar to smoking cobra venom, producing in me an unsettling animalistic body image (I felt like a big, primeval amphibian and spent a lot of time making guttural croaking sounds) and bouts of involuntary telepathy.

"Christ, Forty, he's a fuckin' card, your uncle!"

"I know," he said, chuckling. "He's all right though. I think they'll let him out in less than six months—he's already got the prison guvnor wrapped around his finger, the crafty old sod."

"I'll bet he has," I said, suddenly feeling sleepy, a wave of tour lag producing a series of mosquito-trapping yawns. "Think I'll hit the sack, Fortesque. S'pose we should get on back first thing—unless you fancy going deeper into it . . ."

"Dunno, BP. These bugs . . ." he said, slapping at his hair as he rolled out a particularly scruffy-looking rented sleeping bag. "Christ, look at this thing," he remarked with disgust.

"Looks like someone chundered in it, Forty. How's it smell?"

"Like a sheep's armpit," he answered, gingerly shimmying inside with a grimace.

The infernal buzzing from the wildlife, no less annoying than the clanking of pipes, whoomphing of elevators, and drone of distant TV sets in ancient hotels, conspired to keep me awake despite my exhaustion, and so I attempted to send myself off with a book. I pulled my mini book light out of the knapsack and clipped it onto Abel Zanszoon Tasman's journal (1898), which I had picked up in a secondhand bookstore the day before. But this proved somewhat heavy going—seeing as it was the Latin version. Casting the heavy tome aside I remembered a tape Carruthers had given me on the plane and I fished out my Walkman, certain that this would do the trick.

I had told the soundman how envious I was of people like himself who could sleep like the dead anywhere; at that comment, Carruthers bolted back to his seat and retrieved a black, unmarked cassette tape. "Here, Brian," he'd enthused as he handed it to me. "This'll put you out—it's those great blubbery bastards under the fookin' sea, all squeakin' an' squealing like. S'mega!"

This should do the trick, I thought: the wistful lonesome song of the whales and the deep pull of the ocean's currents; these relaxation tapes were all the rage and I was sure I'd be sleeping like a baby directly.

The tape started innocently enough with the sound of the lulling ocean and the to-and-fro call of the giant mammals. But just as I was getting drowsy, their plaintive songs turned into a hectic battering of screeches, a noise I could only surmise as one of distress. Suddenly, the stereo microphone recording this undersea odyssey appeared to shoot up through the waves to the surface, where Japanese voices could be clearly heard. Amid the yelling Asians, great whooshing effects flew around the stereo picture and the sound oscillated between this racket on the surface, and the screaming whales down below. It was suddenly and appallingly obvious what Carruthers had given me: it was a tape of whales being harpooned by the bloody Japs—a sort of mammalian snuff soundtrack!

I ripped the foul object out my Walkman and threw it at Carruthers' head. It hit him square on his plastacine-like nose but the devil didn't even stir. He just kept right on snoring with a moon-faced grin, hanging out of his sleeping bag as if he were on the most comfortable bed in the plushest hotel. I promised myself to dock him a week's pay for this outrage, and with this angry thought ricocheting around my head, I fell asleep.

Chapter 10

The next morning I awoke to see Fortesque and Carruthers standing on the spit where we had moored our craft. It took me all of two seconds to realize something was amiss—both of them looked as if they were attending a funeral. I groaned loudly and waited until Fortesque trudged into the camp with the news.

"Doesn't look good, mate," he said, which I knew to be tour managerese for serious kimber.

"What is it?"

"Boat's gone."

"Gone . . ." I repeated bleakly.

"Thought I'd moored it good enough. Current's stronger than I realized."

"Ee, never mind that!" shouted Carruthers excitedly. "Look at these greet bolshie bastards!"

He held up the lobster pot, which contained three massive crayfish, kicking and clacking, their green claws snapping viciously.

"Oh great," I said testily. "Well done, chaps. Perhaps we can strap ourselves onto their carapaces and hitch a lift back to Devonport! And if they won't play ball, there's a dirty great kookaburra up in the eucalyptus. Maybe we can tie a message to his foot and tell him to fly to Findhorn. Perhaps he can rouse Tarquin to organize a bleedin' search party! Christ!"

The kookaburra laughed mockingly, sounding oddly Shakespearean, and flew off into the forest.

"Sorry, blue," said Fortesque sheepishly, his unkempt black hair sticking out at all angles.

There was nothing for it but to boil the billy and drop the angry crayfish in, one after the other, for they were too big to cook all at once. So we fired up the primus stove and did just that, tucking into the delicious crustaceans (using clotted cream as a replacement for butter) while lorakeets, fruit doves, and other, less unidentifiable birds flitted in the branches above, cackling at us.

Feeling somewhat fortified, we searched for the boat at the mouth of the tributary, but there was no sign of it. I studied an ancient map at the back of Tasman's journal and figured we were some distance west of a large body of fresh water smack in the middle of the island called Great Lake. Coming up with no better idea, I suggested we follow the tributary in that direction. An area of Great Lake's magnitude must surely have fingers of civilization pointing out from it in all directions—we were bound to hit something eventually. So we strapped what gear we had onto our backs and set off on foot after cutting a few saplings for use as makeshift machetes.

Cursing like construction workers every minute of the way, we tramped laboriously onward for an hour or so, gaining little ground in the stifling heat, our hands blistering from the effort of slashing the unforgiving vegetation. Mosquito bites swelled like boils all over my body and my leg muscles began burning from the effort of trampling down the thorny plants that would not yield under the thrashing of my puny stick.

"Eesh!" Carruthers exclaimed as we came into one of the few small clearings that afforded a glimpse of the bare ground.

"Look at thee. A monkey-faced spider—farff!"

A great leggy arachnid marched across the black earth, pausing occasionally to heft itself back onto its hind legs and wriggle its forelimbs threateningly. I was tempted to imagine Carruthers getting bitten by something poisonous—as this specimen probably was—and had visions of me and Fortesque building the longest stretcher known to man in order to haul the feverish jackass back to civilization.

"Don't mess with it, Carruthers, for Christ's sake," I warned, as he poked at the beast with his stick. I stared up at his blocky head and noticed no bites on his sallow skin. This made me madder even than finding myself in this dangerous predicament—Carruthers was proving quite unpalatable to the biting bugs that feasted so avidly on Fortesque and myself.

"Carruthers, leave your monkey-faced friend to his business and get bloody whacking!" I said sternly, clipping him on the bare leg with my stick. "Nibs," he answered sullenly and resumed thrashing at the wall of greenery.

Our first day lost in the wilds of Tasmania elapsed in nightmarish slow motion. The tangle of exotic flora streamed across my vision, dancing in hallucinatory swirls even when my eyelids were closed, and my insides began to grumble as bilious peptic juices fought over the scant crumbs of dried fish and scones that remained our sole source of sustenance. At times, the jungle seemed to thin, giving us hope that was quickly dashed as it once more returned to its enveloping depths. We had long lost the sparkling tributary, despite our intention to follow it to its source, having apparently veered off course in the first few hours of our blind journey, and as night fell, ravaged and dejected, we collapsed in a clearing by a mercifully clear spring, which bubbled through a dark patch of muddy leaves.

"Something's different here," I panted, poking at the ground from where the water issued. "We must be getting somewhere. This water . . . the land's changing. What do you think, Fortesque?" I asked hopefully.

"Think you're right, BP. Tasmania's not big enough for this to go on forever," he replied, gesturing to the forest. "Still . . . it's *pretty* big—I wouldn't bet on anything yet," he added doubtfully.

Beneath the rotting leaves, shards of volcanic rock poked through and I took this to be a good sign regardless of Fortesque's bleak words. We hacked at the plants surrounding the small clearing to gain a few more precious feet of space, and as the air cooled and the night came on, we threw down our sleeping bags sweating and smelling like a troupe of simians.

As soon as we had sat down to catch our breath, there was a sudden rustle in the undergrowth near Carruthers' head and I bolted upright as a Tasmanian devil, stocky and bear-like, burst through into the clearing and found itself face-to-face with the startled soundman.

"Kimber!" he yelled automatically, but the creature, which bared its teeth in fear at the spectacle, turned and fled, leaving a bone-chilling squeal hanging in the darkening air.

I got up, almost beyond exhaustion, veins stringing across my biceps from the effort, and began thrashing at the vegetation, making the clearing into a larger semicircle in a vague attempt to forge a more civilized area in which to spend the night. Fortesque, ever the stalwart roadie, joined me, and after we had made a fair-sized circle, he went to the knapsack and retrieved the last scone, a dry, hard crumbly thing as appetizing as a piece of deadwood.

"Come on, blue, eat some of this. We'll be out of trouble tomorrow. Great Lake can't be too far off now."

"We're buggered, aren't we, Forty?" I said as I chewed the rock-hard scone and fingered some water from the spring onto my swollen lips.

"Should have tried swimming back up the river."

"Farff. Fookin' kimbered right enough," said Carruthers as he fell into another of his instant nine-hour catnaps.

"Naw," said Fortesque, shrugging off our doomy outlook in order to keep morale up. "We'll make it, mate. It can't go on forever . . . it can't," he added, unable to hide the doubt creeping across him like the rapidly enveloping night.

We crawled into our bags and shared the last tepid can of Boags, and with the rattling of creatures in the forest leaves and the whirring of giant moths spinning across the starry sky above us fell into an exhausted sleep.

Squawking lorakeets, the insect hum and a stab of sunlight knifing through the leaves forced me to emerge from an escapist dream that revolved around myself and the long-chinned English entertainer Bruce Forsyth, bicycling through the suburbs, staring over people's fences and criticizing their gardening skills.

My feverish unconscious was hatching up some interesting stuff in its attempts to take my mind off of my body, which was, even after a night's sleep, beginning to feel like a thing that might stop working at any moment.

Abruptly, between the bird calls and the bugs, I thought I heard stifled a yell of "Kimber!" Was I still dreaming? I forced myself up onto my elbows and immediately realized that all was not well. Instinctively, I yelled at the top of my lungs and leapt from the sleeping bag, grasping for my stick, the aches in my body completely obliterated by a wild surge of fear and adrenaline.

"Fortesque!" I screamed. "Carruthers!" I pleaded, thrashing at the jungle border of our camp, spinning like a dervish, as panicked as a doe in a lion's den. I thought I discerned another muffled yell but from where I couldn't tell. I stood stock-still, straining to hear. The birds were silent but the incessant insect buzz remained steady. A monkey-like hoot cut through the forest depths but the distance of its origin was impossible to gauge.

They were gone. Fortesque and Carruthers were gone, and I stood there tingling with a hopeless frustration, cursing my manager for sending me on this ridiculous tour and, worse still, my compliance in accepting it. Why wasn't I playing London, Rome, or Amsterdam? Why hadn't I reformed the Soulbilly Shakers as every letter I received from every anorak-wearing thinning-haired bifocalled old fart had suggested? I could be headlining Hammersmith Odeon for two nights right now, reliving my one-hit-wonder glory days instead of crawling around the forest floor of some hellish jungle on the wrong side of the globe! Why didn't I take the easy route and mine the lucrative reunion circuit instead of being some clever dick second-grade Dylan knockoff? I was a folk singer, pure and simple, that was the truth of the matter, with all the miserable, dowdy implications that come with that simplistic craft, just as the Penguinites had insinuated at the door of the greasy Marquee Club with its clientele of halfwits and local yokels. How on earth had I allowed myself to go along with this travesty when I could be at home dicking my beautiful wife on a regular basis instead of having to bear the knowledge that that retard Carruthers was getting boffed by every dodgy bint that came within six feet of him? And on my paycheck! What the fuck was I doing in Tasmania anyway, for Christ's sake, playing to an average capacity of twenty-five—and for two goddamn months! And where *was* the teenage sex God? And Fortesque? Where were my crew? What could have happened? Wild animals? Alien abduction?

I stared down at their sleeping bags, empty and rumpled like vacated cocoons, as if some bizarre metamorphosis had taken place in the livid dawn that I in my thick, delirious sleep had not been privy to. They had flown into the canopy and I had been left to crawl across the rotting floor, chained eternally in my caterpillar state, a maggot in the carcass of the forest.

"Steed, you bastard!" I screamed at the trees, shaking my fist for emphasis. And while I was at it, why not give the most popular entertainer on the island a good roasting too? "And fuck you, John Travolta, you great white-trousered ponce!" I yelled. It was an outrage. Ten years too late, I thought. Ten bloody years later and these inbred, wart-nosed, peons! . . . these Tasmanian twats are just getting into fucking disco . . . these . . . grrr!

But my rampage trailed off as I realized the frustrating emptiness of it. I quite liked John Travolta, truth be told, and couldn't actually think of a bad disco record—even "Boogie Oogie Oogie" was a masterpiece of a pop single.

This inspired me to get with the Tasmanians and their retro-chic. Right there, right on that lower Silurian mud heap that my stomping feet had turned our camp into, I broke into a fierce Bee Gees medley, complete with the tight choreography of the Hustle, albeit with an invisible partner. I was well into their greatly underrated "Spirits Having Flown" when I stopped in midstep, dropping the imaginary white scarf that trailed, windblown from my neck. Hysteria was gripping me. No doubt about that. Disco was the greatest era in pop music since Mersey Beat, and I had said so in many a provocative and trend-defying interview. Which probably accounted for the fact that I was not anymore what you might call a viable commodity in London and New York and rarely gainfully employed in those Meccas of cool, but stuck out here, in the back of beyond, losing my bloody mind.

Slapping myself about the face, I fell to the floor and drank from the little, bubbling spring, my heart beating at an alarmingly rapid rate.

Perhaps, it suddenly occurred to me as I guzzled the leafy-tasting water, the Tasmanians were ten years ahead of the curve! Could they possibly be in super, retro-retro-retro mode? So far behind they were ahead? That could be it, my feverish brain decided.

This intriguing possibility occupied my thoughts as I began to hack automatically into the dense shrubs, once again continuing my wasting slog into the unknown. There was nothing else for it, and gradually as the exhausting work took its toll my imagination returned from its febrile flights and I began to look for traces of human passage in the undergrowth—something, anything, to give me clues as to the direction I should take.

I believed—by the discovery of minute dents and wrinkles in branch and fern—that I was somehow on the right track, that Brian Porker, jungle detective, was going to save his cohorts from whatever fate had befallen them, and so I tramped on through the humid murk until at last the lush vegetation appeared to thin slightly. But after a brief respite in the shape of a butte, which I climbed to survey the apparently endless canopy, I was back in the thick of it again and the day disappeared in a chimera of alternating consciousness. One minute I was clearheaded, struggling on stoutly with a colonial "up and at 'em" attitude, the next I caught myself cursing the ridiculous Barry White and his terrible sexist album cover for "I've Got So Much to Give," or spewing venom at cretinous "Northern Soul" fans in Manchester or Birmingham or wherever the hell they lived.

However, the occasional rant did me good, and I had returned my equilibrium to one of general stability by late afternoon; but still, I seemed no nearer to saving myself or my lost road crew. Almost imperceptibly, however, small changes in the environment were occurring and before twilight was snuffed out by total darkness I came across a cave in a rocky outcrop next to a small streamlet and stumbled inside, my trusty brass Zippo throwing shadows on the damp sandstone walls.

In the inflamed neurosis of that morning I had stupidly left my sleeping bag back in last night's camp and was glad of the protection the cave might afford and too tuckered to worry about what poisonous insects and reptiles lurked within its crevices.

Bone tired once again, I curled up on the moss-covered floor and tried to ignore the fluttering bats and giant moths that passed in and out of the cave's entrance. There was an unholy stench in there, but I tried to ignore it as I fell into a sweaty, troubled sleep, disregarding the nagging familiarity of that animal-like odor.

Light was filtering through the shallow entrance to the cave when I awoke and the olfactory messages I again received troubled me immediately. What is that smell? I thought. As I crawled toward the light it hit me—it was reminiscent of damp dog fur, but much more intense: dog to the power of ten. A knot of fear gripped my throat and I felt I would surely gag if I didn't get out of there at that moment, but as I clambered into the light, the most awesome and chilling scene greeted me. For there, not ten feet away from the cave's entrance, stood a conundrum of a beast, standing stock-still in the quiet oppressive morning air.

The creature appeared to be canine, at least in appearance. Its pointy wolf-like face topped by sharp erect ears regarded me with a startled expression. The grayish brown fur of its upper torso broke up into black stripes halfway down its back and went all the way to the tip of its tail. I knew instantly what it was, for an illustration of two such beasts adorned every bottle and can of Boags beer in Tasmania. And I'd once seen a scratchy black-and-white film of what must have been one of the few remaining of its kind—for the last known specimen died on this very island in Hobart Zoo in 1936! Without doubt it was the marsupial wolf, the supposedly extinct thylacine. Cryptozoologists had been studying clues of the continued existence of this mysterious creature for years, and occasionally some joker would bring forth a photograph of dim-striped hindquarters disappearing into the bush, an image that could easily be debunked as a dog with some black lines painted on it—a dog in marsupial wolf's clothing, as it were. Many claimed that relic colonies of the beast still survived—there had been too many sightings over the years for enthusiasts and dreamers to give up on it. But officially, the thylacine was extinct. Yet here in front of me was evidence that at least one specimen—surely indicating a breeding colony—had survived the guns of the colonizing farmers anxious to protect their sheep, on which it allegedly preyed so virulently.

I had no camera, no way in which to record the reality of this Cenozoic vision, and when it casually turned its back on me and displayed its pouch, which opened toward its hindquarters, I caught a glimpse of two sets of eyes therein. It was a female with young!

The black stripes of thylacinus slowly merged into the tangle of plants edging the small clearing around the cave mouth, and I stood there stunned, not fully believing my discovery. Quickly, I strode to the creature's point of exit, hungry for a second glimpse, and saw there a path or track, curling into the wilderness. I followed cautiously, hoping the animal was well fed and not laying some trap, although it appeared more amused than alarmed by my presence, and I could not ignore this revelation and just press on blindly into the forest without further investigation. This was like discovering a living dodo, or a great auk. Much like the coelacanth, the prehistoric fish that was believed to be extinct but had been discovered by fishermen in the Indian Ocean in this century, the thylacine had somehow escaped the net of discovery until now, and I had stumbled right into its rank-smelling den.

Questions exploded in my head as I gingerly picked my way along the vague path. Why did the thylacine react with such calm upon discovering me crawling from the bowels of its lair? Where had it spent the night? Where was the male, and how protective was it? Where were Fortesque and that toggle-headed fool Carruthers? And where was my next meal coming from?

That I would receive answers to any of these questions within the space of the next ten minutes seemed improbable, but as I rounded a bend in the trail, one of them was answered immediately. I again caught sight of stripy hindquarters up ahead, but this was not the same animal I had seen moments before. This one was bigger and even more mangy than the first and lighter in color, and then the former made her appearance again, lifting herself up from a crouch in the bushes. There were a pair of them and the two pups, still tucked in the marsupial pouch. They loped on ahead, halting sometimes as if to wait for me as I laboriously hacked at the overgrown path. Then shockingly, without warning, I encountered something every bit as strange as the thylacine. Standing in front of me, where not a moment before the two creatures had been, stood a man.

He was black skinned with woolly hair, heavy brows, a short broad nose, and a smallish head. His face was deeply etched by scarification and a necklace of shells adorned his neck. Red ocher and charcoal were daubed on his body, and he held a crude wooden spear. Instantly, he turned and disappeared into the brush up ahead. With my heart pounding in my chest, I could think of nothing else but to follow, and exactly where he had vanished I crashed through the foliage and was greeted by the most incredible sight.

I was in a clearing surrounded by a camp of rough shelters plastered with leaves and mud, all of them propped above ground level on heavy wooden stanchions. In the center of the clearing was a pit from which curled wisps of smoke. Standing around the pit were four aborigines, two men and a woman with a baby suckling at her breast. As my momentum carried me forward into this bizarre site, two more tribesmen appeared from the bush at my side, not with a threatening attitude, but with the obvious intention of blocking my exit. All wore only loincloths, save one, a short fellow who donned a lemon yellow T-shirt with the words "Tart Sniffer" emblazoned across it in fluorescent pink. Shocked as I was, I did not immediately realize the implications of this incongruous sight. First the extinct thylacinus, and now this: a thriving group of supposedly extinct native Tasmanians! I gasped and froze on the spot, staring at the ancient-looking faces of the aborigines with their heavy brows and deeply etched bone structures. The white man had supposedly committed ethnocide upon this race, and the Tasmanian Tiger—as the thylacine was sometimes called—was said to have suffered the same fate. But here they were, flesh and blood in some hidden enclave in the forest, almost under the nose of civilization. And not only that, but dodging in and out of the wooden pillars that served to prop up the crude huts were the pair of thylacines. They were apparently pets!

I smiled nervously at the aborigines but they did not smile back. Thankfully, though, hostility did not seem to mark their demeanor and only querulous and suspicious looks came my way. And as if that weren't enough, I noticed a long white leg swinging out of a hammock in one of the shelters and those familiar grating tones of my soundman cut through the domestic scene like a machete from hell. So that's where the garish T-shirt had come from: obviously, they'd confiscated our shared knapsack and one of the natives had taken a fancy to an item of Carruthers' custom clothing.

"Thought we 'ad a spot of kimber there, chuck. Farff. Looks like nibs now, though, don't it?"

"Carruthers?" I began, but stopped short when the trusty Fortesque appeared, rolling out of another nearby hammock.

"All right, mate? They said they was goin' to find you—well, when I say 'said,' I mean one of 'em kept holding up three fingers and pointing to the forest, nodding his head. Think they were just 'avin' a spot of fun with you, that's all. Hey, you should 'ave brought a banjo, mate. I bet they'd love a show!"

"Jesus, Forty, this is unbelievable. These people are meant to be extinct. And these animals—do you know what they are?"

"Thylasomethings," said Fortesque casually. "I know, there s'posed to be extinct, too. There's a fortune sittin' around here. Look, these blokes are none too happy about this, but I get the feeling they've been expecting someone to find them at any time. I don't reckon they're gonna hurt us, at any rate. Keep it cool and I think we'll be all right."

THE OTHER LIFE OF BRIAN

Fortesque's assessment seemed sound to me; I did not feel any immediate threat, although how the aborigines were going to deal with this I had no way of knowing. They must have gotten away with their invisibility for a very long time, and so close to encroaching civilization, despite the forbidding wildness of this extraordinary environment. But I did feel a certain amount of unease about our discovery. The delicate balance of this paradise was now severely jeopardized, and I envisioned teams of scientists tramping through the thylacines' lairs, taking their young off to zoos and research institutes. The missionaries would be in like a shot, too. This innocent lost tribe would be eating aspirin and donning K-mart leisure wear before you could blink.

Just then, a powerfully built aborigine emerged from a hut holding in front of him what looked to be a necklace with a dull green fishhook dangling from it. He approached confidently, shaking the object in front of me. Other tribesmen quickly formed a circle around me, gently pushing Carruthers and Fortesque out of the way as they did so. Outside the circle, the women gathered, giggling shyly.

The man with the necklace gradually changed his expression from a blithe politeness to a threatening grimace as he moved closer and began shaking the necklace not six inches from my eyes.

"Oh, oh. Um . . . Forty? Ah, whaddaya think of this?" I asked nervously; but the group, although not restraining my crew, were making it quite clear that they had no part in this new development.

Fortesque was not stuck for ideas, though. "I've seen this in New Zealand!" he yelped excitedly. "The Maoris do something like it. Face him down, BP! Pick the thing up if he drops it on the ground! Face him down! It's important you don't lose yer bottle."

Indeed, they seemed to have singled me out as the leader of my tribe, and I gathered from my tour manager's comments that I was about to undergo some sort of test, the outcome of which could prove vital to our acceptance here.

"Shit," I said flatly, shaking in my battered sneakers.

"AH, AH, AH!" yelled the big chap with the necklace as he continued to rattle it in my face, along with a nasty-looking spear that he held in his other hand. The others immediately took up the chant and began brandishing their spears, too, thrusting them at me in a very disturbing manner.

The sweating tribesmen, their ever louder chanting, their wide angry eyes and stamping bare feet made my head swim and I thought for a moment that I would pass out. Everything started to spin around like in a scene from an old B movie.

"Stay with it, Beep!" encouraged Fortesque from somewhere behind the encircling natives. "Stay with it, mate!"

With that, I took a deep breath and stared right back into the leader's black eyes, letting him know that no matter what, I would not succumb to intimidation. I was bluffing, of course, but the more I stared this powerful man down, the more I began to trust Fortesque's assessment that this was indeed merely a test and that with any luck, no harm would come to me if I played along with it.

Sensing my intent, the aborigine suddenly flung the necklace down onto the red sand at my feet and stepped back to await results. He then assumed a mighty spear-throwing stance, pointing his weapon at me like a javelin thrower about to break the rules of Olympic competition and murder one of his opponents.

What did I have to lose? I bent down, the tip of my aggressor's lethal weapon almost brushing the top of my head, and picked up the necklace.

A triumphant roar issued from the tribespeople, and, not coming up with a better idea, I lifted the necklace above my head and roared also. They responded with yelps of delight, and smiles broke out all around. The next thing I knew the men were hugging me and the women were dangling their pendulous breasts in my face and rubbing their broad noses against mine.

Next, the instigator of this little charade motioned first toward the necklace and then toward my neck. Picking up on his queue, I put the artifact over my head and gave them a big beaming smile, which seemed to go down very well.

"Bravo, BP!" yelled Fortesque in the background. "Fookin' nibs!" shouted Carruthers. After a bit of congratulatory slapping on the back, the group of aborigines broke up and Fortesque and Carruthers drew near to examine the artifact. The green fishhook appeared to be made of a jade-like substance, dull green and heavy for its size; it was about an inch in length and a few millimeters thick. A small hole was bored into its shaft, through which the string—some kind of hemp-like vine—was threaded.

It did not look particularly valuable, but the manner in which the green stone was carved and polished suggested a reasonable degree of skill, and I hoped that our hosts would let me hang on to it and not expect it returned now that the trial was complete.

"Nifty piece of work, that," announced Fortesque after he had felt the smooth lines of the fishhook in his gnarly fingers. My tour manager, already a slim but gnarly fellow, seemed to have become even more tightly conditioned in the last few days. His arm muscles beneath the cuffs of his dirty white T-shirt were as ropey-looking as jungle vines and his veins streaked along them like red snakes. Carruthers, however, appeared as cadaverous as ever, still white, huge, and larval, a teenager despite himself.

"Right. Now listen up," I said firmly, nodding toward the soundman as I chewed on a leg of roast wallaby provided by our aboriginal hosts. It was my second night in the village, and with strength returning and the recent delirium behind me, I was determined to take charge of the situation, to impose some discipline on future actions concerning our discovery.

I pointed the wallaby leg bone at Carruthers, then flicked it into the shadows at the edge of the campfires' light where it was quickly snatched up by one of the thylacines.

"You know what's gonna go down here if we don't keep our mouths shut, right? Fortesque, convince this great plank here, will you. You know what I mean, Carruthers?" I said, getting annoyed at the soundman's recalcitrance. He sat there with a glum surliness as I lectured about the inevitability of ethnocide, specicide, and the shattering disruption this paradise would receive if we went back blaring like foghorns.

"Okay, look," I continued, assuming a menacing tone as Carruthers remained fixed and cross-legged, a moping expression stuck on his oblong face.

"I'll have your legs broken if you don't keep your fucking mouth shut. Got it?"

He blew out air and rolled his pale wall-eyes around for a moment before giving me a grudging nod of agreement.

Our edgy conversation had kept the sensitive natives away, eating their meals at different fires dotted around the village, but as we relaxed a few of them shuffled over and sat with us, resuming the laborious communications we had experimented with over the last two days. These consisted of sign language, sand drawing, and much facial and body language, which began to reveal some of their secrets to us. There were twenty-six adults in this village and they were apparently on peaceful terms with two other communities within the forest. All three groups had thylacines as regular visitors, as if they were drawn together in their mutual fear of extermination.

But we had to get back. I had work to do and it was possible the boatman, Tubb, had become anxious about his property and called the police; a search party could be screaming up and down the Mersey and we would have some explaining to do.

It remained a mystery why the aborigines had taken our boat and then kidnapped Fortesque and Carruthers. From hints gleaned from our frustrating dialogue with them, we believed that we had crossed some invisible line of territory and had appeared to them to be on the verge of discovering their existence; they were simply anxious to control the outcome of such an eventuality and thus have the upper hand in a potentially threatening situation. But this was more guesswork on our part than fact. Before my stumbling arrival, Fortesque described how their Shaman had danced around Carruthers for two hours and then somehow a decision had been reached. We had been accepted as innocents and not cut from the same mold as other white gods. Possibly the odd countenance of Carruthers had been enough to swing the balance in our favor. Perhaps they saw in him something akin to their own primitive simplicity. He certainly fit in there well enough, playing with the children, flirting with the women (and judging by the interest one such female was showing, I suspected the rotter of something more than flirtation), and gaining instant respect from the thylacines that, although not overtly interested in being petted like domesticated animals, seemed intrigued by the soundman and followed him around the camp, their feral eyes fascinated by his eccentric bearing. The elders too had shown a certain respect for the seven-foot lank that baffled and irritated me. There was, it seemed, plenty of caveman in Carruthers.

Chapter 11

"Letter for you, sport. And a fax," said the wart-nosed receptionist at the Abel Hotel as he passed my room key over the counter. "How's the tour been going? Getting a lot of rumpies are you, eh?" he leered.

"Rum? . . . " I queried, staring at the letter like it was a message from another planet. "Ask Carruthers," I mumbled, heading for the elevator feeling the bile rise in my gut. "He's like a pig in shit," I added, glancing back at wart-nose as he thrust his hand into the crook of his arm, brought it up in that time-honored salute to copulation, and yelled "Wahey!" across the damp, musty reception.

With two shows under my belt since our return to civilization, I still felt disoriented and filled with awe at our incredible discovery. The world we had reentered seemed like the world of savages and the jungle paradise the Eden man had been intended for. Those days of hardship before our capture by the aborigines had been well worth it, an initiation that we had passed, by our very survival. And I wore the jade fishhook on its primitive string under my black T-shirt, reaching inside to feel it now and again, as if it were a talisman.

I entered my room, the same one I had occupied when we arrived in Tasmania in what felt like a century ago. The fax was from Steed and the letter from the rapacious American lawyers who represented those religious perverts the Baedburgers, the couple who had conned my half-uncle into willing them his earthly estate. I read the fax first, anger (that wonderful creative goo) pulsing through my veins with every syllable, an anger not to be defused by the last paragraph, which did, however, cause me to let out a whoop of surprise:

Dear Brian you client:

The new recording is unlikely to reach the projected quantity of unitary sales calculated by Shinto Tool Records in America.

I therefore assess in all due and pursuant presumption, in vitro, divided in toto, mano y mano and quantum profligate, an ergo assumption that Lex, the president is—as stated in clauses 1B, 3A and 13C of our legal and binding document hereafter known as "The Recording Contract"—entitled to the following *imputum creatium*:

A. Tacit agreement of all future recordings as assessed via demonstration materials.

B. Haircut management formulated demographically and effected by a stylist that "the Record Company" has the sole right to select.

C. A multiforce assessment comprising of producers, arrangers, improvers and digital technicians to be exclusively chosen by "the Company" and hired expressly for the purposes of said album project to be remunerated entirely by "the Artist" from recoupable advances.

D. Twenty-two-year-old A&R twat y kunti pratspeak interfero ad nauseam over yer shoulder.

Brian, I know some justifiable pride may have to be swallowed but it is my learned assumption that the key to your commercial future in America is severely hampered by your persistent attitude that you are in some way superior intellectually and artistically to people who work in "record companies."

Please think this over and in due course (preferably before the beginning of the new tax year) fax me your thoughts. I will be in Japan for the next 3 weeks with my other client, the Neanderthal guitarist, and will be completely unreachable. Miss Twark, my secretary, will be accompanying me but hopefully she will be able to access my fax machine in Findhorn and have your reply refaxed to the fax machine in the first class Tokyo hotel I'll be using as a fax base.

In the meantime, please look over these sales figures for the latest Bone Mutha and Richardo Enlighteno projects. According to Shinto Tool both these artists and many more have succumbed to puppet mode and therefore, due to the *imputum creatium* of the people you so despise, have duly increased their sales potential accordingly.

Also, Jay Weinerbaum at Campers Monthly wants another in-depth interview. Shinto Tool consider it very important. You can do it when you get back.

How's the tour going? Oh, by the way, I've canceled the last two weeks as we're just covering old ground: *performo interuptus*, as it were.

Yours without prejudice,
Steed

"Clocked it Beep," said Fortesque on the phone. I had rung his room the moment Steed's final sentence had registered, but Fortesque had received a fax also, bearing the same news. "Couple more shows, mate, an' we're out of here. I've told Carruthers."

"Oh yeah, what's he up to?" I asked, wondering if the road dog would be disappointed.

"He's in his room with that stewardess from the flight over."

"Stewardess? Stewardess? Not that old biddy with skin like a bongo drum?"

"The same," said Fortesque. "Up there with her an' a bottle of Tasmanian vodka."

"Christ," I said, "he's probably gonna set fire to her. What a bloke, Forty, eh? Not playing tonight, am I?" I ventured, suddenly going a blank.

"Naw, rest up, mate. Later."

"Later," I said, and hung up.

I then ripped open the letter from America, hoping those obsequious Shylocks would instill in me the same vibrant hostility that I had gleaned from the first three-quarters of Steed's fax. I was not disappointed and almost began foaming at the mouth as I perused the foul piece of correspondence:

Dear Mr. Corker:

Thank you for your last correspondence. In the light of this recent information concerning John "Sir" Bacon's mental health, we still feel that the Baedburgers are fully entitled to the entire proceeds of his will. The Baedburgers have indicated no such wayward behavior on behalf of Mr. Bacon during the time they, in their Christian hospitality, took him in, nurtured and cared for him.

It is their honest opinion that he was of sound mind at that time and that his only illness, due to old age, was physical. He suffered from mild gout, shingles and chronic diarrhea which they saw fit to treat at the hands of their local medical practitioner, Dr. Rashid Poutenscope, and this, at their own expense.

Therefore, we will begin the process of probating the will and ignore your feeble but imaginative ramblings. Blood, Mr. Corker, is only thicker than evangelical holy water when you have a Will that is weighed in your favor. We await your citation with a large and bureaucratic chuckle.

Very truly yours,
Messrs. Goldtraub, Cardbaum & Silvermein

P.S. It has come to our attention that you are something of a celebrity in the pop world. One of our assistants in the typing pool has a son who owns your first two long playing discs. Would it be too much trouble if we send the aforementioned discs to your home address in order that you may autograph them? If we may enclose a photograph of ourselves for you to sign, which we would thereafter frame and hang on the wall of our palatial offices, we would also be humbly grateful.

Thank you, in your service
Messrs. G, C & S

"Right! Right! Mr. Corker indeed! I'll give them Mr. Corker! I'll give them a right fucking corker!"

I shook the letter in front of me, shouting at their outrageously bland unctuousness. I was not going to be ripped off without a long and convoluted fight. But I would not merely spew forth insults and obscenities in the language of a common fishwife, no sir. I would channel my disgust into a terse yet poetic rhetoric; I would give the bounders what for—no question—but I would also give them a good dose of home truth, a little thing those evangelical wide-bottoms, the Baedburgers, had long kept swept under the static-laden carpets of their tract housing module.

I snatched the personalized water-marked paper from my bag and tested my bottle-green fountain pen like a syringe, then launched into a reply, successfully blotting out the multifarious aches that threatened to drag me into sloth. For if truth be told, our jungle escapade had left me well knackered but damn it if I would not strike while the iron was hot!

To Messrs. Goldenhind, Cardbutt and Silverbum
Dear Sirs:

The chronic mental illness it has been my misfortune to inherit from my melancholy, schizophrenic and maniacal deviationist half-uncle John "Sir" Bacon, has, in recent weeks, kept me bedridden and thus, until this very day, unable to reply to your last correspondence. I fortunately awoke this morning somewhat refreshed and coherent and at last, rid of the ghostly apparitions that have plagued my troubled soul. Bedeviled as I have been by visions of eldritch bestials stretching their fetid tentacles through the portals of hell itself, I have not once considered rescinding my original position of complete obstruction of the deliverance of my half-uncle's estate to those insipid born-again zealots, the Baedburgers.

Furthermore, I consider the Baedburgers not only to be agents of evil coercion, but also to be—not to put too fine a point on it—quite mad themselves.

I in fact stayed with the Baedburgers last August for two days and found them both dysfunctional as a dynamic family unit, and hyper-insensitive to the terminally insane. In short, they had no place taking the old fool in the first place. Are you, good sirs, unaware of "The Kool Aid Miracle?" Let me give you a brief summary of this preposterous story, for surely Loretta Baedburger, from whose lips this very nonsense was uttered, will not give it mention in your presence.

Loretta (an assumed name of course, "Joyce," I suspect is closer to the truth) recounted her tale of "The Kool Aid Miracle" to me one hot afternoon as I tried to force the foul supermarket hormonally altered pig ribs her family considered food down my gagging throat. It was one of a string of "miracles" she, in her permanent "Born Again" delusional state, convinced herself she had experienced.

One afternoon that very summer, Loretta had attended a church-organized garden fete of which she had the task of preparing the usual mass-produced unsophisticated refreshments one would expect at such dire functions. She concocted, if my vivid memory of her tale serves me, a large amount of bologna sandwiches (white bread of course), many buckets of artificially flavoured jello (FD&C yellow and green coloring, natch), and a ten gallon drum of Kool Aid, a substance—if the adverts are to be believed—that works on the human body like some form of biologically replenishing amphetamine. (Personally, I have never tried the stuff but being from the British Isles I think I have consumed similar mass-market poisons in my uninformed youth.)

Amongst the group of tepid Christians who attended the gathering, she described, with forced equanimity, a large group of Africans whose skins where "so black they were blue." I perceived in her falsely amiable description some repugnance on her part, for like all of these born-again Christians, she is also a born-again racist. The Africans, according to Loretta, took quite a shine to this lukewarm fetid brew and guzzled large quantities of the stuff. But as the afternoon bore on, instead of the sparkling liquid disappearing as the laws of physics would normally dictate, the ten-gallon drum remained "miraculously" filled to the brim. The Africans appeared refreshed enough, and Loretta, in her desperate groping for "signs from the Lord," pronounced the event a miracle. Hence, "The Kool Aid Miracle."

It does not take too astute an intelligence to grasp that the blue-skinned sneaks were merely trying to be polite and duly pouring the muck right back into the drum when no one was looking. Loretta, blinded as she is by religious fanaticism, assumed that God in His infinite bad taste had in fact chosen her as a vessel, His wonders to perform.

She told me this story as her loathsome pet ferret leapt about between our feet like some nasty muppet. This is the psychopath who expects to receive the wealth of my dear departed half-uncle? Not on your nelly, good sirs! The money's mine I tell you! It's my money!

As for autographing some God-fearing brainwashed young tossle-head's vinyl collection—please send the articles to me. You in your ignorance are obviously unaware of the vinyl shortage that began as far back as 1974 and continues to this very day. I shall gladly apply my moniker to the cover artwork of these rarities. But the vinyl I shall keep and melt down in my private recording studio where I have collected a large vat of the stuff, ready to be remolded for my next release. Please inform this hair-brained youth that I am a current artiste who releases new product every year, and not some ancient washout from the 70s.

In conclusion gentlemen: my lawyers are working full time on this case and our forthcoming victory is assured. In the meantime, watch your backs.

Yours sincerely,
Brian Porker, M.B.E., O.B.E.

That completed, I sighed with satisfaction and flopped back on the lumpy bed, happy in the knowledge that this tour was now on its last legs and that I would soon be back in London, giving Steed a good roasting and sorting out a few business details with my literary agent before finally returning to the US to give my wife a good shagging.

Chapter 12

"You mean you could have copped the lot?" asked an incredulous Fortesque after I had recounted the Bahá'í incident.

"The lot, Forty," I replied. "I would have been installed in some palace in Iran with servants, concubines, tons of dough I shouldn't wonder—and my pick of the tarts, dirty fingernails and all. That Bahá'u'lláh was like a rat up a drainpipe when it came to his female followers, by all accounts."

We were on the return flight to London, chugging back cheap champagne, in high spirits despite the prospect of hours locked in a stifling tube. Carruthers' friend, the Stewardess From Hell, wobbled past heaving a trolley and gave me an evil wink. As for the soundman—he was a few rows up already passed out after a vodka binge that had begun at 11 A.M. in the airport bar.

The tour, as far as I could ascertain, had accomplished nothing. *Grease* was still the most popular record on the island and the huge influx of my latest product that Steed had promised seemed unlikely. Still, I had been somewhat cheered by the last two shows, in Margate and Dunallay, where I had drawn reasonable houses, half full at least. And the memory of the thylacines, the aborigines, and every detail of our startling discovery filled me with a pulsing renaissance, a warm glow of amazement that inspired flights of creativity that I reveled in, and let rent from my pen in the form of surreal lyrics and vivid insights. So open and flowing did I feel that I had spontaneously begun to blurt out the entire Bahá'í episode to my tour manager, despite the fact that the very thought of it still made me cringe with embarrassment. Before this moment, I'd preferred to keep it to myself, even with the knowledge that if Steed and Smyke had gotten wind of it via those basin-headed Northerners from Slade Two, it was a good bet that Fortesque had heard the gist of the fiasco already.

Fortesque, tactful man that he was, acted as if the story were fresh news to him and listened with consuming interest.

"Blimey, blue," he exclaimed, foaming at the mouth at the idea of being a powerful guru and attaining all the trappings that came with it. "Whew, reckon I would have gone for that . . . still, I s'pose you were right in the end."

"Damn right, Forty. You won't catch me eating dry-roasted peanuts and drinking Worcestershire sauce and chanting like a twit. And besides," I added, getting down to road-scum level, "you should have seen the womenfolk—grim!"

"Ha haaaa!" laughed Fortesque.

"Yeah, Forty—ever seen a good-looking nun?"

"Got ya, Beep! Ha! Say no more, sport. Say no more."

"Hey, listen," I said, an inspired thought causing me to suddenly lurch forward and pull Steed's fax from my bag.

"Do they have a fax machine on these babies?"

"What, on the plane?"

"Yeah."

"I'll go check."

And my trusty tour manager leapt to his feet and shot up the aisle as I busied myself with a suitably astringent reply to my manager's latest heretic balderdash. I ordered more champagne and burrowed in, the words leaping from my pen like soldiers going to battle, and when Fortesque returned with the good news that they did indeed have fax facility on the plane, I palmed him my finished handiwork, which he read, causing him a hearty guffaw as he sped off to dispatch it.

Dear Steed you bastard,

No I will not do a follow-up interview with Jay Weinerbaum of Campers Monthly. In fact, if I ever run into that little snit again, I shall ram my fist so far down his throat he'll need a post-mortem to get it out.

Shinto Tool and that mechanized product manager can take their record deal, force it into a blender, and make an obscene species of guacamole with it. I care not a wit. I'm ready for that inevitable spiral down indie alley. That precipitous plummet into ant-budget land. That gleeful Formica netherworld where guitar straps snap on open-mic night at your local folk club and strings are boiled for tomorrow's meagerly paid performance. In short, I would rather open a drum shop in Sheffield than talk "creatively" with either you or those flaccid-brained plimsoleheads at Shinto Tool Records. And if I hear the names "Bone Mutha" or "Richardo Enlighteno" mentioned by you or Shinto Tool ever again I shall ram my fist . . . etc., etc.

And will you please stop sending me faxes that look like nothing less than legal documents? The last one I received was like a court summons; the one before that, I was convinced my property was about to be repossessed.

Please forward these creative ideas to Shinto Tool.

Yours,
BP, H.A.T.E. F.C.U.2.

That done, Fortesque and I continued chatting merrily for a while but avoided any discourse concerning our adventure in the forest, preferring to keep those events locked in our own minds, protected in a sacred dreamscape. But when Fortesque returned to his window seat, I found myself reflecting again on the aborigines and the deeply mysterious thylacines, safe for the moment in their humid forest home. Surely, it could only be a matter of time before they were discovered and their innocent existence trashed. My reverie was interrupted by a loud groan, and I looked around to see Carruthers' hair flash past like a bag of burning donuts as he tripped headlong down the aisle and disgorged his lunch and half a bottle of Tasmanian vodka onto a sleeping passenger's foot. I smiled secretly to myself. If the true natives of Tasmania—the aborigines and the thylacines—had survived him, they would surely survive anything.

Chapter 13

My one thought on completion of the aborted Tasmanian tour was to quickly return to my North American estate and pick up where I had left off before I was so rudely interrupted. Spring would be in the air, and there was much to enjoy in the spectacular North American scenery. I'd soon be puttering around the woodshed, waxing up the antique cross-country skis, opening the pool in readiness for the coming summer, and ridding myself of seminal fluids by the bucketload with the help of my wife's svelte body. Christ, my groin was aching!

Perhaps I would even push myself into the music room and make contact with my distilled anger (ah, that creative goo!), shored up from my recent experiences, and scribble down a few songs. I might get around to writing a play even. On the last leg of our flight over to Tasmania I had received divine inspiration for a plot in the form of a jug-headed German and a rather effeminate Englishman who sat in front of me. They were deeply involved in a discussion about cannibalism, which the German seemed to think should be encouraged because it was a great way to thin the overpopulated globe and solve the problem of starvation in third world countries. I had began to jot down an outline for a plot tentatively entitled "Cannibalism: Crime and Nourishment." This idea excited me and I deemed it to have plenty of potential.

I had become excited about the prospect of tinkering with it further and getting it to my literary agent in London, who had successfully secured a small-scale church hall provincial production of my last work, *The Man in the Green Trilby*. But as I discovered when I reached my London apartment, this gentle future was not to be. Steed, like a rampaging bull elephant, was determined to stomp every speck of juice out of *Porker in Aspic*, a record that so far had distinguished itself with utterly appalling sales figures. A single fax hung from my machine in the flat. I stared at it, dreading its contents, feeling the emptiness of the living room close in around me, wishing I had flown directly to the States instead of coming back to England merely to meet with my literary agent and go over a few accounts with Steed.

Brian:

Cut short my Japan visit. Got sick. Miss Twark and I had a run in with the fugu. Close call. Now then, great news old boy! Real enthusiasm for *Porker in Aspic* up north. Lining a tour up. You could go back to the States—but what with the preparations etc., it hardly seems worth it.

Come to the office tomorrow morning. A few things I want to go over with you.

Later,
Steed

PS. Hope this fax is less official sounding than usual, man.

I could almost smell Steed's reticence all over the paper; fashioning this loose correspondence had obviously been a great effort for him and he had probably ripped up two other attempts, both of them resembling litigation proceedings, before this one finally exited his pen with great reluctance. What did he mean, "up north?" Watford? Morecombe? Had a Porker appreciation society suddenly blossomed in Steed's bizarre Findhorn locale and did he expect me to drop everything and spend hours shivering in a transit van clanking up and down the M1?

Surely the north of England was no less afflicted than the south by the cult of mediocrity in the shape of dreadlocked rappers, melody-deficient singer/songwriters whose vibrato-saturated voices were routinely thought of by the dullard masses as being soulful, and, of course, the ever popular reunion acts?

No, I would have none of this. Steed was not going to walk all over me because some Northern plebeian had given the record a decent review and a few hairy-arsed Yorkshire promoters had bent his ear. No way. I would stride into his office, dander well and truly up, and tell him that it was just not on. Then I would go back to America where I was appreciated and pick up a few lucrative corporate gigs to help fund the laziness I had planned for the rest of the year.

Yes, that was the ticket. I'd had enough performing to mental defectives and white-trousered Travolta enthusiasts, thank you. Steed could take the job and stuff it. Damn those occasional good reviews, I thought. Always more trouble than they were worth. Far better to receive flagrantly damning press that creates the effect of dampening the enthusiasms of both record company and manager, thus ensuring the likelihood of little, if not zero, promotional effort on my part. I would sort Steed out tomorrow. Right now, in the empty, dead air of my flat, the faint, melancholy trace of my wife's perfume still in the air and the odd piece of some half-forgotten child's toy left on the floor, I would attack the mail, a venomous pen at the ready.

There was nothing from those insidious American lawyers, but Shinto Tool, my US record company, had sent over another batch of reviews for *Porker in Aspic*, one specimen being a prime lubricator of viciousness and hostility. It was from Chicago, a town that normally finds favor in my recording endeavors, but these strongholds of Porkerism often harbor a sly worm in the apple, lurking, honing his mandibles for a good old hatchet job, or more annoying still, a piece riddled with willful insouciance. Yes, some little bifocaled bastard from the Windy City was trying to make a name for himself!

The fax paper came out like a shot and a hasty call to Shinto Tool's publicity department in Los Angeles revealed the fax number of the culprit's publication and I had great sport clobbering the anorak-wearing nerd mightily.

Ah, yes, this was fine stuff!

Next on the chopping block was my indolent European record label, Dreadnought Records. Some cheeky, box-headed dolt from the promo department had apparently arranged a whistlestop promotional tour of Europe between now and my alleged "Tour of the North." Judging by the contents of this piece of heinous correspondence, these mythical journeys I was about to undertake were a done deal and Steed and Dreadnought had been at it, thick as thieves, while I was away. The sheer sloppiness of the Dreadnought employee's idea of a comprehensive itinerary almost made me wretch with bile. I would let this teenage moron know that he was not dealing with some hick who had just arrived on the last train from the suburbs with stars in his eyes, and that in fact I had actually made a few records, done a few interviews, and dealt with more brainless record company persons than you could hurl a cliché at.

I looked at the clock—almost time to call the wife on the other side of the pond. First the fax, then the phone call home:

Dear Record Company Person,

Will I receive a more accurate and detailed itinerary of my forthcoming promo tour, or will the accommodations and routing be left to guess work? Will you and your cronies experience some weird thrill at the thought of my good self, sweating bullets in economy class, surrounded no doubt by religious fanatics, great bolshie women who claim to be my biggest fan and flight imbeciles of every imaginable stripe, and me, without a comprehensive itinerary?

According to you, there are four days to go before this travesty gets underway, and I have but a piece of fax paper bearing the legend:

London/poss Birmingham	Monday
France	Tuesday
Belgium/Holland	Wednesday (no hotel Brussels: drive Germany)
Germany	Thursday
Sweden/Norway/Denmark	Friday
Austria (tbc)	Saturday

This is the itinerary? And I am expected to board an airplane with this nonsense? Get it together you slovenly little indie label or I will not turn up.

As you know, I am refusing to do interviews for Shinto Tool in the USA because the thought of that third hack in a row asking me if I will ever work with that unjustly famous percussionist Biezel Sicks again fills me with dread. It would be true to say that lately I have the misfortune to experience actual physical nausea at interview sessions and it requires great effort on my part not to vomit all over these buffoons. I'm granting Dreadnought Records this favor purely to help stimulate flagging European sales. Therefore, please show some restraint in the scheduling and bear in mind I like talking to the press about as much as I enjoy stepping in dog turd.

Furthermore, if any of the lovely hotels I'll be staying in have less than three stars on their door (two and a half will just not do), I will point it out in no uncertain terms to whichever rep you send to accompany me, and have him ferret out suitable accommodations immediately.

Now, send me that detailed itinerary today. I hate surprises and do not respond well to them.

Yours, BP

I zapped the fax off to Dreadnought and then made the familial call. I was peeved, irritated that my wife and son were so far away and probably expecting me to arrive in the US any day soon. And now this promo tour, which seemed to be a done deal, and some loathsome jaunt above the Watford curtain? How long would it be before I was reunited in the bosom of my family—and more importantly, reunited with my wife's bosom. It had been long enough already—I was beginning to release involuntary emissions of essential bodily fluids and my testes felt like medicine balls.

"Come on. Pick up . . . pick up!" I hissed impatiently as the phone rang unanswered, my thoughts drifting hopefully to a bout of marital phone sex. I was about to give up when I heard that welcoming click and my wife got on the line. After a spot of moo moo's and a dabble of telephonic conoodling, we discussed Steed's recent tour plans. Not surprisingly, Tarquin had made a call to our Vermont home a week ago and blustered over my better half like a steamroller with sincere promises of "widening territories," "cementing relationships," and more tempting than that, "cash flow prerogatives." He seemed convinced that there could be a potential gold mine for me up north and had, in cunning managerese, enlisted the support of my wife with lures of "fiscal bolstering" and a bank account as fat as a goose liver.

"We need the money, Brian," she said. "Especially if we're talking all next fall *and* winter in the Caribbean. "Steed *is* good when it comes to finances—you know that. And with a little extra in the accounts you can really take it easy later in the year."

"But I was hoping to take it easy *now*. Steed's really gotten to you, hasn't he," I stated accusingly, and not in the form of a question.

"Well, you get yourself a new manager every few years and this is what they're going to do: a new broom and all that . . ."

"Uh . . ."

"You know how it is, Brian. He's enthusiastic, that's all, and he says there's some real interest in the record up north. What does he mean by 'up north' anyway? Scotland?"

"Fucked if I know," I confessed.

Might as well have a lobotomy, I said to my wife. I certainly didn't need a brain if this was my future; it didn't call for much independent thought: jumping when Steed said jump, "yes sir, no sir, three bags full sir" to the record company. Might as well take a pointy needle and stick the mother right up under my eyelid.

Our conversation ended, both of us at least agreeing that only a cartload of cash could convince us that yet another tour, so close on the heels of the last, was worth a sliver of consideration. Steed had better produce some hefty figures before I did anything. And then I went out for a run, followed by three toothsome pints of bitter in the local pub, some Thai food, and eight hours of dreamless sleep.

Chapter 14

"Been sprinting again, laddie?" said Steed, not for a minute concerned about my answer, affirmative or negative. He strode off purposefully across the office, tapping a baton against his thick thigh. But before he reached whatever destination originally intended, he spun around and strode right on back to his desk, suddenly clicking the joints in his chunky shoulders, as if exercise had been the sole purpose of his navigations.

It was true, I had combined a mixture of speed-walking and jogging to get to his office in a little known cul-de-sac off Harley Street. It was an unseasonably hot day and I had no intention of sitting in a cab, in the traffic, watching the meter roll into unthinkable sums of whatever nasty new currency happened to pass as legal tender in the British Isles at that particular point in history. Avoiding the Cro-Magnon commentary of a London cabbie was another bonus of my healthy perambulation, and jogging was always safer than the London underground; at least you could run away if a moron attack erupted.

I looked around the office feeling the usual sinking dread as Steed tapped his baton on the desk as if killing flies with it, and wondered, as I had many times before, how I had come to allow the man to manage me in the first place. It had nothing to do with any savvy on his part in the artistic field—Tarquin had trouble tapping his feet in time, let alone recognizing the merits or demerits of any given recording in the history of pop music. No, it was by pure default that I had hired Steed, having appeared in front of him in court a few years before when my former bilingual manager was suing me for everything I owned, including my much imitated haircut, a style that had once become popular not for its flamboyance, but for its disarming ordinariness.

Steed, resplendent in wig and gown, had pulled me aside after drumming my former manager's trumped-up charges right out of court, and had put a little word in my ear. At first, I thought I was receiving the advances of an old fruit, but my barrister informed me that Steed was in fact leaving the bar and had already signed one famous client to a management contract—a very well-off and esteemed Neanderthal guitarist once popular in the sixties.

Steed's cool, clear judgment on that day had extricated me from what could have been a long and convoluted minefield of lawsuits and counterlawsuits, and I found myself free to create again. I had, however, not intended to plunge into another management situation so soon, a bitter taste from the recent debacle still fresh in my mouth. But Tarquin's upper-crust accent, so incongruous in the guttersnipe vernacular of rock 'n' roll, and his expertise in the legal field together with a powerful father figure image that oozed out of his pores like aftershave made him a somewhat irresistible figure, and before I knew it, without quite understanding how or why, I found myself with a new manager.

From that point on, I knew my earnings, at least, were in safe hands, for Steed was a meticulous business manager. But his eccentric and sometimes baffling promotional methods often left me drained, irritated, and mired by a feeling of abject helplessness. His technique in human interaction was often bizarre and unnerving, too. Once, at a high-level bullshit bash peopled by three top record company executives and their various toadies who had gathered together in a suite in London's Montcalm Hotel to discuss a new and lucrative deal I was about to enter, Tarquin, while pacing the lush quarters in his usual hyperdrive mode, dismantled a lamp stand (he often fiddled distractingly with objects as he made deals, which had the effect of putting his opponents thoroughly off guard, thereby leaving himself free to shoehorn bigger advances out of them), which fell to pieces in a hail of sparks and started a fire, forcing the distinguished company to flee the suite screaming for the fire brigade. In another oft-quoted incident, Tarquin, sitting poolside at a similar high-level meeting in Los Angeles, was wildly shaking a disposable cigarette lighter about in order to get it to work. All he had managed to extract from the object so far had been a dull clicking sound, until he finally held it to his ear, as if a diagnosis could be reached by studying the sound the cheap mechanism made. Then, upon striking the wheel, a six-inch flame shot out of the thing and set fire to his hair. In a panic, he jumped into the pool forgetting that it had been drained for repairs and promptly broke a leg.

THE OTHER LIFE OF BRIAN

These Chaplinesque antics were legendary and at least created a folklore of hilarity around the man. But what really irked me was his habit of withholding important information, omitting the essential details of proposed tours until he had me, trapped like a fly in a pitcher plant.

"Well it's looking good for Greenland!" Tarquin enthused jarringly. My mouth opened, but nothing came out. "Getting some reports of radio play up there," he continued, dropping into the swivel chair behind his desk. "Number ten on the playlists! Iceland's coming together, Svalbard's firm and we're waiting on the promoters from Franz Joseph Land to get back to us—shouldn't be a problem though. Might have a struggle with the visas for Novaya Zemlya, but the promoters are raving up there—seems a shame not to do it. Oh . . . and there's this little island just a bit south of Svalbard—Bear Island it's called. Not much more than a rock, really. Now . . ." He paused dramatically, still hitting objects on his desk, which created a dull musical accompaniment. "It's Norwegian at the moment, but the Russians have apparently got nuclear subs in its waters right now, but if we get in there fast enough we could do the show, grab the kronor, and get out before the coup. What do you think? There's only one club in the whole place . . . well . . . more a sardine processing plant in actual fact. But we'll fill it with fish people flush with their monthly pay packets, which are quite hefty as I understand it at this time of year. They're going to be charging the equivalent of fifty quid a ticket! Outrageous! Four hundred Eskimos at fifty quid a pop? Bloody hell! We should go for it I reckon—seeing as you're up there. Wait a minute!" Steed yelled, grabbing a sheath of papers in front of him.

"No, no, no, I've got them mixed up—the fish processing plant's in *Navoya*, Bear Island has a *great* club. And a few surprises, my lad," he added with an enigmatic raise of the eyebrows.

My mind reeled; had England been invaded while I was in Tasmania? Was Birmingham now called Novaya Zemlya? Svalbard? Franz what Land? Were these new names for Yorkshire and Scotland? Iceland? . . . Greenland? . . . Steed had distinctly uttered these words. This was not about a tour of the north of England at all!

Before I could form a sentence the phone rang and Tarquin, who had been gradually tilting backward in his seat as he continued to reel off the list of improbable countries I was to visit on my proposed "Tour of the Arctic Circle," fell to the floor with a thump, his red riding boots sticking up behind his desk like a pair of Mexican chillipeppers. He righted himself with surprising athletic ability and grabbed the phone.

"Hello!" he bellowed into the mouthpiece, not acknowledging his backflip for a single moment. "Giorgi! Great to hear from you!"

He then went on for a good ten minutes, making intricate monetary transactions with a promoter from some hideous hunk of ice named Novaya Zemlya. I walked over to the map on the wall, which was speckled with red pins. Novaya Zemlya was so far north it practically spilled off the top of the earth! It seemed to be almost joined to the northernmost portion of Russia. I was mortified!

"Got it!" bellowed Tarquin clanging down the phone. "Now," he went on as I became increasingly numb. All the managers it has been my misfortune to employ seem to have this same effect on me: I walk into their offices, all geared up to make a stink about their latest ridiculous proposal, and walk out having agreed to practically everything they've put forward.

"That's Novaya settled. We're firm there," he said, raising his thick white eyebrows in a manner that suggested that somehow "we" had achieved a great victory. "Now, remixing . . . The Greenlandians love the single, but for their market they feel it's too . . . I don't know . . . *soft*, is what they're saying. Dreadnought are prepared to put up the money, so I think we should go in next week with an engineer and have another go at it. All right?"

Dreadnought, my European record company, were as tight a bunch of skinflints as you can imagine, but at the sound of the word "remix," *all* record companies seem strangely willing to throw huge sums of money away. I've yet to understand why. Perhaps they feel "artistically involved" when a perfectly good track is butchered to a pulp for the sake of radio play, or the frigid Greenland public.

"Well I suppose it's . . ." I began, numbly agreeing to everything as usual.

"Good," said Tarquin with some relief. There's nothing managers hate more than an artist unwilling to remix at a record company's request.

"Great, great," he continued. "It's looking good, this little tour, and you know, there's bound to be plenty of time for skiing. I'd take your piste gear if I were you. Now, Smyke and Fortesque are on the case with the visas, and Carruthers wants a word about your onstage acoustic sound or something. Give him a ring today, could you? He's up in Kimber."

"Carruthers?!" I said, flabbergasted. "I thought he was out with that voodoo metal outfit The . . ."

"The Zombie's Bollocks," said Tarquin for me. "No, they ran into a little trouble with the authorities up in Glasgow, so Carruthers is free. He's a great soundman."

"Yeah . . . I suppose . . ." I answered lamely, the beginnings of a dejected whine creeping into my voice.

I looked out through the window at the bright clear sky and somehow cheered a little. The thought of escaping Tarquin's office, away from this nightmare tour schedule, was attractive—at least if I didn't put up any arguments I'd be outside quickly and be able to put the whole thing in the back of my mind. The idea of burying my head in the sand spurred me on into blandly accepting practically anything my manager threw at me. Great, I thought. I'll walk up to the Lord's Tavern and sink a few pints in the pub. Put the whole thing out of my mind. Perhaps a war would break out in the Barents Sea and we'd have to cancel. Maybe Russia would invade Bear Island and throw the whole of the Northern Hemisphere into turmoil. With those nuclear subs fishing around, it certainly seemed possible.

The phone went off like a siren and Steed almost dived on it. Here's my que, I thought, and headed for the door.

I left Tarquin in midtelephonic theatrics, walking out of his office feeling totally stupefied as some promoter from one of those subzero wastelands and my crazed manager began an excruciatingly slow conversation. Steed had various weighty tomes in front of him that he consulted as he spoke, announcing into the telephone words like "grohlk" and "krakatnyskiff"!

My thoughts drifted back to Tasmania as I jogged across Marylebone Road toward Regents Park, sweating like a stevedore in the unlikely warmth of the April sun. I was fond of Fortesque, the stout and trusty tour manager; him I could probably stand hanging out with for another tour, so close on the heels of the last. But Carruthers, in my judgment, was a slope-faced oaf of towering proportions. Steed, his assistant, Smyke, and Fortesque seemed to hold his technical abilities in high esteem, even though his roadwork was largely confined to mixing hideous death-metal bands. I couldn't understand it. I was convinced that the rotter had never even seen an acoustic guitar until the first date of my Tasmanian tour, and here I was, being told to call him up and beg for some gems of information on how to make one sound good onstage! The fiend made my blood boil, but I found myself, after a couple of cheering pints and a Scotch egg in the Lord's Tavern, back at my apartment, dialing the togglehead's number.

"Kimber 95959," answered Carruthers, as if in ridicule of the manner in which people in the south of England answer their phones.

"BP here. Tarquin said something . . . some acoustic set up?"

"Eee, Beep! Loovely t'hear from thee. Farff! Aye, listen. Mate o'mine—'is name's Stouffer—s'got a greet set oop fer acoustical guitars onstage."

"Oh," was all I could muster to this barrage of slaughter slathered upon the English language. But that name rang a bell: Stouffer? Where had I heard it before?

"Aye, s'mega gear. Why don't thee coom oop t'Kimber and check it out, man?"

"Er . . . me come up there? Er . . ."

"Can't check it there when it's 'ere, can thee? Heh heh heh. Coom oop. Stouffer's a bright little bastard and the power in Greenland's a right bunch of bollocks. We'll be in t'serious kimber right off if we don't get it nibs now."

I considered his offer for a moment. I had the remix to trudge through on the following Monday and the rest of the week off; why not, I thought? At least I could throw my weight about with the thick-skinned Carruthers, and after my meeting with Tarquin, which as usual had left me drained and listless, I felt I needed a road dog to kick around.

"All right, I'll be up Tuesday. But it better be good."

"Crackin'," said Carruthers. "Take the A13b to Wally, and ask there, they'll point thee straight t'Kimber. Nibs, farff!" And with those precise directions, the clown hung up.

I did the Greenland remix on Monday with an engineer Tarquin had chosen, presumably from the Yellow Pages, judging by his dubious abilities. It seemed the youngster had never worked on a recording with a real drum kit before, and as he pushed up the faders to explore what was on tape, he made no disguise of his utter incredulity.

"What's that fuckin' mess? he asked, wincing.

"Those are drums," I answered flatly. "Big round things that human beings beat on. The clanging things are called cymbals. They are large metal objects that hang in space around the big round things."

"Christ, no wonder they want a remix!" he sneered.

I had to sit through four hours of this, plus an A&R man from Dreadnought Records who looked and acted all of ten years old as he repeated like an automaton, "More guitars, BP! They love that old-fashioned shit in Greenland!"

Chapter 15

I left London at 2 p.m. on Tuesday afternoon, experiencing a pleasant feeling of relief as I gunned the Lancia 2000 Ralleye Beta Coupe up the little known B road, the A13b, toward the North. It was cooler than the previous week, and a recent rain had freshened up the dehydrated countryside considerably. Canals and farmlands flashed by together with endless fields of a bright yellow crop that I believed was called oilseed rape. From my many travels up and down the country in the seventies, I knew this to be a plant that seemed to bloom all year round, even in the mild English winters. I tried to think of a product available in England that listed rape, or a derivative thereof, as an ingredient, but came up with nothing. What were they doing with the stuff? Wherever it went, they must need a hell of a lot of it judging by the number and size of the fields that were awash in its yellow flower.

After three hours of reckless speeding I was well into what I considered to be the north of England, and the usual dense blanket of cloud hung ominously over the increasingly dreary landscape. At last I came to the sign for Wally and turned off the A13b. Ten miles down a narrow country road flanked by thick hedgerows—an increasingly rare sight—and I entered the surprisingly picturesque village of Wally, twinned, according to the sign, with Bødo, a remote town in the very north of Norway.

Carruthers' scanty directions indicated that I had to have a word with the locals as to the location of Kimber. I hopped out of the car and plunged into a crumbling junk store with a thatched roof. Inside a man was perched on a stool behind a rotting wooden counter. He wore a colorless woolen hat and a filthy-looking khaki jacket. His pockmarked face creased into an insane grin the moment I entered, and his huge ears flanked a disturbingly pointed head. He looked like a demented pineapple. Before asking directions, however, I decided to poke around the store for a while; I wanted to first get some idea as to whether this alarming-looking storekeeper was a pervert or merely a harmless local idiot. If he came up with anything funny, I decided, I'd simply say "Thank you" and walk out. With a forced casualness, I picked my way through the piles of old molding paperbacks, automobile parts, and farming equipment that littered every space in the store, occasionally throwing surreptitious glances at the man behind the counter.

"Hi there," I ventured finally, scanning the dim confines of his counter and wondering if he'd had a customer in the last ten years. The fellow had remained in place while I'd poked around the rubbish, apparently staring at nothing, the insane grin still plastered across his lumpy face. Feeling no sense of danger, however, I decided to go ahead and ask directions.

"I'm looking for Kimber, I . . ."

"Carruthers," he interjected alarmingly.

I couldn't believe it. I hadn't even seen a sign for Kimber and this old geezer knew Carruthers? What strange relationship existed between the two I couldn't imagine. Without prompting, the man gave me directions.

"Take the road outside 'ere t'Pipeley, just past Pipeley at t'traffic lights, turn left and follow on five mile t'Quimley and just on t'first bend thee'll see a sign t'Kimber. Follow that 'bout seven mile and just before Kimber there's a mud track on t'right with an old mill 'ouse by it. Follow track 1.7 mile and there's Carruthers' farm 'ouse. Can't miss it."

"Right," I muttered, flustered, trying to keep up with these intricate instructions.

"Got it, thanks." And with that I turned sharply, banging my knee on what looked like a vicious gin-trap, and got out fast.

After my encounter with the pineapple-head I needed a drink, so I strode across the road to a pub named The Fighting Stoat. It's exterior had an inviting country inn look about it, but inside, it was no less gloomy than the junk store. I walked across the beer-stained squishy carpet and stood at the smelly bar, dotted with rusting tin ashtrays and used beer mats, and ordered a pint of the local bitter. The barman regarded me with lazy eyes, which seemed to stare in two directions at once as if they were both made of glass. He said nothing as the frothy beer spat out of the spigot into the mug and splashed onto his already hop-spattered old waistcoat. I took a long gulp and felt the effects in seconds; this was strong stuff and finishing the pint would be an effort. Off to my left, sitting around a small table littered with empty crisp packets and beer mugs, sat three young men dressed in battered laborer's clothes. They ignored me as they stared into their sticky glasses as if they had been frozen there for years in some bizarre tableau. To my right, perched on stools at the bar, two locals in farm worker's overalls shot me the typical, slightly hostile glances one expects when one enters the foreign territory of an English pub. Both men looked like the kind of people who, after six or seven pints on a Friday night, return home to kick their dogs and then treat their fat wives as mere receptacles. Abruptly, one of them performed that uniquely English stunt of asking me a question with an inane grin on his face and his eyes squinted closed, only to open them wide when he looked away.

"Visitin' Carruthers, are thee?" he asked, as if the whole world knew my business. He took a slug from his pint and winked at his mate who also echoed the question silently with the closed-eye technique.

"Well, yes, I'm going to Kimber to . . ."

"Take the road outside 'ere t'Pipeley, just past Pipeley . . ."

"I know, I know," I interrupted, annoyed and deeply unsettled at having another complete stranger reel off detailed directions to an isolated farmhouse about twelve miles away. Did everyone in Wally know Carruthers and his affairs so intimately?

"Oo . . . 'e knows, you know. Bye 'eck!" said the farm fool as he and his thickset mate laughed heartily. I began to think I'd entered some cryptic twilight zone riddled with Druidic descendants and lay lines.

"Yes, thank you," I said perfunctorily, guzzling half the contents of my beer mug and quickly making for the door. "Thanks," I said gulping. "Bye."

"Oo . . . thanks, 'e reckons, ha ha ha!" the clod laughed, joined by the barman and the three other customers in the pub.

"See you in t'Kimber!" was their gleeful parting shot as I flew through the door, the powerful brew attacking my legs like steel bolts boring down into my feet.

"Christ!" I muttered as I fired up the Lancia and roared out of the village. Carruthers must have notified the whole of the north of England proclaiming my arrival. I promised to suffocate the oaf in his sleep if these kind of shenanigans continued.

Within twenty minutes I was bumping along the mud road toward Carruthers' residence, the directions from the pineapple-faced junk man correct to a millimeter. I swept between the thick hedgerows that bordered the open fields and came to a pit-ridden bottleneck drive that led to a sprawling dilapidated farmhouse. I felt sure it was the soundman's house as I squinted through the oncoming twilight at the back window of a rusting crate of a van parked by the front door. It had two bumper stickers on it. One said: "Hunters Eat More Beaver," the other, "Kids Who Hunt, Trap and Fish Don't Mug Little Old Ladies."

"Uh huh," I mumbled to myself resignedly as I stepped out of the Lancia and into the rich country mud outside the farmhouse door. Above me were gray clouds, and a thin mist of rain hung in the air. Two tiny bats flickered past my head and banked off over the thatched roof. A copse of birch and oak stood to the left of the building and a sparse hedge-row flanked the right. Next to the van stood an old crumbling barn. The whole place looked like it needed a serious overhaul and a good coat of paint wouldn't have gone amiss.

Before I could swing the huge rusty horseshoe that served as a knocker, the door flew open. A large young woman with huge bolting black eyes stared out at me. She was dressed in a scuzzy black dress and her frizzy, dyed black hair stuck up around her white dumpy face.

"Eeee!" she exclaimed like an air raid siren. "Coom in, coom in. Did Carruthers tell thee, I'm your biggest fan?"

"Hi. No, no he didn't mention it," I said, with the patient smile I muster for the many large, bolt-eyed women who claim to be my biggest fan. I stepped into the house with a sinking feeling; not only was I going to have to put up with the clod Carruthers, but also with his lumpen wife, who was no doubt going to regale me with questions about my first two albums, recorded all of ten years ago.

"I play your first album all the time!" she exclaimed as the leaden feeling sank in and paved the way for the usual numbness that follows it.

"Drives 'im barmy it does! 'E's into death metal, really," she stage whispered. "S'big pint waitin' for thee in the pit and 'e's just torchin' up a chillum. This way."

More of the gorilla-style local brew, I thought. A chillum? It had been a long time since my lungs and head had been able to even consider such a serious smoking instrument, but I could see a lost weekend on the horizon.

"BP! BP! Coom in fella. Nibs!" said Carruthers, exhaling a massive blast of smoke from the chillum, which he held expertly, an old damp cloth wrapped around its base.

"Wally lads'll be over shortly. Have a suck on this—pull ya right outta kimber, no question!"

He proffered the smoldering chillum, which although I knew would be wise to refuse, I automatically grasped, formed a cup with my hands, made a filter with the rag, and took a good pull on the end of the cone. The thick sensual flavor of prime gold Lebanese flooded through me like a balm. This surprised me: I hadn't seen gold Leb since the early seventies, when it mysteriously disappeared from these shores. A lack of Red Lebanese, Afghani, and Paki black—also prevalent in those heady times—followed soon after, only to be replaced by a constant diet of Moroccan hashish that became blander with each passing year.

"Jesus, Carruthers!" I gasped, it having been a long time, as I say. "Where did you get this shit from?"

"Heh heh. Bloke in Pipeley's clonin' it, farff. Nibs eh?"

"Cloning it?"

"Aye, clonin' it. Ave another blast," he offered. I foolishly accepted, knowing I would be better advised to await the effects of the first hit, which would—in about thirty seconds—most probably knock me on my ass.

I looked around the room amazed at the decor. The dull cream walls were adorned with slightly tattered but rare and original posters from the sixties; Day-Glo jobs of Hendrix, Cream, and those Indian ones with the human-elephant beings. A lead beaded lamp that dappled the ceiling with a subtle light show illuminated the room, which was to all intents and purposes a perfect reproduction of a typical dope-smoking, acid-tripping London flat of the early seventies, and the air was dense with the reek of patchouli oil and hashish. The couch and armchairs were black and sagging, as if the roof had once been taken off and the rain had been allowed to soak them thoroughly. Carruthers slumped on the couch wearing a purple T-shirt with the word "Bong" printed on it in various primary colors. His stand of matted red hair jutted about his head like a field of upturned carrots. He passed me the chillum, which I again partook of together with a frothy pint of the local mad-juice. If the word "Kimber" was both a geographic term and a mental one, I was, within two minutes, in both places at once.

"Sorry BP, didn't introduce meself," said Carruthers' wife, entering with a great vicious-looking black cat draped over her shoulder. "I'm Wiggy. Now, that first album cover—coom on, own up—was that a spliff you were smokin'? I reckon it must 'ave been, eh?"

"Uh . . . only a roll-up, I think," I answered, feeling completely out of it already.

Just then, there was a bang on the door and Carruthers leapt out of his recline and went to answer it. I heard laughter and lots of yells of 'kimber!," followed by a throaty male chant: "E E E . . . E E E . . . 'E's on the way with a E E E!"

Then Carruthers returned to the erstwhile opium den with the pineapple-faced junk man, the two slovens I had met in the pub, and another man I didn't recognize. They rolled in carrying various containers of alcohol and the man I had talked to in the bar winked slyly at me. Being out of practice, the gold Leb had by now expanded my senses to drastic proportions. I felt like I was in a submarine that was leaking and filling up with freakish undersea creatures. A bout of paranoia seized me, and for a moment, as the red-faced Northerners danced into the room in slow motion, puffing their cheeks out like a school of gilled creatures, I fancied that I had fallen into some satanic ritual the like of which was exposed in the gutter press every day, a perpetually lurking menace frequenting the dark gothic realms of olde England.

"BP," said Carruthers. "This is Trevor, and 'ere's Bob the junky," he continued, pointing to one of the men and the pineapple head. "This 'ere's Crouch. And this one's Trevor. That's two Trevors, got it?"

They roared with laughter. Trevor number two whacked Wiggy on the behind and old Bob the junky, incongruously for a man of at least sixty, pulled out a large joint, which he lit, took a deep drag of, and passed to me.

"And we're waitin' for yer man Stouffer with the E!" yelled Bob. Stouffer? Something in the recesses of my memory was tweaked yet again, but I just couldn't place it.

"E E E . . . E E E . . . E's on the way with a E E E!" they chanted, popping the plastic spigots of their beer tanks as Wiggy pulled pint mugs from a dark wood cabinet.

"Another bash of Bishop's Balls?" yelled Wiggy as she refilled my mug. I was gradually acclimating and knew now that with the flow was the only way to go and that any attempt at reversal would have been pointless.

After about an hour of surreal and raucous conversation that seemed to revolve around drug consumption and various items of dangerous and obscure farm machinery, the man Carruthers assured me was the guru of onstage acoustic sound, Stouffer, crashed through the front door without knocking and was greeted by more of the "E E E" chant. He immediately handed everyone a capsule, which they greedily gobbled down. I steadfastly refused this time—I was not about to enter a state of ecstasy with this lot; what they were going to get up to later was entirely unpredictable.

More time dragged by in an orgy of guzzling, smoking, and yelling to a soundtrack of three slightly different but equally frenetic versions of Nico's "Janitor of Lunacy," performed by some deranged punky thrash band named The Nico Teens, whom I later discovered were managed by Carruthers and Stouffer and usually sold a quarter of a million copies of every record they released, mostly in the north of England.

"Ee, Beep," slurred Carruthers, his head nearly touching the low ceiling of the smoke-filled room. "D'yer like the record? Fookin' Nico Teens. Great band, in't they?" Two of them are coomin' later . . . eh oop," he said as he cocked an ear toward the door. "Could be they now, nibs!"

Two of the Nico Teens entered, looking like bank clerks in drab clerical-gray outfits. They were followed by three middle-aged housewives and a policeman in full on-duty gear, helmet and all. For a moment I believed we were being raided, but it soon sunk in after I noticed the constable's ruddy cheeks and pickled-looking W. C. Field's nose, that officer O'Pork—as they laughingly called him—was a regular at these crazed drug sessions. If this was a Tuesday night, I asked myself, what must the weekends be like?

"T'gangs all 'ere! Bit quiet tonight, though, BP—thou should coom up on a weekend!" said Carruthers, answering my question as if by telepathy.

THE OTHER LIFE OF BRIAN

The night was boring on like a drill, and I suddenly realized that I hadn't eaten a thing since morning. After a difficult conversation with Wiggy, she led me to a giant refrigerator in the kitchen, where she miraculously produced a roast partridge, some thick crusty bread, and a bowl of black stuff she referred to as " 'edgehog pate." I wolfed it down, not daring to inquire as to the exact nature of the dish—which was quite delicious—for fear of getting a gruesome reply. After the meal, I returned to the living room and played along with the party antics for a while, even joining in with a few of the primal chants. But I was tired and in dread of what might develop later. The 'E' was beginning to grip them all and the jolly housewives were making lewd and lascivious comments without any provocation and taking it in turns to fondle the big blue policeman's helmet. At about 10:30, I pulled Carruthers aside and asked where I could crash, not wishing to end up on the floor in this rural rampage.

"Ee, pooped, are thee?" he asked, his pale, gray-green eyes swimming in his large head. "Long drive, eh? All right, chum, sure you don't want a pop of E?"

"No, no," I insisted. "You go ahead, I'm feeling a bit . . . kimbered." Damned if I wasn't lapsing into his ridiculous lingo.

"Ee, kimbered are thee? Heh heh heh. This way. Oop t'stairs."

He led me through a labyrinth of small dim rooms and corridors before we came to a steep flight of narrow stairs, which we climbed to a single door. The tall Carruthers almost had to bend double to enter the room, and after much fumbling in the pitch-black he found the light switch and left me to it.

"Sleep well, Brian. Long day with Stouffer tomorrow, nibs. Oh, and I'd lock the door if I were thee," he advised with a wink, glancing toward the floor and the crazed party beneath.

"Aye," I muttered, and Carruthers left the room.

I crawled into the narrow bed, suffering severe alcohol and hashish head spins. Here we go, I thought. Foolishly, I had not inquired as to the location of an upstairs toilet and wondered what to do if I lost control and needed to throw up. Finding my way downstairs in the dark would be dangerous enough, and rejoining the mad crowd in the living room was something to be avoided at all costs, what with the Ecstasy kicking in big time and all. There was nothing for it: I had to judge it dead right and dive into one of the spins from exactly the correct mental angle, thus slipping neatly into unconsciousness and not succumbing to a puke attack.

After three attempts in which failure forced me to sit up straight and concentrate all my efforts toward deep breathing and denial, I finally dropped my head on the surprisingly soft pillow with just the right attitude and fell between the cracks of the spins, going out like a light as I did so.

Deep into the night, I was awakened several times by loud banging sounds and the occasional chant, often followed by groans that indicated either pleasure or pain—I daren't imagine which—but luckily, sleep returned me each time to sweet escape.

Chapter 16

In the morning, I awoke to a deep country silence punctuated only by birdcalls and the howl of a distant cockerel. Two steps covered the width of my garret and as I looked out of the tiny window, I could see that the thin drizzle had not let up. Feeling quite fresh and energetic as one often does after a night of hashish indulgence to the point of saturation, I dressed quickly, excited by the idea of damp country air. I picked my way down to the bottom of the staircase and crept past the living room, which was mercifully shut; loud snoring reverberated from within, so I remained stealthy, not wishing to awaken any of the rural oafs who might still be in the house.

Once outside, I immediately began to explore the wild tangle of shrubbery, car engines, and rusting farm machinery that surrounded the Carruthers' residence. At the back of the house I found several small wooden buildings—more huts than anything—and without hesitation, entered the first one as the drizzle gained momentum and turned into light rain. Inside, I was amazed to find the walls lined with cages and the ground littered with straw. The musty odor of hairy animals gave my olfactory organ a nasty shock at such an early hour, and my ears were suddenly bombarded with the sound of squeaking and chittering that my presence must have evoked. Inside the cages, little feet began scampering around wildly. Looking through the wire squares of each small prison, I at first thought that the skittish rodents were ferrets. This would explain the bumper stickers on the old van out front—Carruthers was obviously an avid hunter and probably used ferrets to root out the local game. The thought of him lurching around the countryside terrorizing rare badgers and innocent rabbits made me instantly nauseous, and I was about to exit the putrid hut when I realized with a shock that these animals were not quite as they seemed. Instead of the usual creamy white or dull buff of domesticated ferrets, these creatures displayed much richer coloration. Some were dark with vivid white markings, and others almost black. Some were tiny, and the ones that resembled ferrets the most still had a wild sleekness and a natural coat too pristine to be the usual pet shop purchases. Then I caught on. These were not domestic animals at all, or even feral. They were wild weasels, stoats, polecats (the ancestor of the ferret), and rare pine martins. I was surrounded by a crazy menagerie of vicious little hunters that belonged in the wild, or at least in a zoo. This lot had to be illegal. I thought of the partying P. C. O'Pork who had turned up for last night's 'E' orgy. Was there no law north of Watford? It appeared that the use of illegal substances had burrowed so deeply into society, that not only was this generation of teenagers acting as though the drug casualties of the sixties were but a blip on the progress of mind alteration, but also the police, junkmen, and housewives—who once would have regarded booze as their only recreation—were getting stoned as coots as well. And collections of Day-Glo posters and exotic animals had somehow been integrated into the scene. What would I discover next?

I left the stoat house by the back door and after struggling through some coarse rhubarb and hollyhock beds found a similar hut at the back of the garden. Inside, there was a hoard of dangerous-looking guns and traps and stacks of shelves holding dozens of books, mostly on animal husbandry. I picked up a few of the guns and examined them. Some were new-looking rifles. Others—although my knowledge of firearms is almost nonexistent—appeared to be antique blunderbusses, such as one might see in history books or in paintings portraying ancient clashes. All were in good condition and very clean. Probably loaded too, I thought. Then something in the corner caught my eye. It was another wire-fronted cage, a good deal larger than the others. I crept up cautiously to investigate. This time, I was to receive the rudest shock of all. Inside the cage, standing straight up and regarding me with black curious eyes, was a thylacine pup. That rotten devil Carruthers had somehow managed to pinch one from the very wilds of Tasmania and bring it back to England!

How the fiendish mooncalf had managed this extraordinary feat under my very nose was quite beyond me and I felt my jaw literally drop in disbelief.

The thylacine pup and I stared at each other with equal wonder, and

THE OTHER LIFE OF BRIAN

I was about to go back to the house and give Carruthers a good clobbering about his flaming red topknot when the rascal entered the hut. He stood blinking in the doorway, holding a pint of beer and wearing a white T-shirt with the word "Pustule!" stamped on it in an evil green.

"Towser," he said, as if introducing a common basset hound. " 'Is name's Towser. 'Is poop pongs a bit and 'e 'ad a bit of a cold for the first week, but 'e's out of kimber now right enough, ain't you boy?" And with that, he crunched over in his size-sixteen army boots and khaki trousers, opened the cage, and pulled out the pup, which looked surprisingly stout and playful as it licked Carruthers' face with obvious affection. I stood dumbfounded, taking in the spectacle in the cramped hut, listening to the rain pattering softly on the roof.

"Carruthers, you bilge rat!" I yelled, but I could see that this living fossil's fate was already sealed. It was not about to get on a plane and fly back to Tasmania.

"Okay, how did you do it? How on earth did you smuggle this animal back? And where the hell did you keep it stashed on a thirty-hour plane flight with three fuel stops?"

"Easy," answered Carruthers, his big pale face getting wetter and wetter as the pup continued its happy licking. "I met this stewardess on the flight over, hooked up with 'er in Tas—you know, I were boffin' 'er like—and she said she'd put 'im in a little doggy box and 'ide 'im in t'hold, see. She reckoned 'ed be warm enough, like. And the chief Abo' gave me some medicinal plant—all crushed up it were—to knock 'im out like. Well, she smuggled me down there at every stop t'check 'im and give 'im a feedin' with a baby bottle with some milk in it. Didn't raise a fuss at all. Seemed to be enjoying 'imself like. Then at Heathrow, she just walked out with the little fella in a little bag. Air hostess, nibs. No problem like. No customs check!"

"Oh I get it, you mean that old dear who kept bringing you free champagne. Her?" I asked, incensed at the idea of the Stewardess From Hell becoming so casually involved with our revolutionary discovery.

"Aye, that's 'er."

"And what about in the jungle, how did you get hold of it? It was a mere suckling in its mother's pouch."

"Well, they were just at weaning time, see, 'im and 'is sister. So they'd pop outta the pouch now and again, and they seemed to like me. Most animals do 'cept the ones I've got chewin' their legs off in gin traps, farff. So see, I gave the big Abo' in charge me Walkman and a couple of death-thrash tapes—well nibs 'e was with that—and 'e sneaked Towser 'ere into me dander bag just before we left. Loovely little fella, 'in't we!" exclaimed Carruthers cheerily, scratching the tail-wagging marsupial behind the ear.

Just then, P. C. O'Pork came in, his helmet on his head and a grin creasing his ruddy face.

"Mornin', all. 'Ow's that Towser then, eh lad? Looks chipper enough, eh, Carruthers?"

"Eh, oop, O'Pork. Aye, 'e's nibs. Crackin', 'e is. Look at 'im. I'll give 'im his partridge n' kibble in a bit. Eh, Towser, you'd like that, wouldn't thee?"

O'Pork walked over and took the wriggling animal in his large hands.

"We've got big plans for thee, lad," he said mysteriously, holding the young thylacine out at arm's length. It had a light brown belly and on its back, the distinctive black stripes of its species were beginning to form. "Big plans . . ." O'Pork repeated.

What sinister ideas they were cooking up I was afraid to ask in the presence of O'Pork. A policeman who smoked dope, took Ecstasy, and dabbled in the illegal animal trade was obviously about as dangerous a character as you could imagine. A Cenozoic beast in the hands of Piltdown man, I thought with a shudder. And as for Carruthers, who had bribed the Aborigine chief with a Walkman to obtain the animal and delivered God-knows-what foul favors to a middle-aged air hostess to have the beast stowed securely on a marathon flight—here was a man who was both resourceful and stupid. Another scary combination.

By about 1:30 in the afternoon, Carruthers and I were in the Lancia tooling into the village of Kimber, which closely resembled Wally and was populated by characters that looked as if they'd just stepped out of *Night of the Living Dead*.

"So, Carruthers," I ventured. "What are these big plans you have for the thylacine? Come on, out with it."

"Hare coarsin'," he said, as if it was the obvious and natural destiny of a purportedly extinct animal from Tasmania transported illegally to the wilds of northern England.

"You mean, you're going to train that animal to hunt hares?"

"Yeah, perfect for t'job, 'e is. We'll run 'im against greyhounds and whippets and the like from other towns—big bets on hare coursing oop 'ere, y'know. Reckon me and the Kimber lads'll make a fortune. Towser's a nifty little mover; 'e'll 'ave the buggers in t'kimber right off. And we'll 'ave plenty of jugged hare in t'larder, too. Crackin'!"

"So you're telling me," I said as we turned into the back street where Stouffer lived, "that you brought that ridiculously rare and endangered animal all the way from deepest Tasmania to chase hares around a field?"

"And for company," said Carruthers, as if talking about a pet Jack Russell. "I like a good dog, I do."

I decided to ask the clown no further questions. The incredible escapade appeared to strike the teenage giant as no more outrageous than a trip to the local pet store to pick up a hamster. I tried to take my mind off of the whole fiasco and braced myself for our meeting with Carruthers' techie friend, whose doorstep my soundman now led me to.

Stouffer, the man I had been assured was a master of acoustic sonics, greeted us at the entrance of his old semidetached and ushered us through into his workroom. I handed him my guitar and we got right down to business.

"Got a pickup in it, Carruthers tells me," Stouffer remarked, giving my ax a quick once-over. He was a short, stocky fellow with wispy, thinning brown hair and spectacles as thick as the bottom of a Coke bottle. This had the alarming effect of magnifying the size of his eyes so that he reminded me of one of those dogs with "eyes as big as saucers" from "The Tinder Box" fairy tale.

"None too clever Carruthers tells me," he grumbled, studying my old Hohner and quickly unwinding the strings.

"I thought it sounded all right," I replied somewhat testily, as in double quick time the surly genius had the strings off and was tearing out the expensive Martin pickup that had served me well for years.

"Won't be worth a thylacine's fart in Greenland!" he said, chuckling with Carruthers.

"Why not? What do you mean?" I asked, as the pickup came out and was rudely plonked onto the work table.

"Cold'll probably do it in . . . and power's weird as 'ell up there. You'll be kimbered before thou know it. Much better to go with the Stouffer Sonic Set-Up. Really nibs, eh Carruthers?"

"Farff. Nibs it is," answered Carruthers with a moon-faced grin plastering his face.

"You see," went on Stouffer, pulling a heavy-looking black object from a drawer in the table, "they're on 295 watts up there, very unusual amperage and at least 350 kilohertz to every main's supply. The wattage is a joke and the MA's all to blazes, 'specially on Bear Island. You'll need my Sonic Set-Up portable generator/transformer to run this gear, and 'alf a mile of cable snakin' down yer trousers, but you'll sound like a bloody dream. 'Alf an hour and we'll 'ave it runnin'. Want a pint?"

And then it clicked. I suddenly remembered where I had heard the name Stouffer before and the image of the egg-headed guitarist from Slade Two blasting through the wall amid the yammering Bahá'í', the soundhole of his guitar emitting puffs of smoke from a similar device, popped into my mind.

"Wait a minute. You're the one who did that guitarist's gear—the one with a head shaped like a boiled egg. The bloke from Slade Two, right?" I asked the exophthalmic technician.

"Slade Two? Oh yeah, that silly bastard with the basin cut. I told the twat not to use it as far south as Jokkmökk—not bloody cold enough there; it were set for much more Arctic conditions. 'E 'ad no trouble when they got into Lapland proper. Now bugger off. Go for a pint—I'm concentrating."

He stuck the vicious-looking black object into my stringless guitar and produced an electric screwdriver and some large screws. I was not keen on seeing this massive-eyed lunatic tear into my guitar anymore than was absolutely necessary and felt relieved at the thought of a drink, so Carruthers and I strolled out of the house to a grim-looking pub across the road called The Weasel's Manifold Revenge, where Stouffer apparently had a permanent tab going. I slugged back the beer with some agitation, studying the pub's frightening decor, the focus of which was a series of horrific hunting tableaus bolted to tables and featuring small rodents ripping each other to shreds.

"Does he know what he's doing, Carruthers?" I asked, staring into the mad glass eyes of a pair of Norway rats locked in a bloody embrace. I would have rather sat at the bar, which appeared free of these awful taxidermal travesties, but Carruthers had steered us to this particular table as soon as we'd picked up our drinks, almost as if this was his regular seat

THE OTHER LIFE OF BRIAN

in the pub. Save for a pair of farmhands Carruthers seemed on first-name terms with, the establishment was empty, and not without good reason, I thought with a shudder.

"Say what?" asked the soundman, stroking the stuffed beasts in front of us distractedly.

"Stouffer. Does he know what the fuck he's doing? I mean, I saw what happened to that egg-head guitarist in Slade Two—not a pretty sight, let me tell you."

"The nibs is Stouffer," he assured me, polishing a rats' glass eye with a damp and spatulate fingertip. "Does all the bands, 'e does. Nico Teens' entire setup is done by 'im."

"But . . . you're talking about thrash outfits. What does he know about acoustics?"

"Ee, you'd be surprised, mate. All the death bands include at least one acoustic anthem. The tarts love it. Aye, got to 'ave an acoustic anthem!"

"Have you been up there?" I asked. "Greenland, Zemlya, whatever it's called, Iceland, Svalbard?"

"Oh aye," answered Carruthers. "Nico Teens is big up there. Been up a couple of times. Cold as a witches arse, mind. Bring yer long johns. Bloody kimber if yer van gets stuck in t'ice. Thou could die within t'hour."

"Great," I said, not for the last time silently cursing my insane manager Tarquin Steed.

We finished our pints and went back to Stouffer's place. The guitar was on the workbench with Stouffer's huge black pickup fastened inside the sound hole by four big screws. Instead of the usual guitar lead, a thick black multicore ran out of the socket, across the floor, and into a complicated-looking four-foot-high generator that sat on the other side of the room. This frightening-looking machine displayed a plethora of toggle switches, buttons, flashing lights, and at least three dozen thin-colored wires snaked out of its side and back to the guitar, where they were fastened under the pick guard. The whole job looked like a particularly cruel torture device, and I was damned if I was going to accept this nonsense from the bug-eyed Stouffer.

"You've got to be kidding!" I steamed. "What in the blazes is this nonsense? It's either going to explode or take off. I'm not going for this. Put the Martin back in, Stouffer, this is outrageous!"

"Try it," said Stouffer stoically. "Just try it."

"Ee, BP, it looks right Gothic! They love all that in t'Arctic Circle!" enthused Carruthers as he went over to the generator and stroked it lovingly. "Nibs job, Stouffer," he added. "C'mon, BP, just stick it on. Give it a go, lad!"

I'd come all this way. What the hell, I thought. I'll give it a strum, hate it, and get him to replace the Martin pickup and get the hell out of there. So with a shrug I allowed them to hoist the guitar—which had become a good twenty pounds heavier with Stouffer's black device inside it—around my neck. The bug-eyed technician then unpopped the tiny colored cables that were connected with mini-mini-jacks, and as Carruthers pulled my trousers out to create some room, Stouffer threaded the whole lot down inside my trouser legs and out the bottom, then reconnected them.

"Is this really necessary?" I asked nervously. "I mean, why can't they just hang out the back or something. This looks bloody dangerous to me."

"No no no," insisted Stouffer. "They won't function properly unless protected by just the right amount of body heat. They adjust to the unnatural condition of the Arctic air and the fluctuating Arctic power source by absorbing human body heat. Each wire is fitted with a tiny micro thermostat that works in conjunction with your growing body temperature throughout a typical one-and-a-half-hour performance. You do about an hour an a half, right?"

"Yes yes," I said impatiently, not enjoying the feeling of dozens of wires sticking between the hairs of my legs. "Come on then, fire it up and let's get this over with."

I was convinced that whatever this drug-addled psychopath had cooked up would sound utterly dreadful, or at least go up in smoke within minutes.

Stouffer ran a cable between the generator/transformer to a small P.A. system while I stood there with the guitar strap cutting into my shoulder, due to the instrument's excessive weight, and the wires snaking down my trouser legs, looking and feeling like something out of a science fiction movie.

"One last thing," said Stouffer, as he produced some black patches that he stuck on my bare arms, completing the cyborg effect. "Radio transmission blood pressure sensors—got to keep right on top of the power/blood ratio when you're up in t'Arctic Circle. Might as well get used to them now. There we go . . . all right. I'll switch the bugger on, see what 'appens, shall we?"

"You mean you're not sure?" I said.

"Heh heh. I've put a few folks into kimber with the prototypes, but I think I've got t'bugs out now—unless of course you have an unusual pulse rate. Anyway, 'ere we go, give it a strum!"

And with that he threw a number of toggle switches on the generator and I closed my eyes, bit my bottom lip, and hit a full, hard E Major. As the sound of my old, ragged acoustic guitar boomed out at me I gasped. I couldn't believe what I was hearing. The sound that came through those speakers was simply fantastic. There was no hint of the bland, compromised signal processing response that usually accompanies a heavily amplified acoustic guitar, and not a trace of that annoying electric guitar sound typical of most acoustic pickups. It was as if my ax was aimed perfectly at an expensive studio microphone and going direct into the P.A., only much, much louder and with perfect acoustic tones.

"Incredible!" I yelled over the sound of the huge chords I was chunking out. "This is it! Amazing!"

I hammered on for about five minutes, marveling at the sonic wonder that filled my ears, for a while completely forgetting that the guitar felt like a cow on my chest. But by the time I'd got through a couple of tunes, I realized that my neck was stiffening up and my back starting to ache. Suddenly, my ears were filled with a strange buzzing sensation and I felt a creeping ticklish feeling that ran between my leg, where the tiny wires were strung, and the black microsensors fastened to my arms. I stopped playing and looked down at my hands, which were beginning to twitch involuntarily. Then the vibrating sensation began to increase from minor to major. Just as this phenomenon began to occur, I noticed a deep hum coming from the P.A. and the generator's lights started blinking like an ambulance.

"Ee up!" yelped Stouffer, diving across the floor in the direction of the pulsating generator. "Why didn't you say you were hyperactive?"

"I'm not!" I screamed with fear. "Get me out of this!"

Carruthers dashed toward me but tripped over the multicore which yanked at the guitar but did not fall out, causing me to topple onto my back, where I lay like a dying crab, my legs and arms stuck up in the air, twitching, as a horrible electric current ran through me.

"Argh!" I moaned, staring up at the egg carton–encrusted ceiling. And then I passed out.

"This man's not hyperactive, Stouffer!" I heard a voice say as I regained consciousness. I was flat out on a hard surface, and as my eyes gathered focus, I could make out a bright light, and above that a white painted ceiling. Standing over me was an old man with deep blue eyes and hair like Einstein's. He wore a white smock, and a black stethoscope was attached to his ears.

"You got your amperage ratio to kilohertz to body temperature all t'cock again," the doctor said scornfully, feeling the pulse in my neck and looking over at a sheepish Stouffer. "I told you about that last time you knocked out one of them Nico Teens—you set temperature gauges as if t'chap were already in t'North Pole. You'll nobble some poor bugger right to t'kimber one day, you big girl's blouse you!"

"I must 'ave done. Sorry, BP. Are you all right? 'Asn't put you off, 'as it?" asked Stouffer.

I could still remember the stunning acoustic sound the dangerous equipment had produced, and even though I had a sizable headache, I wanted that sound.

"No," I said blurrily. "Just test it on Carruthers next time, will you?"

"Won't be much use," said the Doc. "Carruthers'll probably enjoy a good shock. E's the type 'oo sticks 'is fingers into European sockets to see if they're puttin' out AC or DC!"

They all had a good chuckle at this, and I let out a resigned sigh, knowing that the doctor was probably not kidding.

"Now," said the doctor. "Bob Hope and the psychedelics are popular up here, but in this case a little snifter of my patented Chinese . . . ahem . . . blood tonic, wouldn't go amiss." And with that, he thrust a tiny shot glass into my hand and motioned for me to drink it. The viscous, earthy-tasting brown liquid slid down my throat like a raw egg, but within moments I was up on my feet feeling light as a feather and remarkably clearheaded. "What the hell is that stuff, Doc?" I asked, as he took a shot himself.

"It's a ginseng/coca mixture," he replied with a twinkle in his eye. Carruthers and Stouffer seemed most amused by this explanation.

"Well," added the doctor, "it's *half* Chinese . . . the other half's Peruvian!

Kimber, I thought. What a place!

We strolled back to Stouffer's house, the doctor's surgery being conveniently located next to the pub opposite. I had to have that sound. Suddenly the thought of Iceland and all points north didn't seem so awful. Armed with Stouffer's acoustic wonder I felt like I could take on the world . . . or at least the coldest part of it.

"Stouffer," I said, as we reached his door in the drizzle.

"If you can make that get-up a tad lighter and maybe go radio on some of those wires, you might have something there. I mean, I might just go for it."

"We'll see," said Stouffer with a small smile. "I reckon I might be able to rig up a lighter version. We'll see."

"Crackin'!" I yelled. "Wire me up and plug me in!"

And the three of us cried out together like crazed lumberjacks: "Kimber!"

Chapter 17

After my return from the wilds of Kimber, I set off for the planned European press junket accompanied by a bullet-headed promo man from Dreadnought. The jaunt was thankfully somewhat truncated due to lack of interest on the part of the press, and once it was completed I found myself clumping into London's Heathrow Airport on a dank May evening, a chill in my bones as if in preparation for the Arctic endurance test I was about to undergo. The extreme folly of the situation struck further lances of ice into my heart as I glanced around the fluorescent, clanging terminal and spotted a sign saying ICELANDIC AIR CARGO, tucked away in a grim corner. The only redeeming quality about this mission was the sound promised by Stouffer's Sonic Set-Up, and I clung to that idea as if it were an invisible talisman.

The area of the globe I was about to invade would most probably make Tasmania look like rock 'n' roll nirvana, and right then, as I labored through the thronging terminal with heavy baggage of both the mental and physical variety, my reservations were not solely with the airline.

My first surprise, on arriving at the Icelandic check-in desk, was the sight of my infuriatingly lubricious manager at the head of the queue, heaving what looked like some form of sled onto the scales. His wild white hair hovered over his face like a blizzard as he loudly brandished the oily jargon of his previous vocation—a magistrate's court judge—at the intimidated girl behind the desk.

"This is going to Iceland," he said firmly at the poor red-faced young cadet. "This is a cargo flight and as outlined in clause 14b of the Icelandic Commercial Cargo Carrier's requirements for volative passengers, crew and airline employees, as such, does not count as personal baggage. It is a promotional item and therefore covered in the B35 I've just given you."

THE OTHER LIFE OF BRIAN

Steed snatched the huge official-looking ream of documents back over the counter, tutting at the agent, who had been squinting helplessly at the thing with no discernible illumination.

"Here you are!" boomed Steed triumphantly. "Right here, in black and white, clause 14b. I know the bloody rules better than you, and you work here? Tut tut . . . oh, BP. There you are! Just getting the luge on. Have you seen Carruthers and Stouffer yet?"

Steed watched me with a vacant expression as I heaved my baggage forward. He wore a bulky brown parka and thick ski pants and looked well attired for a tour of the Northern Hemisphere. My heart sank: Tarquin Steed, a veritable Clouseau among managers, was obviously joining me on this foolhardy trip. But could I have heard him correctly? Did he really ask me if I'd seen Stouffer yet? Barely had the pretour depression sunk in when, indeed, my fears were confirmed: a raucous chorus of "Wally Wally! Kimber Kimber!" echoed around the ticketing area and that noisome northern duo, Carruthers and Stouffer, suddenly appeared, pushing carts loaded with personal baggage and an armament of sound gear.

" 'Away' t'lads!' yelled Stouffer as the pair gunned their carts up behind me.

"Come up to the front boys," called Tarquin. "We're a party, after all."

"Aye," agreed Carruthers, his matted red hair tied up in a ridiculous bun. "Plenty of partyin' on this tour, eh, Brian?"

Fortesque appeared next, pushing a trolley loaded to the brim and looking like he'd just got out of bed.

"I'm off to the change bureau," announced Steed suddenly. "You boys check in. The intern here has all your details. You can manage that, can you, lovey?" he asked the ticket lady sarcastically. She made no comment as she checked my passport, a scarred and battered item that looked like it had seen front line action in a variety of foreign wars. "Good," declared Steed with mock satisfaction. "See you onboard, chaps." And off he tramped, waving a huge roll of sterling in his hand.

"Tarquin," I seethed, as we finally took our seats on the draughty Icelandic cargo plane. "Why didn't you tell me you were coming? And what is that lunatic Stouffer doing here? And why for God's sake are we on a cargo flight?"

"Didn't I tell you I was coming?" he said blandly, as he worked on the seat's armrest with a screwdriver he had pulled out of his pocket. "I doubt if I'll make the whole trip—probably bale out after Bear Island. Stouffer? Got to have him along with that complicated gear he's rigged you up with. I'd have thought you knew that in Kimber. Cargo flight? Well, we had to do something to offset the price of bringing Stouffer along. Looks all right to me . . . bit drafty I suppose. But it'll get us there. Relax, enjoy yourself!"

"And, Tarquin," I continued, already feeling the lethargy of defeat overcoming me, "what are we packing a luge for?"

"Promotional shots," he replied, pulling the wiring out of the armrest as if it were the most normal thing in the world to do.

"Pro . . ." I began.

"Great luge track south of Reykjavik; you can handle a luge, right? All that skiing you've been doing in recent years up in Vermont? Not much difference really—it's all sliding. Same thing."

I looked at him as he fished some electrical tape out of his parka and began to ball it around the wires he had torn from the armrest. His obscure and pointless work completed, he looked over at me with his usual infuriatingly bland expression.

"Promotional shots," I finally responded in a voice devoid of emotion or interest. I was wondering if either Carruthers or Stouffer were holding any powerful sedatives. I needed unconsciousness badly. "On a luge."

"Some very talented photographers up there, very talented. There's one chap—Tjork or Bjork, I think his name is—he can take a shot of someone hurtling down a luge run at eighty miles per hour and still keep their face in focus. Perfect! We'll spend an afternoon at it, then rush them over to the British press. They'll go wild!"

This idea struck me as both terrifying and useless—the British music press hadn't been interested in me in years, and I could not see how risking my life was going to change anything.

"You'll never get me on one of those things," I hissed flatly.

"Come on," he said, "you'll love it. Couple of runs down, we'll never get you off the thing! You'll be addicted in no time. That's what it's all about boy: addiction! Sex, drugs, rock 'n' roll!"

This coming from a man pushing sixty who was rich. From what I could gather, he had only tried illegal drugs once, in Los Angeles, back in his roaring forties, and the result was another legendary episode of pandemonium. One evening, or so the story went, as Steed and some friends were about to visit a fairly posh restaurant in Santa Barbara, someone offered Tarquin a powerful joint of Hawaiian wacky weed. He saw no harm in trying a few pulls, seeing as everyone in the company he was in appeared to be in particularly good humor from the weed's effects. About an hour later, while ensconced in the restaurant over an arugala salad, Tarquin suddenly decided that the drug had imbued him with the power to walk through solid objects: tables, people, brick walls—anything seemed fair game to his distorted perception. So up he leapt from his seat and began to test his newfound power, plowing into everything in his path like a bull. Apparently, the establishment suffered some fairly extensive damage before Steed's friends and the maitre d' managed to wrestle him to the ground and the medics had been called to administer a tranquilizer.

"Right, Steed," I mumbled numbly, thinking of my manager in pinstripe and polka dot bowtie smacking head first into the beige wall of a trendy nouvelle cuisine Californian bistro as startled diners in Polo shirts and loafers looked on in amazement.

"Addiction. Rock 'n' fuckin' roll."

Steed ignored me, and after a few more cheering remarks concerning luging techniques, fell into a deep, snore-ridden sleep, the remains of the armrests' electrical system still grasped firmly in his left hand. I looked around the cabin. We were in the middle portion of the plane, a craft that seemed to have been hastily converted from passenger to cargo flight, then halfheartedly back again in order to maximize the thin appeal of Icelandic tourism. Rows of seats were interrupted intermittently by bulky items of cargo mysteriously covered in heavy canvas tarps. Carruthers, Fortesque, and Stouffer were further up, acquainting themselves with the stewardesses, whose scruffy appearance suggested that they were probably alcoholic castoffs from other airlines. Indeed, they appeared to have no qualms about flopping down into the many empty seats and pouring themselves glasses of cheap champagne—of which there was a seemingly endless supply—and talking up a storm with the passengers.

After a monotonous hour of bumpy flight, I looked up from my English/Icelandic translator and found a gargantuan woman leaning over me. She was dressed in a great off-white ski outfit with fake fur sticking out of every possible crevice. Her huge googly eyes bolted out of her head like glass cannonballs, and worse still, they were the kind of eyes that, without any effort on her part, showed large areas of white even *above* the pupils. The kind of eyes that are usually associated with certified psychopaths.

"Eh, Brian Porker! How are you, blue? Mind if I sit?" Before I could answer, the Amazon had dropped her huge landing gear into the vacant aisle seat next to me.

"I'm Hilda. I'll be doing your lights. I'm single and traveling the world. Fuckin' great, eh?" she bellowed in a guttural and coarse Australian accent. Leaving me no time in which to protest, she then launched into that familiar oft heard refrain I had come to associate with enormous googly-eyed women.

"Eh, Brian, I'm your biggest fan! Love your first two albums to *death*, mate! Christ, it's great to be doing this. Now listen, I'm actually workin' with your support act—the Tiny Brocil Fishes—but Carruthers reckons I can have a bash at your show. I mean, better to have someone who understands the lingo on the case, right? Better than some fuckin' slope-headed Eskimo. Right, sport? S'gonna be great! Do you do any of yer old stuff? Bloody hope so!" And she elbowed me in the leg with the force of an all-in mud wrestler, emitting a crude bellow of laughter that made Steed flip around in his sleep like a fish.

What, I thought, is the point of having managers, tour managers, soundmen, technicians, roadies, accountants, secretaries and office staff—a whole system of alleged professionalism at my disposal—if I'm going to be hurtled off to the North Pole only to discover, one hour into the flight, that someone I have never laid eyes on before is going to be spending the next five weeks clumping around in hotel rooms, probably next door to me, and committing goodness knows what atrocities with a lighting board at my expense? Carruthers, is it? Carruthers reckons this frightening giantess can do my lights, does he? I'll bury the blockhead in the first snowdrift we encounter—if I can find one deep enough. I'll feed the stinker to the huskies, I decided.

Heaving a sigh, I refrained from arguing with this monster. I'd scream at Tarquin later. No sense in angering Hilda the giantess—she could probably break my hip with a well-aimed nudge.

THE OTHER LIFE OF BRIAN

"Um . . ." I hazarded, recalling her other cryptic announcement. "The Tiny what?"

"The Tiny Brocil Fishes—your support act," asserted Hilda. "Carruthers is managing them and I do their PR and their lights. Got some great oil gels, raging stuff; back projection, strobes—that sort of thing. You don't mind smoke machines, do you, sport? Jeez I'm looking forward to this! Like I say—biggest fan! When are you coming back to Aussie again? You only did Tassy last time you were down there, you wicked rascal!"

And with that comforting monologue loaded with references to totally unsuitable sixties lighting effects, Big Hilda again hammered me in the leg with her powerful right elbow. She droned on for what seemed an eternity, giving a detailed account of the formation of the Tiny Brocil Fishes (who were, she informed me, already in Iceland doing a club warm-up date), their eclectic taste in death thrash, and the address of their hairdresser. I consoled myself with thoughts of the frozen North: perhaps I could permanently numb my sensitivities in the subzero climate and block out the nagging nausea that would doubtless enfold me if I had to endure this brutish bunch of liggers for an entire tour.

Hilda finally gave me a parting wallop, and with the help of a couple of stiff vodkas I dropped off into a feverish mind surf. When I regained half-consciousness an hour or so later, the first sound I heard was Hilda's powerful vocal cords clanging in the front of the cabin: "You smooth-talking bastard!" she screamed. "I'm on the rag at the moment, but you can fuck me up the shitter if you like!"

"Wahey! Kimber! Wally!" chorused Carruthers and Stouffer in perfect synchronization.

Finally, after what seemed like a week, we landed in Iceland and deplaned on a grim and icy runway. As I stepped down the shaky gangplank, I was greeted by a cold so deep, I felt I would be paralyzed before I got to the hotel. Inside the airport, it was hardly any warmer, but at least the customs officials seemed entirely uninterested in us and waived us straight through; dressed as they were in a variety of animal skins, they looked as if they couldn't wait until their shifts ended and they could all get back to their igloos or whatever it was passed as dwellings in this godforsaken place.

"Bracing, isn't it," said Tarquin as we exited the terminal, and not in the form of a question.

"No it isn't," I answered anyway. We followed the crew into a van driven by a woolly-looking man named Kric, who claimed to be the local promoter. "Can you please put the heat up, Kric?" I whined hopelessly. "They obviously don't call it Iceland for nothing," I added, to no one in particular.

"Wait till we get oop Wandel Land! Now that's fookin' *cold!*" shouted Carruthers, his teeth chattering noisily.

"Where's that?" I asked, thinking perhaps another nightmarish country had been added to the tour schedule without my knowledge.

"Northern inspectorate, Greenland," Stouffer filled in. He had already torched up a joint and was passing it on to Big Hilda, as the Australian giantess seemed to be known. This lot were probably going to get us all thrown into the slammer well before we reached Wandel Land. I could see it now: a horrendous concrete structure smack in the middle of Greenland (by all accounts an enormous country), completely unregistered and full of brain-damaged alcoholic Greenlandian peasants, doing life sentences for performing deviant sexual acts with beasts of the tundra.

After half an hour of driving over what appeared to be solid permafrost peppered with clusters of desolate utility buildings, we reached our hotel, which looked as welcoming as a police station in the middle of a South London council estate. This did nothing to weaken my foreboding of imminent imprisonment, and I quickly dumped my bags in the freezing lobby, unconcerned about theft or damage, and headed toward the sound of a jukebox, in search of comfort and alcohol.

Fortesque joined me in the dark hotel bar, but he didn't have a lot to say. I began guzzling double shots of a foul local vodka, which instantly made my head spin; dead brain cells began scooting across my eyes whenever I turned in the direction of the garish ersatz Wurlitzer. Tarquin and the crew had rushed off to a club called, "Ja, Reykjavik Rockingk!" to watch a set by the Tiny Brocil Fishes. This, apparently, was the joint I was to perform in the following evening.

"Don't like the look of this luge bit, mate," my tour manager remarked glumly.

"You think I do?" I said, studying the squinty-eyed bartender, who busied himself washing glasses in a light blue plastic tub that sported fringes of ice and small pieces of what appeared to be potato peelings, bobbing about in the sudsy waves.

THE OTHER LIFE OF BRIAN

"I wouldn't do it, Beep," said Fortesque, jutting his lips dubitably. "You'll come a cropper. Need skill to do that."

"Tell me something I don't know!" I retorted impatiently. "Christ, Forty, I've seen that stuff on TV. Still . . ." I pondered, imagining the adrenaline produced from such a dizzying flight. "Be nice to be able to do something like that, don't you think?"

"Steady on, mate, the vodka's getting to you—oh! By the way, nearly forgot."

"What?"

"On TV tonight, here in Iceland. That Donovan Tribute's on."

"They've got TVs in the rooms?"

"Should have in yours, sport. Why? I thought you hated that show."

The memory of the debacle made my ears burn but still, to arrive in this wasteland and find a rerun of one of my rare TV appearances being shown on that very night was, I had to admit to myself, at least minutely cheering, even though the circumstances of the event were heinous in the extreme.

I ordered a quadruple vodka and left Fortesque at the bar, a worried expression on his gnarly face after I had admitted a small sparkle of interest in the idea of a luge run. I staggered along a blindingly bright and lonesome corridor, sometimes stopping to reread the number on my key and straining to hear the sounds of TVs behind the brown plywood doors.

At last I located a room number that matched my key and fumbled through the door into the icy confines of the chamber. The cell I had entered had nothing save white walls lit by a rack of fluorescent lights, two army-like bunk beds, and a tiny, dusty old TV festooned with aerials and evil black wires that sprouted from its back like filthy dreadlocks.

I dumped my bags on the top bunk and turned on the TV. The opening credits and camera angles zooming into the crowd at Madison Square Garden sputtered on the screen in foggy black and white. I flopped onto the khaki spread on the lower bunk, holding the vodka skillfully unspilt in my right hand.

Immediately, and with a deafening roar of approval from the balding, flatulent audience, I was thrust into the shallow end as some talentless Okie rock singer whose name I could never remember strutted onto the vast stage accompanied by two underdressed female backing singers, one Caucasian, one Black. The cocky snit launched into a rock version of Donovan's great "Sunny Goodge Street," butchering its subtleties into submission as he dared to leap around like a prat and wiggle his blue-jeaned hips as if performing at a cheap disco.

This rerun was mercifully cut and edited, but still found time to show the one small segment that created interest and controversy: this featured that bald tart from Ireland bouncing expectantly to the microphone as if in the throes of a Gaelic dance only to find herself soundly booed by the entire audience!

The wide-bottomed, godfearing Americans had apparently taken extreme offense when, not a few days before, the young Irish bint had announced on late night TV that she had recently met with the Pope on his last visit to Ireland and had smoked dope with him in his suite at Dublin's Grand Hotel! She had referred to His Eminence as a "right little drug fiend," and "a bit of a lad with the ladies, too."

The poor waif stood at the mic attempting to begin her assault on Donovan's incendiary "Mellow Yellow" but was not allowed to utter a note due to the crowd's fearsome roars of disapproval. The MC, a country singer of no fixed ability, sheepishly crept up behind the lass and clumsily attempted to comfort her. But true to her spunky little vixen image, she brooked none of his sentimental hugs and whispers, perhaps rightly divining them to be some form of bizarre public come-on, and, with the swiftness and expertise of a Dublin street waif, turned on our hapless MC and administered a snappy knee to the groin followed by a sickening head butt, which resulted in a howling nosebleed and a probable rupture for the unfortunate chap.

I gulped more vodka and writhed as the holier-than-thou audience continued booing the bald girl (but not until they had issued a split-second sickening groan at the knee to the groin, which made me roar briefly with joy) until she finally left the stage, which she did with what I considered great aplomb: as she reached the curtain, she deftly flipped up her deconstructed hospital gown and cocked a snook at the whole, fatuous stadium load. (The close up of her exposed bum, however, had been obscured by a jiggling blue spot, which I thought negated the power of her courageous act somewhat.)

I scanned the narrow room for a phone with which to call Forty, figuring by now he would have left the bar to enjoy this spectacle, but could find no trace of one. Due to extreme jet lag and the fierce Icelandic vodka, the ceiling had begun to sway dangerously, and I sought one more distraction other than the Donovan tribute to regain my equilibrium. A swift chuckle with Forty was out of the question, unless I was prepared to negotiate the freezing corridors in search of his room. I decided to stay put, straightening out the spins with the occasional slap on the cheek as there, upon that tiny screen, I appeared, ironically attired in white trousers and a red caftan that I had purchased in the Kensington hypermarket in 1971 and dug out especially for the show.

Unlike the rest of the performers, the technicians had decided not to emblazon my name across the screen upon my entrance and had conveniently mixed out the smattering of applause I had received from the very few in the audience who had actually heard of me. I sucked in breath through my teeth in pure vitriol at this cruel editing, feeling the veins in my neck trace through my skin like the canals of Mars. I was solely tempted to get up and kick the TV screen in, but checked myself. At least I was on there, being beamed into the depths of the Arctic and not discarded completely, a heap of tape on the cutting room floor.

The song I had chosen to perform that night was a stunning little Donovan obscurity that had the crowd, already confused by my non-superstar presence, further scratching their balding pates and suburban perms in dim-witted consternation. But what had really incensed me on that very night—after the excruciatingly dull performance of some black female one-hit-wonder feminist folkie and an obscene American white wench whose career had spanned all of one whole year—was the incredible sight of the alleged superstar Thomas Poultry, taking the stage with his sterile backing band the Throbs, and doing a "rocked out" version of that very song! There was that heathen blond thug, singing as if a plum had been stapled into his palate, belting out a version of that extraordinary ode "Jersey Thursday," as if I did not exist! As if I had not, in fact, been on that very stage barely ten minutes before, sublime, stark and solo, giving that rare gem a sparkling polish through which the cretinous audience had fidgeted impatiently, waiting like sheep for the next "superstar" appearance. And to add insult to injury, as Poultry butchered his way into the first chorus, the audience roared their approval, as if they actually *knew* the song!

"Grrr grrr grrr!" I seethed, and then with a deep swig finished the remainder of the vodka and promptly passed out.

Chapter 18

In the morning, I slumped down to the breakfast room, which had the atmosphere of a foyer in a mental asylum, and there found Tarquin, a trifle disheveled looking. I helped myself to the buffet, which consisted of a few pots of gray-looking tea, some biscuits, a large bowl of wrinkled old grapefruit segments, and some slivers of a gross-looking meat, spitting on a griddle. I selected a portion of each and sat down next to Tarquin, who was leafing through a pile of faxes.

"Well well well, my boy," he said brightly, immediately taking the upper hand. "Looking chipper, looking chipper!" He reached into the deep folds of his parka and fished out a gold fountain pen and proceeded to dash around the faxes with bold strokes. "Don't want him . . . don't want him . . . we'll take her, that sounds good."

"What's this lot?" I asked glumly, wincing as the slippery meat passed over my furry tongue. The local hooch I had drunk last night was certainly good value for money—it felt as if its effects would probably last well into next week.

"This?" he said, giving me that irritatingly nonchalant stare from his blank blue eyes that meant noisome tasks were about to be hurled in my direction. "Didn't Fortesque tell you?"

"What?"

"Press conference, 11 A.M., in the lobby. Now," he bristled, taking advantage of my delicate state. Rule number one, I thought (too late as usual): don't have breakfast in the hotel on the first morning of a tour if the manager is also in the building; *always*, head right out of a side door, find a quiet cafe, and stay there for at least three hours.

Steed continued like a drill in my head.

"We've got the Arctic Associated Press lady coming over—can't go wrong with that—gets to all the islands simultaneously. *The Icelandic Foghorn*—small, but influential," he noted, raising his thick white eyebrows above his gold-rimmed reading spectacles. "*The Greenland Crossbow.* Good, good. *Franz Joseph Land Herald, Nuuk Weekly, Ja Porg Mettal*—not your cup of tea, I know, but the kids buy it by the bucketload. Let me see . . . ah yes—*Folkenzinger Underground Newsletter, Porkars Weekly Entertainment Guide*—ha ha ha, named after you, that one! Ah . . . *Hemisphere Hoedown*. Now that's a cracking little glossy, and they've picked up on your country influence, we've got to do that . . . um . . . then there's a couple of phoners, one to Zemlya—we can't leave them out, they're starving for it over there. Aaaaand . . . one to Bear Island. Oh, wait a minute . . . here, this morning, we've got three or four teen fanzines may or may not be turning up—depending on how much space they've got this week. Enjoying the fried seal blubber?"

"Argh!" I exclaimed, as I spat a portion of the slippery meat onto the floor.

"Stock up on that my lad. It'll give you strength—and insulation!"

I composed myself as quickly as I could, not wishing to allow Tarquin's deviations to confuse me, this being, as I've noted, his standard approach to negotiations.

"OK, Steed," I began, forcing a little steel into my voice. "This luge business—forget it, OK? Get a stunt man to do it. Do it yourself—whatever. And why was I not told that this Amazon—Broom Hilda, or whatever her bloody name is—is 'having a bash' at doing my lights? I mean, do I have to find this out from her, and on the bloody plane over, too? Makes me look a complete idiot. And . . . and now, you spring a four-hour press conference on me with what sounds like the most unsuitable collection of publications I can imagine? I mean, don't they have an Icelandic *Rolling Stone* or something?"

"That's a good point, BP," boomed Tarquin in his usual counterattack mode, which consisted of agreeing with his opponents' (opponents being the appropriate word) disagreement, thus defusing their ire just enough to begin the subtle process of *getting the fool to agree with everything* . "They *don't* have *Rolling Stone* up here, but they've got MTV. Maybe we can get an interview on their news section—a couple of songs even. That's a jolly good idea, I'll make a note of it."

"I've been ostracized by MTV," I snapped.

"Not up here," countered Tarquin. "They don't have demographics; they've no idea how unpopular you are."

GRAHAM PARKER

There seemed little point in fighting the press deluge—they were probably lining up in the lobby right now. I made a few more whining noises about Big Hilda and her *Laugh In* style of lighting ideas, but Steed shrugged them off, saying he'd have a word with her about toning it down for my act and saving the Vietnam backdrop footage, the psychedelic oil gels, and the strobes solely for the Tiny Brocil Fishes, whose acid death rock was more suited to such histrionics. As for the luge run, when I brought that up again, he just sucked his lips and stared at me blandly with face lowered and bushy white eyebrows raised.

We traipsed down to the lobby and sure enough, about eight so-called journalists were patiently waiting, microphones and notepads sticking out of their parka pockets ready for action. The slovenly-looking young man from reception eyed me suspiciously as he led Steed and me into a conference room, bright and soulless and over-endowed with fluorescent lights. A table had been laid out with more of the same sticky offerings that I'd found in the breakfast room, only there were some larger, even more slippery pieces of flesh simmering on a griddle.

"Oh, BP," whispered Tarquin, as the press lunged into the big flabby steaks and began devouring them as if they were some delicacy. "Don't make any comment about the whale blubber. They love the stuff. They think nothing of harpooning great herds of sperm, blue, and Minke. You might even come across the odd Narwhal fillet. Just don't say anything, OK? They get a bit touchy about armchair environmentalists. They depend on blubber up here." He looked around surreptitiously. "They can't exactly grow avocados—got to feel sorry for them, really."

"Ahem!" he exclaimed before I could respond, addressing the journalists with a jaunty smile. "All right, ladies and gentlemen, Brian's here to answer your questions—no rush though, enjoy the buffet!"

I stifled a gag reflex and sat down in the hot seat, literally right under a large set of fluorescents. The cameras started clicking and I went through my usual routine of dead poses. Then the questioning began. They all spoke a strange convoluted language that made Swedish seem like the Queen's English.

"Welcome here, Iceland it is," said a bulky, grinning woman with huge red lips. "You like, do you, our very own Sugar Cubes group?"

"No, I don't," I shot back. "Like the French, the Germans, the Fins, the Danes, the Swedes, the Spaniards, the Moors, the Bolsheviks and

153

any other nationality north, south, or east of the United Kingdom—until you reach the continent of America—Icelandics are not fit to play rock 'n' roll. They make," I said with relish, getting back to the simple question, "a horrible squeaking sound."

"Ah! Yes, I'm seeing you!" said the lady, quite enthusiastically.

This was turning out to be more fun than I thought, I could heartily abuse these blubber heads with virtual impunity. Now, if they'd only stay away from the mundanities . . .

"How," began a fur-swaddled chap, a mic in one hand and a plate of whale in the other, "did meeting Soulbilly Shakers—your fine big group—starting off your career happen?"

I should have known better: the mundanities had arrived. To spice things up, I decided to lie through my teeth.

"I was working in a bone factory at the time," I began, knowing full well they all knew my well-documented history, but as usual, had to have it from my lips. The press in backward nations, like Belgium, always plunge me into a depression by showing keen interest in the early part of my career while totally ignoring the fact that I have a new record out.

"I was working in a bone factory," I continued, "when a black Daimler pulled in to pick up some femurs. A tall behemoth of a guitar player leaned out of the limousine and ordered me to fill the boot with product. While doing my good work, I was absently humming 'Small Town Talk,' a great single—in case you don't know—by Bobby Charles. The back window opened and a mad, balding keyboard player looked out. 'You sound good,' he said, 'sing up a bit!' So I broke into the chorus in full voice. All the windows of the old Daimler opened and a sly Irish voice in the back said, 'You're hired!' That," I concluded dramatically, "is how I came to join the Soulbilly Shakers."

There was a brief flutter of Icelandic conversation combined with a good deal of thoughtful head nodding. They seemed fairly satisfied with my fantastic story. A skinny young man with bad skin chimed in next:

"What are you thinking on the rapping?"

"I think it's music made by morons for morons," was my Zen-like answer. " 'Come back when you can write a tune, pal,' is my usual response to this loathsome genre. And as for hip hop," I added, warming to the abuse, "hip hop into the nearest refrigerator and close the door behind you—then, you can call yourself 'Ice' if you like."

The questions and answers continued for an hour or so in this pleasant manner until it was time for me to do the phoners. They were similar in nature, although my historical accounts became more and more outlandish with each retelling. The interviews finally over, I bolted to my room for a nap before joining my crew and heading down to Ja, Reykjavik Rockingk! for a soundcheck. There, I encountered the Tiny Brocil Fishes, who on first impression were as clueless a bunch as one could imagine. But later that evening, when they took the stage, their animal magnetism was apparent in every move, even if their musical skills required about twenty years of honing. To my horror, when they had finished their set and left the stage—after a distressing double encore—half the audience left too!

In the claustrophobic dressing room thick with crawling Icelandic graffiti, I strummed my guitar and tried to calm myself. Fortesque entered, carrying a can of frozen puffin meat and a bottle of spring water. I asked him why we had hired an opening act with such devastating audience support. He glumly explained that their latest single, "Head Cleaner," had suddenly begun bulleting up the Arctic charts and they were fast becoming a bit of a sensation; their video was on heavy rotation on MTV, too. Fortesque wiped the black strands of hair from his eyes and poured me some water.

"I must say, BP," he added, "I wasn't sure about this one from the beginning; I don't think they know shit about you up here. But look at it this way," he said, ever the enthusiastic road dog. "If the Brocils weren't opening for you, you'd probably only get fifty people in here—at least you're doing twice as good as that!"

"Oh thanks, Forty," I sneered sarcastically. "In this cavernous thousand-capacity club, I've got one hundred punters out there? Can't fuckin' wait! Where's that bastard Steed?"

But it was too late for recriminations—I had a show to do. I survive well under pressure, often turning in my best work, and tonight I had nothing to lose. I took the stage with a devil-may-care righteousness, armed with the incredible sound generated by Stouffer's Sonic Set-Up and the jade fishhook from the Tasmanian aboriginals still on its crude twine strung around my neck, and began blasting out the hardest-hitting set I could conjure up. After a couple of tunes the word seemed to filter out onto the street (the capital being a small place where a grapevine had instant effect) and some of the kids who had left after the Brocils' show began to reappear. Soon the place had a respectable enough crowd of three hundred or so and I hammered through my stuff with ever-increasing vigor. After the show, the local hundred-proof vodka ensured the usual forgiving party atmosphere as the Brocils and I exchanged compliments as Big Hilda slobbered on about how great this tour was going to be. Foolishly, I even agreed to Steed's proposed plan of traveling down to Vest Mannaeyjar to at least *look* at the luge run. Amazing what a decent gig can do for an egomaniac!

Chapter 19

And so, on our day off, before the second show, which was to be in Siglufjørdur on the north coast, we bumped along an icy road heading south toward what I was convinced would end this freezing uncomfortable tour, not to mention my life—the publicity luge run. Although I had protested violently at first, something in me relished the idea of relinquishing my harness of safety, and the notion of treading that fine line between looking like either a complete prat or a triumphant Olympian seemed more and more intriguing. To lie back on a prong of metal and hurtle down a winding tube of ice, unskilled and untrained, seemed magnificently stupid and probably as close to enlightenment as I would ever get. What the hell? I'd take a look at the track at least. If the sight of it automatically loosened my bowels, I could just stick my trademark briarwood shades on Steed, and tell him to do it for me. Expert as he was at surviving self-inflicted disasters, he could self-inflict himself right into this one.

Three hours later we arrived in a small sports complex, and before I had time to argue, I was led into a changing room by two fanatics who gleefully offered some pointers on luging techniques as they measured me up and quickly produced the neccesary clothing, which I shoehorned myself into with some difficulty. They then led our entourage around the back of the building and suddenly I found myself staring into an abyss of shimmering blue ice, shaking in my unfamiliar luge shoes.

"Why can't I just lie on it, on the flat ground, have Teal wobble his camera a bit, and pretend I actually did a run," I protested as I stood by the awesome track, adjusting my freezing crotch in the skintight sealskin luge suit.

"Nonsense!" laughed Tarquin. "Look at those bends! Just lie back and let the bugger go! Think of the dizzying speed! Think of the record sales! Front page of the NME with this one—well at least you'd share front page with the Brocils, seeing as they're slated for next week. Where're your balls?"

"I don't know," I answered, feeling around in the suit. "I think they disappeared when I looked over the edge—the banks of this thing must be ten feet high! I'll break every fucking bone in my body! What do you mean: 'just lie back and let the bugger go'? How the hell do you know? Why, don't you try it first? Come on, Steed, get on the bastard! Here you go."

I grabbed the blades of the ice-cold machine and shook it at him, but he waved his hands in a negative fashion.

"No no no," he said, laughing. "Too heavy, my boy. This luge is specifically designed for a maximum body weight of 150 pounds, I'd only scratch up the track and stall halfway down—come on, let's get on with it. Teal's protesting about the failing light: it drops like a stone in the Arctic as soon as it hits 4 P.M. at this time of year. Go for it BP! We're rooting for you! First aid's nearby, and if you do flip over, they tell me you'll slow from eighty miles per hour to about forty in a tenth of a second—can't do too much damage at that speed."

"Bastard," I mumbled, as I lay back on the biting steel of the luge and stared up at the dirty Arctic sky.

Teal, the photographer, had rigged up a series of cameras along different sections of the track, all of them hooked up to a little black timing device he held in his bluing hands. He grinned at me through the gap in his big white front teeth. He looked like an Eskimo with a hydrogen bomb.

"This will be excellence!" he exclaimed. The blotchy faces of Carruthers and Stouffer bobbed over my head as they began to rock the luge to and fro in preparation for my descent.

"Quick! The light!" roared Teal as a dark cloud scudded over.

Suddenly, I was off, the machine rattling and crunching on the ice as I picked up speed. Whatever the lugers had told me in their pigeon English back in the dressing room had evaporated from my mind by the time I hit the first bend. I was moving so fast, making sense of anything was difficult. But I did notice Teal's string of Nikons popping their flashes in my eyes and illuminating the glassy ice walls of the run as I plummeted down. The adrenaline rushed to my head like methadrine, and I found myself anticipating the bends beautifully, my brain sending accelerated messages to my prostrate body, which tightened into a streamlined muscle, bending and bracing synchronously with the curves of the track. The awesome speed, the tight bends, the great walls of shimmering translucent blue ice as solid as concrete spun and elasticized in my vision, conspiring to rupture my apparent Zen state with fear. But I would have nothing to do with that emotion, and grimly held on until at last I reached the long straight run that signaled the final hundred yards. I'd survived!

"Let me at it!" I yelled. "One more for luck."

I peeled my body off the machine and found myself shaking like a glob of blubber, but nevertheless exhilarated by my success. The crew gathered around me with much back-slapping and Teal, after punching the keys on his black box, announced that everything had functioned correctly and that he had a collection of stunning shots in the bag. The adrenaline was wearing off and I felt drained; I realized once was enough. If I tried it again, I'd probably be thinking too hard about the brilliance of the first run and make a fatal mistake. Even the lugers—who claimed to be practicing for the next Olympics—were surprised and even slightly miffed by my success.

"Let's get back to the city," I said. "A drink might go down well."

Suddenly Carruthers let out a cry of alarm: "Eh oop! Here Comes Steed. 'E's gone ballistic!"

I spun around just in time to see the empty luge banging around the final bend of the track, closely followed by Steed spinning down the chute in his oversized parka, curled into a fetal position. We stood paralyzed as both my manager and the heavy steel device came out of the curve and shot down the final straight toward our feet.

"Quick!" I screamed. "The first aid man!" But as the luge slowed to a stop on the slight upward gradient of the final ten yards, my manager's flight was checked also, and he uncurled himself from the fetal position and quickly scrambled to his feet, his face ashen, but his expression giving nothing away.

"Whew, that was good," he said, as if he'd just been for a swim in a comfortably heated pool. We gasped and ran to him, expecting a broken bone, skull injuries, some blood at least. But he seemed fine. He smoothed out his bulky parka and looked at us.

"What?" he queried, knowing full well our reason for concern, but not giving way for a moment. "No no," he bluffed. "Nothing really. Took a little spill on the first bend. Too heavy for the luge. Had to try it though. Shall we go for a drink then, or what? Having another run, Brian?"

Once again, Steed shrugged off one of his classic clumsy stunts, so near to total disaster, as if it were merely a missed footing on an icy path.

Chapter 20

The next evening, without notable incident or calamity, I performed in Siglufjørdur on the north coast, right on the edge of the forbidding Denmark Strait. The Brocils seemed to be pulling the crowd, but most of them lingered for my set, and it was with less trepidation that I boarded a hulking ferry the next morning to King Christian IX Land in the vast ice floe known as Greenland. After two nights, one in Brewster, the other in Godthåb, the capital, we headed north to Wandel Land, where we were to take a short ferry ride over to the improbably named Disko Island.

I suspected that as in Tasmania, a strong John Travolta cult was in the offing, but was quite unprepared for the sight that greeted me as I took the stage in Disko Island's only nightclub, Boysworld. Halfway through my second song, my mind was doing its usual racing routine: *'Why do the monitors sound so different from soundcheck? Shit! I strained my upper register two nights back. Was the applause really that feeble after the first song? They don't like me—I'll sing louder and faster, that'll fool 'em. Damn! Why have I got a ballad third on my set list? That won't help. The guitar sounds like a banjo. No it doesn't, there's a bloke tapping his feet. They like it after all . . . no, he's stopped again . . . shit. He's going to the bar. I'm dying up here! Why is it an all-male audience? And why are so many guys holding hands? Why? . . .*

The last thought nearly stopped me in midlyric. My paranoid thought processes, which always enmesh me at the beginning of a performance, dropped away in shock as I realized the true nature of the audience. For although there was a good-sized crowd in the club, I couldn't for the life of me pick out one female face. And there seemed to be a lot of earrings flashing, a lot of neat haircuts, plenty of tight trousers, and an inordinate amount of touchy-feely stuff going on right under my nose. I was singing to an audience comprised totally of homosexuals! Disko Island indeed! Well, they would surely have preferred Gloria Gaynor or that midget from Minneapolis, but, gradually, after four or five numbers, they seemed to be making the best of my ardently heterosexual material, and when I threw in a quasi-protest gem, their applause was quite appreciable. Carruthers and Stouffer, however, who manned the soundboard, which, owing to the bad design of the premises, was on the side of the small stage, seemed much put out by the seething males. Between songs, as I reached for my glass of glacier water, the loutish duo would crack vicious asides into a microphone that fed into my monitors, and although at a fairly low volume, were clearly heard by the boys in the front, who minced and wiggled mockingly at these comments.

"Fookin' shirtlifters!" Carruthers would shout, and then dip his head down into the controls of the board.

"Bunch of fookin' Michaels!" yelled Stouffer.

"A bunch of what?" I said off mic to Stouffer.

"Bunch of Michaels," he yelled back, attacking the gear with a soldering iron. "George fookin' Michaels!"

"Shut up, Stouffer!" I hissed. "They've paid their money, and George isn't here to defend himself."

To this, the squat, bug-eyed boffin shaped his left hand into a wedge and jammed it into the crook of his right arm, which he lifted and shook at the crowd, this being that peculiar English signal that can be taken as either a term of endearment, or a nasty "up yours."

The audience assessed it as the latter and a few atmosphere-damaging boos followed. This gig threatened to go downhill fast but I was determined to entertain to the fulfillment of the contract, which, in all the dives I've played in my career, never ever specifies giving a bad show due to the gender or sexual preference of the audience.

"Fuck you, Stouffer," I said with a well-measured degree of intent.

I leaned back over my amp at the back of the stage and shouted to Fortesque, who was crouching in the wings ready to hand me my Gretsch for the electric segment of my show. "Forty, get Steed to deal with Stouffer, will you? Before there's a riot!"

But Steed had already decided to take the initiative. I felt the flimsy stage vibrate heavily and wheeled around to see Tarquin, his thick hands wrapped around Stouffer's neck, wrestling with the soundtech between the mic stand and the soundboard. They tussled on the floor of the greasy black stage, Steed in a magistrate's pin-stripe suit with a yellow polka dot bow tie, the young Stouffer in khaki combat trousers, Doc Marten's, and a purple T-shirt apparently advertising an obscure indie label, "Stuff It! Records."

The boys on the dance floor gave out a loud, if high-pitched, cheer. Big Hilda turned on the strobe, and on the stage the pair could be seen, arms and legs flailing like a cartoon in the hard white flashes. I grabbed the Gretch from Fortesque, deciding not to miss a chance at embroidering the reviews with a touch of dramatics. I knew the local press were out there and this little fiasco would certainly spice up my reputation a tad, so I launched into my old hit, "Knee Trembler," as Steed and Stouffer thrashed on, not four feet away. Right on cue, as I blasted the climatic E major at the song's conclusion, Stouffer broke free from Tarquin's clutches, and rushed to the lip of the stage, curled into a cannonball, and sailed into the audience with a cry of "Kimber! Fook the Michaels!"

A space in the floor cleared instantly and Stouffer landed like an egg. He stood up and looked around aggressively, ready to throw out a few punches but eventually thought better of it as he studied the sheer volume of pooftahs with increasing trepidation. Some of the bigger, leather-clad types, pushed to the edge of the circle and stared little Stouffer down. But before they could beat him to a pulp, Carruthers waded in, grabbed Stouffer by the shoulders, and muscled him to the backstage entrance.

I looked over at Steed, who was still lying on his back on the stage, one leg stuck up in the air, prostrate and seemingly mesmerized by the flickering strobe. Fortesque helped him off and the show continued with renewed momentum. Later, we discovered that Steed, due to the effects of the psychedelic lighting, had experienced some kind of flashback to his one disastrous experiment with mind-altering substances, and was beginning to view solid objects, once again, as no obstacle to the passage of the human body. After the show, we pumped him full of vodka in order to bring him down and so prevent him from attempting to leave the club the hard way.

Tomorrow we would fly west to east across the country for a show in Scoresbysund, our last show in this vast, forbidding land before heading on to Svalbard, smack in the middle of the Arctic Ocean.

THE OTHER LIFE OF BRIAN

* * *

After a thankfully uneventful engagement in a small but fairly normal club on the east coast, we finally left Greenland with our sexual identities intact, if not our reputations, and the tour cranked on, assuming as all tours do, a life of its own. Steed had chartered an old pranged-up relic of a plane that one morning we crammed into, clutching various publications all running the luge shot with detailed descriptions of the Disko Island debacle.

I studied the press in horror, staring at the photograph that screamed from the front page of the *Greenland Crossbow*. There I was, lying stiff as a board, my face etched with a deathly pallor and my body looking like a seal that had been skinned, had its blubber removed, and then the skin sewn back onto its bones. And one of the ridiculous rags, much to the amusement of everyone on the plane, had mistakenly shown a picture of Tarquin, his head between his legs as he spun around a bend following the overturned luge. (Teal's cameras had apparently carried on clicking.)

"You see, Steed!" I yelled, above the sound of the screaming props, "I told you—you could have done it for me! These bastards don't know the difference!"

But I certainly felt a twinge of rare satisfaction. With a little help from my crew and the Tiny Brocil Fishes, I seemed to be taking the Frozen North by storm. Why not? It made a change from yelling for yen, or krooning for kroner. Hardly Madison Square Garden, but better than a kick in the head. With renewed enthusiasm, I took a hit from a small flask of vodka and decided to enjoy the ride.

The plane, piloted by a kamikaze enthusiast named Njørker (pronounced "Dik"), clanked and farted in crystalline skies toward Svalbard, also known as Spitsbergen and apparently owned by the Norwegians. Below us, the massive Greenland Sea swept out in every direction. Occasionally, Dik would swoop the old crate down low over the ocean surface for no obvious reason, then heave the controls back and take us up again in a gut-wrenching climb. Stouffer's stomach appeared to become uncontrollably delicate after these helter-skelter stunts, and more than once he had to open a window and vomit toward the brooding sea. This act was usually applauded by a loud yell of "Wally!" from Carruthers, who sat next to me.

"What's all this homophobic crap from Stouffer then?" I asked

Carruthers, as the sickly fumes of Stouffer's vodka retching permeated the plane. "And you too, you ignorant sod. What's your problem, Carruthers? A bit of latency lurking in you somewhere, is there?"

Terry, the lead singer/bass guitarist of the Brocils, who was sitting in front of us, leaned over and answered for the heathen pair.

"They can't stand queers," he said in his hard Dorking accent: the Brocils hailed from Surrey and spoke like Londoners but with the coarseness of football hooligans. "The Brocils don't give a shit, know what I mean? I mean like . . . if they're payin' good fuckin' money, I don't care where they stick their truncheons, know what I mean? S'long as it's not up me. Stroll on!"

The whole band had a good guffaw at this. I studied their retro clothing and haircuts. The lot of them seemed to have latched onto that transitory black hole of English fashion, the period between '72 and '76, when brainless hooligans from the suburbs finally discovered acid, but still, due to the dwindling appeal of hippiedom, dressed and acted like alcoholic morons. Seeing as none of the entire band could have been born before 1960, this affectation filled me with a mixture of dread and wonder. They wore either parallels or stay-press trousers, brown shoes with great chunky soles and heels, those awful shirts with enormous collars that football players of the period often sported, curly hair, just growing out from an earlier "suede head" look, and denim jackets with strips of fake wool around the collar.

"See," continued Terry, his large nose and spotty face not six inches away from me in the cramped quarters of the plane. "Brocils like 'cid, scrooms, booze, dope, chicks—an' queers is no threat to our philosophy of life, know what I mean? These two . . ." by this he meant Carruthers and Stouffer, "they're from up north, right? All that fuckin' trappin' of little 'armless animals 'as turned their brains. They smoke n' trip, but queers turn 'em right up. Different, Northerners, ain't they?" he mused, closing his eyes in a tight toothy smile every time he spoke to me.

" 'Armless animals?" I asked, for some strange reason not understanding him.

" 'Armless!" he shouted over the roar of the engine and the loud moaning of Stouffer, who retched another installment of last night's vodka out of the window. "You know, 'armless! HARMLESS!" he enunciated finally, using the "H" with much distaste. "Poor little bunny rabbits," he went on. "They got that fuckin' great thylawotsit chasin' up and down the bloody fields, too!"

I was stunned. Terry had made a reference to the legendary animal as if it were common knowledge; Carruthers had the specimen housed with his collection of vicious hunting beasts, and, despite my warnings to keep a lid on the matter, appeared not to be keeping it a secret in the slightest.

"My God," I gasped, addressing my infuriating soundman. "You mean that thing is really in action, Carruthers? It's been in the fields? How did it grow so quickly?"

"Aye, big now, 'e is. Kibble, partridge, and a shitload of vitamins—packs the weight on, nibs," explained Carruthers, instantly warming to the subject. "But the bugger's a dead loss at hare coursin'. I dunno . . . 'e don't run proper—'is tail's all bloody stiff and it slows 'im down. Mind you, Towser scares the bugger out of t'other dogs—they run a fookin' mile when they so much as smell 'im! But he's marvelous to see—love that bloody animal. Love 'im! And 'e did pull down a local farmer's calf and crushed its jugular in about two bloody seconds—I 'ad a bit of explainin' to do with that one, I did."

"Well for Christ's sake, Carruthers, I could have told you he'd be useless chasing hares. And the animal is not a dog; not even remotely related to dogs, in fact. It's more of a giant fucking biting kangaroo, is what. Hence the stiff tail. I've been reading up on them, something you should be doing."

Ignoring my comments, the incorrigible Carruthers blithely continued describing the progress of the animal without a hint of conscience. By all accounts, it had grown into a strong and faithful pet and was menacing the local canines and serving as great entertainment for Carruthers and his roguish crew of deviants on the farmlands of Kimber. Judging by the growing number of people who knew about this incredible phenomenon, I wondered how long it would be before the story leaked to the press and I would awake one morning to find my name and this remarkable story splashed all over the front pages of the gutter press, and eventually, I thought with a shudder, the corridors of the law courts.

I studied the teenage giant Carruthers as he continued to enthuse about the thylacine's impeccably ruthless cow-killing abilities. Even on this freezing plane flight the buffoon wore only a pair of black sweat pants with his trademark lime green silky boxing shorts pulled over them, yellow hiking boots, and an orange T-shirt the size of a tent with the words 'Pooftahs Out!' printed on it in Rastafarian colors. His white gangly arms were studded here and there with what looked like cigarette burns. His fire-red hair boasted a volcanic eruption of styles. He was in midsentence, pouring over the minute details of the thylacine's blood curdling 120 degree jaw stretch, when a surge of outrage flashed through my blood, and I quickly rolled the Greenland Crossbow into a tube and whacked him fiercely over the head with it.

"Carruthers," I said, as he looked at me stupidly, blinking his pale, vacuous eyes and bringing an ungainly hand up to scratch his errant hair. "Carruthers, you ought to be certified, you rotter. If my name ever comes up in connection with that thylacine I'll have your guts for garters. Have you got that, you oaf?"

"Nibs," he mumbled sheepishly and then added with some enthusiasm: "But you've got to coom oop and see 'im, BP! Aye, it's a mega-sight it is. Fookin' mega!"

"Twat!" I spat, and whacked him a few more times about his enormous block-shaped head; but quietly, I found myself intrigued by the idea of that lupine-striped marsupial bounding across a field in the early-morning mist, hot on the scent of a local dog or some unfortunate calf too slow to get out of the way.

Chapter 21

The gig in Svalbard's capitol, Longyearbyen, seemed a pointless exercise to me. Steed assured me that the money was good, but the audience, comprised mainly of fish-processing factory workers, husky breeders, and various pilots and seamen whose age and obvious debilitation suggested that the Arctic Circle was the last stop on their plummeting careers, was enough to stifle the excitement of this morning's front page press. A grim pall settled on our party after the show, and the thought of tomorrow's four-hour sled ride to the South Cape did nothing to lift it.

The next morning we bundled up in as many layers of clothing as we had, and set out on an enormous sled pulled by a team of eight devil-eyed huskies and captained by a surprisingly frail-looking little fellow named Njark. Old Njark was a taciturn chap who for the most part kept his thoughts to himself and let his dogs do the barking. As we bounced along over the bleak pack ice, the only thing that came out of his mouth was the occasional yell of "Tushky tushky!" directed at his crazed, powerful brutes, followed by a celebratory globule of spit fired expertly into the air above his head, where it caught the stiff wind and promptly boomeranged back toward myself and the crew, necessitating much dipping and weaving as we tried to dodge its trajectory. After each shot, Njark would look back over his shoulder, the leather reins of the sled gripped firmly in his gloved hands, and give us a big weatherbeaten gap-toothed grin.

Somehow we arrived at South Cape, despite two attempts from Stouffer to strangle Njark after he became the recipient of the driver's phlegm attacks. Tarquin intervened each time and held the boffin down in a full-nelson wrestling hold until he'd regained a semblance of calm. God knows, I had a mind to deck the cretinous Njark myself, but Steed showed correct prudence in this matter; if we had so much as laid a finger on their master, no doubt those evil-looking beasts of burden would likely have torn us to shreds.

In South Cape, a town distinguished by a permanent howling gail and a weather condition known as "ice crystals" (a self-explanatory term that nonetheless filled me with wonder that anyone could put up with the bitter cold, throat-choking effect of this phenomena for more than a day), an audience identical to the Longyearbyen crowd turned up. My performance, however, which took place in a cod processing plant hastily converted to accommodate entertainment only hours before show time, turned out to be a little more uplifting than the night before due to the drunken enthusiasm of the factory workers. Still, I couldn't see the point of it all. There wasn't a record store in the entire country. When I pressed Tarquin on the subject, he just shrugged it off with a cryptic, "You never know, my boy, you never know."

"Never know what?" was my incredulous response.

"The old knock-on effect," he said slyly, tapping his nose. "Could pay dividends on Bear Island, a show like tonight's. It was full here, you know."

"Yeah," I said, "full of a bunch of moronic fish cleaners who smelled like dead seals and danced like Captain Bird's Eye. And Bear Island—I've looked on the map—it's about the size of Neasden! Knock on effect," I sneered. "You must be joking."

Stouffer, who was just edging past us in the walk-in freezer that served as a dressing room, said: "Big Drugs on Bear," and trundled off, followed by my uncomprehending stare.

"What?" I said to Steed.

"Well, laddie, let's just say Bear's a little livelier than you might suspect. A little livelier."

I could glean no more information from Steed, who rushed off to bag the Norwegian kronor from Jalfie, the slick man who called himself the promoter who also, I discovered, organized fish-skinning tournaments when entertainers were thin on the ground in Svalbard, which was usually 361 days of the year.

Fortesque offered no further enlightenment on tomorrow's engagement on Bear Island either; this was Carruthers' and Stouffer's turf, apparently. The idea that Steed knew something of the realities of a show on Bear Island buzzed in my head as I covered myself with the skins of Arctic animals that lay across the rude dagswain serving as my bed, and tried to snatch some sleep in my coffin-like room in South Cape's only hotel, the Northern Njarl.

Early the next morning, Tarquin Steed, Big Hilda, Carruthers, Stouffer, Fortesque, myself, Jalfie the promoter, and a pilot named Flyte bent ourselves into yet another clanking relic of a seaplane for the voyage to the remote and minuscule Bear Island. The Tiny Brocil Fishes were waiting for another pilot to shake his hangover, one plane being too small for the lot of us. Big Hilda was in an ebullient mood. The night before she had met the man who installed the hideous fluorescent lighting that seemed to festoon every habitation and workplace in the entire Arctic, and a romantic interlude had ensued. She garbled on endlessly about the contents of my often tender love ballads—especially the scant few that had appeared on my first two LPs—and how she found them so "relatable," or some such tosh. I told her emphatically that they were inspired by no actual personal experience, but were rather gleaned or more bluntly, stolen, from TV soap operas. This of course, had the desirable effect of bursting her bubble about sensitive artists and their moody affairs, fueled (she believed) by years of starving in garrets, wrestling with drug addiction, and practicing self-denial as a means to obtain enlightenment. I informed her somewhat bluntly that I was, "Well thought of, well fed, and well fucked." This statement at last dampened her mood and stifled her lovelorn waxings—which were beginning to grate on my hangover—and I managed to sit out the rest of the flight in brooding silence.

We shuffled into the Bear Island Boogie Bar later that day, and although the place smelled like a sea lion's whelping pit, Carruthers and Stouffer appeared quite at home and on first-name terms with the staff, who cleaned and generally readied the place for show time. Two barmaids—who were, much to my surprise, svelte and attractive Californians—busied themselves behind the well-stocked fifty-foot-long bar, washing glasses and bandying comments about with the two soundmen. What with Carruthers' and Stouffer's familiarity with the club and its staff, the banks of neon advertising American and imported beers, and the collection of up-to-date pinball and video machines that lined one of the dank walls, I suddenly felt quite disoriented. Apart from the rank odor of sea life that seemed to permeate most of these Arctic gigs, I could have been in Chicago or Washington.

"Big Drugs," repeated Stouffer enigmatically as he careened across the floor toward Steed, who was on his back on the tacky dance floor, taking a screwdriver to the bottom of Stouffer's Sonic Set-Up generator. "Gerrout a there, ya bastard!" yelled the boffin as he hauled my permanently fidgeting manager away from certain electrocution.

"Just having a look," said Steed with the innocence of a baby.

"Don't fookin' touch," ordered Stouffer testily before turning to me as I adjusted a mic stand on the stage, readying for soundcheck "Like I say, BP," he said with a gleeful grin, "Big Drugs on Bear, heh heh!"

I decided to ignore the clown. I imagined the only drugs that they had on this frozen block were hormones for pumping up the blubber on the local seal population, and Stouffer was just pulling my leg or indulging in some wishful thinking.

But I began to think differently later that evening as I played my first song and gazed through the stage lights at the bizarre audience my show had attracted. The fish cleaners and salty dogs of the previous two performances on Svalbard were almost entirely absent, and in their place was as eclectic a mix as one might find in the latest fashionable New York hotspot. Out there, in the writhing mass, was a much different kettle of fish than the typical Arctic crowd I had encountered so far, barring perhaps the queers of Disko Island. Below my feet were a riot of night world denizens of every stripe. Where did these misplaced ravers come from? I could see well-dressed young women and grunge-clad young men, looking like they had just stepped out of fashion ads in hip magazines; punky types with green hair and ripped-up leather jackets; Japanese businessmen in pinstriped suits with expensive-looking western courtesans on their arms; and dotted here and there, middle-aged men who would not have looked out of place strolling from high class Saville Row tailors and into chauffeur-driven Rolls Royces. They hadn't just come here for the younger and more fashionable Tiny Brocil Fishes, either. Incredibly, they seemed quite well acquainted with my material, and some, much to my amazement, cheered heartily when I started tunes from my latest album.

I left the stage after twenty-two songs and five encores, completely bewildered, and flopped down in the well-appointed dressing room to open a bottle of champagne. (Incongruously, again, a fine vintage Moet and Chandon.)

"I can't believe this place," I said to Steed and Fortesque as they joined me for a drink. "What," I questioned, "is going on here?"

"We' off t'casino, or what?" asked Carruthers, entering the dressing room looking hot and sweaty. Stouffer followed him; his eyes, already amplified behind his bottle-thick specs, were spinning like Catherine wheels.

"Casino?" I asked. "What are you on, Carruthers? Have the Big Drugs arrived?"

"Come on, Brian," said Steed, "it's just out the back here."

I slugged back a glass of Moet and followed them through an exit in the dressing room, which led us along a narrow corridor to a white door, this with the word "Private" stamped upon it in black packing crate–style letters. Steed took out a key and opened the door. I could dimly hear a muted cacophony coming from within and felt a weird flash of nerves in my gut. When the door flew open, a startling scene greeted my eyes, and I felt as if I had just wandered into a Fellini movie. Before us were roiling, animated groups of people gathered around various gaming tables, the bets and chips flying from hands to green felt like confetti. Well-dressed gentlemen swished by carrying flutes of champagne, and women yelled and laughed in the thick fallout of cigarette smoke. The plush red carpeting, gold-plated appointments, and rich solid wood tables told me that whoever put this lot together had enough money to raise the *Titanic*.

"Jesus!" was all I could say, as we walked from room to room, each one as lively as the last.

"Nice bar in the next one," claimed Carruthers, as we shouldered through the crowd into a luxuriously furnished room dotted with groups of people relaxing on sofas around large glass tables. The bar was, in fact, stupendous, stretching the entire length of a hundred-foot back wall and made seemingly out of one massive piece of some spectacularly expensive hardwood. We sat on red leather stools and leaned over the fine polished grain, waiting only moments before an impeccably dressed barman appeared in front of us.

"Good evening, gentlemen," he said, in an accent I couldn't place. "My name's Snarl and I'll be serving you this evening. What'll it be?"

"A round of Vodka Icebergs I think, Snarl," ordered Steed, his eyebrows raising toward me. I nodded mutely, ready to guzzle anything placed in front of me.

"Oh, and by the way, gentlemen," said Snarl, standing directly in front of Carruthers and pointing a clean finger at him. "This gentleman is banned from here, he's under age."

And with that, both Carruthers and the barman locked hands and began to arm wrestle with a vengeance that within moments gave way to a dual bellowing fit, quickly taken up by Steed and Stouffer. What a setup! They were all obviously well acquainted and the brief bout of mock argy-bargy became fond handshakes and polite queries about the welfare of friends, families, and the names of various obscure rock acts with whom my soundmen had passed through Bear Island on previous tours.

Snarl went off to get the drinks, giving me a wink and flipping his palm in the air, a gesture I took to be vaguely welcoming, but still, I felt I was in the presence of a club that I was not quite a member of.

As I drank the head-clearing Vodka Iceberg, Stouffer sidled up and pulled two sheets of what I at first took to be postage stamps out of his combat jacket.

"These ones," he said very slowly, pointing to a sheet divided into small squares with blue and red shields printed on each one, "these ones are Supermen. Very mild, actually." He looked at me with his huge swirling eyes. I thought I could see his black pupils shrinking and dilating, even in the dim lighting of the bar. "I'll bet it's been a long time for thee, but if you want to get reacquainted, these are the boys for you."

I blinked and examined the sheet, having no idea as to what he was talking about. They looked like something a child would have, like those transfers that wash off.

"Now these," he added, pressing the other sheet into my line of vision, "them's Jokers. Work thou way oop, I would. A good deal more serious is Jokers."

I studied this sheet carefully, finally catching on to what Stouffer was showing me.

"Acid!" I gasped, staring at the tiny but unmistakable image of Jack Nicholson, printed beautifully on each square. "Very tempting, Stouffer," I said, handing them back to him and examining my fingers for fear of skin ingestion. "But," I continued, "just finding myself in this situation is trippy enough, thanks. I mean, I'm just beginning to handle this externally. I wouldn't want to deal with it internally, too. Thanks all the same, Stouff. You carry on, there's a good chap."

"Nibs!" yelled Carruthers from two stools along. "More to coom too, BP. More to coom. These ain't even the Big Drugs, right Stouffer?"

"Right," said Stouffer cheerfully.

Steed got up from his stool and strolled over. An immaculately dressed couple brushed behind us, looking flushed and intoxicated. I glanced around the room and noticed that the thick smoke wasn't just emanating from tobacco. Large hashish joints were being handed around with no thought of discretion.

"All right, Stouffer," said Steed, twirling the ice in his glass, "I think it's time Brian met the Clermont Set." This sounded exceptionally ominous, and I wondered, with a hint of paranoia, if a speckle of Joker had rubbed off into my skin.

I followed my crew out of the bar, feeling like I was being led to my execution. We struggled back through two of the gaming rooms we had navigated previously on the way to "Snarl's Den," as the bar we had just left was known as, and came to a door behind a blackjack table, roped off and guarded by a large goon. Without a word, he lifted the thick red rope and opened the door. We entered, and for a couple of minutes zigged and zagged a labyrinthine corridor that Carruthers had utter confidence in negotiating, even in the livid darkness. Without warning, a room opened up before us and quite suddenly I stood before a shining roulette wheel and was being introduced by Steed, to a distinguished-looking middle-aged gentleman.

"This is Lucky, BP. He runs the place." I shook hands with the man, noticing his black mustache, his graying hair, and his aristocratic forehead. Obviously, he was no used car salesman made good, but carried himself with the air of a man whose ancestry was not of the common stamp.

So what? I thought to myself. Hardly an execution, or an initiation come to that. Steed had just introduced me to some old upper cruster with more money than sense. But there was something gnawing away in the back of mind; I felt sure the face was familiar and not just the type, many of whom can be seen on English television every year, hooraying their way through Ascot.

"Good to meet you, Brian," the gentleman said. "Great show tonight, I'm quite fond of your first two LPs, actually. The new stuff's pretty top hole too. How's the remix doing? I've been pulling a few strings with my friends on the Arctic radio circuit, but they're awfully slow to pick up on quality up here, awfully slow."

In his rich upper-class accent, he sounded quite out of place discussing my material, but I felt that secret thrill that all working class people succumb to when they feel they have made an impression on the gentry, despite their usual loathing for such buffoons.

"Oh thank you, er, sir," I stammered, "but I don't think they're going for it. Still, the gigs are doing pretty well."

"Excellent, excellent," he said, and then turned to Carruthers, who was edging in beside me. "Carruthers, old chap, have you been winning? Is it taking all right?"

"Ee, I've done bloody marvelous so far, Lucky. 'Ad a couple of rounds of blackjack before t'gig and a few spins on the wheel. Won every time! Big Drugs is workin' a treat, I'd say. I'll be off for a few more shots in a while. It's great, I can almost see the balls landing in the slots split seconds before I place me bet, and the cards flash before me eyes like a great girt vision! Nibs it is! Mega nibs!"

"Splendid!" exclaimed Lucky with satisfaction. "I think they're finally getting the dosage right; that nasty triple vision stuff that occurred last time you were here seems to have been eradicated, don't you think?"

"Oh aye," said Carruthers, continuing with what seemed to me an utterly incomprehensible conversation. "I'm feeling it nibs now, Lucky. Crackin' stuff. I think they've got t'formula bang on. In fact . . . I feel lucky! I feel lucky!"

This last quip caused chuckles all around, and as Lucky himself turned and began throwing chips onto his private table, I looked stupidly toward Steed, as if begging for clarification. He put his arm around my shoulder and quietly led me off. As we walked I happened to glance over into a very dim corner of the room. I made out the shape of what I took to be a huge hairy man, sitting with a drink in his ape-like hand. I also caught a glimpse of a silver choker flashing dully around his neck that was attached to a thin chain. The end of the chain was held by a woman, apparently dressed head to toe in leather bondage gear. I immediately dismissed this vision; it had to be a trick of the light or perhaps—I thought with another flash of dread—a minute quantity of that damned Joker blotter had seeped into my bloodstream. I had to keep cool here; I wanted to know in non-multidimensional terms what the heck was going on. At last, Steed filled me in, at least partially.

"Now, BP," he said quietly, "take a good look at Lucky. Think about it . . ."

I stared over at the languid sophisticate, idly collecting a big win at the roulette wheel, his lordly countenance calm and unruffled by his successful play. Lordly? Why did that word spring to mind? Then it hit me. I remembered in a flash where I had seen that face before. I'd seen it in a magazine article in recent years; and in fact, the story behind that upper-class physiognomy had remained an irrepressible force of mystery that returned to the mind of the public imagination year after year, like an ancient riddle. Of course! He was none other than Lord "Lucky" Lucan, the 7th Earl of Lucan, the wastrel English peer who had disappeared almost twenty years ago after a botched attempt to kill his own wife. By all accounts, he had miscalculated horrendously and instead, bludgeoned his children's nanny to death. He vanished from the face of the earth the day after the murder and left in his wake an enigma that had stymied the law ever since. But here he was, large as life, and enjoying the one vice that had by all accounts threatened to drag him down so many times in his, as it were, previous life—gambling!

"You've got it, haven't you?" said Steed, studying the lights going on all over my face.

"It's Lucan, isn't it," I said, not in the form of a question.

"The Big Drugs that big mouth Stouffer was rattling on about," Steed explained, "are a little development Lucky's got going up here. He was a terrible loser, back when he was a free man. So, with a bit of funding from the Clermont Set, he put this enormous underground casino together—we're fifty feet below ground, you know—and hired a team of scientists—Russians, mostly—to develop drugs that help you win. I don't know . . . they enhance your perception in a very specific way apparently. Something about "luck DNA," as they call it. Never tried it myself. Seems like he's getting somewhere though."

We looked over at Lucan, who with a satisfied smile stacked up another win. Carruthers stood beside him yelling "Nibs!" as he too raked in the chips from Lucan's smiling personal croupier.

"Isn't he just winning from himself though, Steed?" I asked, not seeing the point apart from the purely hedonistic value.

"Oh yes, it all goes back, of course. Not out in the main rooms though . . . that's real gambling. Helps to fund the research. Ah look, there's Goldie now, and Aspers . . . hi, chaps." Steed addressed two older gentlemen who were just joining Lord Lucan at the table.

"John Aspinal and Sir James Goldsmith," said Steed in my ear. "Part of the Clermont Set. These blokes have got so much money, they make the crown jewels look like small change. As long suspected of course, those two engineered Lucky's escape after the murder. Whisked him off to the Orkneys at first, then they built this place up here. They pay off the Norwegian government handsomely I hear. There are Russian subs patrolling the shores right now, but I think they're just a new clause in the deal; protection I believe. Bit sad really, I think they're just using Lucky as a pawn. You know . . . a guinea pig. God knows what damage these Big Drugs are doing; hardly anything like official safeguards in their development. Could be rotting out his liver for all anyone knows. But apparently—though I don't know all the ins and outs—when they've got this drug perfected, they're going to take over the entire world's gambling industry. They don't think they're rich enough already, you see, ha!"

"Greedy bastards," I said.

"About the size of it," agreed Steed.

"How come you know this lot then, Steed?" I asked.

"Oh, we go back a bit, you know. Our paths crossed a few times long ago. Old school tie and all that. Old school tie."

Steed explained a few more intricacies of this fascinating situation, but after a while I had stopped listening. The monstrous hairy fellow I had spotted earlier regained my attention. He stood up in the shadows, the chain jangling from his neck flickering in the bondage lady's hands. The monster gave himself a good scratch, then shook himself down from head to toe in a frightening rhythmic doglike motion. I couldn't make things out too clearly, owing to the dungeon-like darkness of his corner, but he looked like he was covered in hair from head to toe, and had to be a good deal over eight feet tall. He sat down again and gave a deep rumbling grunt that shook my insides from ten feet away. I must be hallucinating, I thought. This place was getting to me— I was seeing giant apes. Still, I had to investigate, so I wandered away from Tarquin who had suddenly been commandeered by Big Hilda and the fluorescent lighting man, who seemed to appear from nowhere. I approached Lucan as he took a break from the roulette wheel to snag a drink from a passing waiter. I sidled up beside him, grabbing a glass of vintage champagne from the overflowing tray.

"Er . . . Lord Lucan," I ventured. "Um, Lucky, old chap. I may have been spiked by one of Stouffer's Jokers, but I'm sure there's a very peculiar fellow over there in the corner." I pointed in the direction of the hairy apparition, not knowing if I was committing some faux pas by even mentioning it, for now I was fairly convinced that if it was an hallucination, it was unusually specific; no one else in the room seemed to be sprouting huge masses of thick simian hair.

"Oh," said Lucky vaguely. "You've spotted George, that's all. I suppose someone ought to introduce you. You are, after all, a bit of a guest of honor. I expect you'll want to see the eagle, too. I'll round them up for you, old boy. Now, you see the door over there?" He pointed to the corner of the room, about five feet from where we were standing and diagonal to the entrance where the crew and I had at first entered this private den. "You go through there . . . Carruthers!" he snapped to the teenage giant. "Take Brian through to the paddock, there's a good chap. Introductions to be made."

"Nibs, Luck," answered Carruthers, pushing two roulette chips into his eye sockets with a daft grin.

"Mush mush," ordered Lucan, "haven't got all night—lots more testing to be done, old boy."

"Nibs it is, farff! This way, Beep."

The ungainly redhead led me through the door and sat me down inside "the paddock" on an old wooden bench. It was very bright in that room, the fluorescent light man having overextended himself to the point of painfulness. I blinked and winced and looked up at Carruthers, whose blotchy skin looked like an ordinance survey map of Pirbright Heath. My eyes gradually adjusted until I noticed sawdust on the floor of the cell-like white room, two other old benches and another door in the back wall. Before I could adjust to this new and—compared with the plush glamour of the gaming rooms—rather hostile environment, the back door swung open and in walked Lord Lucan with an enormous bird of prey on his arm. Lucky's wrist was encased in a thick leather gauntlet and the massive raptor's talons gripped it ferociously as it shuffled its giant black and white wings. I recognized the species immediately, being an amateur ornithologist and an avid fan of nature shows. Its unreal dimensions and heavy orange beak revealed its identity as a Stellers sea eagle, the largest eagle on the planet Earth, boasting a good eight-foot wing span.

"He's a Stel . . ." began Lucky grandly.

"Stellars sea eagle," I interjected, eager to impress these showoffs with my knowledge. By now, I was feeling quite out of sorts and was glad of the firm ground my education in natural history placed me on.

"Oh . . ." said Lucky, a little taken aback. "Well . . . anyway. You'll probably know that there are only about two thousand of them alive today. This one, we rescued as a fledgling. It can fly, but he doesn't seem to want to. Likes the free seafood I expect, don't you, Earl?" he said to the bird, which let out a blood-curdling caw. He then turned around stiffly, the sea eagle balanced awkwardly on his arm, its wings flapping gently for balance, and shouted through the open back door into the darkness that lay beyond.

"Tamby? Are you coming? Bring George through so's Brian can get a good look at him in the light, will you, darling? Ah, here we are, there's a sweetie."

Tamby, the bondage woman, slid into the room, her black leather pants swishing softly. She held the thin silver chain, her enormous charge obediently at heel introducing a ripe apish odor to the paddock and a sight too surreal for my baffled senses to correctly register. "George"—as Lucan had referred to him—was indeed some steps away from being entirely human, being the height of a basketball player suffering from severe encephalitis. He was massive, totally covered with coarse brown-black hair with small beady eyes and a prominent forehead that angled down to a flattened nose displaying deep black flared nostrils.

Tamby, a wraith-like blonde with a mascara overload, issued the simple command "Sit!," which George obeyed with a small pensive whimper, and collapsed in a heavy sulking heap onto a bench.

"Don't worry, Brian," said Lord Lucan, "he's a harmless fellow. I believe they have them in America where they go under the silly name of 'Bigfoot.' 'Sasquatch' is more suitable perhaps, although up here in the Arctic the locals call them 'Ingloot,' meaning 'Mountain Man.'"

"An Abominable Snowman?" I gasped.

THE OTHER LIFE OF BRIAN

"Ah," said Lucan. "Another totally unsuitable moniker. 'Yeti' isn't bad, but I prefer Mountain Man—closer to the truth I reckon. At any rate, that's what we're going to call him when the exhibition is finally up and running. So, there you have it. Aspers has always been fascinated by the idea that these boys exist—arranged a few partially successful hunts in the Himalayas some years back, in fact. But he finally got lucky up here. Bagged George in Franz Joseph Land, on Graham Bell Island. You've got a gig there in a few days I think. Watch out! The whole audience might be comprised of these chappies! That'll be a laugh, eh? Ha ha ha!"

A rock 'n' roll zombie if I ever saw one, Tamby sat mutely next to George, who swung his endless monkey arms between his great thick thighs. Carruthers sloped over and scratched the Sasquatch behind the ear. They obviously shared a lot in common, those two.

Steed entered, and he and Lucan loosely explained the bizarre enterprise to me. The world gambling monopoly was a dead cert, now that the Big Drugs were having all the quirks and side effects hammered out of them. And what with the thylacine that Carruthers had safely ensconced in the wilds of Kimber (Lucan made it quite clear that the animal would eventually end up here), the Stellars sea eagle—a creature doomed to extinction, probably within the next thirty years or so—and the Abominable Snowman, they had the beginnings of a private cryptozoo that seemed created purely for the pleasure of the Clermont Set and their rich cronies, many of whom were apparently willing to pay large sums for the capture and nurturing of such beasts.

"And that brings us," said Lord Lucan, after this explanation, which included the names of various other animals, some of which even I, with my fairly well-read knowledge of such matters, had not heard of, "to some form of remuneration . . . uh, regarding Towser, the thylacine pup. What I mean is, people are going to be paying to see and be in close proximity to these creatures. As I said, the thylacine's eventually going to come up here to Bear. Sorry, Carruthers." Lucan looked over at my soundman.

"Aye, I know it," said Carruthers sadly, adding: "I like the word 'remuneration,' though."

"Don't worry, old stick," Lucky assured him, "we pay well for good specimens."

"And also, you see, Brian," Lucan went on, turning to me. "It was you, in a way, that discovered this little beauty. It was on your time and on your tour. The creature is almost—if not for George here—the pride of our little collection so far. Fifty million yen OK? Sorry it's in yen, but our two disgustingly rich Japanese investors are most keen on extinct marsupials, most keen. I've spoken to Steed here about it, and we can wire it through to your account in the Caymans tomorrow. Carruthers I'm taking care of separately. The fifty million's yours, save 15 percent for this rogue," he laughed, meaning Tarquin, my manager.

"Whoa. Wait a minute," I stammered. "I don't have an account in . . ."

"Opened it yesterday," interjected Steed. "Personal account in the Cayman Islands. Can't be got at. The Clermont Set have an airtight ring around the bank. Tax free, the lot. I got it up and running the minute we agreed to the figure. Tried for more, but these rich aristocrat types are tight bastards." With that, Tarquin and Lucan broke into chuckles and manly banter.

"What other stuff are you after? You mentioned some other creatures just now," I asked Lucan, fascinated by the idea of a collection of animals that contained near-mythical beasts like the Yeti and supposedly extinct creatures like the thylacine.

"Well, apart from the ones I've already mentioned," he said, somewhat cagily, "we now have positive proof of a group of giant amphibians living in Loch Ness and at least ten other Northern hemisphere deep water lakes. The plesiosaur idea is claptrap—they're obviously giant urodeles."

"Obviously," I agreed, stunned at the breadth of the research going into this rather frivolous project.

"Yes," continued Lucan, "big fellows actually, but some of the reports over the years have been vastly exaggerated of course."

"Of course," I murmured.

"Giant amphibians they are indeed," continued Lucky. "The remains of urodeles have been found in the vicinity of Loch Ness many times in the past, but only one or two researchers have paid any attention to it. The press, as usual, have ostensibly quagmired the reality in ridicule forever. But, they *are* there. Matter of fact, we've got a tank waiting for the first one to arrive. A tank I say: more of a whole environment, actually." He pointed to the back door. "It's a mess in there now," he explained, reading my mind. "You really must come back within a year—we'll have the whole thing up and running. They'll be marvelous exhibits, believe me. Marvelous. Um . . . let's see now," Lucan went on, rubbing his cologned chin in a speculatory fashion.

"In about three days' time my Russian contacts are delivering a creature sometimes known as 'Bergman's bear,' named after Swedish zoologist Sten Bergman, who examined the skin of one of these giants back in the twenties. Bloody huge thing—makes George over there look like a midget.

"Oh yes! A tatzelwurm's coming in from Austria in a week or two. Now they're *really* interesting," enthused Lucan, now thoroughly warming to the subject.

We stood under the harsh fluorescent lights of the paddock, Lucan immaculate in his pinstripe, me in black jeans, my beat-up Dutch army parka, and a badly designed freebie T-shirt from an Icelandic radio station, enmeshed in the coarse odor of Bigfoot and sawdust.

"A tatzelwurm! Can you imagine? I'm very excited about this one!" raved Lucky, pulling a silver cigarette case from his inside suit pocket and offering me a Black Russian. I declined, having been on a rare non-smoking binge since the beginning of the Arctic tour. Lucan lit up, the click of his heavy solid gold lighter echoing ominously against the stone ceiling. I stared into the Lord's slate-gray eyes, riveted, dying to hear more.

"Yes, the tatzelwurm!" he went on, sensing his utterly fascinated audience of one. Steed meanwhile, was poking around with an electric socket in the wall, trying to get a screwdriver into it. Carruthers sat on the bench next to Tamby, who rubbed his leg in a completely nonsexual manner, as if it were a piece of cardboard. The soundman seemed uninterested in Tamby. He was staring across her and making eye contact with the Sasquatch, who responded by staring back, expressionless and glum, bored out of its mind.

"Yes, sometimes known as the 'tunnel worm' or 'mountain stump,'" Lucan went on, sucking deeply on his powerful Black Russian. "They appear to be an entirely unknown genus, not quite reptile, not quite amphibian, very nasty looking and quite hostile, too. Three feet long, scaly, and rather resembling some form of giant, obnoxious skink, they haven't even been spotted since the 1800s, but I was fascinated enough to launch an extensive expedition in the Austrian and Swiss alps—couple of my chappies died of exposure in the process, as a matter of fact. But at any rate we've got one now. Fine specimen by all accounts; they've just got to ascertain what the bastards eat before we ship it out here. We'll need a good supply of their feed, whatever it is.

"And naturally, we're hoping for one of those blasted three-foot dun-colored almond-eyed alien chappies that keep abducting Americans for cross-breeding experiments, too. You know: 'the Grays,' they call them. Just a matter of time, old boy. A matter of time." Lucan twisted his fine gray-black mustache between his manicured fingers and looked over at the Bigfoot wistfully. My head was spinning. I'd just been handed almost half a million dollars for an accident and was standing fifty feet under the permafrost of the obscure Norwegian-owned Bear Island talking to Lord Lucan about the imminent capture of Loch Ness monsters and alien beings. I looked over at Tarquin Steed standing in the glare of a potent quadruple fluorescent fixture impaled in the white stone ceiling, holding the screwdriver he'd been using to poke into the electrical socket in front of his squinting eyes, as if it held more secrets to its simple design than he'd previously imagined.

He shrugged and said, "It's a life, I s'pose," and then returned to the outlet with renewed vengeance.

"I think I'll hit the sack," I replied to Tarquin's cryptic comment, feeling suddenly drained. "I've got a show to do tomorrow. Long flight too. Thanks for everything, Lucky. Do you know the way out of here, Steed?"

But as I uttered my manager's name, a hail of sparks flew out of the wall socket he'd been fiddling with and blew him halfway across the room like a cannonball.

"Bloody hell!" he moaned as Carruthers and I rushed over to assist him.

"You all right, Steed?" I asked urgently, pulling him to his feet and dusting the sawdust off of his shoulders.

"What?" he responded, already acting like nothing unusual had occurred.

"No no no. I'm fine," he said, staring quizzically between the screwdriver, which he still held tightly in his hand, and the smoldering socket in the wall.

THE OTHER LIFE OF BRIAN

"Lucky, is that alternating current, or what?" he asked blandly.

Lucan shrugged and laughed quietly, as if he were used to such antics coming from my manager. "You *are* OK, Steed, yes? We've got a hell of a medical staff if you need it, you know."

"Medi? . . . No. Not a bit of it. Right as rain. Now, BP. What were you saying? Ready to hit the sack?—And it *will* be a sack! Was that it?"

I nodded agreement numbly, amazed once more by Tarquin's invincibly thick skin.

"Let's away. Hotel's just a labyrinth away," said Steed, beginning to yawn, the electric shock apparently already forgotten. "If we don't take a wrong turn at the North Pole we should find it all right. Come on, let's go. Long day tomorrow."

We made our way back to the dressing room where this odyssey had begun and walked out across the empty club floor to the entrance door. Outside, it was so cold that each breath was like swallowing a lungful of tiny shards of glass.

I thought about the Cayman Islands and all that money sitting, tax-free, in a bank. I suddenly felt like I'd been suffering this climate for years and the thought of blowing out the rest of this tour and going straight to the Caymans to lie on a beach for the rest of my life struck me like a beacon of light. Franz Joseph Land? Novaya Zemlya? Two of the coldest, most hostile environments on earth—and Russian territory, too? What was the point? I could practically retire with all those yen.

This tempting idea percolated in my mind and I shared it with Fortesque and Tarquin. We sat down in the dark empty lounge of our chilly, brooding hotel and drank some fiery unidentifiable alcohol we had managed to prize out of the night porter.

"So what about it, Steed? I said, after he had at first ignored my remark about quitting the tour now and going to the beach. He took a deep breath and leveled his eyes at me.

"I don't think that would be too wise a move, Brian," he said solemnly.

"Come on, man!" I shouted, banging back another glass of hooch with a flourish. "Let's get out of this dump. We're freezing our arses off and all those yen are languishing in the bloody sun! Come on, this place is doing me in; surely after tonight, the gigs are downhill all the way?"

"Come on, Brian," he continued, still in a serious mood. "Look," he said. "The Clermont Set have got their fingers into every pie up here; most of the clubs you've been playing are either owned or part-owned by them." Steed sucked his teeth as he let this bit of information sink in.

I loaded my glass further with the nasty Bear Island brew; if I kept downing the stuff at this rate, I'd probably go blind in my sleep. But I knew what Steed was saying. I'd inadvertently been responsible for the discovery of the thylacine pup and they'd paid me handsomely, but if I crossed them, they'd probably have my guts for garters, and even worse, get their fifty million yen back in the blink of a computer transaction. I suddenly felt like I was on their payroll. The idea that those sinister aristocratic bastards had something over me was most unpleasant; they were probably all Satan worshipers and God knows what else.

I quickly shrugged this idea off, however, letting the booze do its good work. There seemed no reason why they would want to lord it over me. I had delivered the rare animal, if only by default, and I had been rewarded with wheelbarrow loads of money. Deal closed: so long as I fulfilled my commitments in the Arctic. Hell, I thought, why rock the boat? I may be endowed with no small measure of moral fiber, but I'm not a complete idiot. I'll take the cash.

"How's the first gig in Franz Joseph Land looking, Fortesque," I asked my trusty charge with a slight mustering of enthusiasm.

"Not looking too good, mate," answered the doomy black-haired Aussie. "Only sold thirty tickets so far."

"Ah, but hold on a minute," slurred Steed, the moonshine finally clouding his vocal abilities. "That fairly accurately tallies with the population figures. I wouldn't be too hasty on this one. And we're only talking about one island, remember, the others will improve markedly!"

"Ha!" I jeered and tossed back the alcohol. "What kind of Sasquatch crap is that, Steed? Pull the other leg, it's got an endangered rock singer on it!"

And with that, we clanked our glasses together and continued drinking until the steel gray of the dawn shocked us up to our rooms.

Chapter 22

"I was on Bunkum," said the little old lady sitting next to me. The Icelandic cargo-cum-passenger flight was just pulling through a patch of gut-wrenching turbulence and the drinks had been hastily delivered, encouraging a bout of relieved camaraderie that manifested itself in warm pockets of conversation throughout the icy tube.

The tour of the Arctic Circle was over and I could feel the various pressures of work and exposure to hostile locales breaking down in my system, producing as they did a relaxed exhaustion that left me somewhat undefended against any slings and arrows that might come my way in the form of conversational strangers on airplanes. And so, for no other reason perhaps than lack of energy, I refrained from hoisting up barriers of indifference or hostility and left the headphones in my bag, prepared to at least give the old girl a few minutes of my time.

I looked down at the shrunken figure to my left, huddled in a pink padded ski jacket with the fur-lined hood up. By her accent I divined that she was American.

"I'm sorry?" I queried.

"Bunkum," she replied, flashing a pair of twinkling mascaraed blue eyes, perched like sentries astride a prominent nose, to which she dabbed a clean white handkerchief.

"I was on Bunkum. I was having a colon operation when, bang! I went out. The blips on that goddamn machine that tells you whether or not your heart's stopped beating went flat. It's all on film. It was on TV. Allen, my son, videotaped it for me, too. He's such a mensch, that boy."

"Oh . . ." I had no answer to this and for a moment felt a Flight Bore attack approaching. But she seemed a sweet old dear, so I whacked down the rest of my Vodka Iceberg for strength, and raised my eyebrows at her, encouraging continuance.

"I was lucky," she went on, touching the back of my wrist with her wrinkled fingers, which seemed to be attached to her hand by various items of excessive goldsmithery. "Rolf Greenbaumstein was there with the whole crew from Bunkum. Steinglass, the neuropsychiatrist, was watching over the equipment that week; they had aura enhancers, paranormal detector guns—all that stuff! They just happened to be in St. Vincent's on that day going from ward to ward, looking for NDEs for the show, and I was the lucky one!"

She beamed at me and I felt a tic go off under my right eye; she was no Flight Bore but some other, hitherto unrecorded species. I hadn't a clue as to what she was talking about but decided to stick it out, not wishing to move to the one empty seat on the plane next to the motor-mouthed Big Hilda, who sat further up, partying heartily with my crew, The Tiny Brocil Fishes, and most of the cut-rate air hostesses who were working the flight.

"Bunkum!" she exclaimed, perceiving my uncomprehending expression with a rapier-like sensitivity. "The TV show on NBC. Sometimes they feature apparitions; sometimes UFOs or hobgoblins—you've seen it, surely?"

"Oh right, Bunkum!" I answered, finally getting it. "Very entertaining, very entertaining. Used to be called *Hokum*, didn't it?" I asked.

"Right. Now you've got it!" she enthused, twisting her little frame around in the seat, a Tom Collins swirling in a plastic cup in her glittering hand.

"ND . . . a whatta?" I begged clarification.

"Near Death Experiences!" she boomed, her New York accent becoming richer as the beverage warmed her vocal cords. "Steinglass said to me: 'We recorded a number of unusual readings on our equipment when you were *out there*. Can you tell us please, Mrs. Weissmuller, if you were conscious of anything during the ninety seconds when your heart stopped beating?' This was on TV! I'm famous in Brooklyn!"

"Great, great," I said, grabbing a hostess who had managed to tear herself away from my partying crew to work the aisles. I ordered us more drinks.

"So I said to Steinglass—now remember: I was flat on a hospital bed at the time, but they brought in a makeup girl, very professional—I said, 'Oh . . . it was wonderful! Suddenly there was this light. A bright white

THE OTHER LIFE OF BRIAN

light and I floated up into it. I looked down and I could see the doctors and nurses . . . and myself, lying on the operating table! The next thing, I'm moving along a tunnel of white light, just drifting up through it. I felt at peace, beautiful, happy. Then, I'm on the other side of the tunnel and I'm in a sort of room. It's white, but I can't make out any walls. And then the most wonderful thing! All my relatives are there! Mother, father, uncles, aunts. My brother Abraham is there . . . my sister-in-law, my grandparents—on both sides—all there to meet me!'

"We communicated without words. It was just this warm feeling of love. Quite overwhelming. But then, suddenly, something told me I was not ready. That I shouldn't be there yet. That I had more work to do on earth—then pop! I'm back on the operating table and my heart's beating and I'm coming to. So I tell Steinglass all this and he says to me, 'Mrs. Weissmuller, what is your occupation?' And I say to Steinglass, 'I'm a squid cleaner in the Long Island Fish Processing Factory.' And he says, 'I see.' Then they cut to the other feature about this Russian man who sticks steel needles through his arms, attaches cables to them and pulls trains up hills."

The old biddy looked up at me and grinned, raising her fresh drink in a halfhearted toasting gesture before downing a goodly slug.

At that point we were interrupted by Carruthers, who plonked himself down on the floor in the aisle next to me and attempted some end of tour banter that I did not respond to with any enthusiasm, preferring the old lady's most intriguing tale. He quickly plummeted into a dense stupor before Stouffer lurched up, poured some water down his neck, and managed to rouse him enough to return to the front of the plane, where the jollities were still going on full swing. Carruthers had left a fresh Vodka Iceberg on my tray table, though, which I downed in one gulp, having chugalugged the last one, doubtful as to whether the stewardesses would ever bother to get back to normal service again.

"Ah, thank you," the lady sighed gratefully as she finished her drink, apparently not noticing ten minutes had passed since her last utterance. "You're a nice boy. You're that pop singer, aren't you?"

I mumbled a vague affirmative, but the old dear didn't say a lot after that; she just sat there in a glassy reverie. I tried to think of the relevance of meeting one's relatives on the other side. I could imagine Aunt

Maude and Uncle Ted, drifting through the light to welcome me, as if on wheels. Uncle Ted, bald as a coot singing "Green green, it's green they say, on the far side of the hill," just like that old 45 he used to play every Christmas. And Aunt Maude, caked in talc and Revlon products, utterly sexless, a woman who, in life, probably directed no more than half a dozen sentences my way and all of them chastising, in the course of the sixteen or so Christmases that we had found ourselves in the same house, together with the rest of the family.

My granddad on my mother's side was bound to be right up front of the welcoming throng. There he'd stand, a grizzled old geezer, totally unrecognizable to me seeing as he died when I was about four years old. I'd probably assume he was some old pervert attempting to molest me. Who the hell is this old sod, I'd think, showering me with affection? Then there'd be Granny, on my father's side. Old Nancy was a volatile little vixen who for the rest of her life never spoke a word to me after I turned up one year for the annual holiday wearing a T-shirt with "Rolling Stones" emblazoned on it in some red gukky stuff that you ironed on. Not another word.

Her husband was a doozie, too. Old Pop would get into the Ford Ruby and we'd set off for a day trip to some hellish, tarry English beach, and as soon as we'd arrive, he'd creak out of the car, lie down on the ground (car parks were all grass then), and promptly fall asleep! Nancy would rage at him and make these extraordinary little "cottle cottle" sounds with her ill-fitting false teeth, but to no avail: the old bugger could sleep anywhere, anytime.

One by one, I paraded the relatives across my mind's eye and could not think of any single reason, any display of love or affection that we showed to each other on earth that could possibly warrant a reunion in heaven. I was convinced that not a one of them would be hanging around in the ether, dying, as it were, to shower their young relative with warm and bosomy familial love. In fact, I would have given them damn short shrift if they did; the very idea made my skin crawl!

I glanced at the old biddy. She was asleep, or meditating or something. She looked straight ahead, eyes closed and stock still, the near empty plastic glass in her bony hand standing upright on her knee. I watched the drink in fascination as her grip, before my very eyes, went limp and the vessel tilted over, loosing the remains of its icy contents

THE OTHER LIFE OF BRIAN

down her legs. I went to grab it, but it was too late and the cup flipped over her knee and bounced on the uncarpeted metal floor.

Studying her face, a twinge of apprehension began broiling in my gut. I glanced at a stewardess up front momentarily, then back to that face, which was drained, white as frost despite the substantial applications of old lady pancake and eyeliner.

"Shit," I said, reaching for a pulse. Her little wrist, cooling under my thumb revealed no pulse; not a blip. I could picture that machine in the episode of *Bunkum*, the machine that tells you whether or not your heart's stopped beating, its dot hanging on the screen like an imploding sun as the show's thickly German-accented crew stared into it, scratching their scientific beards in anticipation.

The old girl was dead. Dead as a doorknob, probably halfway on her around-the-world trip. Expired, right there in the seat next to me. She'd probably saved up for this trip: a last adventure before the kin on the other side, in that white, loving light, were finally ready to embrace her fully, into the heavenly fold.

An air hostess finally negotiated the aisle as we hit another pocket of turbulence. She smiled at me quickly but I made no move to respond, lethargy having gripped me, as if in sympathy with the corpse. I remained there for a while, stiff and reluctant, accepting the finality of the situation and in some way gaining quiet inspiration from that vacant mortal coil. I could see her soul, drifting up, the strains of "Hava Nagilla" reaching her spirit eardrums and the sight of her friends, relations, and all the rest of the mensches in her life materializing in her ethereal eyeballs. They were probably going to have a damn good nosh presently: matzo balls in chicken soup, blintzes and bagels and all washed down with a gutful of that Manischewitz muck, sweet as molasses.

I saw no point in raising the alarm: surely one NDE in a lifetime was enough? High time for a simple DE, I reckoned. The good work she had been ordained to continue at the Long Island Fish Processing Factory was over, and that was that. I wasn't going to risk rousing some heart-thumping medic who might be onboard tearing over here and squeezing the life back into the old dear. Let her go, I thought, looking down at that little pixie face, now slumping out of the hood of the ski jacket, a completely blank expression engraved upon it.

Then I saw the thylacine, my imagination suddenly activated, feeding on the spirit essence I fancied still dusted around the cadaver. The thylacine, in a cage, in Kimber, waiting for Carruthers to return, only to find itself yanked off by some brutish emissary of the Clermont Set to a distant, lonely, freezing destination. Oh, I had no doubt that Lucky and his crew would have some cute Tasmanian environment scenario ready for the pup, but I felt a catch in my throat just thinking about it. There seemed a sacred, mythical quality about the beast, and I suddenly experienced a frustrated tingling in my blood that evolved into great shards of remorse and longing. The longing sprung from some deep unfathomable memory, almost cellular in its genesis, and the sudden, shocking vision of my cousin Billy placing a toad in the indentation made by a seesaw, and then letting the seesaw come down on it, flooded my inner eye. "I thought it might like to live there," he'd said, the rotten sadist, barely concealing a chuckle in his voice as I had stared down at the exploded amphibian, its guts oozing out like white cream.

This incongruous childhood memory of the local playground was whisked away and I was back with the corpse, which hadn't moved an inch. Thylacines, corpses, squashed toads, a career reduced to tours of the outback, the frozen north, and God knows where else Steed had up his sleeve—what did it all mean? Extinction. That was the final word at the end of my personal tunnel. No loving relatives, no cozy retirement plans, no welcoming white light. Extinction, plain and simple. And then I knew what I had to do.

Chapter 23

"Carruthers?"
"Aye?"
"BP."
"Ee, Brian! Mega, mega. How are thee? All right?"

I paused for a moment, straining to hear through the clicks and pops in the miles of fiber optics, satellites, or whatever the hell modern technology linked London to Kimber by telephone. I was worried about phone bugs and had been paranoid since we'd returned to London, watching for shadows on the streets, imagining the Clermont Set to be an arm of Orwell's Thought Police now that we were literally into the proverbial 1984.

It was old Mrs. Weissmuller and her sudden demise that had plunged me into this state. I had been existing on parallel levels since the moment she'd pegged it on the plane, flip-flopping between normal senses and some unusual radar-like wider arc. I thought I could see through a person's skin and perceive a glowing intangible within. I walked as if my legs were folded up into a lotus position beneath me; I had to look down occasionally to see if they actually appeared so, fearing the whole of London staring at me.

"Carruthers, is it still there?" There was no immediate response, as if Carruthers were looking around the room. A clear vision of the oaf flashed into my mind. He was glancing down at his lime green boxing shorts, the telephone held out from his ear. This mental apparition was so tactile, I could feel the country silence in the hall where the phone was. I could smell bread, hedgehog pâté, and damp, chilly air.

"What's that, Brian?"
"The fucking thylacine, Carruthers!" I hissed through my teeth. "Is it still there?"

"Oh aye, Towser's in t'cage. Went out early this morning an' 'ad a good workout, 'e did. Got on the scent of rabbit. Couldn't catch 'im— 'e's too slow for that, but the bugger can smell 'em a mile off and flushes 'em out so's I can get a good shot at 'em. Crackin!"

"They haven't come for him yet then?" I asked, a stunning rendition of that great lummox Carruthers and the stripy thylacine, now big as a Labrador, appearing suddenly on this new movie screen in my head.

"Not yet," he answered glumly.

"Good. Listen Carruthers. Are you still in touch with that air hostess?"

"Which one?"

"The one who smuggled the animal over, you twit!"

"Oh, Miss Mepps. Aye, nibs. Got Miss Mepps's phone noomber. Lives in London, she does."

"Give her a call and ask her when she's going back to Tasmania. Ask her when her next flight is. Got it?"

"Aye . . . are you thinking what . . ."

"Just do it, Carruthers, there's a chap."

"Nibs. Call thee when I get 'er. Farff."

I paced around the flat, butterflies traversing my stomach as I awaited Carruthers' call. I kept going over to the big bay windows and looking down onto the wide tree-lined street. Two young, svelte Arab lads were hanging around by an ancient plane tree three doors down, both wearing trench coats and tossing the prickly casing of a plane tree seedcase back and forth to each other. Something about their witless game was making them chuckle. They made me uneasy. The whole gusty vista of that street in fact, and the empty creaking of the floorboards under the royal blue carpet, had me nervy and lonesome. I wished I could just get on a plane and go to America and be with my family and forget the harebrained scheme that I was about to embark on, a scheme that could well land me in very serious kimber indeed.

I picked through the mail I had brought up from downstairs on my return from the Arctic. Sure enough, the Baedburger's tiresome lawyers had concocted a reply to the last imaginative gem that I had sent them in what felt like years past.

THE OTHER LIFE OF BRIAN

Dear "Sir" Porker:

Since receiving your last correspondence, which we have had photocopied, enlarged and framed, we have received a bill from the Holy Order of American Jaffas, amounting to the sum of $30,139.15. This, they claim, is their rightful due in compensation for your half-uncle's "criminal and scandalous" neglect of duties while in their employ, and is to be paid in full in lieu of the Baedburger's receipt of his estate.

It appears the Jaffas have received word of Mr. Bacon's death and in their impoverishment have decided legal action is a necessary step to restore the once grand order he allegedly brought down.

The Lombardi Memorial Hospital of Franklin D. Roosevelt Island, NY. have also filed a claim for $15,000.00 in recompense for their boarding and treatment of Mr. Bacon in the last five months of his life. This leaves a total of $25,010.35. Our legal fees for handling the claim on behalf of the Baedburgers are $7,000.00 Presumably yours will amount to a similar figure. This leaves $11,010.35, $5,000.00 of which will be demanded in state taxes which leaves a grand total of $6,010.35. One moment . . . the telephone is ringing—excuse us Mr. "Sir" Porker. That was the Canadian government informing us that $5,953.10 is due to them in back taxes for the seven hectares of land Mr. Bacon owned in New Caledonia. This leaves a grand total of $57.25. Would you accept a check? Loretta and Gaylord Baedburger have decided not to continue with their claim. The money's yours.

Very truly yours,
Messrs. Goldtraub, Cardbaum & Silvermein

I fumbled for my fountain pen, ready to dash off a suitable opprobrious reply when the phone rang and the dulcet tones of Carruthers grated into my already cranked-up irritability.

"Aye, BP. Carruthers." And once again, my febrile brain projected a pristine vision across my inner eye; I could see the thylacine, loping through the English countryside, slinking across a misty meadow with the gangly Carruthers floundering behind, a long-barreled rifle in his right hand.

"Yes," I said, trying to focus on the job in hand.

"Got Miss Mepps, nibs. Very lucky, she's on a flight tomorrow night, 7 P.M., Heathrow. Could 'ave missed 'er easy."

"She's going to Tasmania, Carruthers?"

"Aye, farff. Tassy it is."

"OK, Carruthers," I said, thinking of Miss Mepps, the Stewardess From Hell, with her trampoline skin from the cut-price facelift.

"Where is she?"

"She's in 'er flat on the Peabody Estate—Victoria, down by Scotland Yard."

"She's in London? Great. Carruthers, listen to me carefully . . ."

Chapter 24

With nothing more than a large shoulder bag for luggage, I strode out of the house at noon the next day and muscled through the chilly wind toward my car. My eyes went immediately to the young, sloe-eyed Arabs who were in exactly the same spot as the day before, as if they had been there all night. There they were, standing not two feet from my silver Lancia, nonchalantly tossing their prickly seedcase about until they saw my determined figure striding down the front steps in their direction. Quickly, and with a slick insouciance, the pair eased off down the street a little, still tossing the seedcase, their trench coats flapping out behind them in the breeze as they threw glances back at me. I could afford but a cursory assessment due to the minefield of dog turds I routinely have to dodge on my street (the richer the neighborhood in London, the more remiss the dog owners), but I could see by their clothing and assured demeanor that these boys had spent a good deal of time in England and were most probably educated here. They lacked the coarseness of your general Edgeware Road fundamentalists who always appeared to me to be uncomfortable on concrete, as if sand would be their chosen medium.

I made it to the car, my feet free of dog shit, and watched the youths speeding up as they turned the corner of my street into the adjoining crescent. The outlandish, almost psychotropic effect I had been experiencing since my time with the old Maven of Death on the plane returned with a vengeance, having been relatively calm for most of the previous day after my phone conversations with Carruthers. Now, as I sat in the Lancia's cracked custom leather seat gunning the throaty engine, I could swear I saw the black sickle of the Grim Reaper himself protruding from the arm of one of the Arabs just before he disappeared around the corner.

This vision hovered in front of my eyes, repeating and superimposing itself wherever I looked, and I had to slap myself hard across the cheek to get rid of it.

I drove off toward Marble Arch, struggling to remain in earthly consciousness by studying the London scenario: the Pakistanis in the windows of their video and computer stores that flanked Edgeware Road before the overpass; the rich Saudis in their Mercedeses, cruising past casinos not one hundred yards further down; the occasional bum, skulking along in search of a rare rubbish bin from which to extricate his rotting dinner.

It all seemed to help, and my hallucinatory state decayed somewhat after an altercation with a spud-like cabby who attempted to cut me up at Marble Arch.

"Fuckin' eye-ties!" he yelled, as I forced my way into the swarming stream of traffic on the roundabout.

"Get off an' milk it!" I shouted back, this, in my best cockney accent from my mother's side.

Gunning the Lancia down past Victoria Station, I hooked a right opposite New Scotland Yard, finding St. Peters Street and the brown brick buildings of the Peabody Estate. I parked the car at a meter and hurried into a courtyard, hoping it was the right place. Everything seemed to go into slow motion as I glanced back at the street and saw a red Ford Escort going by and a youthful, tan face flash a pair of dark almond eyes in my direction. Then quickly, a hand came up, pulling the lapel of a trench coat to conceal them.

Bahá'í! That's who those slippery Arabs were—the thick-fingered sect with the lulling hypnotic tones who believed me to be the reincarnation of their guru! They were back, stalking me again, just as they had in Sweden. I thought back to yesterday in my flat, trying to remember any phone calls that had resulted in mechanical, dreamlike behavior on my part. But I drew a blank, recalling only my words with Carruthers and a quick call to Fortesque full of terse orders and instruction dumped onto his answering machine, and I divined that whatever leaps my imagination was taking were most probably stimulated purely by the bizarre transmutation I had glommed from the corpse on the plane. But surely, a Bahá'í attack could not be far behind.

I found the right building and bounded up the steps, suddenly feeling feisty, taking strength from the knowledge that if I had beaten them once, I could beat them again. I rang the doorbell and the suspicious, darkling eyes of Miss Mepps greeted me, her dyed black hair swept back off her forehead to reveal the taut and artificially tanned skin of her pinchy face.

THE OTHER LIFE OF BRIAN

"Carruthers? He's here," she said, vaguely ushering me in, her affected middle-class accent as transparent as the face job.

"Hi, Miss Mepps," I said, trying to warm up the chilly reception she'd given me. "How's the hound?"

"Carruthers?" she repeated in the direction of the back of the apartment. For some reason, the Stewardess From Hell remained true to my initial impression of her; just as she showed on the flight to Tasmania months ago, her attitude toward me was one of disdain, as if my mere presence offended her. I tried to recall any action on my part that could have initiated her attitude, but ordering a beer slightly too soon on the flight seemed the only thing that could have set her off.

"Coom on, Towser, coom on, lad!" Carruthers came swiveling in from a door at the back of the room, the thylacine on a leash tangling between the great white poles that served as the soundman's legs. The sight of the creature sent a chill down my spine. There it stood, straining on the leash in my direction, bestial and wolfish, the trademark stripes black as coal across its upper body, saliva dripping from its great, gnarly jaws and its powerful feet firmly planted on the cheap, paisley patterned carpet. Carruthers wrestled with the leash and grinned at me inanely as the thylacine began beating its stiff tail into a dusty aspidistra that stood glumly in a tinfoil wrapped pot.

"How the devil are we going to keep that thing quiet?" I asked, feeling my plan collapse around me. "Its bloody *huge*, Carruthers!" It's a full grown specimen. How are we going to get this monster onto the plane?"

"Tranks" was the teenage giant's one word reply.

I suddenly felt dull, immersed in ennui and close to calling the whole thing off, but I asked for the bathroom, deciding a spot of water on the back of the neck might do me good. I had no idea what "tranks" was supposed to mean and took it to be the dark side of "nibs," or some such Northern nonsense. But when I studied the open medicine cabinet in Miss Mepps's bathroom, its meaning became apparent as the sight of numerous bottles, clearly labeled and crammed with a variety of tempting-colored capsules and pills greeted my eyes.

Tranquilizers, and lots of them. Miltown, Valium, Librium, Ativan, plus a bottle of yellow tablets with a long word ending in "drine" on the label. Speed, obviously—the air hostesses little helper. I stifled the urge to gobble a cocktail of the stuff and headed back out into the living room.

"How?" I asked, crashing a cuddling session between the middle-aged air hostess, the thylacine, lolling its girt tongue around their faces, and Carruthers, his red hair presiding over the whole spectacle like a flaming spaceship.

"Oh aye," he said, unfolding up to his feet from the ghastly red velvet sofa where this display had been enacted. "See, in t'jungle, where I got Towser 'ere, the chief Abo' stuffed 'im full of medicinal plants like I told you. Sent the little booger right off. Chap gave me a supply and Miss Mepps kept slippin' it to 'im at every fuel stop. I've got a set of works, we'll just crush some pills up like, an' shoot 'im up, farff. Kimber an' goodnight. Not a problem, nibs."

"Not a problem? What about the stench?" I queried, my nostrils flaring like black holes at the powerful canine-like whiff that permeated the room. "This animal may not be related to dogs, but he sure stinks like one—and a dead one at that."

Miss Mepps gave me a look, as if I had insulted her yet again, and for a moment I wondered if the marsupial was entirely to blame for the stench in that place.

"Don't worry, darling," she said sarcastically, "I'll smother him in eau de something or other—it's the size I'm worried about. I'll have to put him in that giant over there." She pointed to an oversized canvas bag rumpled around the base of the TV stand. "You just relax and do the pop star bit. Get drunk or whatever it is you blokes do all the time, all right?" she said, her voice beginning to drip venom. "But I'm coming clean if I get nailed with the thing," she added, snooting her pinchy nose up in a superior manner.

"Hey, it was you who brought it here!" I said firmly, the temptation to stride over and clout the bitch around the ears gathering momentum.

"Stop moaning, *pop star*. We'll pull it off."

"I'm moaning?" I exclaimed, unable to contain myself any longer and reaching for the nearest object, which happened to be a ragged-looking pineapple sitting atop a bowl of fruit, most of it in various stages of decomposition. I lurched toward Miss Mepps, the prickly item shaking in my right hand before me and a low growl escaping from my curling lips. Her black eyes popped out as if on stalks as I lunged, fully intent on pole-axing her with a rotting pineapple. But Carruthers was off the mark with surprising speed and stuck out one of those dog-bone legs without even moving from the couch and I tumbled over like a felled tree. The spiky pineapple, however, was still firmly in my grasp as I came down, my arm extended before me, and found its mark in the crotch of Miss Mepps's navy blue polyester skirt, which raised a doglike yelp from the shocked woman.

Nanoseconds later, my face hit the floor between Miss Mepps's feet, and the thylacine leapt into the imbroglio followed by the top half of Carruthers, who was trying desperately to separate the tongue-lolling beast before danger ensued.

After a confusing eternity immersed in the duel attack of Miss Mepps's feet and the Tasmanian tiger's rank breath, Carruthers managed to pull the animal back with one hand and lifted me up with the other as if I were some kind of motorized toy that had gone berserk.

Miss Mepps sat holding her heart and panting fiercely. I stood, also short of breath, staring stupidly at the pineapple's stalk, which I still gripped firmly in my hand; the fruit's semirotten flesh lay in the stewardess's lap, oleaginous, adding yet more offensive odor to the atmosphere. Towser the thylacine sat at Carruthers' heel, panting and letting its tongue pick up what few cooling molecules of air were left in the room.

"Well," said Miss Mepps standing up, her normal disdainful expression back in place. "That pineapple came all the way from Hawaii, you bastard! Try to control this fool will you, Carruthers?" she pleaded, giving me the evil eye.

"I'll just go and change my skirt and get the tranquilizers ready, shall I? We'd better get going, I want to get that animal on the plane in good time, in case the hold gets short of space."

She went to the bathroom, giving me a wide berth. I made to apologize to Carruthers but caught myself. It wasn't my fault we were in this predicament—I was merely following the trail my vision of extinction had prompted; the vision produced by my proximity to the old lady's corpse as its spirit fled into the unknown. Carruthers had snaffled the animal up from its rightful home and started this whole mess off. What with the Bahá'í and the Clermont Set on my heels it was no wonder I was attacking air hostesses. Plus, I was throwing away fifty million fucking yen!

"Spot o' kimber, there," said Carruthers cheerfully as he pulled a syringe from the pocket of his shorts. He was wearing a tentlike brown T-shirt with the word "Tupperware!" imprinted on it in a ghastly avocado shade.

"Enjoyed that little romp didn't thee, Towser, eh lad? Time for your nap now, boy. Aye, off you go . . ."

The brown van with the black tinted windows had been tailing us since the junction of Kensington Church Street and Kensington High Street, and not far behind that hovered the red Ford Escort. Wind whipped the streets ominously as I hung a left and gunned the Lancia down Warwick Road. Through the blustering raincoats and flapping shopping bags, I caught occasional glimpses of eerie, glowing spirits beneath the human vessels of pedestrians. Again, I wondered if I'd picked up a dose from Stouffer's damned joker stamps that I'd fingered so carelessly back on Bear Island, and if I was having some kind of delayed reaction. I'd certainly experienced enough acid flashes years after the late sixties to know the feeling by now, but this seemed even weirder than that, and I began to doubt that merely sitting next to a corpse on a converted cargo plane from the Arctic had been enough to cause this kind of psychic upheaval. At first, I made no mention to Carruthers of either my expanded consciousness or the down-to-earth fact that we were being followed; he stretched his ungainly frame across the backseat, seemingly unconcerned with my sudden throttle-jamming bursts of speed, staring gormlessly ahead as if watching a dull movie.

But as I began to think back on that return flight from Iceland, turning the details over in my mind as carefully as my flashing brain would allow, I recalled an incident that had occurred only a half hour before the old lady had snuffed it. I remembered Carruthers drifting back and drunkenly planting himself on the floor of the aisle next to me. He'd attempted some kind of emotional end of tour–type conversation, the kind of inebriated male-bonding celebratory rant that often follows weeks of hardship mixed with triumphant shows, some of which the Polar gigs, despite my cynicism, most definitely were. Our feeble attempts at chumminess had fizzled out within minutes, however: I was more interested in what the old lady had to say, and the soundman had suddenly fallen into a deep sleep in midsentence as if hit on the head with a mallet. Before I'd begun to resume conversation with the old Long Island Jewess, Stouffer lurched back to our section of the plane and poured some water down Carruthers' neck in order to rouse him and return his lanky frame to the partying up front, and as he'd dragged the half conscious teenage giant away, I'd noticed Carruthers' beverage sitting on my tray table next to my empty glass. There'd been a lull in the drinks service, mainly because the stewardesses were hanging with my crew, yukking it up and pouring out the freebies, so I'd taken a sip of Carruthers' drink, and, deciding that it was merely a nice, refreshing Vodka Iceberg and nothing more, had downed it in one. This sudden reminiscence disturbed me thoroughly as we slowed at the lights on the Chiswick roundabout leading to the M4; I felt compelled to investigate the nature of that drink.

"Um, Carruthers?" I ventured, dreading an answer that would actually explain my predicament.

"Aye?" he replied dully.

"Do you remember on the flight back from the Arctic sitting next to me and leaving a drink on my tray table?"

"So that's what 'appened to it!" he exclaimed, suddenly enthusiastic after his recent lassitude. I feared the worst.

"What was in it?" I hazarded, gritting my teeth with anxiety.

"Fookin' poison dart frog toxin!" he unhesitatingly replied.

"Uh huh," I said, as stoically as possible. "Poison dart frog—"

"Aye, when we said 'Big Drugs on Bear Island,' we meant drugs, plural, meaning more than one like—not just the KP3."

"KP3?"

"Aye, that's what they call the gamblin' potion—actually a very refined form of the poison dart frog stuff—the stuff you drunk were much cruder—although I'm not sure I'm supposed to spell it out like that to anyone not in the know, like. But I suppose you are in the know now, aren't thee?"

"Yes, Carruthers, I suppose I am," I said, beginning to seethe and already looking around the car for some heavy object with which to crown the bugger with.

"OK, Carruthers," I said, measuring my words very carefully. "What does this shit do, exactly?"

"Well, the crude stuff you took is like the early stages of the development of KP3—the gamblin' drug. Those fookin' Russian scientists like to catch a buzz, no question, and they managed to isolate a very discreet—I say *very discreet*—and selective amount of the *exact* molecules from the fookin' dart frog like, leavin' out the stuff that puts you in't serious kimber—the fookin' bit what kills you, like. Oh, and they're also faffin' around with some Arizona Diamondback rattlesnake venom—now *that* I'm lookin' forward to givin' a bash. Nibs."

"I see," I said, staring at the soundman in the car's rearview mirror as he sat in the backseat, curled across its length, the twin towers of his long legs, bent at the knee, jutting out of his lime green boxing shorts and obscenely hairless, almost touching the tan material of the Lancia's roof.

"Aye," he went on nonchalantly. "With the poison dart frog, they isolated the useful chemicals, kept a batch of the crude form—the one that makes thee see skeletons walkin' around and shit—the one you're on—and then moved on from there till they finally sorted the finer stuff that pulls up your luck DNA; you know, the gamblin' drug."

"And pray tell me, my little amateur chemist," I said sarcastically, guessing that abject anger would soon replace it. "How long is this stuff going to affect me?"

"S'different with everyone, so far as I know. Comes in rushes. Couple of days . . . a few weeks. But drink takes the edge off, Brian!" he announced cheerily. "Aye, if I were thee, I'd keep a steady flow of booze goin' down yer trap—that'll keep thee out of serious kimber, farff."

"I see," I said, feeling something boiling inside me, something akin to homicidal, psychopathic rage. And then I could not help but yell at the top of my lungs: "Why the fuck are you walking around fucking airplanes with drinks full of fucking poison bloody dart frog toxin? You brainless twat!"

"Aye, steady on, Beep," the rotter replied blandly. "Fookin' Stouffer gave it to me. I'd already 'ad two hits of Superman and 'alf a Joker already, plus enough vodka to bugger up a battleship. What the 'eck are you doin' snarfin' back other people's drinks for anyway? Not even *I'd* do that."

This last sentence he'd uttered with some indignation, and I had to admit, he had me dead to rights.

"Right," I finally responded, the anger suddenly draining from me and a dull acceptance taking its place.

"So I need to take the edge off with a few drinks, and it'll go away eventually?"

"Far as I know, nibs. At least I haven't heard of anyone being *permanently* damaged by it . . . yet. Course, hardly anyone's taken it to speak of—it's not exactly on the streets y'know."

We had left Miss Mepps behind in the traffic driving her bottom-of-the-line Peugeot, the thylacine like a sack of spuds in the backseat, pumped full of hypnotics and tranquilizers. Carruthers had worked out some outlandish equation for the mix, which seemed equal parts Valium, Ativan, and Miltown, with a two-capsule topping of Nembutal.

"For dreams," he had insisted, as if this dangerous cocktail were a commonly prescribed relaxant for subduing wondrous, officially extinct species.

As we hit the M4, I lunged the motor into the eighties but still the ominous van with the tinted windows that had been following us all along weaved in and out of the traffic, doggedly keeping pace. I prayed that whoever was at the wheel did not know that we had separated from Miss Mepps and thus had no idea that the thylacine was with her, asleep in her undistinguished Peugeot. If this was the case, we had a damn good chance of at least getting on that plane and getting the animal out of the country. But as I crunched the Lancia into a space in Heathrow's long-term car park, I saw the brown van pull in also, its tinted windows flat under the gray sky.

"Move it, Carruthers," I exclaimed, "there's the shuttle!"

We grabbed our bags and dashed for the bus, which promptly pulled off. I sat down in the back and watched out the window as two men who looked like nightclub bouncers leapt out of the van and gave the Lancia the once-over, then leapt back in, parking their vehicle in a space nearby.

"Ee, thou look a bit pale, BP," said Carruthers. "Are thee all right?"

"Aye," I answered, not for the first time slipping into the soundman's lingo. "I mean yes . . . yes, Carruthers, I'm fine. I need a drink, that's all."

"Ee, farff! That's the ticket. Plenty on t'plane. Miss Mepps'll be doling out the freebies by t'bucket load! Nibs it'll be, no question!"

I could well imagine the ossified air hostess pouring alcohol down Carruthers' gannet-like gullet but figured her role with me would remain Stewardess From Hell, and I would have to buy my own.

We picked up our tickets and joined the check-in line even though I had pleaded with the ticket agent to give us boarding cards; we had only large shoulder bags and no luggage to check in but had to join the queue anyway. I shuffled impatiently, wincing at the clamorous amplification of voices and the clanging of metal trolleys, willing the line to move faster, silently cursing the slow-motion responses of the officious ticket cadets as they went through their mechanical rituals, asking Pakistanis, Jews, Arabs, and English alike if they had any explosive devices tucked away in their luggage. And then a tap on my shoulder made me jump. I spun around and there were the goons, blobby-faced and shoehorned into their cheap suits—one even wore black sunglasses as if he were working for the CIA.

"Where is it?" asked the one who had prodded me.

My intestines rippled like snakes and threw my stomach into a spasm; the saliva on my tongue seemed to take on a life of its own, dividing into separate rivulets before drying out completely. The tic under my right eye went off, closely followed by a similar physical dysfunction under my left eye. I nudged Carruthers, who had not noticed the impending danger. The goons looked up at the teenage giant and reacted, their violent superiority taking a slight dent at the spectacle of this pole-like human, his expression no less stupid than theirs. I saw a policeman directing a squat Japanese lady nearby and took courage from the sheer publicness of the place.

"What?" I said, a cheeky edge in my voice.

"The dog," said the goon, his monotone south London accent dulled into flatness by years of supreme thickness. The Clermont Set might be aristocrats, but they certainly didn't hire Sloane Rangers to do their dirty work.

"We were s'posed to be collecting a dog from ginger 'ere," said the other thug as he closed in on me, "but we 'eard 'e'd left for London last night with it. We were told it comes from Tasmania . . . that's where this flight's goin', right moosh?"

It had been years since I had heard anyone use the word "moosh," and I snorted involuntarily. The policeman walked by again, chatting amiably to a uniformed pilot. The two thugs stepped back slightly, trying to act as if they were in the queue. Something snapped in me: if the Clermont Set wanted the thylacine, they could come and get it themselves.

"Fuck off," I said, right to the hired thugs' faces, and then the line suddenly cleared and it was my turn at the check-in desk. Carruthers bellied up to the counter with me, casting back cocky smirks at the two performers, who seemed at a loss for ideas.

But they soon gathered their paltry sum of wits about them and made for the ticket counter, closely followed by the two sloe-eyed Bahá'i.

Chapter 25

Miss Mepps doddered down the aisle as the plane taxied toward takeoff position. She looked both calm and jumpy as she adjusted the seat belt on a child, a speed/tranquilizer cocktail obviously to blame for this obscene phenomenon. As her wrinkled hands alighted on the little girl's torso, her face was a paradigm of diligent kindness, but as she tightened the seat belt, I saw her jaw clench and her ears move, causing the tacky koala bear earrings she wore to jiggle menacingly.

She returned to her slow motion journey, giving me the speedy side of her humor as she passed by my seat, flashing a tense, disdainful grimace in an infinitely tiny space of time. I was already wired to the teeth with the knowledge that the hired marsupial wolf-nappers were onboard, ten rows back in the smoking section, and presumably, the young Bahá'í were on the plane, too. And I hoped to Christ that the message I had left on Fortesque's answering machine was picked up by the stalwart fellow in time—certainly, so far, there was no sign that it had been. At least I had Carruthers with me and his unusual countenance seemed to confuse the two thugs; but I didn't fancy our chances much if they were to remove us from a public place. There would be a huge amount of kimber delivered at the hands of those two monsters if we didn't cough up the beast, and I wasn't sure that withstanding torture would prove something my delicate system would approve of.

My eyes bounced around in their sockets as the jet lifted off, and the altered consciousness that had plagued me since the demise of the Maven of Death and the ingestion of Carruthers' poison dart frog derivative returned with a vengeance. It had been somewhat quelled by the recent adrenaline rush ignited by the Clermont Set's hired muscle, paranoia and fear being comparatively normal states. But as the plane thundered into the air, I was quite suddenly catapulted into deep hallucination, and every passenger's head in front of me shed its layers of hair and skin until I was thrust into the deathly apparition of a vessel peopled by skeletons, and the very fabric of the interior of that vessel began to crinkle off as if burned and rotted in the fires of hell. Thinking of the purpose of this mission, I immediately flipped back into normality, albeit tainted with trepidation induced by my various pursuers.

This sudden grounding gave me strength, and I glanced over at a normal-looking Carruthers, who was deep into a tattered hardcover entitled *Curing Wolverine Fur for Pleasure and Profit*, and became heartened by the bizarre ability I seemed to have developed in turning the visions off at will—if not as yet finding a use for turning them on in the first place.

Gradually, as the constant thrum of the engines and the warming tingle of two quarter bottles of bad Chardonnay took effect, I relaxed and took courage from the idea that I was on a righteous mission. And with my enemies apparently unaware of our collaborator Miss Mepps, and hopefully, another trump card up my sleeve, the chances of success seemed suddenly quite high. If only I could fend off the hypnotic deviltry of the Bahá'i, and once out of the airport in Tasmania, the brutality of the goons.

A splash of red caught my eye, just beyond the bulkhead—a woman in a hideous satiny muumuu, spinning around out of the service area with a drink in her hand, as red as the curtain-like garment. I did not need to look at her face for identification as my eye fixed on the thin splash of brown, viscous and oily, like old blood, that dissolved into the redness of the liquid: tomato juice and Worcestershire sauce! Without doubt, floating down the aisle toward me like a grotty peacock, closely followed by her two young chappies-in-waiting, was herself, the Mata Horror.

"I knew it, I knew it," I said resignedly as she wafted into the spare seat next to me, her bare feet thonged up in some cruddy old Himalayan sandals.

"Brian," she said, fixing me with her googly brown eyes and flipping the tray table open for her drink. "Things are going well for you in the Arctic Circle, aren't they? But some of your subjects were disappointed that you didn't include our songs in your set. You do remember the songs, don't you Brian? Bahá'u'lláh lláh u'áhál u'lláh . . ."

"Yes, yes! I remember the bloody songs, but you're not getting me this time!" I said firmly as I reached into my bag, pulled out some earplugs, and quickly inserted them. "There!" I said firmly. "Now why the fuck haven't you people got the message, eh? Look, you: tomato juice with Worcestershire sauce and . . . and dry-roasted peanuts, right?" I said, pointing to her foul beverage. "Me: large quantities of alcohol and steak and chips, OK? That's a *big* difference in sensibilities. Now leave me alone. I'm going on holiday with my good friend Carruthers. Go on, piss off!"

She looked at me as if I were a naughty boy throwing a tantrum. The two young acolytes (whom I recognized as the fellows who had been hanging around outside my flat for days) lounged in the aisle next to her, incredibly, still tossing the plane tree seedcase casually between themselves.

"And tell Mutt and Jeff here if I ever catch them buggering about near my motor again I'll bang their little tinted heads together until their ears bleed."

The Mata ignored the violence of my threat and laid a thick-fingered hand on my knee. I grimaced at the sight of those still grubby nails, left unclean in what I now assumed to be some cryptic reading of the archaic rules of the cult.

"Oh, holiday is it, Brian?" she said, mild chastising sarcasm edging her voice.

"Ee oop. Oo's the tart, Beep?" asked Carruthers, folding the top half of his body over into the seat next to me and staring straight at Lolla's face.

"Carruthers, this is Lolla," I said dejectedly, fearing a match made in hell on the horizon. "She's a Bahá'í who believes I am in fact the reincarnation of Bahá'u'lláh, the long dead founder of her alleged religion."

"Ee, nibs!" exclaimed Carruthers guilelessly. I could see I would have to fill the soundman in on my previous experiences with these people—and quickly, in the hope that he could continue with the mission if I succumbed to their mind-bending tactics.

"And it is written," said Lolla alarmingly, " 'the manifestation shall return to earth and he shall initiate the dying as they spring free to the eternal and the beasts of mythology shall be his subservient attendants.' "

I started sweating under my Dutch army parka and a buzzing went off between my temples identical to the sound I had heard an infinity ago, under the water of my pool in America, when Steed had called to press me into the Swedish tour.

"What a load of tosh!" I exclaimed, a crystalline reenactment of the old lady dying next to me on the plane and my first view of the thylacine in the rain forest exploding into my inner eye. Lolla was on to something, no doubt about it. They'd obviously been keeping tabs on me all this time and my admonishment came out flat and unconvincing. But I had a strand of grit within me that would not be crushed into a listless and malleable powder. Come what may, I was convinced that somehow I would make it through this time, individuality intact.

"Touch o' kimber 'ere, eh Beep?" asked Carruthers, finally twigging that Lolla might not be such an easy lay.

The Mata Horror got up, not wishing to tangle with the teenage giant, and her slippery companions made way for her, ready to rope themselves around her if trouble threatened.

"Damn right, Carruthers," I said. "Kimberish as it gets. Don't let these bastards sing to you, OK? On no account let them get into your eardrums. Got me?" Carruthers looked up at Lolla uncomprehendingly.

"If thou say so, Beep. If thou say so."

"We'll be seeing you, Bahá'u'lláh incarnate," said Lolla, as the three of them swished off up the aisle.

"Jeez," I sighed, tugging my jacket off and gulping for air.

"Nice-lookin' tart," said Carruthers, watching the red curtain disappear past the bulkhead.

"Are you kidding, Carruthers? And what is this disturbing literature you're thumbing through here?" I demanded, grabbing the crusty book that he still held in his hands. Inside were depictions of those vicious giant weasels, forty inches long and forty pounds in weight, hung up in various stages of skinning. *"Curing Wolverine Fur for Pleasure and Profit?"* I sneered disgustedly. I slapped the thing back into his hands and at that very moment, a minute molecule of tobacco odor from the back of the plane teased my nostrils, instantly curing me of a nonsmoking binge I had been on since the beginning of the Arctic Circle tour.

"Fuck it. I'm going to the back to scrounge a smoke. You're coming too, Carruthers."

"Nibs," said the soundman, twisting his difficult frame into an upright position.

THE OTHER LIFE OF BRIAN

We shuffled into the space around the toilets at the very back of the plane. It was crowded down there, like some kind of party was going on fueled by the excessive amounts of booze typically consumed by smokers on airplanes. My eyes stung and teared up as I entered the curtain of noxious chemicals that hung across the very back row of seats like the door to a private nightclub. I wanted to turn back but the nicotine bugs were already filing through my bloodstream, marching like army ants from my brain to my heart, which pulsed excitedly in anticipation.

Inside the cloud, people were laughing and holding beer cans, thick streams of smoke rising from their hands and mouths. On these long flights, even Stewardesses From Hell refrained from forcing people back into their seats and the bodies joggled about merrily, easing left and right as folk edged between the throng into the toilets. I studied the faces—the usual lot were there: tubby English businessmen, red nosed and hurtling toward their first heart attacks, on the way to Bombay to rip off a few peasants in the spice trade; trim, chain-smoking Japanese, dutifully plowing through three packs a day to hold up their country's revenue as their government dictates; a few neurotic-looking young women, going along with the chatting-up process but not about to disappear into the toilet with one of the paunchy businessmen; a couple of pasty youths, getting shit-faced and talking football. I squinted through the cigarette fallout, seeking out a likely candidate who might graciously give me a coffin nail without insisting on boring the pants off me. But they all seemed equally likely to prove irksome, and as the nicotine lust reached a mindless fever pitch, my patience was revoked completely; salivating like an idiot, I lunged toward the back of a big fellow in a cheap, dark suit.

"Excuse me, could you . . ." but the words dropped away as I stared up into the smoke-shrouded face of one of London's finest performers, standing there with his clone buddy.

" 'Ello, Brian . . . what? Oh, you wanna fag, do yer? 'Ere ya go, mate. Rothmans. Lovely, eh?"

I knew I could not avoid the Clermont Set's goons for the entire flight and figured earlier that they'd be smokers and would be in the back somewhere, but the craving had made me lose my mind and momentarily forget their presence on the plane. Borrowing cigarettes from them had not been part of my agenda, and I cursed my stupidity.

"Yeah . . . yeah, thanks," I said, resigning myself for the sake of the worst drug known to man. Without hesitation I took the perfect cylinder from his ham-like mitt, ripped off the filter tip, and accepted a light from his chartreuse disposable lighter. Carruthers edged in next to me, nudging a laughing blonde out of the way with his white elbow. After two quick pulls on the Rothmans, I felt the poison drill through my bloodstream, turning my legs to jelly instantly. My head spun and I felt my lungs go mushy as old wounds were reawakened. I cursed myself silently but kept dragging away, staring through smarting eyes at the pie-faced hooligan whose chest was almost touching my face in the confines of the narrow gangway.

"Oo," said the goon, flicking his head back to his partner, "breaks the filter off, does Brian. Tough little bastard, are we, Brian?"

I said nothing, grinding the dappled tip into a cottony mush in my sweaty fingers. Both goons loomed over me, smoke swirling around them like the horns of hell, and I felt the door flip open in my head and groaned slightly as both men transformed into seething Halloween devils, their cigarettes now the great prongs of pitchforks.

Concentrating hard on the tobacco fix, I managed to dispel this deathly vision and shrink the world back into the friendlier dimensions of braggadocio and fear. A stewardess, already loosened up by the gathering of flight hours, fought through the bodies and actually took drink orders. The goons wanted whiskey and Coke, Carruthers ordered neat vodka, and I asked for brandy, remembering my soundman's advice about keeping the alcohol level up in my bloodstream in order to keep the poison dart frog toxin down. A Japanese businessman laughed heartily, smoke spewing from his head like a steel factory. I just stood there, inches from the thug's chest, smelling Brute aftershave spiking through the baccy in waves.

Muscle number two, who stood so close to his pal that they looked like unlikely Siamese twins, brought a hand up to his face and casually scratched his jaw. A heavy gold knuckleduster caught a glint of light, then he smirked at me and Carruthers before slipping the hand back in his pocket to shake off the brutal weapon.

"Ee oop!" boomed Carruthers, leaning over my shoulder as the hand disappeared. "Knuckledusters is fookin' illegal! 'Ow dyer get through t'metal detectors with that then, eh? Give us a look, will ya?"

The thug looked around nervously as people who weren't in the midst of high-volume conversation threw glances in our direction. He stepped forward and hissed up Carruthers' nose.

"Shut the fuck up you great bastard stick insect," he said in a tone that made the word "menacing" sound positively convivial. Carruthers, however, appeared amused, and I found myself feeling a touch of pride creep into my heart, perhaps even a little admiration for the togglehead, albeit grudgingly. And when he leaned into the goon and brought one of his massive army boots down upon those cheap Cuban heels I could not restrain a grin of wonderment from crossing my face.

"Ow! Oi! Oo, you . . . fuckin' cunt!" exclaimed the brute, barely able to keep his voice down. He balled up his fist and readied himself for a punch, but at that moment an air hostess appeared through the curtain of smoke, holding a tray spilling over with drinks.

"Two whiskey and Cokes?" she said cheerfully as the goon's fist unclenched automatically and a forced smile was quickly hoisted across his piggy face.

"And vodka and a brandy for us, Miss," I said grabbing the plastic cups. I was beginning to take a perverse pleasure from the atmosphere of tension and malice; one stray punch could have these turkeys flung off the plane in Bombay. They knew they had to control themselves.

Like a bad pickpocket, I openly plunged my hand into goon number one's jacket, fishing out his Rothmans, which caused him to visibly exsanguinate. " 'Ere, what dyer think? . . . " he began halfheartedly. But I was already placing my drink into the mug's hand and lighting up. I took the cup back from him and stood there, guzzling and puffing smoke into his face. "Want your coffin nails back, pal?"

"Little bastard," he muttered, snatching them out of my hand and fumbling out one for himself. Out of nowhere, Miss Mepps appeared and gave Carruthers a little squeeze as she passed. And in slow motion I saw him twist around, give her a kiss, and say "Ee oop luv, nibs!" before I could do a thing to stop it. The hired nasties tensed their faces up, tiny glimmers of awareness fighting through their congenitally sluggish synapses.

"Well well well," said the one with the cigarettes. "Know each other, eh, Mr. Carruthers?" I elbowed the dolt in the hip before he could blurt anything out but it was too late.

"I might 'ave boffed 'er once, farff," he said cockily. Flummoxed, I reached up and pushed Carruthers back, turning myself to make a hasty getaway. The goons exchanged glances and stared hard at us.

"He . . . ah, he just means . . . you know?" I muttered stupidly. "He's done a few of these stewardess birds in his time, that's what he means. Thanks for the smokes." We broke through the cloud curtain and left the goons standing there, trailing us with their beady eyes.

"Bint's a bit old for you, isn't she Carruthers?" one of them yelled after us, and they cackled viciously, sending a chill down my spine.

"They're both as thick as two short planks," I said to Carruthers as we got back to our seats, "but I think even *they* might have got the picture now."

"Sorry, Beep," he said miserably, pulling at his unruly red hair as if rearranging the gray matter beneath it.

"Ah, don't worry about it, Carruthers. What else are we doing on this flight but smuggling the thylacine back to Tas? They knew that anyway—they just know how now. Makes little difference in the end."

Carruthers sat next to me fiddling idly with his wolverine book, running his spatulate fingers over its crumbling blue spine. He'd gone up in my estimation, proving himself to be a good egg in a pinch, his loyalties to his on-the-road employer impeccable, and I felt that finally, despite his annoying demeanor and habits—qualities that make themselves known instantly in the torturous conditions of rock 'n' roll tours—I was warming up to the lad and perhaps it was time to show him something other than disdain.

"So, Carruthers," I began, shifting uncomfortably in my seat, "do you have, er . . . parents—family and stuff—up in Kimber? Is that where you were born?"

"Aye," the soundman answered, stuffing his book in the seatback and pulling two mini vodkas from the same receptacle.

"Mum's a furrier—makes coats and stuff outta mink mostly. She gets her fur from a mink farm just outside Kimber, plus the gear I supply 'er with from hunting, y'know? And dad's got a garden center just outside of Wally."

The furrier bit made me bristle, but I soldiered on, determined to conjure up some kind of camaraderie no matter what. I looked up at his face, perhaps seeing the man behind it for the first time. There wasn't a great deal going on in there, but I decided to give him the benefit of the doubt for the time being. We slugged the vodka straight from the bottle and continued cagily.

"Hm," I responded finally. "Sounds fairly normal, I suppose. And when did you get into the rock 'n' roll game?"

"Aye well, I used to 'ave a little band—I was playing a fair bit of drums when I was only fifteen like. We was called The Macabre; real goth, like. Nibs guitarist, too—'e's livin' in America now, doin' session work. Jimmy Turkle is 'is name."

"Oh yeah? I've heard of him."

"Aye, makes a fookin' fortune, 'e does. Anyway, when we split up, I did a bit of roadie work for some local outfits and then me and Stouffer teamed up and did a tour with the Neanderthal guitarist. That's 'ow I met your man Steed what manages 'im, and Fortesque. Stouff' and I manage the Nico Teens and a few other little bands and put 'em out on our own label, Fook It! Records."

"Very good, very good. Those fuckin' Nico Teens sell more in the north of England than I do in the entire world by the sound of it."

"Aye, they're doin' all right, but they've got no international cred like you—know what I mean? That counts for a lot. They can't get arrested south of Watford."

"And the Brocils? What's their story?"

"Aye, Tiny Brocil Fishes is headed for t'big time, I reckon. They're on our label at present, but that won't last long: big guns is already sniffin' around; they'll probably end up on Shinto Tool or somethin'."

There was no doubt that Carruthers was a resourceful young chap and had his finger in a few pies. Damned if I wasn't beginning to like the clown.

"Well," I continued as Carruthers caught Miss Mepps's eye and signaled for more drinks. "If I ever need a label I might have a word with you."

"You? On our label? Fookin' 'ell BP, that'd be bloody mega! We'd do you a nibs deal—better than you're gettin' outta Shinto Tool and fookin' Dreadnaught. The advances might not coom up to snuff for you though," he concluded, his ebullience dampening a bit.

"Well, look," I said, warming to the idea of actually going all the way and getting right down to real indie land. "Those labels ain't gonna be coming up with the cash either, the way things are going. New fish to fry—know what I mean?"

"I s'pose . . ."

"And they all just piss me off anyway. What's the point?"

"Ee fookin' 'eckers like BP, we *are there* for you, mate! Fookin' *there!*"

Carruthers seemed so excited at my absurd suggestion that he fairly bounced up and down in his seat.

"All right, we'll talk about it when my deal comes up," I said, already regretting my words but not wishing to burst his bubble just yet. "I can't see Shinto picking up the option anyway. I sometimes feel like our Towser the thylacine: about to become extinct."

At the thought of extinction, the seatback in front of me began to ripple until its cloth padding appeared to peel away, revealing a flaking, bony, skeletal frame. I shook my head rapidly until the image subsided, leaving only a ghostlike residue superimposed upon the gray seat covering.

"You all right, BP?" asked the soundman with some concern.

"Frog toxin lurch," I replied as calmly as possible. "It's passed."

"Aye, well—back to your point," said Carruthers. "Towser and 'is kin are not extinct, are they? And nor are thee. I must admit, I thought 'Knee Trembler' was the only good thing you'd ever done until I worked for you. Now I see all yer stuff is nibs—just different, that's all. Thou has plenty of go in thee, plenty of go. Never say die, Brian. Never say die."

Carruthers looked down at me, his pale gray-green eyes blank as ever but his intent sincere.

"Well damn it, Carruthers, You're a good sort," I said. "A damned good sort. Cheers! And by the way," I continued, another thought regarding my soundman popping into my head, "where did the name 'Carruthers' come from? I mean, it doesn't sound like a Northern name at all . . ."

"Well," he began cagily. "Um, me dad's from an old, old family—ah . . . sort of royalty, actually."

"Royalty? And what's your first name, anyway?"

"First name's Archibald—don't fookin' laugh!"

"Ha! Archibald?"

"Aye, I'm like, fourteenth in line for t'throne."

Carruthers said this with the most sheepish look on his long pale face, almost flushing red with embarrassment. But I was not following his drift at all and looked back at him with a quizzical expression, the neat vodka jockeying for position with an extreme fatigue that had suddenly begun to wash over me.

"What the fuck are you on about, Carruthers?" I slurred. "What *throne*?"

"Er . . . the English throne? Like, y'know, King of England and all."

"Christ!" I exclaimed, almost spitting a mouthful of alcohol onto the seatback.

"I'm actually Thane Archibald Carruthers. His nibs."

I gritted my teeth, suddenly becoming irritated with the jackass again.

"You mean to say, we have two extremely nasty thugs on our tail, armed with knuckledusters and God knows what else, hired by a bunch of upper-crust bastards, and here you are, more upper crust than the fucking lot of them and you're not using it to get us out of this very serious piece of kimber?

"Carruthers," I went on, the boozy slur disappearing from my voice as I digested the full implications of my soundman's admission. "This little bit of information could have proven very useful to us, Carruthers. Do you understand me, man?" I demanded with complete exasperation.

"Aye," replied Carruthers, still looking miserable about his lineage. "I just don't make a big fuss about it, that's all. I mean, it's all in the past, really. Dad prefer's being a bloke who runs a gardenin' center, like. And I just want to bugger around. Besides, I was born oop north and that's 'oo I am, not some poncy southern royalty pooftah. More fookin' trouble than it's worth, all that. I don't need the 'assle."

"Don't need the? . . . "

But I gave up. The man was a conundrum, just like a living, breathing thylacine, and I had to admit it took a lot of gall to throw away the kind of connections that Carruthers could have cultivated had he wished to live an easier life than that of rock 'n' roll roadie.

"Well damn it, man!" I exclaimed after a lenghty pause in which two more mini vodkas appeared from the gangly hand of Thane Archibald Carruthers, which we unceremoniously swallowed in short order. "You're all right, Carruthers! Bollocks to royalty! And God save the Queen!"

And with that, we chinked plastic bottles and grinned at each other.

Then Carruthers closed his eyes and immediately fell into a six-hour catnap.

Chapter 26

"Is this it? Is this all your baggage, sir?"

"That's it," I answered the spotty youth who was pumping his bony chest out under his uniform, cocky and officious in his official persona as immigration moron. I glanced through the glass booth and noticed a familiar figure exiting the area, a lank strand of black hair hanging out of a black baseball cap and a false mustache draped across his lip.

"Yeah, I'm only staying a couple of days. I was working here last year—but I'm just here for a spot of birding this time."

"A spot of whating?" asked the jerk sarcastically.

"Bird watching," I said, fighting to keep cool, restraining the urge to bounce my fist off the top of his dandruff-flecked head.

"All the way from Blighty for a couple of days' bird watching . . . on a thirty-hour flight?"

"Correct," I answered, battling a sarcasm drip. The little prat scrutinized my passport, blinking at the various expunged work permits, visitor's visas, and exotic stamps scattered like a butterfly collection throughout its well-thumbed pages.

He gave me a final once-over with his vacant, lobotomized eyes, shrugged, then waved me through. Carruthers followed, miraculously passing muster with his similarly improbable story. We had bolted from the plane, leaving the goons straggling through the sluggish denizens of the smoking section, who had hampered their progress somewhat, dragging their enormous cargos of cigarettes and alcohol from the overhead compartments.

Miss Mepps, no doubt fortified by her little helpers, had scurried off through the crew exit like a cockroach and was by now presumably in another section of the airport, waiting for the three of us. Lolla and her two Bahá'í toadies were nowhere to be seen and I scanned the arrivals hall anxiously, expecting them to pounce like Hare Krishnas at any moment. But

Carruthers and I made it to the curb, and following a nod from the stalwart in the baseball cap and black mustache, hopped directly into a taxi.

The doors closed and we were off, but as I turned in my seat I spotted the Clermont Set's hired heavies hustling for the next cab in line, closely followed by those fiendish religious perverts.

"Shit! They're on to us, Forty. And the goons have got a pretty good idea Miss Mepps is in on it."

"Which hotel, lads?' asked the cabdriver, slovenly draped around the steering wheel.

"Terminal three, private craft, by the goods hanger," said Fortesque, pulling off the baseball cap and giving me a high five.

"What? Sorry mate, I don't go there. I'll drop you at Qantas and you can get another bloody cab, all right?"

Fortesque leaned out of his seat and was at the driver's side, giving him an earful and pressing bills into his top pocket. Sitting down again, he peeled off the mustache with a painful rip.

"Cool?" I asked.

"Cool," he assured me.

"Nibs," piped Carruthers.

Wiping sweat from my brow, I then extracted a pair of miniature high-powered binoculars from my shoulder bag.

"Thank God you got my message," I said to Fortesque, pressing the lenses to my eyes. "Is Bruce go? Are we happening?"

"Bruce is go, sport, no worries. Called him before I left for Heathrow. Bloody lucky—only been out of stir for a week."

"Good man. Oh, how'd you get through immigration with that getup on, by the way?"

Fortesque pulled his passport out and flipped it open to show me the photo. There he was, sporting a black mustache and wearing a baseball cap.

"Looked like this when I got the passport," he asserted with a wry chuckle.

"Not a good image, Fortesque," I said.

"Look a bit of an idiot, don't I?" he agreed.

Handing the passport back, I returned my attention to the view out of the back window and saw a cab picking up speed, exiting the last passenger terminal.

"Oh oh, I hope your uncle's where he's supposed to be, Fortesque, engine gunning. And Carruthers' bint, too."

"Aye, Miss Mepps'll be there. Towser should be coomin' to by now, I can set 'im onto them if need be, that'll give 'em some kimber right enough, farff!"

Our cabdriver, attempting some Grande Prix tactics under orders from Forty, pushed the vehicle to its limits, and as terminal three came into sight, I looked through the binoculars back at the following cab, catching glimpses of it between the concrete blocks of airport utility buildings. Within minutes, we screamed to a halt next to the weather-beaten carcass of a twin-engine six seater. The door was open and there inside was Miss Mepps and the thylacine, strangely similar expressions on their faces as they peered out at us. The beast saw Carruthers and began panting, doing its best to control its great lolling tongue as it fought off thirty hours of tranquilizers.

Fortesque's uncle hopped out of the cockpit with a bottle of Boags in his hand, a smile squeezing his eyes shut and his mouth cracked across his face like a busted mattress. He lifted his canvas hat and jiggled it at us, making the corks, hung on fishing line around its rim, bounce like tiny marionettes. I could almost smell his breath from the inside of the taxi.

"Uncle Bruce!" yelled Forty, rushing to the stout geezer and embracing him. "Your lookin' bonzer, mate! Crate's gone downhill a bit, though, ain't she?" he added, gesturing toward the heap of sun-bleached tin that coughed and spluttered alarmingly in the hot morning air.

"Aw, she's a beauty, Forty. No problems, mate!" Bruce assured him with gusto. "Where we goin', Devonport?"

"Right, Bruce."

"Get a fuckin' move on then—looks like company."

The cab screeched to a halt not fifty feet away, plummeting me into another death vision. I stared dumbfounded as the vehicle rippled through layers of reality, reversing its evolution as if from a complex life-form back toward single-celled bacterium and became in a twinkling a macabre black hearse. In a thick, timeless motion, it disgorged its cargo of five animated skeletons, who stood swaying slightly, twitching their nervous fingers, their yellow teeth parting soundlessly.

THE OTHER LIFE OF BRIAN

"Come on, BP! Quick, onboard!"

It was Fortesque, grabbing the collar of my dun-colored Dutch army parka and dragging me backward like a sack of spuds. I snapped out of the death trance, the grotesque premonition of extinction, and then saw clearly the Clermont Set's thugs in their cheap, tight suits, and with them, the trench-coated Arabs led by herself, the Mata Horror, bundling toward me across the steaming tarmac.

Bruce was revving the engine and had already began to rock the plane into a taxi while Fortesque, feeling the ancient hood of my parka rip, dropped out of the door and instantly slipped in front of me in an act of selfless protection. On came the thug in the sunglasses, his piggy-faced companion at his heels.

I yelled: "Go! go!" into the air, ready to have my teeth kicked in for the sake of a great, smelly, near-mythical marsupial.

But then that oft-heard cry rent the air, plump in timber amid the thin whine of the twin engines: "Kimber!" bellowed Carruthers. "Away t'lads! Go sic 'em, Towser!"

The thylacine, obedient to the soundman's every command, flew past my ear at full stretch, its stripes blurring across my eyes, dragging with it that powerful canine odor I had first noticed in its mother's very nest an infinity ago, tickling my nostrils with its organic complexity.

The Clermont Set's dullard emissaries ground to a halt and then, before they could barely flinch, the Tasmanian Tiger was upon the nearest one, its teeth embedded in his crotch, growls issuing from its massive drooling jaws. The other thug tripped back toward the taxi but the driver was already flooring it, screaming across the asphalt back toward the main airport and away from this frightening spectacle. Towser hung on like a leech as the wailing heavy hit the ground howling for mercy and would not see release until Fortesque and I were safely aboard. Only then did Carruthers issue a short sharp "Nibs!" followed by a full-throated "Nibs, laddieee!" At this command the thylacine finally broke its hold, looking around stupidly as if a wave of chemical somnambu-lism had once more returned to its pumping bloodstream.

The clanky plane was now gathering momentum and Bruce roared incomprehensibly above the engines' racket. Fortesque still held me by the collar, and above the pair of us Carruthers' flaming head arched out, "nibsing" and "laddieing" like a lunatic until at last the beast snapped to its senses. With a good turn of speed, the thylacine bounded down the runway and up into the plane, causing the three of us to tumble back like skittles, sweat and blood spraying over us as Towser happily licked Carruthers' smiling face.

"What a laddie, aren't thou? What a laddie, farff!" sang Carruthers as a stream of curses came from our pilot followed by a defiant, "Whoa! Fuckin' 'ell, we're up!" as we looped around over our assailants.

"You mean takeoff was in doubt, Bruce?" I shouted, shimmying into a seat.

"Well . . . not really, sport . . . well, all right, sort of. Ah, don't worry about it. I couldn't get the bastard to start half an hour before you blokes turned up, let alone take off. All right, Sheila? Lovely!" Bruce slapped Miss Mepps, who sat shotgun, across the knee with a big farmer's hand, the corks on his hat doing a merry dance.

"Oh oh, look down there," said Bruce, banking once more over the small terminal with its three hangers and small craft dotted around like toys.

There were the Bahá'i and the bozos talking to a man in blue overalls and pointing excitedly to a red and white six seater.

"Fuck it!" bellowed Bruce. "That's Pikey—he'll do anything for a buck. I told the bastard to go to pub—gave him a five-spot, I did, too. Buy yourself a couple of frosties, I said, go on. I'll take care of things here, mate, no worries. Bastard can smell money a mile off; he was my connection in the toad gland importing business over here. Cunt didn't do any time though, oh no—*I* took all the heat. Got caught in New Zealand, see. Your friends'll get a lift from that bugger, I'm afraid," he asserted, looking back at me and slugging on his beer. "Oh, boys," he continued with a healthy belch. "Case of Boags under the seat by the pooch. Welcome to Tas!"

Chapter 27

"**BP, nearly forgot**—letter for you, arrived at the office the other day."

The small plane, rank with the odor of male thylacine, droned across the farmlands and towns of Tasmania, heading north to Devonport and the ostium of the Mersey River. The animal sat in the tiny gangway, its body pressed against Carruthers, its head level with me. I took the letter from Fortesque and held it in my lap for a while as I studied the thylacine's Cenozoic features: thylacinus cynocephelus, the marsupial equivalent of canis lupus or canis rufus, although not a wolf at all, but absolutely the top predator in this neck of the woods; the Tasmanian answer to the Bengal tiger or the lions of the African plains.

The creature reacted to my stare and met my eyes with a bout of panting and yawning, enunciated by little whines and snuffles. Then it turned its long jaws and faced me directly for a moment, ceasing its puppyish heaving, and went still and quiet. External distraction disappeared for a split second, and the thylacine and I locked eyes, finding some personal thread of destiny relating our lives on a most primitive, primal level. The propinquity riffled between us in molecular currents and I at once experienced the ancient vistas of the thylacine's existence and perhaps, or so it seemed to me, the thylacine experienced my tiny speck of life, and the understanding of what had brought us together became crystal clear: we were both about to cheat extinction. The marsupial wolf may well have been hanging on grimly to its fast disappearing sanctuary, as I most certainly was hanging on to my last slivers of communication, to a shrinking audience reduced to tiny islands bobbing in a sea of ever-expanding insouciance, as sure an extinction as if a farmer's gun had been pointed to my head and its lethal cargo ejected into my brain. But we lived on despite the ambivilent world. We would defy it and survive, no matter what. Well, the thylacine would, I thought, with a sudden twinge of doubt. Whether I'd pull it off or not, I had no idea.

* * *

"BP? BP? You all right mate?" said Fortesque, his etched, gnomish face coming into focus in front of me as the buzzing engine noise flooded back over my senses. "Look like you've seen a ghost mate—you hearin' this on the radio?"

"Ghosts?" I responded sluggishly. "Seen a few of those lately, Forty. What is it? I added, his second remark slowly sinking in.

"Turn it up, will you Bruce," demanded my tour manager.

"I 'eard this earlier," said Bruce cheerily as he fiddled with the volume on the dashboard. 'Knee Trembles,' is that what it's called? Forty told me you were a popular bloke—top twenny, eh mate?"

"Top? . . . " I mumbled as my old warhorse came in and out on the plane's radio.

"I'm not supposed to be tuned to this, of course," said Bruce, "but I like a bit of pop when I'm stuntin' around the skies. Fuck it, I'm losin' it . . ." The station crumbled into static as Bruce banked the plane sharply to the left. I looked down through the grubby window, feeling as if I could reach through it and touch the green Tasmanian landscape below.

"Well, it was a hit about ten years ago," I finally agreed as the station went out of range and was replaced by a strangled mixture of Australian news coverage and sputterings of a cricket score. "But only in England."

"Nah, they said top twenny in Tas—I'm bloody sure of it."

I shrugged. He was obviously mistaken. My attention was then drawn to the letter Fortesque had handed me.

I opened it and was instantly grounded: it was not from those noisome Shylocks in the law firm that represented the Baedburgers, but from the Baedburgers themselves, those born-again zealots who had received my late half-uncle's inheritance.

I read the thing at arm's length, holding it up to the plane's ceiling as if it carried a bad odor. My anger (ah, that comforting creative goo!) rushed back into my system like an old friend:

Dear Brian,

We have received various correspondences from you to our representatives in law, Messrs. Goldtraub, Cardbaum and Silvermein. I'm sorry to say that we are deeply offended by most of it.

THE OTHER LIFE OF BRIAN

When you were our guest here in our own home you seemed such a nice young man and were enjoying the pig ribs thoroughly. When our son Adam said to you "I haven't seen any of your songs on MTV, Brian," your explanation of this strange discrepancy seemed satisfying at the time. But now I don't believe for a minute that we've ever heard of you because the people who run the radio stations and MTV are all "bastards," as you called them. I believe now that perhaps you are at fault, Brian. Perhaps your temper and hostility are what turns people against you. Now that I have seen your sickening letters to our lawyers I feel more than ever that Hell will take you unless you quickly learn the truth of God, Our Lord through His Son Jesus Christ.

Only then will you be saved and perhaps this will reflect in your work and our son will then see your songs on the television. (We think a perm would help, too.)

We are sending our prayers to you and hope you will soon be hearing His word.

And by the way, due to your slanderous letters, we are suing the pants off you.

Yours sincerely,
Loretta and Gaylord Baedburger

"Ha!" I snorted, crushing the despicable document in my hand. "Pendulous, wide-bottomed, God-fearing . . . twats!" I yelled, reaching for my personally embossed writing paper and bottle-green fountain pen.

"Bloody hell," Uncle Bruce uttered, "pull that toothbrush out of yer freckle before more crap backs up out of yer mouth!"

"S'cuse me, Bruce. It's just these right-wing moralist wide-bottomed . . ."

"Wide-bottomed?" said Bruce, interested. "Is there a woman involved, sport? I like a girl with a big bum. All right, Sheila?" he said again to Miss Mepps, whose pinched face had taken on an aggrieved, pained expression. Bruce then broke into an explicit song of the bush, an unpleasant ditty about flying doctors, pregnant women, and kangaroo intestines. I gathered my writing equipment and tore into a suitable riposte to the Baedburgers' heinous moralisms.

GRAHAM PARKER

Dear Loretta and Gaylord:

Due to the twisted strand of DNA it has been my misfortune to inherit from my late half-uncle John "Sir" Bacon, I have been wracked with tempestuous visions both mystical in genesis and revelatory in outcome. Your personal, oleaginous sightings of the divine are like viewing dog-turds on the wet cobbles of Montmartre compared to the crystalline, Blakian, sweeping profluent *religiouso* I myself have recently been subjected to.

This, I bear with a martyr's acceptance and an avatar's courage. Yourselves, hoodwinked by false morality and leaden oversimplifications, could not in your dullest imaginings conceive of the awesome force and frightening splendor of true revelatory insight. No, it is I who must inherit the tightrope of sanity which I must walk for my entire life.

Short on gray matter and long on gluteus you may well be and this may serve you in the short-run of piratical tyranny. But in the long-haul, I believe that karmic forces will eventually swell against you and my righteous replevy will indeed come to pass. In the meantime—stick a fucking bung up it you flatulent bastards!

Yours sincerely,
Brian Porker, M.C. (Knighted)

"Better, better, better!" I yelled as I folded my handiwork into one of my personal envelopes. I had indeed received a vibrant kick from penning this reply and could feel the mighty weights of jet lag, pessimism, and any lack of balls that might be attempting to threaten this mission, encapsulated and compartmentalized behind my sheer bloody-mindedness to succeed.

"Not that much better!" Bruce shouted over the engines roar as he banked the plane down toward a small landing strip at the edge of Devonport. "Pikey's Cessna's got more throttle than this old girl—seven o' clock, take a gander."

Carruthers, Fortesque, and I twisted left and peered through the dirty windows at the red and white craft in the blue sky not too far

THE OTHER LIFE OF BRIAN

behind, crawling with religious maniacs and hired bully boys. It was going to be tight, but I figured providing Bruce could get this wreck down in one attempt and the previously arranged taxi was there ready to move, we could lose them before we hit the river.

"Hang on, kiddies!" shouted Bruce as we plummeted toward the strip, a sudden turbulence knocking the plane around like a toy.

"Crickey, that northwind picks up a beauty here."

The thylacine let out a yawning whine and pressed its head down on the floor between its paws. I stroked its back, nervously marveling at its solid lines, its muscularity under the brash fur; kibble and partridge had almost certainly given its growth hormones an advantage over its wild brethren. I imagined the little kin Towser had shared a pouch with to be naturally smaller due to the rigors of the wild, although not too much so; I remembered the roast wallaby leftovers thrown to the thylacines in the flickering shadows around the aboriginal campfires.

"Where did you get your pilot's license?" asked Miss Mepps, throwing Bruce an angular look and popping a couple of pills into her thin mouth.

"Pilot's license?" yelled Bruce. Miss Mepps's eyes widened with annoyance.

"Just kidding, darlin'," he quickly added, sensing a sound clocking in the offing from the old biddy. "Tangalooma actually, darlin'. I'm one of the Tangalooma Phantoms. Bonzer division let me tell you, blue . . . whoa! Shut up, I gotta concentrate."

Bruce took his bloodshot eyes off of Miss Mepps just in time to level the craft out for a landing. Sweat rushed to my forehead as the wheels hit the asphalt. We bounced up and down, our pilot fighting the controls and flipping switches with a maniacal grin on his florid face.

Once safely down, the plane lurched toward the terminal, which consisted of a large tin hut with a radar dish on its roof, shimmering in the heat haze coming off the asphalt. The cab sat there with no driver, but the keys were in the ignition and we launched ourselves into it, Bruce, in the driver's seat with Fortesque riding shotgun, Carruthers, Miss Mepps, and myself in the back and the thylacine obediently squeezed into the trunk with a greasy spare tire and a bag of tools for company.

"Bastard's been on the blower!" yelled Uncle Bruce as we careened along the pot-hole-ridden exit road almost colliding with another taxi cab entering the tiny airstrip. We looked back and saw Pikey's Cessna hit the runway. No doubt that the cab was intended for its odious passengers.

Bruce followed the exit road, which practically encircled the airstrip until joining a main road, and between the rotting hulks of abandoned biplanes strung with prickly climbing plants on the perimeter, we caught glimpses of the Bahá'i and the goons dashing for their taxi.

"Rough-lookin' tart . . . what's her game, Brian?" asked Bruce, scratching his stubble with his left hand while his right fought with the steering wheel on the pockmarked road. He had seen Lolla, her red curtain garment shimmering in the heat haze.

"Religion," I said flatly, not in the mood to elaborate.

"Worth running from," said Bruce.

Chapter 28

Bruce reluctantly skirted the speed limit as we headed south of Devonport toward the docks in the mouth of the Mersey River. Getting stopped for speeding now would bring our aggressors right onto our heels, and I feared that Fortesque's uncle, who constantly popped the caps off Boags bottles with his teeth and guzzled their contents, would prove to be shitfaced in the chemical analysis of a Breathalyzer.

The constant momentum caused me to doze a little, or at least mind-surf. I closed my eyes and found myself visualizing Miss Mepps, whose stockinged leg was pressed against mine and whose cheap perfume blossomed in the hot confines of the backseat. The simple nastiness of these twin assaults suddenly kicked in a lurch from the poison dart frog toxin. My awareness seemed to fold inward, away from the mind's usual housing in the cranium, and traveled inward to my heart. From there it flowed like decoagulating oil into the bloodstream of my leg, through my black jeans (experiencing in exquisite detail each fine thread of denim as it did so) and from there swiftly through Miss Mepps's sticky stockings. With an alarming jolt, this liquid awareness then bore right into her very corpuscles. Through her pointy body I traveled and onward into the beanpole leg of Carruthers. Messages sped to my inner eye which formed intimate details of the pairs' physiology: the regrowth of shaved black hairs on Miss Mepps's legs, pushing up microscopic plates of dead skin into the weave of her blue skirt; Carruthers' knee joints, stiff as steel cables from their perpetual crumpled position in cars, airplane seats, and anywhere else designed for normal-sized humans; and the boy was still growing—he wasn't yet twenty years of age!

My tactile bubble awareness raced up through his bloodstream to his blocky head and floated there, as if in amniotic fluid, finding nothing resembling a brain. Then some liquid synapse in that darkling pond clicked to simple thoughts of Towser, sweating in the boot of the car, and I rolled back through the plastic seat covers, molecule by molecule into the spongy seat itself and then right through the steel skeleton of the vehicle and into the pungent microclimate of the living marsupial. I drifted there awhile, sensing its breathing, like tides breaking ancient shores, tasting its dim awareness of its master Carruthers, inches away. It would be hard for the creature to see the last of him, but that was how it was going to be.

Without warning, a nauseous pumping motion kicked in and the entire alarming process suddenly reversed itself and I found my mind back in my head again.

The groan of downshifting gears and shifting of human weight in the backseat, a throat-clearing from Fortesque, and a muttered curse from Bruce signaled some form of arrival and I blinked awake in the mid-morning brightness, catching a glimpse of sparkling water as the screams of gulls reached my ears.

"Tubb's the man we want, lads," said Bruce. "Just around the bend here. You all right, Brian?"

"Just a spot of jet lag, Bruce," I answered, grabbing a Boags from the taxi's floor.

Tubb? Did I hear him right? Bruce *would* know him; but at least the boatman made no complaint last time we were here, returning his craft four days late; Tubb it would undoubtedly be.

And there he was, bending over a pile of rotting ropes and nets, his stained, baggy jeans halfway down his behind, exposing his ass crack like the back of a sow. Bruce brought the cab to a halt and Tubb turned his head, cracking a smile under a dirty white baseball cap. He wobbled up to Bruce, who heaved himself out of the driver's seat and marched forward. The two men embraced each other and made manly comments; Tubb looked more rotund than I remembered but his wares had not changed a bit: the very same ice-blue motorboat that we had rented only months ago for our fateful journey into the distant past bobbed in the current off the floating dock, in close proximity to a few other craft in varying stages of dilapidation, tossing in the eddies of the bay.

"Come on, Brian!" barked Uncle Bruce. "And you, nephew, and that long streak of piss and his charmin' air hostess—and don't forget

THE OTHER LIFE OF BRIAN

Rover! Let's get the fuck out of here before that bunch of perverts arrive. Here, come and meet old Tubb."

"We've met," I said, nodding to Tubb, who threw us a wave and a gap-toothed grin. He showed no sign of recognition however and busied himself pulling in the ice-blue launch as Bruce had words in his ear and pulled out a wad of Australian dollars, which he began shaking near Tubb's face. Very little negotiating transpired and soon Tubb was stuffing a handful of uncounted bills in his shirt pocket and motioning for us to board the craft, which we quickly did. Within moments we were cast off once more, the motor creating white horses of foam at the rudder. The thylacine, standing bolt upright in the prow, flared its nostrils and fixed its wolfish eyes upstream, a living, breathing figurehead propelled from the Cenozoic into this very space in time.

"Away t'lads!" hollered Carruthers. "Kimber!"

The marsupial remained in locked position, smacking its lips, which now appeared dry and sandpapery. Carruthers stroked its striped hindquarters, looking sad as he sensed the inevitable parting of man and beast, master and pet.

"Oh, a life on the ocean wave
Is better n' goin' to sea
A life on the ocean wave
Is the only life for me, Tarrum!"

Bruce sang merrily as he manned the rudder and I gripped the starboard side, my eyes roaming the numerous floating docks, ramshackle huts, and fish cleaning sheds that lined the banks of the river. Various craft bobbed past us: some tatty vessels in need of a paint job, like Tubb's old junk; the odd ketch in full sail, meticulously maintained by crusty enthusiasts with severe nautical bents, and one or two high-powered speedboats peopled by pickled-looking rich folk who leaned back victorious, as if in control of giant phalluses.

"What if the bastards rent something like that?" I said to no one in particular. Miss Mepps again sat beside me and answered in a dull, dazed fashion: "I've met those Bahá'í's, they're not that bad. I've learned to like dry-roasted peanuts."

This I could well imagine. There must be many occasions on long flights when those devilish confections are the only form of sustenance left to devour. Perhaps this phenomenon contributed to the stickish dryness of most air hostesses, who often appear to me as though their ovaries and other important organs have shriveled within during the first year of their noisome employment.

"You'd be the boss, though, wouldn't you? If you went for that reincarnation bit, I mean. We'd all have to kowtow to you," continued Miss Mepps in a vaguely accusing manner. "We'd be *under* you," she said ominously, unbuttoning her blue tunic to reveal a cheap St. Christopher medal nestled in her bony cleavage. Well this was very fine, I thought. Miss Mepps was obviously about to undergo a major mental breakdown, possibly of psychotic proportions, and almost certainly fueled by the dizzying array of amphetamines and tranquilizers she had been stuffing herself with for the last thirty hours.

"Don't worry, Miss Mepps," I said, not in the mood to console her for a single minute. "You'll *never* be under me, I can assure you."

She did a little hoity-toity wiggle with her head, lips thrust out like salt-dried slugs, and then stared straight ahead, uncannily assuming the very expression worn by Towser as he sniffed the air upstream for ancestral memories.

It was not yet noon and well up in the eighties, but dry; the humidity would doubtless come later as we entered the more forested regions. I had no real plan, other than deliverance both physical and spiritual and had, until discovering the two groups of adversaries on the flight over, foreseen no real problems: dump the thylacine back in the forest with the aborigines (if we could find them again), or near as damn it, jet back to London and explain to Steed how I just threw away 50 million yen for the sake of a rank-smelling marsupial, and then spend the rest of my life wondering whether the evil Clermont Set were going to bump me off for such heinous and dishonorable conduct. Nothing to it. Piece of cake. But now here I was, trying to fulfill this simple destiny with a serious complication on my tail. And where were they? What was keeping them?

I scanned the sparkling river behind us but saw only a few small fishing vessels with local salty dogs at their rudders, cramped up with their nets and poles and lines.

"No use, lads. I know there's a lady onboard, but I've got to take a piss."

THE OTHER LIFE OF BRIAN

Bruce signaled Carruthers to slip aft and man the rudder as he knelt by the port side and pulled out his penis, which looked like a small red parrot with a purple beak, and with a wet belch pissed over the side.

"Ah . . . that's better. 'Please release me, let me go,' " Bruce sang, buttoning up his canvas shorts. He sat down next to Fortesque on the narrow plank that served as one of the seats and scratched at his whiskery jaw.

"Well, come on, lads and ladesses! What could be better? Lovely day, cruisin' upstream followed by a couple of blokes who look like they'd murder you as soon as they look at you, big ole fuckin' extinct bastard stinkin' the boat up out front there, the lovely Miss Mepps . . . marvelous! Cheer up for Christ sakes!"

Bruce eyed Miss Mepps's backside on the seat in front of him with a lascivious lip curl and resumed the entertainments:

"You're the one that I want
(You're the one I want now, oo oo oo honey!)

"Yeah! Love that one, don't you, Brian? What's that other one I heard recently? Now how does that one go? Oh yeah:

'Nebuchadnezzar and Pontius Pilate
Lazzaro Spallanzani and Venus De Milo
They hunted him down, inflicted many pains
But he suffered erysipelas and lived on seven planes
King of the Senses
King of the Senses'

"Great, that one is. Love it!"

"Hear that, Beep?" piped up Fortesque as I strained my memory around this most familiar song.

"Yeah, what . . ."

"Bruce is singing 'King of the Senses.' Where did you hear that then, Bruce?"

"On the fuckin' radio of course. Heard it a good few times. Catchy number that—who's it by then?"

"Brian Porker himself!" answered Fortesque, reaching diagonally across the rear of Miss Mepps and slapping me on the back.

Of course! With a shock I realized it was a track off my latest record, *Porker In Aspic*.

"Jesus, that *and* 'Knee Trembler'? Where, Bruce," I demanded excitedly, knowing he must have heard it numerous times to be so familiar with two of its many dense couplets. "Where d'you hear the one you were just singing?"

"I dunno . . . I've been moving around Tas' for the last week—been hearing it a lot. One of yours, is it? Good on yer, blue. Bit long though, sport. Reckon you could 'ave knocked off a minute or two and no one would be any the wiser—it is a novelty song after all."

Fortesque and I chuckled at Bruce's assessment of my epic seven-minute psychodrama. Perhaps the sheer weight of the thing was cutting through the tight Tasmanian playlists, scything its way into the armies of disco dervishes and divas with a refreshing ferocity. Whatever, I was aghast that perhaps after all, my poorly attended tour of Tasmania had actually produced results; after years of nonsense, this was a new one to me. Extinction suddenly seemed a distant memory.

Chapter 29

Almost three hours upriver and the thylacine still held the bow, twitching and shuffling excitedly every time some errant steering took us from midstream toward the banks, which now began to lose all traces of civilization and regained that wild primeval look I remembered from our last visit. Steam hung in wisps between the lush flora, and brilliant green rosellas dipped between the branches.

I felt a queer uneasiness that attacked me from all fronts at once: the drone of the boat's motor seemed to drill into my bones; the thylacine's fur became tangible, and even though my fingers were a few feet away, I could feel its coarseness like horsehair on my skin; and a crushing sensation, as if the very canopy of the forest were bearing down on my skull, made me blink and shake my head in an effort to shrug it off. Fucking Carruthers and his experimental Big Drugs! He should be going through this, not me.

Suddenly, Bruce lowered the revs of the motor to virtually idle and the water plipped against the old craft's prow as the current tried to jostle us to a standstill.

"Well, will you look at that," said Bruce softly, quiet amazement replacing his usual rowdiness.

And there, to our left, almost blending into the dappled foliage, the naked camouflage of his skin as natural as a rotting tree trunk, a mud bank, or a termite mound, was the aboriginal leader I had first set eyes upon when I blindly stumbled after the pair of thylacines into that ancient, secret habitation.

He did not look at us as our boat caught an eddying flash and dollied up to within ten feet of his presence. His black body was arched as if in a martial arts stance with the right arm bent at the elbow and the right hand open by his bushy hair. His left arm was thrust straight out from his shoulder, pointing upstream. His bare feet were planted in the mud on the very lip of the bank as if he grew there, like an ancient tree that refused to bend with erosion, and he held a catatonic expression beneath the pale white and ocher daubings that accompanied the scars on his face.

The forest canopy above the river suddenly became transparent to my senses, as if I had become a human epidioscope, and I knew that no one else on the boat was experiencing this phenomenon and that the strange posture of the aborigine had set this off in me. I braced myself for further embellishments of the death awareness. Sure enough, the forest cringed as if its very sap had been removed and each twig transformed into brittle witches fingers that curled menacingly over, all but powdering off the branches.

Carruthers, Fortesque, Miss Mepps, and Bruce became doughlike figurines in the boat beside me, and only the thylacine remained normal, as if caught in another wave of time. But I became irritated suddenly with these psychotropic party tricks and cursed loudly at the aborigine, delusionally believing that he surely must have some link with the Maven of Death herself and the frog toxin; it seemed perfectly normal to me that those three elements would be connected and intrinsic to the next few hours of my existence. All the same, I recalled Carruthers' advice about tempering the toxins' affects with alcohol and reached down into the boat for one of Bruce's cans of Boags, wishing I'd brought a bottle of brandy along. I downed the drink in one but felt nothing.

"What are you trying to tell me?" I finally yelled at the black man (to me he was a black man, and I was damned sure *he* would not have thought of himself as an "African Tasmanian") on the bank as I crushed the beer can in frustration. Instantly, his right hand made a circling motion and his hips gyrated to some unheard rhythm. Although this display may have appeared merely a graceful yet meaningless piece of native mumbo to my companions, in my resonant state pure imagery had been transmitted to my inner eye and I divined the meaning of his posturing without a second thought.

Abruptly, the silence that had enveloped me since having sighted our aboriginal guide was shattered by the roar of what I knew with uncanny certainty to be a powerful motor-launch.

"Bruce, step on it!" I yelled, and staring literally through the dense forest, back around the river bend, as if with X-ray vision, I saw an expensive-looking speedboat powering toward us, the Bahá'í at the helm and the goons, like foolish figureheads, gripping the rails on the prow.

"Up ahead, Bruce, another river joins us—a whirlpool! A whirlpool! Go for it!"

"Bonzer mate, aye aye, cap'n!" roared Bruce as he gave the outboard full throttle, making Miss Mepps fall back like a bowling pin onto the wet planks of the deck.

At that precise moment the aborigine broke into a perfect dance routine from the seventies, a bang-on Travolta job, right out of *Grease*, and frugged off into the undergrowth, blending into its cover like a giant chameleon. My synapses fired with heightened clarity, but as if induced by a three-mile run and a cold shower and not by the mystical portents transmuted upon me by aborigines, speckles of Joker, poison dart frog toxin, or dying old ladies on airplanes.

I knew with assured finality that the death visions were over; the final glimpse through the impenetrable forest at our aggressors and the telepathic bout with the aborigine signaled their demise; at last, they had served their obscure purpose and I felt the macabre door closing with a deep resounding boom.

"Kimber! eh oop, Towser!"

Ah, those oh so earthly tones completed the impression of a return to sweet normality as Carruthers, like an enormous ignited matchstick, hurled himself at full stretch over the side, the thylacine alongside him, and they swam toward the mouth of the very tributary we had entered months ago, back in another age.

"What? What? Up ahead where?" begged Bruce in delayed reaction to my orders to get going. "What's the rush sport? Have I missed something?"

I explained, vaguely, to Bruce and Fortesque, that I had just had a weird feeling that a thirty-foot speedboat carrying two great ornery bastards from south London and a herd of religious nutters known as the Bahá'í was closing in rapidly, not wishing to elaborate on my recent skeleton vision and that I had in fact just seen through impenetrable forest, round a bend in the river, and spotted the oncoming launch probably a good half mile from the spot where we had encountered the signifying aborigine.

"Bollocks!" boomed Bruce. "My ears are as sharp as a bloody bat's I'd be hearing the motor by now."

"Cut the engine," I ordered flatly, which he did, and as the current of the crystalline upper Mersey began to push the powerless boat back downstream, the growing drone of a motorboat could be faintly discerned amid the babbling water, screeching parrots, and buzzing insects.

"Well I'll be buggered," whispered Bruce, "you're on the case, BP."

"Buggered?" questioned Fortesque. "S'pect you were . . . in prison, right, Unc'?"

"You bastard, Forty! Nobody got their rotten Rodney up my freckle! I *ruled* in that slammer mate, *ruled.*"

The stalwart road turf and his ex-convict uncle had a damn good chuckle and popped a couple of Boags before Bruce reengaged the motor and thrust us back upstream, heading toward what I hoped would be the fulfillment of my aboriginal telepathy: there we would discover another river disgorging its liquid body into the Mersey, and forming a whirlpool at that juncture. This I could see in my mind's eye in normal mnemonic fashion, a simple picture of a scene grafted into my memory banks by the obscure pantomime witnessed earlier on the riverbank, but left in place, as if I had actually been there. But what to do with this whirlpool, this potentially dangerous natural wonder, I hadn't the slightest notion.

Chapter 30

Now that Carruthers had taken it upon himself, without a word of discussion, to expedite the mission by launching into the wild with the thylacine, I expected some reaction from Miss Mepps. But the stewardess seemed unaware of his ballsy flight and sat stock-still in the boat as if nailed there, staring ahead catatonically, her purplish mascara smudged from the humidity and the pancake on her cheeks coming off in flakes, each piece indented with visible pore prints.

For a short while we chugged along the ever narrowing river in silence, the drone of the high-powered launch behind us increasing its volume incrementally by the minute.

"Dorking," said Miss Mepps suddenly to no one in particular.

"I'm sorry?" I responded, as Fortesque and I turned to study her with raised eyebrows. But she made no attempt to clarify this cryptic reference to southern England and remained prim and steady in the rocking boat.

Suddenly, rounding a bend we saw the realization of my vision up ahead: sure enough, there was another river, ejecting its stored energy into the Mersey, which indeed created a thundering crash of foam and cascading currents overshadowed by a fine cloud of hazy mist.

In a still pool under the bank to our port side I caught a glimpse of a dark, sleek shape gliding underwater into a dense tangle of tree roots. I knew immediately that it was that marvel of nature, that absurd egg-laying conundrum, that bafflement of science, a duck-billed platypus. I was tempted to instruct our helmsman Bruce to give chase, but my reverie was rudely interrupted by a yell from Fortesque's uncle.

"Now what, Brian? You're the bugger with the ideas!" he begged, pointing behind us. I looked back downstream and there were our pursuers, right on our heels.

For a moment, my mind frizzled with escapist fantasies; I would have loved to linger and catch another glimpse of the platypus and, as if the thought were connected by its very strangeness, delve into Miss Mepps's bizarre utterances to ferret out their meanings, even though they were quite probably unfathomable. She was, I felt, going through a severe psychotic episode. This idea gave me a sudden urge to tackle the aging air hostess and toss her overboard in order to knock some sense into her. The very nerve of the woman! (I have never been able to stand people who were weak enough to let their psychoses get the better of them in the presence of others.)

But the big white power boat was only 100 feet behind us with Lolla and her pals hanging onto the railing, her dread crimson muumuu like a battered flag heralding religious idiocy, and the ruffians, one at the wheel with his black shades catching the sun and the other smoking a Rothmans and grinning madly, sensing victory. It seemed they had not yet noticed that Carruthers and the beast were no longer with us, and before they could get close enough to see that the pair were not lying flat, hiding beneath the bench seats of our craft, I had to shrug off any delightful ideas of trouncing Miss Mepps or studying platypuses. It was undoubtedly time to act decisively.

"Brian . . ." moaned Fortesque.

"Okay," I gasped, my head clearing of extraneous baggage. "Bruce, hit it! Make an arc around that mass of foam where the tributary joins."

Bruce did as I instructed, hammering old Tubb's boat through the shallows at the edge of the turbulence, and as he spun the craft behind that roiling tangle, I felt the perfection of execution raise my adrenaline as if I was about to survive a mighty luge run, hit an ace in the tennis court, or complete a fast slalom with consummate skill. For as we bobbed in the skirts of the turbulence, the goon at the helm of the powerboat headed their vessel straight toward us, ignoring as he did the dangers of the seething white water. And as they hit that junction, that very pinnacle of unpredictability, the speedboat spun like a cork gripped in the talons of the foaming maelstrom as if its motor had been ripped away.

Its onerous crew tumbled about the deck like toys as the launch swiveled around and around in circles, tilting from port to starboard, the engine flooded and useless. Bruce and Fortesque cheered as we watched from the safety of the deep pools upstream of the churning vortex. The poor thugs and the Bahá'i slid fore and aft, struggling to maintain equilibrium. Their anguish was evident; their tortured faces told the story: they were up the creek without a paddle, in mortal danger and the object of their chase no longer within reach.

"Where's that fuckin' dog?" barked one of the thugs as he twisted like an eel on a hook, desperately gripping the deck rail.

"Free! And it's actually more closely related to a kangaroo than a dog, you idiot!" I yelled, intoxicated at our success and determined to lord it over our adversaries with a little well-researched knowledge. Bruce gunned up the outboard and we edged around the whirlpool, cruising slowly back downstream.

"Not extinct, and not in bondage!" I added as a parting shot.

Looking back at the crippled speedboat, now almost completely on its side and taking water with its sharply pointed hull cutting into the foam, I could see Lolla diving for it, followed by the svelte Arabs, the straps of their lifejackets flapping in the air before they hit the river. I didn't rate their chances too highly, but if they jumped far enough away from the center of the whirlpool where the boat was slowly going down, I reckoned they might just make it, if they were lucky. Their problem, I figured.

Bruce and Fortesque seemed well cheered by the matter; Miss Mepps, on the other hand, remained static and wall-eyed, gripping the bench seat and staring ahead in a blank, chemical trance. I had a sudden impulse to turn around and help the hapless Bahá'í but fought it—the chance of encountering more aggro from the Clermont Set's goons did not seem worth the risk.

A black cockatoo swooped across the river up ahead, cackling, as if mocking the folly of humans. Fortesque pointed out the mouth of the tiny tributary where our adventure had begun, and we tilted into it and chugged upstream, soon reaching the very spit of land where the aborigines had taken our boat months ago.

"Next?" queried Bruce, as we moored and disembarked, already slapping the biting insects that jockeyed for position around our flesh.

"Where the hell is Carruthers?" mumbled Fortesque.

"I guess . . . we wait?" I ventured, ignoring my tour manager's question altogether.

"You mean you haven't got *all* the answers, Brian?" said Bruce with a cheerful sarcasm.

And so we sat around on our haunches, quietly, listening for telltale sounds, occasionally glancing at Miss Mepps, who reclined with her back against a fine eucalyptus, a glimmer of cognizance returning to her face as the alien surroundings impinged upon her consciousness.

The shadows slowly lengthened as we waited and Fortesque busied himself whittling a stick of she-oak. Bruce clumped around the clearing, scratching his stomach and emitting sounds from various parts of his body.

"Nectarine," said Miss Mepps suddenly, causing the three of us to silently cease our obscure endeavors and peer in her direction. I had been studying a small lizard that sat on a strand of button grass, its gimlet eye occasionally appraising me in full reptilian sneakiness. Seemingly startled at the sound of Miss Mepps's voice, it suddenly leapt from its fragile perch and disappeared into the brush. From beneath my knees I felt a faint rumble, intermittent at first, but rapidly increasing in velocity.

My first thought was of the aborigines: at last they were on their way, creeping through the secret corridors of their dense, primeval home. But with growing alarm knifing through me like a cold stone arrow in my entrails, I knew that the true natives of Tasmania would appear silently, as if beamed in molecule by molecule with no vibration, no crashing of timber.

I leapt to my feet, trying desperately to pierce the dense jungle of foliage with wholly inefficient eyes. True to my feelings of unease, the actual crashing of timber erupted beyond the wall of green surrounding us, and unless bull elephants had been transported from Africa, the only thing that could cause such wanton commotion in so pristine an environment was a brace of thickset white men.

Fortesque and Bruce stiffened and I instinctively grabbed a stick, holding the frail object in my hand. But its effectiveness as a weapon would be no more than that of a feather against the oncoming weight of two of London's finest, and I dropped it, glancing panic-stricken around the clearing in search of the most likely escape route.

"They're 'ere!" yelled one of the Clermont Set's thugs as they thundered through the last wave of undergrowth. With no thought of the power of unity, Bruce, Fortesque and I bolted into the forest at tangents, swallowed immediately by the leafy oblivion.

THE OTHER LIFE OF BRIAN

"Follow Brian!" yelled the heavies, and I hurtled into the thickets making excruciatingly slow progress, bogged down in a nightmarish sequence, my legs hampered by the tangles of vines and creepers and the sheer unevenness of the terrain beneath them.

The thugs bumbled through behind me, benefiting from the slight crushing of branch and bush that my flimsy weight delivered upon the vegetation, and I felt them gaining on me, inch by terrible inch. There would be no airport police to protect me this time; no crowded aisles in the planes' smoking section to keep the brutes in their place. If they got hold of me here, fingers would surely be bent backward, a nose undoubtedly broken, a kneecap or two shattered by iron-hard knuckledusters. Talk about kimber—the very essence of it was on my tail.

"Where's the fuckin' dog, Brian?" they yelled, and I could almost perceive the faint obnoxious whiff of Brute aftershave, mixed in a devilish alchemy with their sweat, which poured profusely from their bodies, now shed of the tight suit jackets and bulging through their ripped and soaking shirts.

I continued to claw into the forest, oblivious to the cuts and bruises, possible bites from venomous insects or reptiles, and the distinct chance of breaks and fractures of my overextended bones. But as I reached a shallow clearing, the canopy seemed to spin around me and the cry of a startled bird reverberated in my head mixed with the panting and grunting of the pursuing hard nuts, and I felt my knees buckle beneath me as I went down, rolling onto my back, spinning around with my neck craned forward, my eyes bugged out and staring as the men lurched at my body.

Their great mitts reached down to me and I gave up, cringing as I readied myself for some serious thumping. But as their bloodied hands hovered over my face, they seemed to freeze on the spot, both men wincing at the same moment with an uncanny synchronism. Looks of uncertainty crossed their blobby, malevolent faces. They slapped at their thick, short necks. With a wince of pain, one of the thugs reached around behind himself and pulled a sharp object from his skin and stared at it, uncomprehendingly. Then, with strange muted thumps, the pair of them keeled over and hit the leafy floor. I lay still, absorbed in the sudden dead silence of the rain forest, my heart pounding in my chest seemingly the only sound in the entire universe.

The silence continued for a few minutes, and, assuming my aggressors were either dead or out cold, I tugged my foot from under the stomach of one of the stricken gangsters and stood up, surveying the depths of the leafy tangles, passing over what I at first took to be a patch of dappled foliage before realizing that it was in fact a human face. Leaves parted, followed by branches, and other faces appeared. Slowly, four aborigines slid into the clearing, one of them holding the instrument of the goons' demise—a small bow of rough stick and vine, shorter than a man's forearm and delicate in design.

The aborigine chief moved fleetfoot toward me, his three bowmen fanning out around the white bodies which they kicked gently until satisfied that they had been rendered harmless. The chief's eyes met mine and I smiled weakly, humbled in his presence.

"Nibs," he said.

Chapter 31

I could picture the scene when scientists finally discovered the secret tribe: there they'd be, handheld videocams dipping around, shaving mirrors, pots and pans, wristwatches, and knives proffered as gifts to the bemused aborigines; and when the linguists attempted that first tentative communication between modern and ancient civilizations, the first word up for detailed research and analysis would be an obscure, ambiguous single syllable from Kimber, near Pipely, not far from Wally: "nibs."

Nibs it was to be then, and the chief took my arm and led me through the forest, leaving his aides to deal with the deadweight of the unconscious white men.

When we reached their village, Fortesque, Bruce, and Miss Mepps were already there, rounded up by the tribesmen and united with Carruthers, who had been taken almost as soon as he had left the crystal waters of the Mersey and hauled himself up onto its primeval banks.

That evening, we sat around the fires as Towser the much traveled thylacine and his smaller sister dipped in and out of the shadows under the star-filled infinite mantle of the sky. We spoke quietly and ate, occasionally glancing over at the awning of a hut where the two brutes swung in hammocks, moaning in their sleep under the powerful effects of the plant extracts that had knocked them out.

Once again I wondered—as I had on our previous visit to this very camp—at the wealth of discoveries that lay around us: the perfectly balanced lives of the natives and their apparently stable sustenance and interaction with their surroundings; their intimate knowledge of the plant life and the substances contained in root and leaf, and of course the thylacines, magnificent and strange, semidomesticated, an object of salivation for zoologists the world over.

Awakening the next morning, I heard Miss Mepps talking to Carruthers nearby and was glad to notice a semblance of normality in her speech; it seemed a serious psychosis had somehow been averted and she spoke of returning to England with natural relief and excitement, vowing not to breath a word of our adventure to anyone.

I swung out of my hammock and rubbed my eyes in the brightness but jolted wide awake when Carruthers stopped his conversation with Miss Mepps in midsentence and gasped loudly.

"Ee, fook!" he exclaimed, edging backward around the side of the hut toward me. "The tart and the wogs are back! Eh, BP, check it out—fookin' kimber!"

I stepped out away from the awning and followed Carruthers' gaze and there, entering the camp with two aborigine males behind them, were the Mata Horror and her young Bahá'i charges, a tad disheveled but nonetheless still sporting that moony two-feet-above-the-ground look of your typical religious zealots.

"Oh no," I groaned. "Forty?"

Fortesque and Bruce appeared, taking in the spectacle of the Bahá'i's approach with as much trepidation as I. The natives who had brought them in I guessed to be members of another tribe, for I did not recognize them from our last visit here and their appearance held subtle differences. They melted quickly into the goings on about camp with complete ease, however, mingling with their brethren and staring in fascination at the goons, stretched in their hammocks under a nearby awning, the knock-out dose apparently wearing off.

"There you are, Brian," said the Mata, as if addressing a naughty boy. She then followed this annoying opening gambit with a dose of typical gooey sanctimoniousness: "Our belief in the mighty Bahá'u'lláh has sustained us. Open your heart and let his spirit be released Brian for he is within you!"

"Crickey!" exclaimed Bruce.

Just then, the two thugs began to slowly make their way toward us, shakily wobbling across the brown flattened earth in their bare feet, all but their white Y fronts having been removed the night before. Two aborigines quickly flanked them, seemingly alert for signs of trouble, but the goons seemed altered, mellow in disposition and altogether unthreatening.

They stood near us swaying slightly, breathing the clear air and taking in the beauty of the village and the forest, bemused by the situation.

"Nice 'ere," said the one I had borrowed the Rothmans from on the airplane.

"Lovely," said the other one, looking down at his white bare skin as if seeing it for the first time. Their former threatening demeanor seemed banished and a softness was on their features, a condition most likely absent since the day they were born.

The aborigine chief crinkled his broad nose mischievously and slipped his hand into a little bag that dangled from his loincloth. He pulled out the gold knuckledusters, slipped them on his fingers and held his hand up in front of his face. A glint of sun dashed off the smooth surface like a living elfin presence and flickered around the camp, alighting on our faces for a brief moment before flitting away as he moved his hand.

The big white men smiled with wonder at the glowing light, showing no sign of recognizing the vicious instrument they were once so attached too; they just stood there, subservient; another aborigine stepped in front of them and with a skillful flourish, daubed brick red and buff stripes down their cheeks, and then stepped back in appraisal, satisfied with his artwork.

"Christ," said Carruthers. "Whatever they shot 'em oop with, I want a couple of pounds of it, farff!"

"Carruthers!" I snapped, sensing more smuggling on the horizon.

"Just kiddin', Brian," he quickly responded.

"Let's just leave everything in its rightful place this time, shall we?" I said, almost imploring, for I was beginning to feel drained and fragile, wondering how on earth I could finally persuade the religious clowns in front of me that I was absolutely not the reincarnation of their wretched guru.

No sooner had that thought passed through my mind when Lolla fished into the folds of her dread muumuu and pulled out what I at first perceived to be a scroll, no doubt inscribed with insidious religious tenets that were about to be hurled my way. But when she unrolled it with a sudden chorus of the tuneless tunes of Bahá'u'lláh, I saw that it was the very same picture I had stared up at from the wooden throne eons ago, in Jokkmökk, at the Bahá'í's' bizarre crowning ceremony.

With her lank black hair and dull eyes perched atop the open scroll, I was forced once again to confront that slick Arab's features, and a gasp from Fortesque confirmed that the resemblance to me was indeed uncanny.

"Heh heh heh," laughed Carruthers. "It do look like thee, Brian. Heh heh . . ."

"Oh bollocks, Carruthers," I whined.

But Bruce, who was standing there with us, jiggling the corks that hung from his canvas bush hat as he shook his head in surprise at the portrait, suddenly lurched forward and pointed to something that hung below the neck of the likeness of Bahá'u'lláh.

"What's that then, darlin'?" he said, poking the painting with his finger. "What's that signify?" he asked, peering closely. "There's a face in there . . . looks like a medallion or something."

Lolla turned the picture around and looked at it for a moment.

"Oh, its nothing really. Just the likeness of an old mountain man whom the great Bahá'u'lláh met in his formative years. It is said that Bahá'u'lláh received wisdom from this wise man and learned much of what he later organized into the religion we now call Bahá'í'."

"W . . . wait a minute," I stammered. "You mean Bahá'u'lláh wasn't the actual originator of this load of nonsense—there was someone else before him?"

"Well . . ." Lolla looked a little put out and her sloe-eyed Arab companions peered into the painting intently, sporting quizzical expressions. The sun was rising above the clearing and sweat began beading my forehead. I edged up to the Mata Horror, anxious to see the heathen who was really responsible for this travesty, and when I saw the likeness on that medallion, etched finely in exquisite detail, I jumped involuntarily, as if poked in the eye.

"Fortesque," I said shakily to my stalwart tour manager. "Take a gander at this will you—go on."

Fortesque stepped forward and peered at the likeness. I watched his craggy features crease with mirth as he took in the image of the pale, bland eyes, the familiar pursed lips of a man looking like he'd just conned an artist into accepting a string of singing engagements in the North Pole, and the shock of wild, white hair perched atop a rectangular head.

"Whoa!" exclaimed Fortesque, "got a spot of suntan, but there's no mistaking that dial!"

"This," I said triumphantly, jabbing the medallion depiction fiercely, "this is the man you want. This is the *originator* of the load of old tripe you people cling to like limpets. *This* is your guru!"

"What are you talking about?" said Lolla, dropping her arms down with exasperation.

"He lives in Findhorn," I said. "In the north of Scotland. He's an Englishman. He used to be a magistrate, now he's a rock 'n' roll manager. He's got a brain the size of a watermelon! His name is Tarquin Steed! He is the reincarnation you seek. I'm but a humble minstrel. Believe me, he's my boss, so I'm sure he's yours, too."

A flicker of uncertainty crossed Lolla's face as my prophetic assessment began to make a dent on her tunnel-vision awareness. Then I remembered the speech her cohort Mukraik had oozed into the telephone that morning in Jokkmökk and the words came to my tongue with all the familiarity of a nursery rhyme: " 'And in the frozen wastes his eminence shall shine forth and his glory be made manifest," I quoted, realizing I had hit the nail on the head. " 'The frozen wastes' must mean Findhorn!" I explained. "It's not referring to me on a tour of Sweden at all; it's about Steed in Findhorn—it's always bloody freezing in Scotland. That's where your guru is!"

And I turned to Fortesque and said from the corner of my mouth: "That'll keep Steed busy for a bit, eh Forty?"

"Blimey!" chortled the old road dog. I smiled into the rising sun as the aborigines gathered around the Bahá'í who continued to stare at the likeness on the medallion with fascination and a growing mindless belief. Towser the thylacine emerged from the bushes, casting a baleful eye at Carruthers before it slunk back into the forest depths, its stripy hindquarters disappearing into the rippling foliage.

Chapter 32

"Brian, can you hear me? I say, Brian?"

It was the plummy English Public School accent of Steed, bellowing through the static, piercing the calm of the cockpit as if addressing the troops on the front line of a war zone. I could just picture him sitting there in his Findhorn farmhouse, surrounded by thick stone walls, wearing a forest-green Burberry parka, lolling back in a brown leather chair, his chili pepper-red hunting boots propped up on some fine hardwood desk scavenged from a retired solicitor's London office, a wide-eyed look of complete innocence beneath those bushy white eyebrows.

We were on our way back to London and somehow my persuasive manager had conned both the air-traffic controllers in Heathrow and the pilot of our Quantas jumbo jet into allowing him to communicate with me via the plane's radio.

"Now," he roared, and I felt the very same lassitude and hopelessness I had experienced in what felt like an age ago, way back in that halcyon Summer as I'd loafed by my pristine blue swimming pool, my lovely wife within tantalizing reach in her fawn camisole, and the insect life of our Vermont mountain valley location buzzing around my ears in all it's chitinous glory.

"The Clermont Set aren't too happy about your little, er . . . *statement*, or whatever the hell it is you think you're up to," asserted Steed. "But I think I've smoothed out the wrinkles—with a little help from *Lord* Manquill Carruthers, your soundman's dad!"

"Ah," I said, remembering the teenage giant's royal heritage, divulged on the flight over. "So rank was pulled after all, eh?"

"Enough that you won't get killed, Brian, at any rate. Came in handy, that did, I must say. We've lost the yen though, of that there's no doubt. And you know of course they'll be back for Towser sooner or later anyway, regardless. You do know that, don't you?"

THE OTHER LIFE OF BRIAN

I hadn't thought about it. But now that Steed had forced me to I realized that nothing short of United Nations intervention was going to stop Lucky Lucan and his crew from getting their hands on a thylacine eventually. Strangely, the idea filled me with lethargy.

"Whatever," I said flatly into the intercom, glancing at the pilot and his copilot who flanked me in their trim suits, both men sporting identical solarium tans. They ignored me and continued aiming the enormous vessel into the endless expanse of blue.

"Anyway Brian, come around to the office as soon as you get back. Great news! The single's taken off in Greenland—Iceland and Franz Joseph Land are reporting substantial airplay. The Tiny Brocil Fishes and the Nico Teens want to do a package tour and Big Hilda's working on a topping light show. Also, as you probably noticed, the Tasmanians have finally gone through their disco stage, ignored the rest of rock history altogether, and are now going absolutely ape for Soulbilly! "Knee Trembler"s bounding up the charts. If you weren't on that bloody plane I'd have had you stay there and I'd fly the old Soulbilly Shakers over for a reunion tour. Down the road that'll be my laddie—couple of months and we *must* get back there with a band to capitalize."

"Reunion. Right . . . wait a minute. You mean "Trembler" is *really* selling down there." I asked, determined not to get too excited until I heard some hard figures.

"Oh Christ, yes! We've racked up almost 800 so far."

"What? Is that all? And it's in the charts?"

"Well, come on, BP—it is only Tas, after all."

"It is," I responded glumly. "But what about the new stuff? I heard Forty's uncle singing "King Of The Senses." Claims he heard it on Tassy radio."

"One step at a time, laddie. One step at a time. It might take them a while to catch up on your new stuff . . . *intellectually,* that is. I'm pulling some strings to have that song taken off the air for the time being. Can't push them too hard, you know. They are *Tasmanians,* after all"

I tried to calculate the logic of Steed's plan but came up short. Trying to take one of my songs *off* the air was a new one to me, and so original I was too confused to even criticize it.

"Right, whatever," I finally agreed, dumbfounded as usual.

"So anyway, about the Polar regions. Let's get up there, Brian, strike while the iron is hot I say! And it *is* your new stuff that's moving up there—those Northerners are *ready* for the challenge. Mind you, this'll give the back catalogue a hell of a kick, laddie, a hell of a kick!"

"A kick," I said, feeling tired to the bone already. "Um, Steed," I added, one last stab of independence slipping into my mind like a dying slug. "If you mention Japan I'm gonna throttle you."

"Japan! For Chrissakes! Miss Twark? Hang on Brian, I've got the intercom going to London. Smyke, are you there? Good. Get Miss Twark on the blower to Yooky. Tell her to find out what's happening in Tokyo. Bloody good thinking, Brian—now, where was I?"

"What about England, Steed?"

"You're kidding, right?"

"But they published the luge shot, didn't they?"

"Only to be sarcastic, Brian. Only to be sarcastic."

"Right," I agreed sullenly.

"Oi, mate?" The Australian pilot interrupted in a most irritable voice. "Can you *please* get that pooftah off the line? Christ, what does he think this is, a bloody board meeting?"

"Steed, I gotta get the fuck off now—"

"Oh, and by the way," my manager went on oblivious, "we're suing the Baedburgers for copyright infringement. Apparently they've been sending your letters to a local magazine who've been publishing them regularly. Been making a pretty penny out of it from what I've gathered. Miss Twark has served notice on them. Should have them behind bars on this one with any luck.

"Anyway, must sign off now—got a lot of record companies to kick into gear. It's all happening, boy!

"Yours without prejudice, over and out."

I returned to my seat to digest Steed's manifesto for world domination, suddenly feeling rather pepped up by the idea. Miss Mepps doddled by in a fresh uniform, delivering drinks. She appeared a little drained but had somehow miraculously escaped a major mental breakdown; she plonked a free miniature champagne on my tray-table, a semblance of a smile crossing her pinched features.

Two rows up were the Bahá'i, intently studying a map of northern Britain, their intentions finally completely directed away from me and aimed toward bigger game, game that lumbered through the halls of a renovated farmhouse somewhere in Findhorn on the wild coast of Scotland.

Spud and Chip, as we had come to call the Clermont Set's hired heavies, sat together across the aisle from me, altogether changed men. A sweetness had descended upon them since those tiny arrows had shot organic chemical messages into their bloodstreams. They were now innocent as babes, sponging up information and experience as if each moment were their very first.

Lolla, of course, had been in like a shot and Spud and Chip were well immersed in Bahá'í doctrine before the plane had made its first fuel stop. Why not? I thought—they were the perfect candidates for imprinting and perhaps in this case the simplicity of religious belief was well suited and even useful in directing their future lives. And, I figured, they'd come in handy helping Lolla and her chaps persuade Steed to take on the position that was so rightfully his—Progenitor of the Great Bahá'u'lláh and Potentate of the Faith!

"Ee, fookin' great!" barked Carruthers from the seat in front of me as I recounted Tarquin Steed's latest plan of attack. "Mega, Brian, fookin' mega!"

"What?" gasped Fortesque excitedly from the seat next to the soundman. "A hit in Greenland? Nice one blue!"

"Let's do it, boys!" I exclaimed, enticing the pair of them to stand. And we slapped high fives, yelling in unison: "Kimber! Away t'lads!"

After this burst of exhilaration, I plonked myself down, and thought about calling home as soon as we landed to insist that my wife and son join me in England for a few weeks before I continued this apparently never-ending tour of the outer reaches of the planet Earth. And then I fell into a sound and contented sleep.